STILL LEARNING THE RULES
OF HIGH SCHOOL . . .

"Whoever decided that chickens belonged in nuggets was clearly confused," I said.

"Sophomore!" Richard shouted, punching me hard on the shoulder.

"Ow! What was that for?" I asked. I rubbed my shoulder.

"You used an oxymoron," Richard said. "'Clearly confused.'"

"So?"

"So, if you hear someone use one, you get to hit them on the shoulder and shout *sophomore*."

"When did that become a thing?" I asked.

He shrugged. "I don't know. Always, I guess."

I put my fork down. "Is that a wild guess?" I asked.

"No. It's an educated guess."

I could tell from his eyes that it had just dawned on him what I'd done.

"Sophomore!" I shouted, hitting him hard for his *educated guess*. I could get into this game.

"You're both acting like big babies," Lee said. "And *educated guess* isn't necessarily an oxymoron."

Big babies! That was probably an oxymoron.

Before I could even launch my brain into the train of thought wrapped around what my response should be, Lee looked me right in the eyes and said, "Don't even think about it."

OTHER BOOKS YOU MAY ENJOY

SOPHOMORES AND OTHER OXYMORONS

another novel

by DAVID LUBAR

speak

SPEAK
An imprint of Penguin Random House LLC
375 Hudson Street
New York, New York 10014

First published in the United States of America by Dutton Books,
an imprint of Penguin Random House LLC, 2015
Published by Speak, an imprint of Penguin Random House LLC, 2016

THE LIBRARY OF CONGRESS HAS CATALOGED THE DUTTON EDITION AS FOLLOWS:
Lubar, David, author.
Sophomores and other oxymorons : another novel / by David Lubar.
pages cm
Sequel to: Sleeping freshmen never lie.
Summary: Following a difficult freshman year, Scott Hudson is hoping that sophomore year
will be easier, but after a disaster of a first week he finds himself faced with new challenges—
including a particularly demanding English teacher, a school board member whose budget
cutting is covering up a crime, and the discovery that his friendship with Lee,
the Goth girl he met last year, is turning into something else entirely.
ISBN 978-0-525-42970-8 (hardcover)
1. High schools—Juvenile fiction. 2. Dating (Social customs)—Juvenile fiction.
3. Friendship—Juvenile fiction. 4. Self-confidence—Juvenile fiction.
5. Families—Pennsylvania—Juvenile fiction. 6. Conduct of life—Juvenile fiction.
7. Pennsylvania—Juvenile fiction. [1. High schools—Fiction. 2. Schools—Fiction.
3. Dating (social customs)—Fiction. 4. Friendship—Fiction. 5. Self-confidence—Fiction.
6. Family life—Pennsylvania—Fiction. 7. Conduct of life—Fiction.
8. Pennsylvania—Fiction.] I. Title.
PZ7.L96775So 2015
813.54—dc23
[Fic] 2015014160

Speak ISBN 978-0-14-751764-7

Printed in the United States of America

1 3 5 7 9 10 8 6 4 2

Designed by Irene Vandervoort
Edited by Julie Strauss-Gabel

... or "oxymora"...

For the writers who've always had my back:
Jordan Sonnenblick, Paul Acampora, Dan Gutman, Chris Crutcher,
Neal Shusterman, Cynthia Leitich Smith, Greg Leitich Smith,
Steven Gould, Terry Trueman, Pete Hautman, John Scalzi,
Dian Curtis Regan, and Bruce Coville.
No worries, mates. Reciprocity is not mandatory.

ONE

This year is going to totally rock," I told Lee. We were sitting on the top step of her front porch, badly bloated and overfed from the heaping platters of an outrageous Labor Day cookout hosted by her parents, attended by mine, and peppered with a rotating assortment of both families' coworkers, friends, and neighbors. My folks loved Lee. Her folks appeared to tolerate me, though I had a feeling it would be a good idea not to turn my back on her father if we ever went hiking near the edge of a cliff. Dads are excessively protective of their daughters. I think my parents were pretty smart to have nothing but boys, even if they were less than smart about the spacing.

"I admire your enthusiasm," Lee said. "It's cute."

"You're thinking of the wrong Hudson." I pointed to the curb, where my parents were loading my somewhat amusing but essentially useless and frequently damp baby sibling into the backseat of the car. "Sean is cute."

"Agreed," Lee said. "But there's no quota on cute. And there's a strong biological argument for shared traits among siblings. Sean's cute. Bobby's cute. You're cute. It's a Hudson thing. Suck it up and deal with it. What's wrong with being adorable?"

"That's for puppies and toddlers," I said. "We're sophomores now."

"Don't stay out too late, Scott," Mom called after she'd clicked the seventeen buckles and tightened the half-dozen harnesses that locked Sean's Kevlar-reinforced car seat securely in place. "You have school tomorrow. It's a big day. You want to be ready for it."

"I know, Mom. Thanks. Bye." I waved and watched my parents drive off. I wasn't concerned about tomorrow. I'd spent my freshman year mastering the art of functioning without sleep. I'd survived a series of stupid decisions, and scattered brushes with death and destruction. What a difference a year makes. Last year, I'd been clueless. This year, I had a clue.

The door opened behind us. "Big day, tomorrow," Lee's dad said.

Lee and I exchanged amused glances, but she didn't protest. "See you in school," she said, giving my hand a pat. She closed the book she'd been reading, but kept her place with her finger. *Of Mice and Men.* That was our summer-reading book. She was near the end. I'd already read it, on my own, years before it had been assigned. Twice, actually.

"What are you wearing tomorrow?" I asked as I got up from the steps.

"What's the matter? Afraid we'll show up in the same outfit?"

"I think that would be the first sign of the apocalypse," I said. Lee had a fondness for dark, disturbing horror-related T-shirts, which she alternated with dark, disturbing obscure-band-related T-shirts. For the picnic, she'd made her parents happy by wearing a solid brown shirt, adorned with nothing except one tiny Jack Skellington pin. Her hair, which had started the summer a bright orange, was now a muted shade of deep purple.

"The apocalypse has been here for a while," Lee said. "Have you been to a bookstore or a movie theater recently?"

"Quite a few. Good point."

"Thanks. And I actually haven't given school clothing any thought yet," she said.

I took one last look at summer-vacation Lee, then headed for home. When I'd met her last October, she had so many piercings, I was surprised her spine hadn't snapped under the weight of all the metal. Most of this summer, she'd only worn a handful—I mean, a faceful. Wait. "Faceful" sounds like a lot. But "handful" sounds like a little. I guess I'll settle for saying she had a handful of piercings on her face.

With Lee, I was never sure what sort of personal questions were okay, and what sort would earn me an *I-can't-believe-you-*

just-asked-me-that glare, or a bucketful of scalding sarcasm. But curiosity was killing me. I thought back to last week, when she'd come over to show me the camera her parents had given her for her birthday, and I'd finally asked her about it. "You're wearing a lot fewer piercings."

"Your powers of observation remain impressive." She didn't look at me. She was busy snapping her 235th (by my rough estimate) photo of Sean's hands. But I didn't detect any sign of annoyance in her tone. I decided to press on.

"Is it because . . ." I paused to find the right way to phrase my question.

Is it because we're hanging out a lot?

No. That sounded presumptuous.

Is it because we're sort of dating?

Nope. That was probably even more presumptuous, and slightly delusional. Besides, I couldn't honestly call our relationship *dating*. I'd taken her to one dance. I guess that was a date. But *dating* implies an ongoing relationship. This summer, we'd mostly hung out in town when she wasn't working. In my mind, we were more than just friends. Or, at least, close to being more than friends. Though, at the pace things were going, our next real date would coincide with our tenth high school reunion.

"Is it because of what?" she asked.

I grasped the next thought that floated through the vacuum chamber of my mind. "Because your current social clique sports far fewer piercings?" Zero, to be exact.

She pointed the camera at me and captured my digital soul. "Do you think that would be a good reason?"

"No. Absolutely not."

"Neither do I." She switched on her flash and fired several shots at my retinas. "I almost put everything back on right after the dance. I didn't want people to think I'd been motivated to make some sort of drastic change in an effort to gain social acceptance. But I try not to let people's assumptions guide my actions. So I left them off because I didn't care whether people thought they knew why."

As twisty as that might seem, I got it. Though all she'd told me was what *didn't* influence her. I still didn't know her motivation. I realized it didn't matter. I liked Lee. I didn't care how many piercings she had. Though, if I wanted to be totally honest, I liked her more without the excess. But even if she decided to wear an iron mask, I wouldn't mind.

No. That's a lie. An iron mask would bother me. I liked her face. I liked looking at it. And I liked the way looking at it made me feel.

While Lee could be indecipherable at times, my friend Wesley was just the opposite. He'd been the most feared kid in the school, last year. But he was totally open about his thoughts and goals. Like most guys, he followed a self-created code of honor. Wesley could knock out pretty much anybody with one punch, and he had no problem exercising that ability when a situation called for it. But he would never hit you from behind.

My thoughts about Lee and Wesley carried me for several

blocks. It's a little less than two miles from Lee's place to mine. I enjoyed the silence of the suburban streets. Things were rarely quiet at home these days. Sean managed to blow a fair number of decibels out of his tiny lungs and miniature larynx. And when a baby appeared, as Sean had in May, it seemed like every person in the universe had to stop by at some point, spout gibberish along the lines of "kitchee kitchee coo," and fabricate remarks about the adorable nature of such unremarkable, unadorable fabrics as crocheted blankets, quilted bibs, and knitted caps.

My parents were waiting for me in the living room when I got home, perched on the couch that faced the front door. The last time I'd seen them both sporting mingled expressions of joy and fear, they'd just found out Mom was pregnant.

"We have great news," Mom said. She had Sean cradled in her arms. He was asleep. Car rides were his kryptonite. They knocked him right out. Resistance was futile. I wish we lived in a tour bus.

"You're not . . . ?" I pictured our house slowly filling up with babies, while a convoy of dump trucks carted off the diapers that spilled out the doors and windows.

"No!" Dad said, after a brief pause to fill in the dots.

Mom's head snapped toward him as if he'd just spewed a half-dozen swear words, instead of a single relief-filled negative. "I'm not pregnant, if that's what you were thinking," she said. "Not that it would be so terrible." She beamed a fond gaze at

Sean. I think babies get their vitamin D from gaze-beams.

"It would be great. Totally super. The more, the merrier." Now that I knew it wasn't happening, I could be generous with my enthusiasm, and my clichés. "What's the news?"

"I'm opening my own garage," Dad said. "You know that little place on Sibert Street, between the Taco Shack and the dry cleaner?"

"The two-bay service station?" I asked.

"Yeah. They have to rip out the old pumps. Instead of installing new ones, the owner decided to sell the place. It's perfect for a repair shop. And the price is reasonable."

"That's awesome." This really *was* good news. Dad ran the repair department at Linwood Mercedes in Allentown. He'd always wanted to open his own garage. He was an amazing mechanic. He could figure out most problems with cars just by listening to the engine. "I thought you needed to save up a lot more money before you could do that."

"I got a partner," Dad said. "We've been working on plans for a while. He's handling the financing and the paperwork. I just got off the phone with him, and we definitely have a deal. I didn't want to tell you until I knew it was really going to happen."

"But we're still going to have to economize a bit," Mom said. "I'd planned to go back to work last year, but that got sidetracked." She flashed another gaze-beam at our little sidetrack.

I didn't see how any further economizing was possible. We were already funneling all the family's extra money into diapers and baby food. From what I'd seen, a baby's digestive tract is a sort of specialized ecosystem that serves merely to turn money into crap.

"What are you going to do?" I asked. "Rent out Bobby's room?"

Mom and Dad looked at each other with calculating eyes, as if this was actually an excellent suggestion on my part.

"I hadn't thought about that," Dad said. "Rental rates are pretty high around here. We could probably charge a decent amount."

"Stranger danger!" I shouted. "You want a stranger bringing diseases into the house? There are a lot of sketchy people out there. And you don't want Bobby to feel like he has no place at home. At some point, he's going to need that room."

That seemed to yank them back from the fantasy of becoming wealthy landlords.

"We'll manage with what we've saved so far," Dad said. "I'll work at the dealership through the end of the year. The garage goes on the market in January. After we buy it, I'll give notice at the job, so they have plenty of time to find a replacement. We'll fix the place up this winter, and we can open in March."

"Who's the partner?" I asked.

"He doesn't want me to tell anyone until after the contracts are signed," Dad said. "He has another investment he needs to sell, first, to help fund this. It's good to keep quiet about these things. He told me you never want people to know you're motivated to sell, or you won't get a good price. But I think you'll be pleasantly surprised when you find out." He tossed in a wink.

I could tell Dad was excited. I didn't ruin the announcement by sharing my thoughts. It was great he was going to make his dream come true, but the timing was terrible. Mom was busy with Sean. Bobby just started the second month of a six-month tour with his band. That left me as the go-to guy for any tasks that didn't require a six-foot reach, an intimate understanding of socket wrenches, or a driver's license. As for Bobby's room, I still had hopes of eventually turning it into the site of a slot-car track.

I went up to my room to get ready for tomorrow. As I was digging through my desk drawers for blank notebooks, I found my journal. I hadn't touched it all summer, but the memories rekindled by my encounter with parental announcements inspired me to flip it open and start writing.

September 1
    School starts tomorrow, Sean. I know I said I was finished with these journals after you were born. But when parents spring exciting news like "we're going to be even poorer next year," it's a hard habit to break.

So I guess I'll keep it up. Though I'm not expecting anywhere near as much drama this year. I don't think anyone needs a sophomore survival manual. Juniors and seniors will be less of a threat. I'll have a whole class of freshmen who get to suffer the role of buffer.

Hey, that was a halfway-clever phrase. I guess I sort of missed this. It feels good to be writing in my journal again. And, just to be clear, this is not a diary. It's actually not a journal, either. See if you can figure out what it is. I'll give you a couple days to think about it. I need to get ready for tomorrow. Which basically means I have to put some notebooks and pencils in my backpack, and remember to zip it up.

TWO

I was trying to cross a six-lane highway. Cars shot toward me from both directions. Just after I leaped over the center divider, the highway turned into a football field. Cars converged from all directions now, as if I'd wandered into a demolition derby.

Horns blared.

What the heck!

I sat up, and tried to blink away the darkness. But it remained blinkproof. I checked my clock. 5:30. A horn blared again. I stumbled to the window. There was a delivery truck at the curb. Bongo's Bagels. Both the *o*'s in "Bongo's" were made of sliced bagels. And the l in "Bagels" was a knife with cream cheese smeared on it.

I saw upstairs lights flick on in two of the houses across the street. I suspected lights might also be turning on in houses on either side of us.

A guy wearing a white cap got out of the bagel truck

and headed for my front door. Even from above, I knew that walk. It was Wesley. My pal. My scary, dangerous, awesome friend. And, apparently, my friend with no concept of time or adolescent sleep requirements.

I opened my window, and tried to get Wesley's attention with a whispered shout before he started pressing the doorbell. "What are you doing?"

He craned his head back and waved at me, then pointed at the truck. "I got a new job. Delivering stuff. To the *school*. How's that for a lucky break? I can give you a ride every morning, just like last year. So you don't have to take the bus. Come on down. I'm running late."

Teeth unbrushed. Bladder unemptied. Stomach unfed. Eyes unfocused. Brain unactivated. No way. "Thanks. But I'm running late, too. I'll call you after school."

"You sure?"

"I'm sure."

"Hey, a couple bagels spilled out when I hit the curb. They're still hot. I'll get you one."

"That's okay," I called. But he was already sprinting back to the truck. He leaned in through the passenger window and grabbed something from the foot well. I was still sliding up the screen when he chucked the bagel, flinging it at me with the form and force of a champion Frisbee thrower. Both my hands were occupied. The bagel hit my head, then ricocheted into the room.

Ouch.

It felt like a salt bagel. At least he hadn't been delivering pies. Or bricks.

I slid the screen down, closed the window, and went back to sleep.

Briefly.

Sean started crying at 5:45 A.M.

This was going to be a long day.

The third time I rose—with the help of my alarm—it felt like someone decided to explore the depths of my ear canal with an electric drill. And something seemed to be missing. But I couldn't figure it out right away.

As I walked downstairs, I realized the two things that weren't there—bacon and blueberry pancakes. That's what Mom always made for the first day of school.

There was nobody in the kitchen. I guessed Dad had already left for work. I opened the fridge and grabbed the milk, then hunted through the cabinets for cereal.

Mom walked into the kitchen. "You're up early."

"That's because I have school," I said.

Her eyes widened as the words sank in. "Oh, Scott! I'm so sorry. I totally forgot. I got so involved talking with your dad about the garage. He's really excited. Then Sean woke up several times. And somebody was honking a horn right outside the house. Sit down. I'll make breakfast."

That's what I call "the Sean effect." Last night, Mom had mentioned school. So she knew about it. This morning, after getting up two or three times to take care of Sean, she'd totally forgotten about school. I wished I could let my teachers borrow Sean when it was time to hand out homework assignments.

Mom snatched an egg from the fridge and the milk from the table, and then grabbed the pancake mix. I checked the clock and did the math. As good as Mom was with a spatula and a frying pan, pancakes would take a while. So would the bacon.

"That's okay," I said. "I don't want to miss the bus."

"I can give you a ride."

I pictured her trying to make breakfast, get dressed, buckle Sean into the car, and then drive me to school.

"It's really okay." I retrieved the milk and poured some on my cereal. Mom looked so sad that I added, "We can have a first-week-of-school breakfast on Saturday. That way, I can take my time and enjoy everything. Your pancakes are too good to eat in a hurry."

"That's a great idea," she said.

While there wasn't time for pancakes and bacon, there also wasn't any need to gulp down my cereal. Freshman year, I'd been so anxious about everything, I was the first kid at the bus stop. This year, I took my time.

"Have a great day," Mom said as I headed out.

"I will."

"Be sure to make a good first impression."

"No problem."

When I was a block away from the bus stop, I saw that half a dozen kids were already there. I recognized some of them from middle school. I was pretty sure, based on their neatly ironed clothes and lack of height, that they were all freshmen. I paused at the curb to study them. Which one would have been me last year? There was a boy reading a book. Even from far off, I could recognize the cover. *No More Dead Dogs.* Good choice. Another boy and a girl were talking. The remaining three freshmen, two girls and a boy, stood there in isolation. The boy standing the farthest to the right was wearing a knitted hat with a pompom on top. Bad idea. He was the shortest of the group, which was also a bad idea.

A cluster of older kids—mostly sophomores, along with a handful of juniors and two seniors—headed toward the stop from the other direction. When I'd started ninth grade, the seniors had looked like giants to me. This year, the new crop of seniors still looked big, but they no longer reminded me of mythical monsters. During the past year, I'd gained a bit of height, and they'd lost a bit of stature.

The cluster reached the reader. One of the new juniors, Liam Dortmund, knocked the book out of the kid's hands as he passed by him, almost as an afterthought. The kid waited until the whole group moved by, then reclaimed the book and resumed reading. He was safe for the moment. The mob had spotted the pompom.

Another of the juniors, Bram Eldicott, snatched the hat from the kid. He tossed it to Liam. The kid who'd been de-cap-itated let out a yelp of protest. If the cry had been one octave higher, I think windows would have shattered. Bram and Liam tossed the hat back and forth, while the kid played the monkey in the middle, leaping fruitlessly in an attempt to snatch the hat in flight.

I remembered the mindless bullying that had victimized Mouth Kandeski and some of the other freshmen at the bus stop last year. I'd had my own problems with bullies on the bus, and in the halls of Zenger High. I decided to test the theory that one person could make a difference.

Liam had his back to me. I walked up behind him, waited until Bram lobbed the hat his way, stepped past him, and snagged the hat before it landed in his hands, like a defensive end intercepting a touchdown pass.

"Hey!" Liam shouted.

I ignored Liam and returned the hat to the kid. He was skinny and had frizzy blond hair that still bore evidence of his recently removed headwear. He wore glasses with thick lenses that made his eyes seem enormous. Beneath his jacket, his tan button-down shirt had become halfway untucked, thanks to his failed attempt at airborne-hat recovery.

"Here," I said. "Put it away. It's too warm for a hat." I didn't bother to add that it's always too warm for a hat if you're a freshman at a bus stop.

"Thanks!" He plucked the hat from my hand and started to put it back on his head.

"Seriously," I said, pointing to his backpack. "Stow it."

"My mom said—"

"Your mom isn't here. Trust me. She'd want you to do this."

As the kid shoved the hat into his jacket pocket, I shifted my attention to Bram. He was the one who could take this to a more aggressive level. Liam was his henchman, blindly following Bram's lead. The fact that Bram hadn't tackled me from behind was a good sign. He was casually mean, as opposed to being pure evil or a full-time bully. Still, I'd ruined his fun. Our eyes locked. I kept my face calm, though my heart was getting an aerobic workout. I really didn't want this to escalate. A fistfight wasn't the best way to start the school year.

Bram shrugged. The bus turned the corner, giving both of us something safe to look at. As our city-supplied transportation pulled to the curb, I checked to see if we were going to be stuck with the same driver as last year. Nope. No sign of The Shouter. That was a relief. Maybe he'd exploded during the summer, like an overused pressure cooker forced to make one meal too many. This driver was an old guy, wearing a Sixers Windbreaker. He didn't even bother to look at us as we piled on. That was fine with me. I'd rather be ignored than yelled at. I walked toward the middle of the bus, dropped into an empty seat on the left side, and slid over to the window. Julia Baskins, who I'd had a huge crush on last year, boarded the bus with her friend Kelly Holbrook. I hadn't seen them since school ended. Julia, still heart-wrenchingly gorgeous, smiled at me when I caught her eye. I nodded and smiled back. Kelly nodded, too. I guess we'd both moved on from harboring bad memories. They grabbed seats together near the front.

"Thanks for the rescue. You're awesome."

Hatboy had plopped onto the vacant part of my seat. Apparently, even now that I was over my crush, Julia had the power to distract me from environmental hazards.

"It was no big deal." I looked out the window, hoping the kid would take the hint and stop talking.

"Oh, wow. She's beautiful."

I knew who he was talking about even before I checked. He stared at Julia with the dazed eyes of someone who's just gotten his first look at a Michelangelo masterpiece.

"Don't even think about it. You'll just do stupid stuff in a doomed attempt to get her attention. Trust me. I know all about these things." I returned my attention to the world beyond the window.

"So, what's it like?" he asked.

I pretended I hadn't heard him.

That earned me a triple tap on the shoulder, and a repeat of the question. I don't like getting tapped on the shoulder. I spun around and glared at him.

He cringed and let out a whimper. I felt like I'd just snatched a bowl of food away from a puppy. I guessed it wouldn't hurt to answer his question.

"It's big, crowded, and confusing at first," I said.

His shoulders slumped. "I'm dead."

"Keep your mouth shut and your head down, and you'll be okay," I said.

"That won't help. I'm still dead. It's like I was born with a target on my back." He leaned forward in his seat, as if to allow me to admire the imaginary bull's-eye between his shoulder blades. "Today will be terrible."

I looked at him, all hunched and scrawny in his seat. "You'll be fine." I doubt he believed me, especially since I didn't believe myself, but it seemed like a charitable enough lie. Sort of like how they used to offer the guy facing the firing squad a last cigarette. It wasn't good for him, but it really couldn't do any harm.

He said it again. "I'm dead."

"Probably." I realized there was no point giving him false hope. "But it will be a survivable death."

He lapsed into silence. As did I. Then he pulled something from his backpack. At first glance, I thought it was a game. That would definitely be snatched from his hands before the ride ended. But it had only a small display window. I realized it was a calculator. I turned my attention to the scenery as we rolled through the free world, toward the captivity of school.

Two minutes later, another tap interrupted my motion-lulled mind.

"What?" I asked, snapping again.

He had quite a leap for a little guy. After he got up from the aisle and climbed back onto his seat, he said, "According to the blueprint I studied, the school has nine doors, not counting the loading dock, which I assume might be inaccessible. Is one entrance to the building safer than the others?"

"They're all risky." I took a moment to picture the maze that is Zenger High. "But the door behind the left rear corner of the building, near the Dumpster, puts you in the hall by Mr. Pangborn's room, and he likes to keep an eye on things, so nobody will bother you when you come that way. Just don't linger by the Dumpster, or someone might toss you in."

"Great. Thanks. And what about—"

"Stop it!" I said.

Man, he startled easily. Long ago, I'd read a book called *5,000 Amazing Facts*. The title was about thirty percent accurate, but that still left plenty to savor. One of the amazing facts I'd read was about fainting goats. If you shout at them, they pass out and drop. Hatboy was more of a leaping goat. As tempting as it was to see if I could get him to hit new heights, I decided to try not to startle him again.

After he'd dropped back onto his seat, I told him, "Look, I just spent a year giving advice to a fetus. I'm not in the mood to mentor another embryo."

"A fetus?" he asked. "You gave advice to a fetus?"

"My little brother. Before he was born."

"Your little brother is a llama?" he asked.

"What are you talking about?"

"It would be nine months, at most, for a human, assuming you learned of the pregnancy immediately. Not a whole year. Even llamas don't always take that long. Horses and dolphins do."

"Whatever." I turned away.

"I learned that in a book called *10,000 Amazing Facts.*"

Oh, great. I was riding through town with a mini-me.

"Gestation is highly variable," he said. "I came out in seven months. I was really small."

You still are.

He laughed. "I know what you're thinking. I still am small. But I'm due for a growth spurt. I researched it. Maturation is even more fascinating than gestation."

He talked for a while longer, but I sort of zoned out. The bus rolled along, picking up more students, but getting only about half full.

About five minutes before we reached the school, my subconscious handed me an idea. I didn't want to start up a prolonged conversation with Hatboy, so I waited until the bus pulled into the school lot. When the driver opened the door, I tapped my seatmate on the shoulder.

Apparently, I wasn't the only one who reacted to shoulder taps. After the sound of his scream stopped echoing in my ears, I said, "How would you like to buy a freshman survival manual?"

"Really?"

"Really."

"That would be awesome. Do you have one?"

I sort of did. My first day of school freshman year was such a miserable experience, I'd decided to make a manual for my unborn sibling by writing down any survival tips I could think of. That's how my journal had started. There was a lot of good advice in it. I could take out all the personal stuff, leave in the practical material, and sell it to this kid. Why not?

"I don't have it with me," I said. "But I can bring it tomorrow."

"How much would it cost?" he asked.

Good question. I named a figure that seemed fair. He didn't blink. Maybe I should have asked for more.

"Plus shipping and handling," I said.

"Shipping and handling?"

"That was a joke," I said. But I had the feeling he wouldn't have objected if I'd bumped the price up.

"Good one. You're funny. So you're probably smart. Humor requires intelligence. A lot of famous comedians have philosophy degrees. I can be quite amusing. Except people don't always get my jokes. Though I'd bet you would. Want to hear my favorite one?"

Resistance, apparently, was futile. "Sure. But let's get off the bus first."

The instant his feet hit the asphalt, he said, "How can you tell you're near a murder?"

"I don't know."

"Probable caws."

It took me a second to connect the punchline with the name for a group of crows. Despite myself, I laughed.

"I knew you'd get it. Good one?"

"Yeah. Good one." I pointed to a rear corner of the building. "That's your safest bet. Good luck. Keep moving."

"Thanks."

"Don't dawdle by the Dumpster," I called after him.

I watched for a moment, to make sure his superabundance of fear pheromones didn't attract lions, tigers, or thugs. After he'd turned the corner, I went in the front entrance and threaded my way through the crowds to my new homeroom. I had no trouble finding it. I knew my way around the school, even though I hadn't been there since June.

Okay, sophomore year, I thought, *I'm ready for you. Bring it on.*

THREE

I saw a lot of familiar faces when I reached my homeroom, including Mary Abernathy, Diane Zupstra, and Chuck Peterson. Chuck, whose mom worked in the ER at the hospital, was a good source of news whenever something major happened.

We all exchanged nods, as if to say, *yeah, nothing new here.* It was a big change from freshman year, when everything was new and confusing. We launched into the familiar morning routine and, just like that, it was as if summer had never existed. The homeroom teacher, Mr. Ruiz, took attendance. After the pledge, read over the intercom by the student pledger of the day—who, true to form for student pledgers throughout history, seemed to be encountering "indivisible" for the first time—Principal Hedges welcomed us, shared a brief inspirational message about how a new year meant a fresh start, and reminded us that we could reach our full potential as long as we believed in ourselves and understood the value of hard work and striving to reach our full potential.

The homeroom teacher passed out assignment books and copies of our schedules. I looked at mine. It matched the one I'd gotten online.

Period	Class	Instructor
1st	CP Geometry	Mr. Stockman
2nd	AP U.S. History	Ms. Burke
3rd	Lunch	
4th	CP Biology	Ms. Denton
5th	Life Skills	Ms. Pell
6th	Spanish 2	Ms. Morena
7th	Gym/Study Hall	Mr. Cravutto/Staff
8th	Art 2	Mr. Belman
9th	H. English 2	Mrs. Gilroy

My guidance counselor had suggested I try at least one AP class for college credit. The choices were bio or history. I knew AP Bio would be a mistake. I had barely survived chemistry last year. History, on the other hand, pretty much just requires a good memory and the ability to wade through dense volumes of dreary prose without getting too weak and weary. I'd heard geometry was pretty cool. Trig, which came next year, was supposed to be harder, but I wasn't going to worry about that at the moment. I'd picked up a Spanish language magazine in July, when I was in New York with my dad, and managed to understand a fair amount of it. So I hadn't completely lost my language skills during vacation. Lee was in geometry, lunch, and biology with me. After that, we'd go our separate ways again until English.

When the bell rang, I headed off to my first class. It was interesting seeing the freshmen bubbling through the halls like guppies in a piranha tank. Lee was already in the room, sitting in the third row, on the aisle. She'd saved a seat for me.

She was wearing basic black. Black jeans, black T-shirt, black nail polish, black makeup of various sorts that girls use around their eyes and whose names I could never keep straight. Her piercings had remained stable, except for several additions to her left ear.

There was a test on each desk. Nothing like starting school with a bang. "I hope this isn't an omen," Lee said.

I folded mine diagonally so the top edge was lined up with the side, forming a triangle with a rectangular base, and held it so it cast a shadow on my desk from the morning light coming through the windows. "If it's not an omen, it could be a gnomon," I said.

"Scott, it's too early for wordplay," she said. "Though that is sort of clever, in an obscure, geeky, word-nerd kind of way. But, really, it's too early."

Mr. Stockman, a thin man dressed in a tan suit and plaid shirt, with a fringe of hair encircling three-fifths of the geometry of his head, walked over and stared at the origami in my hands. Or maybe it was testigami. He didn't say anything. I contemplated explaining that I'd folded the test to look like the thing in the center of a sundial. But I realized that would mean explaining about Lee's "omen" comment, and hoping that the teacher knew the shadow-caster in the sundial was called a *gnomon*, while also hoping he had a sense of humor.

"Sorry." I unfolded the test and put it back on my desk, where it no longer lay flat. I hoped I hadn't made a bad first impression. I reminded myself that my teachers would be meeting me for the very first time today. It would be smart to sit back and let someone else stand out in each class as the problem student.

Mr. Stockman headed back to his desk. Halfway there, he turned, pointed at my test, and said, "Gnomon?"

"Yeah." I guessed maybe he'd heard Lee's comment.

"Cool." He awarded me a smile. "Nice example of gnomon-clature."

Lee groaned, then whispered, "You found your tribe."

"Score one for the geeky word nerd," I whispered back.

"This test won't be graded," Mr. Stockman said after he reached his desk. "I just want to get an idea where you all are, as far as core concepts."

That seemed fair. I looked at the first problem. It was basic algebra. Solve the quadratic, give the two values of *x*. I had no trouble remembering how to do that. The next two questions, about slopes and coordinates on a graph, were also pretty easy.

Then there were some questions about points and lines. For the handful of questions where I wasn't positive about the answer, I was able to make a good guess. The fact that we weren't being graded made the test pretty stress-free for me. As I scanned the room, I saw a range of reactions. Most kids seemed pretty relaxed. But one or two were hunched over, gripping their pencils like they might be called upon to switch tasks and kill a vampire on short notice.

Lee finished before me. I wasn't surprised. She had a good head for math.

After Mr. Stockman collected the tests, he introduced us to some of the basic concepts of geometry, and tossed out a pun or two. The best one was "Are Euclid-ing me?" The worst one was the well-known joke about the acorn saying, "Gee, I'm a tree." So, yeah, I was back in school, back to learning things in a classroom environment, and pretty relaxed about everything. It was going to be an easy day. My little glitch with the gnomon had turned into a good thing. And I'd participated enough in the classroom discussion to show him I wasn't a slacker or a clown.

When the bell rang, I said, "See you at lunch."

"Stay out of trouble," Lee said.

"That's the other Hudson," I said.

"Bobby or Sean?" Lee asked.

"I think they'd prove equally problematic in the classroom." I double-checked my schedule, then headed to history.

"Welcome to AP U.S. History. The study of history isn't about dates. It's about people, and the things they do," Ms. Burke said. She looked the way I'd imagine the stereotypical Mrs. Claus would have looked in her late forties, before her hair had turned white, but after she'd developed her rosy cheeks and sunny smile. "We are going to be working very hard all year. We have a lot of material to cover. But there's no reason we can't take a few minutes on our first day to get to know each other. Write three interesting facts about yourself. Share a bit of your history."

The air filled with the scribble of pens. Everyone else started writing immediately, as if they'd entered the room with a fact on hand. Or in mind. I glanced to my left, at Phil Nelson's paper. *I once ate a whole pepperoni pizza.*

I knew I could do better than that. Better fact, I mean. Not better pizza consumption. Five slices pushed me pretty close to my gastronomic comfort zone. I wanted my facts to be good. What was interesting? I guessed the fact that I'd read *5,000 Amazing Facts* would make a cool fact. Yeah, a fact about a book of facts. I loved the self-referential aspect of that. One down. What else? My mom just had a baby. That would work. I'd probably be the only one in class who could say that. Two down. But I needed something really awesome for the third fact.

As I stared at the page, I heard the clicks and clatters of people around me dropping their pens. I glanced over at

Phil. His list was finished. Besides the pizza, though hopefully during the course of a different meal, he'd eaten an entire rotisserie chicken. Not surprisingly, his third fact was that he'd recently bought a new belt and several pairs of pants.

"Okay," Ms. Burke said, "pass them up."

Kids passed their papers forward. Kristen Valence, in the seat ahead of me, twisted a quarter turn and held out her hand.

I couldn't give Ms. Burke two facts when she'd requested three. There had to be something I could add.

Kristen cleared her throat in an obnoxious way.

At this point, the fact didn't even have to be good. It just had to *be*. What did I do this summer? What did I do yesterday? What did I do ten minutes ago?

Think!

I dug deep and found something. Lee had given me three Venus flytraps on the Fourth of July. I never did figure out the connection, if any, between carnivorous plants and declarations of independence. But the plants were definitely cool. They eat insects. You can give them hamburger, too. I fed mine flies and the occasional ant. That was sort of a fun fact. I could even do it as a couplet: *I just feed my plants / live flies and dead ants*. I figured everyone would appreciate a bit of light verse during the readings.

I hesitated. I actually had only one Venus fly trap, since two of them had died soon after I got them, but *plants* worked better in the couplet, so I needed to take some poetic license. Though I guessed I could go with *flies and an ant*.

As I was mentally tweaking the words, Kristen reached for my paper.

I scrawled *I just feed my plants—*

I dashed off the rest in a sloppy line as Kristen yanked the paper out from under the pen.

Shoot. But at least that would make three.

Ms. Burke took the gathered sheets and started reading them aloud. The class had to guess who'd written each one. That was pretty easy, since most of us knew one another.

About midway through the pile, she got to mine.

"'I read a book called *5,000 Amazing Facts,*'" she said.

A couple heads turned my way, and I heard at least one whisper of, "Hudson."

Ms. Burke read the second fact: "'My mom just had a baby.'" Most of the heads turned my way, and I heard my name whispered by several other kids. Sean's arrival was far from a secret. The third fact would be sort of stupid, but I didn't care. At least I wouldn't be branded a slacker.

Ms. Burke frowned at the sheet in her hand, tilted her head slightly to the left, squinted, tilted her head slightly to the right, lifted her glasses up, put her glasses back down, then shrugged and read, "'I just peed my pants.'"

"No!" I shouted. "That's not what I wrote!" Not that anyone would hear me over the laughter that bounced around the room like a barrage of jet-propelled dodgeballs.

As the class settled down from howls and guffaws to

chortles and snickers, I said, "'I just feed my plants flies and ants.' I have Venus flytraps."

It was pointless.

Someone behind me whispered, "Venus flytrap," but substituted the obvious rhyming body part for *Venus*. In other circumstances, I would have found that amusing.

Ms. Burke studied my handwriting for a moment, then said, "Oh, right. I see. I guess that word could have been *feed*. And, yes, *plants* would make sense. It even rhymes. Were you aware of that?"

I nodded.

"Very clever," she said. "I love poetry. Well, I guess we can move on, since we know who wrote this one."

Great. Halfway into history, and I was history.

At the end of the class, some kid I didn't know pointed at my crotch and said, "Hey, you peed your pants."

I could ignore him. But that might inspire him to try again, or get others to join in, preventing the whole thing from fading away. On the other hand, I could smack him down so hard, he never got back up. Maybe even so hard, it would scare off others. I don't mean with my fists. There's an old saying: *Never get in a war of words with a man who buys ink by the barrel.* If I was as good with words as I thought I was, I could end this decisively, right now. But I had to act immediately. If I hesitated, he won.

I planned to stagger him with a lightning-quick one-two

punch, then take him out with a knockout blow.

First jab—surprise him by agreeing.

"Yeah, my pants are wet . . ."

I saw his brows knit closer as he tried to decipher what I was doing. Little did he know he'd just been disarmed.

Second punch, make it about him, and go for the stagger.

". . . because I was laughing so hard at your face, I lost all control of my bladder."

And, now that he was stunned, throw an uppercut, to put him out of my misery. I pointed at my opponent, and addressed the mob: "The next time you're constipated, give Zitgeist here a call. If he can empty a bladder so easily, think what he can do to clogged intestines."

I could tell from the smirks of the crowd that I'd scored a victory. I headed out.

Yeah—two classes down. One disaster averted. One set of bus-stop bullies thwarted. One pun-loving teacher discovered. Sophomore year was definitely rocking. It wasn't even lunchtime, and I'd already come back from the dead.

I met up with Lee down the hall from the cafeteria.

"How was your history class?" I asked.

"Dated," she said. "How was yours?"

"Epic." We got in the food line. "This is a ridiculously early time to eat lunch."

"Think of it as brunch," Lee said.

"Brunch is for adults," I said. We weren't close enough to

see the food yet. I sniffed the air. "And I don't think tacos or chicken cutlets are traditional brunch items."

"How do you do that?" Lee asked. "It all just smells like a barely contained grease fire to me."

"It's a gift. Hey, speaking of which, why did you give me three Venus flytraps for the Fourth of July?"

"Because I know from numerous sad experiences that two-thirds of them die right away," she said. "How many do you have left?"

"One."

Lee grinned. "As my dad likes to say: asked, and answered."

We both got the tacos. I bought chocolate milk. Lee got a soda from the machine. They'd tried to replace all the soda with water and juice last year, but the mayor's brother is a hotshot executive for a major soda company, so carbonated beverages had a lot of support in our town.

If I'd been by myself, I would have stood amid the tables for five minutes, trying to figure out where to sit. Freshman year, my social circle had been torn apart and stitched together. I'd lost old friends, and gained new ones. But Wesley had been a senior last year. So he was gone, leaving Lee and me as our entire high school clique.

Lee grabbed a seat at an empty table. She would have done the same thing even if we weren't together. Or she would have sat with the most popular kids in the room, like she did last year, just for fun. She didn't seem to worry about stuff like social structures, clique hierarchies, and the intangible nature of popularity.

I joined her. I was happy not to have to figure out where I'd fit in best.

Richard Elkhart hovered nearby. I knew him from the paper. I pointed at the empty seats, inviting him to take one. Edith Cutler, also from the paper, joined us. We compared schedules. We all had the same English class. That was good. Richard was in my Spanish class, and Edith was in bio.

The kid I'd thrashed in history walked over. I clenched my fists, ready to protect myself if he took a swing at me, or flung the food on his tray at my face.

"That was funny," he said.

"Funny?"

"Yeah. You really got me good." He looked down at the table. "Can I sit here? I don't know anybody."

"Sure."

"Thanks." He sat, and doled out basic data.

His name was Bradley. He'd just moved here from Upper Saddle River, New Jersey. Apparently, where he came from, insults were exchanged between adolescent males as readily and forcefully as high fives, and didn't lead to fights.

That was a new way to make friends. One more miracle this morning and I was going to apply for sainthood.

I scanned the room to see whether there had been any major social upheavals or revolutions during the summer. Things looked pretty much the same. Except for one thing.

"Kyle and Kelly aren't together anymore." I pointed to where Kelly sat.

"Maybe the alliteration was too much for them," Lee said.

"That theory is as good as any," I said. I examined "Scott and Lee" for any signs of intolerable cuteness. The conjunction seemed fine, marred only by its current status as just a theoretical pairing.

"I heard she dumped him over the summer," Edith said.

"Ouch." No matter what had happened between Kyle and me, I felt a bit sorry for him. I knew how badly he'd wanted a girlfriend last year.

I turned my attention to my lunch. I ate the French fries first, since the cooler they got, the less they resembled food. The tacos weren't bad. They were only flawed by being small and few. As a rule of thumb, a taco should never be smaller than your hand. Or your thumb. I ate both of mine pretty quickly. My tacos. Not my hands. Lee nibbled at one of hers, made a face, and put the other one on my tray. "Want it?"

"Sure." There are some things you never turn down. After I finished my taco, my cubed pale crunchy fruit in sugar water, and my red sugary gelatin desert, I wiped the tortilla-shell grease from my hands and grabbed my notebook. As I sipped my chocolate milk, I compiled a list.

Scott Hudson's List of Things You Should Never Turn Down

A pristine taco of any size.

A ride in a sports car.

The volume.

Advice from a magical talking fish.

Scott Hudson's List of Things
You Should Always Turn Down

A seat next to Lyle "Sardine Breath" Sabretski (even if
he ever gets a sports car).

A bite from a half-eaten caramel apple.

Advice from a talking fly-infested pig's head on a stick.

Lee took a small sip from her soda. This was only her third tiny
slurp, at most. She held the soda out to me. "I can't finish this.
Want it?"

"Sure." I put the nearly full can on my tray, slugged down
the rest of the milk, then chugged the soda, and added it to my
list. I'd never seen Lee drink a whole soda. That worked out
pretty nicely for me.

The bell rang. "Time to conquer the next class," I said.

"Someone's feeling invulnerable," Lee said.

"Hey, we're sophomores," I said. "There are no pitfalls left
for us."

"Here's hoping irony doesn't bite you on the butt," Lee said.

Irony, it turns out, has a big mouth, sharp teeth, and a
craving for Hudson butts.

FOUR

Despite the popularity of various housing clusters of little pigs, assorted tradesmen in a tub, gruff billy goats, blind mice, and other well-known trios, three is not always a good number. I probably could have survived the smell, if it had been alone in its assault on my senses. I might have survived the sight, if it hadn't struck me immediately after the smell. Toss in the third element, which in this case was itself a dangerous trio in the form of gobbled cafeteria tacos, and I didn't have a prayer. Or a convenient tub.

The smell hit me right after I walked through the classroom door, as I turned past the large lab table at the front of the room. If you mixed nail-polish remover with paint thinner in a bucket, tossed in a couple of raw chicken thighs, a mackerel, and assorted slices of deli meats, and let the whole thing sit outside in direct sunlight for a week or two, the stench would seem like fresh-baked apple pie compared to the air in the classroom.

Nothing solid, liquid, or gaseous that Sean had blown out of his lower intestines came close to being this awful. And Sean could clear a room.

The sight smacked me as I looked for the source of the smell. A cat—actually, make that something that had once been a cat—was pinned, belly-up, to a wooden board on the table. Make that belly-up and belly-open. His mouth was agape, as if he were still trying to come to grips with the horror of his current situation. I turned away from the sight as the third taco, which was the last one to go down, exploded from my stomach and rocketed up my throat. I guess it was eager to clear a path for the second and first tacos, which enjoyed a flume ride on the waves of chocolate milk and soda that had tasted so good going down.

I hadn't thrown up in a long time. Not since I had the flu in sixth grade. I saw another splatter of vomit near mine. An instant later, I heard someone behind me joining the puke party.

Now what?

A young teacher stood by the far wall, leaning against the windowsill, her arms crossed in front of her chest like she was waiting for a bus. I guessed that was Ms. Denton. When I caught her eye, she pointed next to her, where five buckets and mops had been lined up. On the windowsill behind each mop, I saw a bottle of water.

I walked across the room with my fellow upchuckers, and

grabbed a bucket. I was relieved to see that Ike Yamamoto was part of our wretched trio. He was a wrestler, and pretty tough, so nobody was going to make fun of us. At least, not as a group. Our third gastric buddy was Chelsea McCabe, whose father was the chief of police. I was pretty sure she was immune from teasing. From what I'd heard, guys were even afraid to ask her out. Nobody wanted to get on the wrong side of the law.

After I'd mopped up my mess, and rinsed my mouth with one of the water bottles, Ms. Denton had us take the buckets back to the janitor's closet. At least Lee had saved a seat for me. I dropped down in it and assured myself that the worst part of the day was over.

"That is totally unacceptable," Lee said. "I'm writing a letter to the school board."

"Yeah," I said. "It does seem kind of cruel."

"Cruel? What are you talking about?" she asked.

"What are *you* talking about?"

"The bottled water," she said. "There's no excuse for that. It's a waste of resources, and an unnecessary expense. The local tap water is fine."

"I thought you were talking about the cat," I said.

Before Lee could respond, Ms. Denton, who'd moved to the front of the room, got things started. She leaned against the lab table, just to the left of the cat. "Welcome to biology," she said. "You'll get used to it." She paused a moment before adding, "Or fail."

Sheila Bergstrom, who was about to regret her decision to wear pink today, and her parents' decision to pass along their Nordic heritage in the form of blond hair and blue eyes, raised her hand. "Is that . . . ?" She pointed at the cat.

"Relax, Barbie. That's for AP," Ms. Denton said. "College prep biology doesn't require you to dissect a cat."

Relief flowed through the room, mingled with scattered sighs of deep disappointment from the science crowd. My own relief was two-pronged. I was happy that I wouldn't be getting intimately familiar with the inside of a cat. I was also pleased that Sheila might have just won the role of least-favorite student. If so, I could add another slick escape to my achievements for the day.

"No cat for this class," said Ms. Denton. "We'll have to settle for a fetal pig."

The image of baby-sized strips of unborn pig sizzling in a pan almost booted the few remaining drops of digestive juices and tortilla sludge from my stomach, but I managed to choke back the nausea.

Lee patted my arm. "Fear not. I'm sure little Hamlet died of natural causes."

As I got ready to point out the unlikeliness of that, she laughed and shot me a *can't-you-tell-when-I'm-kidding?* look.

I returned my attention to the front of the room, where Ms. Denton had started taking attendance. She frowned when she reached my name. "Scott Hudson . . . ," she said. "Any relation to Bobby?"

Oh, great. . . .

I contemplated lying, but settled for saying, "Brother."

Last year, I'd managed to live down, or transcend, my brother's reputation with any of my teachers who'd encountered him during his stormy and incomplete passage through Zenger High. I guessed I was going to run into a new batch of teachers who'd encountered him during his sophomore year.

"You're not like him," she said.

Her tone was so flat, I couldn't tell whether her words were a statement, a question, or a wish. I settled for replying, "No. I'm not."

When the bell rang, I swung to the side of the room, keeping as far from the front table as possible. Lee walked over to the cat, pointed at something within, and asked, "Is that the heart?"

Ms. Denton moved to her side, glanced down, and said, "Yes, Morticia."

Lee ignored the name, though I'm sure she recognized the Addams Family reference, and shifted her finger. "Liver?"

Ms. Denton nodded. Ironically, she was the one, like Morticia Addams, who had long, dark hair and a pale complexion. She picked up a probe and touched something.

"Kidneys?" Lee guessed.

Another nod. "Very good. You should think about transferring to AP. It's not too late."

"I'll give it some thought," Lee said.

As we left the room, I said, "Maybe you really should. . . ."

"Nope," Lee said. "That would cause all sorts of parental expectations that I really don't want to have to live up to."

"You shouldn't not do something just because your parents would approve if you did it," I said.

Lee patted me on the back. "Double negative with a half twist. But you stuck the landing. Nice job, English geek."

"I'm not an English geek," I said.

"My apologies," Lee said. "You're a multi-faceted geek, with broad skills in a variety of disciplines, and a brain crammed with more than five thousand amazing facts."

"Okay. I'll admit to that. But you're dodging the issue. If you don't take AP just because it would please your parents to see you strive, you're cheating yourself."

"If I take AP, who's going to pat you on the back and offer comforting words after you spew tacos and fudgy bubbles?" she asked.

I let it go. Sometimes, arguing with Lee was like playing table tennis with an octopus. There was no way to get a shot past her.

She checked her schedule, pressed the back of her hand against her forehead in a fake swoon, and said, "Alas, it is here we part. I will try to be brave until we reunite."

"See you ninth period," I said. I added, "Morticia," when she was almost out of earshot.

She saluted at me over her shoulder with her middle finger. I took that as a sign of affection.

I headed for Life Skills. I had Ms. Pell, again. That was fine. She told us we'd be spending our first week learning how to balance a checkbook and reconcile an account statement. That was also fine. After an uneventful 5th period of checks and balances, I headed for Spanish.

"*Hola, mi estudiantes. Me llamo Señorita Morena,*" sayeth the teacher.

"*Hola, Señorita Morena,*" sayeth the class.

And that's pretty much all there was to sayeth about sixth period.

I had Mr. Cravutto again for gym. I'd sort of hated him last year, until I'd started to get in shape. Kyle was in my class this year. We'd been friends since kindergarten, and then, one day, we weren't friends anymore.

He caught me staring at him as we headed into the locker room. To my surprise, he smirked, like he'd played some sort of joke on me. That was a change from the guilty look he'd worn right after he'd betrayed me last year, and the ensuing anger at one's victim that often followed guilt. The look worried me. I made a note to keep my eyes open. Especially in the locker room.

We suited up and went outside. Mr. Cravutto didn't bother giving us an introductory talk. We didn't need it. We knew the drill. And talking wasn't a big part of his skill set.

"Renzler," he said, pointing at one of the kids from the JV football team, "warm-up exercises."

"Yes, COACH!" Renzler said.

Apparently, among those who participate in a large amount of extracurricular athletics, the word "coach" can never be spoken at a conversational volume.

Randy Renzler got in front of the class and ran us through the usual exercises while Mr. Cravutto stood to the side and scanned the double doors that led in and out of the gym as if he were waiting for an important package from UPS.

After we'd been thoroughly warmed up, Renzler shouted, "Now what, COACH?"

Mr. Cravutto pointed to the track. "Laps," he said.

Sadly, he didn't mean for us to sit and form them.

Right before we finished our first lap, the girls' class came out, carrying field-hockey sticks. They headed to the field. Mr. Cravutto headed over to the girls' teacher and started talking.

So that's where his mind was.

We ran.

He talked.

Apparently he had a lot to say. I couldn't hear the conversation, but I could guess parts of it, based on his hand gestures. He was telling her all about his sporting skills. Or he was playing a very active one-sided game of charades, trying to get her to guess the phrase, "struck by lightning." She kept nodding and glancing toward the field, where the girls had divided into two teams and started a game.

We kept running.

Eventually, a couple kids flopped to the grass next to the track. Soon after that, several more draped themselves over seats in the bleachers. I slowed down, but I figured I could keep jogging for a while. Mr. Cravutto had to notice us sooner or later.

Or so I thought.

When my legs and lungs signaled that they were going on strike, I dropped out. It pleased me that I'd lasted so long. The only remaining runners were three kids from the cross-country team, and two football players who must have been desperate to impress their coach, but were totally unaware that he would never notice their amazing acts of loyalty and endurance while a female member of the sweatclothes-and-whistles clan was in the vicinity.

Mr. Cravutto had more stamina than I did. He was still shooting his mouth off when the bell rang.

The bell!

We were supposed to be showered and changed before the bell.

Both gym teachers looked at the building as if they'd been startled out of a deep sleep, then turned toward us and blew their whistles.

Some of the kids ran for the locker room. I didn't care if I was late for art. I walked. There was no way I could sprint. After I took the quickest shower in the history of perspiration removal, I got dressed and headed for Mr. Cravutto's office for a late slip. There was a line of kids ahead of me. I heard Mr. Cravutto repeating, "You don't need a slip. Tell your teacher I said it was okay."

I figured that waiting around until I reached the front of the line would just make me later. So I headed for art.

The late bell had already rung.

The teacher, Mr. Belman, lobbed a sneer in my direction. "Nice of you to join us."

Oh, great. I didn't want to get on his bad side. I liked art. I launched into my excuse. "Mr. Cravutto—"

"Say no more," Mr. Belman said. The sneer melted into a grimace of sympathy. "You're excused."

"Thanks." That was a relief. All the seats were taken, except for one next to "Sardine Breath" Sabretski. Great. But I guessed, right then, I could give him some competition in the aromatic department. It could have been worse. At least it wasn't a class that required massive exhalations, like chorus or candle snuffing. I dropped down on the stool and drew in a big sigh of relief, just as my neighbor let out the sigh of someone who's lost personal space.

As I sat there trying to purge my lungs, I noticed that one of the counters under the windows was filled with empty glass bottles. There were all sorts, from tiny perfume bottles in fancy shapes to large bottles that looked like they once held wine or olive oil. There were even several milk bottles from the dairy store that had closed way back when I was little.

"Pick three bottles," Mr. Belman told the class. "Make sure they are different in as many ways as possible—height, circumference, profile, shape."

Before the last long vowel of the last word of his sentence had left his mouth, we'd all leaped to our feet and stampeded toward the windows. I snatched at bottles, trying to get the best ones, even though I had no idea what defined "best" in this situation. It reminded me of those scenes on the news from Black Friday, when people trample their fellow humans in a frenzy to get the best bargains.

After I'd returned to my seat with my trophies, I thought about the way my whole nervous system had responded to the unexpected competition. My immediate fear had been that there wouldn't be enough bottles for everyone. I had to make sure I got mine. It turned out to be an empty fear. There were plenty of bottles left on the counter after the onslaught, though not all of them were still standing. The unchosen bottles didn't look any better or worse than the ones I'd grabbed. I couldn't shake the worry that I'd made bad choices. As I scanned the room, and noticed how my classmates sat slightly hunched over their bottles, as if to protect them from being snatched away, I wondered what would have happened if there'd been a shortage.

We spent the rest of the period drawing our bottles, and seeing how they fit into a rectangle whose proportions Mr. Belman called the golden ratio. Then, the penultimate end-of-period bell of the day rang. Finally, after eight periods of regurgitation, sweat, triumphs, averted disasters, and misunderstandings, it was time for English.

And hubris.

FIVE

I ran into Lee on the steps to the second floor. "I hope the teacher is good," I said. "I can't imagine anybody topping Mr. Franka. Know anything about her?"

"Nope," Lee said. "I mean, I've heard her name, and I think she's been here for a long time, but I have no idea what she's like."

I shifted my bloated backpack—which had been fed a steady stream of textbooks—in an effort to find a more comfortable relationship between it and my shoulders.

"'He walked heavily,'" Lee said in a deep voice.

"Huh?"

Lee gave me a funny look, and repeated the phrase.

"What are you talking about?" I asked.

"It's from *Of Mice and Men*," she said. "Right near the opening. Lenny is described as walking like a bear. You *did* read it, right?"

"I read it twice," I said.

"When?" she asked.

"Uh . . . toward the end of sixth grade. And the summer after seventh." As I spoke, I realized how long ago that sounded. I'd piled a lot of books onto my "finished it" list since then. A whole lot of books. A mass of paragraphs. A slew of scenes. A heap of descriptions.

"Risky," Lee said.

"I'll be fine," I said.

"Of course you will. You seem to have a fair amount of Teflon on your surface," she said. "From what you've told me, today seems to be no exception. You probably have nothing to worry about."

"Yeah. It's not like she's going to slap us with a test the moment we walk in. I can skim the book tonight, to refresh my memory. It's a quick read."

We'd reached the room. Something seemed familiar, but also strange. The school was pretty old. Most of the classrooms had gotten dry-erase boards to replace the chalkboards over the years. And many had SMART Boards. But not this room. It had chalkboards. And it had faded grammar and literature posters that looked like they were from half a century ago.

Mrs. Gilroy, who was dressed in black slacks and a white long-sleeved blouse that seemed a bit too large for her, reminded me of the sort of young grandparent you see on the tennis courts, or in the ads for active retirement villages.

"She's some kind of mythical creature that's half Lee," I whispered, pointing to the black pants, "and half pirate."

"Very amusing," Lee said.

"Welcome to Sophomore Honors English," Mrs. Gilroy said. "It should come as no surprise to you that we'll be immersing ourselves in literature this year. We'll devote much of our time to savoring the joy and magic of our language."

That sounded perfect for me.

"Words are my passion. I hope you'll come to share that sentiment," she said.

This will be great, I thought as I settled into my seat.

"Who knows what *sophomore* means?" Mrs. Gilroy asked. She wrote the word on the board.

Wonderful. That's the sort of thing Mr. Franka would do, to make the class interesting, leading us somewhere by way of questions. And it was the sort of word he'd pick to make the lesson special. There was something very cool about sophomores discussing the meaning of *sophomore*.

While Mrs. Gilroy's back was turned, Josh Rosen said, "It means one year down, three to go."

Mrs. Gilroy took her time turning back to the class. She shot Josh—who hadn't lost his stupid grin—a glare that pretty much said *Don't say another word for the rest of the period*. Josh slunk down in his seat. I felt a twinge of happiness as I realized that, unless she'd had Bobby in her class and held grudges, our teacher had already discovered her least-favorite student. Even if she'd taught Bobby, I'd never be a candidate for problem student in English class. It was my best subject, by far. Still, it was a relief to see the position filled by a highly qualified candidate. Josh was a bit of an ass.

Mrs. Gilroy underlined the first four letters of *sophomore*. "Where else do we hear *soph*?"

"Sophisticated," I said. This was definitely my kind of lecture.

"Softball?" Josh said, quietly enough so Mrs. Gilroy didn't hear him.

I tried to dredge up another example. A word danced in my mind, just out of reach.

"Philosophy!" Lee said, beating me to it.

Mrs. Gilroy snapped her fingers, then pointed at Lee. "*Philosophy* means . . . ?"

"Love of knowledge," Lee said.

"Right," Mrs. Gilroy said, awarding Lee a smile. "Let's break it apart. We know *philo* is love."

That was true. Anyone who's lived in eastern Pennsylvania has learned that, thanks to constantly hearing how Philadelphia is the city of brotherly love.

"That leaves us with *soph* meaning what?" Mrs. Gilroy asked.

"Knowledge," I said.

Mrs. Gilroy shifted her attention from Lee to me. "Technically, *wisdom* is more accurate," she said. She underlined the last four letters of *sophomore*, then scanned the class. "What about *more*?"

Josh held his hands out like Oliver Twist, cupping an imaginary bowl. "May I have more?"

"Moron," I said.

Josh glared at me. "Not you," I said. "I was answering the question."

"Put it together," Mrs. Gilroy said. "Soph . . . more . . ."

"Smart, stupid!" Julia said. "Cool. That's us."

Heads nodded throughout the room in a moment of self-awareness.

"Not cool," Josh said. "We're not stupid."

"Nobody said you were," Mrs. Gilroy said. "The fact is, sophomores do tend to be smart-stupid. A little learning is definitely a dangerous thing. Anyone can amass a head full of facts. It's more difficult to make use of them, or to put two separate concepts together to create a new idea. Let's see what wisdom you've gleaned from your summer reading. I hope you've been looking forward to this discussion as much as I have."

As I got ready to discuss a great novel and impress Mrs. Gilroy with my grasp of literature by being all *soph* and no *more*, she added, "Before we begin our discussion, please take out a pencil and clear your desks."

Lee shot me a worried look.

"I'll be fine," I told her.

"I trust that most of you took the summer-reading

assignment seriously," Mrs. Gilroy said. "For those of you who might have slacked, I am offering a one-time-only opportunity. You can take the test tomorrow."

I felt the stress go out of my spine when she said that.

"There is one stipulation." She paused to stare briefly at each row of us, then said, "No matter how high you score on tomorrow's test, you will not receive anything above a seventy-nine. Is anyone interested in this option?"

Nobody raised a hand. I figured I could score higher than a seventy-nine taking the test today, even if I hadn't read the book in a while.

Mrs. Gilroy handed stacks of tests to the kids at the front of the rows. They passed back the sheets. I looked at the first question.

How is Lenny described in Chapter One?

I flashed a grin in Lee's direction.

"Eyes on your own paper, Mr. Hudson."

I looked down and wrote, "Like a bear."

And that was the high point of my test. I could tell you what happened in the novel. I could narrate the entire plot about simple-minded Lenny and the dreamer, George. I could discuss and debate themes, voice, viewpoint, and all that jazz. I just couldn't dredge up the right details to answer the very specific questions on the test. I fudged my answers as well as I could, but I had a feeling I wasn't going to fool Mrs. Gilroy. At the moment, I was all Lenny and no George.

Thirty minutes later, when we passed up the tests, I realized that whatever first impression I'd made during the discussion of *sophomore*, I was going to make a very bad second impression with Mrs. Gilroy when she graded my test. But maybe I could bump the test to her third impression. With luck, we'd have some class discussion.

After Mrs. Gilroy stuck the tests in a folder, she said, "I hope all of you like to write. We are going to be doing a *lot* of writing this year."

Okay. Now there was hope for me to redeem myself. If there was one thing I was getting pretty good at after working so hard last year on the school paper, it was writing. I'd make an extra effort to dazzle her when we did our first assignment.

As I was imagining her reaction to my creative efforts, she called up two students to pass out textbooks. As soon as I got mine, I flipped it open to the table of contents, and saw the usual gathering of plays, stories, poems, and essays, some of which were familiar. I was pleased to see one of my favorite Ray Bradbury stories among the selections, and a great Billy Collins poem.

We also got a booklet called "A Guide to Effective Writing." I glanced at the first page. It started with a paragraph about picking active verbs and avoiding passive sentences. Definitely rookie advice aimed at kids who didn't inhale books and write for fun. That was followed by a section about making good word choices. Yeah, yeah. Blah, blah, blah. I cloistered the booklet. No, wait. That was a terrible word choice. Let me try again. I stashed the booklet in my backpack. Yeah, much better choice. The writing tips were definitely aimed at babies. Maybe Sean could use them.

By that time, class was almost over. We started a discussion of our summer reading, but it only lasted five minutes. I didn't get a chance to dazzle Mrs. Gilroy with my insights.

The bell rang. Lee and I headed for the hallway.

"Well, she sure shot down a big part of my identity," I said.

"What do you mean?" Lee asked.

I parroted Mrs. Gilroy's words, "Anyone can amass a head full of facts." I paused to admire the way I'd captured her tone, then said, "I guess knowing a bunch of facts doesn't mean anything."

"But loving the knowledge does," Lee said. "That's the first thing I noticed about you."

"It wasn't my biceps?" I asked.

"I'm not even sure you have those," she said.

"Of course I do." I curled my right arm, pumping up my bicep. "Check it out."

"Seriously? You want me to feel your muscles. I don't know. I'm afraid I'd swoon."

I unflexed. School was over. But the best part of school was still ahead of me.

"Want to come to the newspaper meeting?" I asked Lee.

"No thanks, Jimmy Olsen," she said.

"I'm not a cub reporter," I said. "I have a whole year of experience."

"Knock 'em dead," she said. "Or am I supposed to say 'Break a pen'?"

"Either will do, I guess."

SIX

The conference room felt both familiar and strange. Last year's seniors had moved on, including editor Mandy. I'd had a minor crush on her last year, on top of the major crush I'd had for Julia. Crushes aren't like relationships. I don't think it's cheating to have more than one. It's probably self-destructive and delusional. But it's not cheating.

By the time the meeting started, nearly every seat around the room-length table was taken. I saw the other sophomores who'd joined the paper last year, including Richard and Edith. There were two boys and a girl who looked like they were freshmen. One of the boys had a stack of cartoons in front of him. I recognized him from middle school, but didn't know his name.

Just as we were about to get going, the door opened, and Hatboy from the bus raced in. He closed the door, pressed his back against it, and looked around with wild eyes, as if trying to make sure he hadn't just leaped from a lion's den into a tiger's lair.

His eyes downshifted from terrified to merely fearful when he spotted me. "Hi. You're on my bus."

"I'm aware of that."

Before he could continue reminiscing about the good old days of this morning, the door flew open, pinning him to the wall behind it. A big guy—the kind who can't find shirts with collars that fit his neck—looked in from the hallway. Fortunately, he wasn't smart enough to check behind the door for his quarry.

"Anyone seen a little jerk with a big mouth?"

"It's mostly big jerks with little mouths in here," I said.

Gargantua glared at me, but I guess he couldn't process anything that complex right then, while his mind was locked into search-and-destroy mode. He snorted and walked away. The door swung closed. Hatboy, with his back to us, looked a bit like a mounted butterfly. But as he unpeeled himself from the wall and turned around, I didn't see any blood, or jagged protrusions of fractured bone. He staggered toward the table and realigned his glasses to within ten degrees of their proper horizontal orientation.

"What did you do?" I asked the kid.

"I corrected his grammar," he said.

"Some people don't appreciate that," I said. From what I recalled, that was one of the things I'd covered in my survival manual.

"I'll say." He pointed at us with both hands. "What's this? Some kind of club?"

"Newspaper meeting," I said.

"That sounds safe." He checked to make sure the door was shut all the way, then dropped into one of the two remaining empty seats—the one that happened to be right next to me. "Can I join?"

"Can you write?" I asked.

"I know grammar," he said. "And I'm great at math."

"Perfect," I said. "We've been looking for someone who could number the pages correctly. We keep stumbling over the best way to divide primes."

He started to reply, then laughed. "I get it! That's a good one. I told you that you were funny." He held out his hand. "I'm Jeremy Danger."

"Seriously?"

"Yeah. I know. Not a good fit. That's one of life's many jokes. *Disaster* would have been a better match."

The hand remained extended. I shook it. His grip reminded me of times when I'd caught an undersized trout and had to hold it as gently as possible while I removed the hook. Jeremy was also the name of the main character in one of my favorite books, *Jeremy Thatcher, Dragon Hatcher,* but I didn't share that information. I wasn't planning on bonding with Master Danger.

"Coincidentally, Jeremy's a character in one of my favorite books," he said, still enthusiastically pumping my hand.

The door opened again. Jeremy screamed and leaped for cover. Fortunately, he let go of my hand on the way down.

But it wasn't a reappearance of the Incredible Dolt. It was just Mr. Franka, our adviser, and one of the best teachers I'd ever had. Like last year, he wore a beard, and a blue shirt with rolled sleeves.

"Welcome," he said. He gave me a small nod after he'd scanned the room, barely blinking as Jeremy crawled out from under the table. Instead of taking a seat, Mr. Franka walked to the front of the room. "Let's get the bad news out of the way. Our state funds got cut again this year. Something had to go. Unfortunately, the newspaper, along with a cluster of other programs deemed inessential by those who should know better, is now a supplemental budget item. It's part of what they call 'Question Two.' The voters—your parents and neighbors—have to approve it separately from the main budget issue. If the package doesn't get approved we'll lose our funding after the elections."

Rumbles arose. Mr. Franka waved his hand for quiet. "I know. It's a terrible system. But it's the one we have to live with, unless one of you has an idea how we can turn newspaper writing and production into a popular spectator sport. For now, let's make an amazing paper—a paper everyone will love. People don't kill what they love."

I cleared my throat the way people do when they have an obnoxious point to make. We'd read a great poem in Mr.

Franka's class last year, called "The Ballad of Reading Gaol," by Oscar Wilde. It kept using the line, "Each man kills the thing he loves."

I guess Mr. Franka realized what I was thinking. "Good point, Scott. Let's hope nobody goes Wilde with the paper." He turned back to the group. "Okay, first piece of business, we need an editor in chief, because I am only here to advise. Who's up for the job?"

After the briefest flicker of ambition tickled my mind, sending a twinge into my shoulder that almost made me raise my hand, I sat back. I figured I could do an okay job as an editor, but I liked writing my own stuff a lot more than reading other people's articles or handing out assignments. And, traditionally, the editor was a senior. There were four seniors in the room. Lisa Athenos was new to the paper. Ben Sabin and Orlando Fry had joined last year. Sarah Klein had been on the paper since she was a freshman. It didn't take much discussion before Sarah rose to the top. Everyone seemed pleased with the choice.

We assigned other editorial positions, and then got to work figuring out the best department, or *beat*, as we journalists like to call it, for each reporter. Last year, I'd been dying to write book reviews. But, as much as I loved reading, I'd discovered that there was more pleasure in writing about things I'd observed than things I'd read. I figured I'd do sports again. But maybe it would be good for me to try something new. I hadn't even wanted to do sports when I got stuck with it, but it turned out to be fun. I decided to sit back and see what Sarah gave me.

Richard got restaurant reviews, like last year. His parents had both gone to cooking school, so he knew all about food. Edith was doing movie reviews and concerts.

Dan, the freshman with the cartoons, showed us his stuff. We all liked it. We had a couple of cartoonists already, but we'd be able to fit in one more. The other two freshmen, Teresa Braxton and Doug Zolner, loved sports, so Sarah assigned that to both of them.

"You two figure out how to split it up," she said.

I liked her approach. She was going to be a good editor-in-chief. While I waited for my assignment, everything got assigned. Finally, Sarah checked her notes, looked at me, and said, "What about doing some opinion pieces?"

"Sure. That could be fun," I said.

"Keep an eye out for feature ideas, too," she said. "I liked your stuff last year. It was very creative. I want to give you free rein and see what you come up with."

"Thanks."

"I'll let you kids carry on from here," Mr. Franka said. "I have a staff meeting. We're dealing with possible cuts in several departments, too, if the increase in the main budget doesn't get approved."

As he slipped out the door, Sarah said, "We really need to make the paper essential. Especially if it's up for a vote. What can we add? How do we make everyone want to read it each week?"

"We could have a crossword puzzle," Jeremy said.

"Those are hard to construct." Back when I was in middle school, I'd tried to make a real one, like they have in the local paper, where the words are at least three letters long and the pattern is symmetrical. I eventually gave up, after determining that *claxbre, remeeev,* and *drlbuvo* weren't words in any known language. Nor were the nine or ten other linguistic monstrosities that had invaded my grid as I struggled to fill it with interesting words that crossed each other.

"I can do them," Jeremy said. "They're almost trivial."

I had a feeling his idea of a trivial puzzle would be most people's idea of a fight to the death against a killer dictionary.

"We'll think about it," Sarah said. "They take up a lot of space when you add in the grid, all the clues, and the solution. Any other ideas?"

We kicked around a variety of suggestions, but they all needed too much space. Still, I liked the idea of a puzzle. I thought about other things I'd written.

"Got it!" I explained about Tom Swifties. Mr. Franka had introduced us to them last year, so some of the staff were already familiar with the concept. I tossed out several simple examples for those who had never seen them.

"I have total control over my computer," Tom said mousily.

"A softball is harder to pitch than a baseball," Tom said underhandedly.

"*I killed Dracula and the Wolfman,*" Tom said demonstrably.

Jeremy got the idea right away, and shared a good one:

"*Learning handwriting makes me want to swear,*" Tom said cursively.

"Good one," I said.

"That's kind of funny," Sarah said, "but how does that have anything to do with the paper?"

"Some of them are a lot trickier. We can make a puzzle by leaving off the last word. Everyone would want to see the next issue to find out if they'd guessed right, or to learn the answer if they couldn't figure it out."

"If *he or she* had guessed right," Jeremy said.

"What?"

"*Everyone* is singular," Jeremy said.

"How have you managed to live this long?" I asked.

"Part luck, part panic-induced bursts of speed," he said.

It was Sarah's turn to clear her throat. After she recaptured my attention, she said, "Give me an example of a good puzzle."

I dredged up one of the trickier Swifties I'd written for fun last year. "*I am going out with a mermaid,*" Tom said . . .

I left it hanging. Now, they were all staring. I realized I'd given them a pretty tough one. I tossed out a clue. "Where do mermaids live?"

Answers spilled out:

"Ocean . . ."

"Disney World . . ."

"Sea . . ."

I had a weird flash of not *déjà vu* but *deja who*? I didn't have a strange feeling I'd done this before. Instead, I felt I'd become Mrs. Gilroy, leading the class toward the meaning of *sophomore*. But better dressed and less cranky.

I dangled the second clue. "You go out on a . . . ?"

"Tangent . . ."

"Whim . . ."

"Date . . ."

"Limb . . ."

Jeremy got it first. "Sedately!"

"Yup," I said. "See how it works as a puzzle? I've got a ton of them at home. I wrote a bunch for fun last year. I can make up more, if we run out. We can do seasonal ones, or tie them to school events. It would take up almost no space."

"Let's do that." Sarah jotted a note on her pad. "We can add other puzzles if we get more ideas."

"Can I still do a crossword?" Jeremy asked.

"I think we should let the resident cruciverbalist go for it," I said.

Jeremy stared at me as if I'd just plucked a vanished playing card from his shirt pocket.

"You're not the only one in the room in possession of extraneous vocabulary," I said.

■ ■ ■

After the meeting, I figured I'd have to walk into town to catch a metro bus home. But Wesley was parked in the side lot of the school in his bagel truck. Asleep. I didn't want to disturb him, but he woke up when I got close. I doubt it's possible to sneak up on him.

"What are you doing here?" I asked.

"Figured you'd want a ride home."

"Thanks." I climbed in.

He glanced at his watch. "Don't tell me you finally did something worth getting detention."

"Nope. Newspaper meeting," I said. "So, you've been delivering bagels all day?"

"Mostly." He handed me a paper bag that was sitting between the seats.

"What's this?" I asked.

"Extras." He switched on the ignition and backed out of the space.

I opened the bag, grabbed a poppy-seed bagel, which seemed to be all there was, and took a small bite. I figured my stomach was far enough away from the memory of Splitty the Cat that I could keep my food down.

"Tasty." I risked a larger bite. Bagels aren't designed for nibbling. I hadn't realized how starved I was. I'd spent most of the day with an empty stomach. I bit off another hunk before I'd even swallowed the previous one.

"Yeah. They're not bad. They spilled out when I was

70

unloading a delivery. But I brushed them off pretty good. We're supposed to throw them out if they touch the ground, but that seems like a waste."

As those words penetrated my brain, I realized that poppy seeds weren't normally quite as crunchy and gritty as whatever it was I was chewing.

Wesley glanced over his shoulder. "That reminds me. I'm supposed to sweep out the back of the truck each day. Guess I'll do it later."

I didn't join him in contemplating the space behind us. I decided I'd rather not know what the debris on the floor looked like—especially since I was in the process of grinding part of it between my molars.

I spat my mouthful of dirt bagel out the window. It splattered against the asphalt like a doughy snowball.

Wesley was busy enough taking a corner on fewer than four wheels that he failed to notice my review of the food.

"Call me later if you want to do something," he said when he dropped me off.

"Okay. I'm not sure how long my homework will take. I'll call if I get it done early enough."

I spat a couple more stray particles of grit out of my mouth. Then I headed inside.

The first thing I heard when I walked through the door into a cloud of beef-laden air was Mom's voice, coming from the kitchen. "Hi, Scott. I'm making tacos for dinner."

Mom's tacos were infinitely better than the school cafeteria's, but the smell of spiced shredded beef, mixed with the memory of biology, almost launched that initial nibble of bagel back out of my stomach.

"Great," I said, barely managing to speak as I choked back my nausea. Normally, I'd stop in the kitchen after school for a snack. But I figured the farther I got from the smell of food right now, the better, so I headed for the stairs. "I have a ton of homework. I should get started."

"How was school?" she called.

"Fine."

I did have a fair amount of homework. But that wasn't a big surprise. After I finished, I took my journal from freshman year downstairs to the computer and typed up all the parts that contained the advice I'd written for Sean. I left out the personal stuff, like Bobby getting into trouble, and my pathetic yearnings for Julia's attention.

That still left a fairly impressive amount of material. I made the font large, so there were lots of pages. I wanted Jeremy to feel he was getting plenty for his money. As I was tweaking the layout of the pages so they looked nice, I remembered how badly I'd gotten lost in the building on my first day. I added a quick and easy color-coded guide to navigating the halls of Zenger High, with special attention to safe and dangerous areas. I even found an image online of the "here there be dragons" warning from ancient maps, and changed the key word to "seniors." The map brought the count up to thirty-one pages. When I was happy with the way everything looked, I printed out the manual, complete with a cover, and put it in my backpack.

September 2

Good news, Sean. It looks like I'll be compiling more survival advice for you. I'm too fried to go into details, so I'll just summarize what I've learned. Don't trust your memory when it comes to summer reading. Don't eat right before biology class. If someone mocks you, hit back hard and fast. Take no prisoners. Keep track of the time when you're in gym class. And just because something looks like a poppy seed doesn't mean it is a poppy seed. Generally, it's a good idea to know the entire history of anything you plan to chew. In cop shows on TV, I think they call that "the chain of custody."

By the way, I read through my journal this afternoon. When I did, I saw a couple mistakes. I'd told you O. Henry had messed up in the opening of "The Gift of the Magi" unless there were two-cent coins back then. I just looked it up. They did have two-cent coins for a while. But it still makes a pretty interesting puzzle.

This wasn't in my journal, but I stumbled across another mistake Mr. Franka, Lee, and I all made last year. We thought that "Ninety percent of everything is crap" was Sturgeon's Law. (Named for the writer, not the fish. Though it would be fun if he'd written that ninety percent of everything is carp.) It turns out the real name for it is Sturgeon's Revelation. Like most common mistakes not involving explosives, heavy machinery, or high speeds, it is of no importance in the real world.

SEVEN

Jeremy ran toward me when I was half a block from the bus stop. "Do you have it?" he asked

"Yeah. *Ssshhhh.*" I noticed some of the kids at the stop were staring at us.

"Great!" He pulled a cloth wallet—the kind you make in summer camp—from his pocket, extracted several bills, and waved them in my face. "I've got the money."

"Not here," I said. "Wait until we get on the bus." Oh, great. Now I guaranteed that he'd be sitting with me. But I didn't want people seeing me selling something. I guess I sort of felt I was ripping him off. Or, at the very least, exploiting his fear. I was suddenly sure the manual was a worthless bundle of crap. On top of that, the whole thing reminded me of a spy-movie scene involving the sale of government secrets. I almost expected a SWAT team to descend on us with weapons drawn the instant I exchanged the item for the cash. Or maybe that would be a SWAP team.

When we got to our seat on the bus, I pulled the manual from my backpack. "Here."

"Thanks!" He snatched it from my hand, gave me the money, then immediately started reading.

As weirded out as I was by all of this, I couldn't help watching his face as he read my words. Yeah, *my* words. I was used to kids reading my articles in the school paper, but this was more than that. It was a book. Okay, an extremely thin book. A manual, really. But, it was a manual I'd created, filled with my hard-earned wisdom. His eyes moved rapidly. He nodded. His respiration rate increased in a way I found oddly gratifying.

"Yeah. Wow. I never thought of that . . . ," he said. "This is brilliant!"

He kept reading, as absorbed as if he were holding a tale crafted by one of the masters of modern fiction. Once in a while, he'd say a sentence out loud, as if tasting it. It felt strange to hear my words spoken by someone else.

When the bus stopped, he looked up at me and said, "This manual is amazing! Great advice. It makes so much sense."

"Thanks."

I managed to stay awake in geometry. Mr. Stockman's puns helped keep me listening to the lesson. Nobody in history seemed eager to resurrect the issue of bladder control. Bradley had no interest in stepping into the ring for round two. The lesson, about ice-age residents of our land, was fine. I wasn't sure what to do about lunch. I decided to see how hungry I got if I skipped a meal. I'd had a big breakfast. I could make it through the school day without food, and then grab something as soon as I got home.

When it was time for biology, I navigated a path that skirted Splitzkers. But as I walked along the side of the room, Ms. Denton opened the round glass hatch on some sort of small oven. An odor wafted out. My whole body spasmed as I fought to keep from heaving my breakfast cereal into the air in a gastric rainbow. I managed to force everything to remain where it belonged.

"It's an autoclave," Ms. Denton said. Not that I had any desire to know the name of that foul thing.

"Phew . . ." The response spilled out on its own.

"Wait until you hold your first child in your arms and he empties his bowels into his diaper," she said.

"Been there," I told her.

Her eyes widened somewhat. "How precocious of you."

"Baby brother," I said.

She smirked. "I guess your parents could use a refresher in biology."

I could have shot back with something, but I knew there was nothing to be gained from waging war against authority. I'd seen kids try to win a battle of words with a teacher. Even if they won, they lost. I kept my mouth shut and took my seat. One of the oldest and truest clichés out there is *You can't fight*

City Hall. Though I guess it's actually only as old as City Hall itself. I'm sure there's a prehistoric version along the lines of *You can't fight Gronk's cave.*

"Looks like you made a friend," Lee said.

I nodded, but remained silent, just in case Ms. Denton was listening.

"Teacher's pet," Lee said. "Hudson charm is irresistible."

I didn't know about that. But Hudson hunger was definitely hard to ignore. I made it through biology, where hunger would never be a driving force, and Life Skills, but started to feel the pangs of emptiness in Spanish class. It didn't help that we were reading a story about Luis and his mother making tamales. I was starving in study hall. By the time I got to art, I was ready to eat some paste, just to have something in my stomach.

Then I got to English and forgot all about hunger. There it lay, in all its red glory, waiting for me on my desk, as if Mrs. Gilroy wanted to make sure I had every possible second of ninth period to wallow in regret. A sixty-seven. That was about a D+. As if that wasn't bad enough, she'd put a sticker in the upper right corner of the paper, next to the grade. It wasn't a gold star, of course. It looked like Mr. Yuk—the guy who sticks his tongue out to warn toddlers that the sweet tasty syrup in the bottle is really bad for them.

Lee got a ninety-two. A happy yellow duck gave her a wink and a big thumbs-up. Or a wings-up. Stickers are stupid. I stuffed the test in my backpack. I had to do something about this. I was too dismayed by the grade to participate much in the book discussion.

At the end of class, Mrs. Gilroy said, "I'd like to thank those of you who cared enough to participate in our discussion." She looked right at me as she said that.

I really had to do something about the hole I was digging for myself before the top of my head slipped below ground level.

"Go ahead," I told Lee when the bell rang. "I'll catch up with you."

"Good luck, Lenny," she said.

"Enough with the Steinbeck references," I said.

Lee flashed me an evil grin. "Okeydokey."

"Thanks a lot." I knew that Steinbeck's *The Grapes of Wrath* was about people from Oklahoma—Okies. And Lee knew that I knew.

I waited until the room was clear, and then walked up to Mrs. Gilroy's desk. "Can I talk to you about my test grade?" I asked.

"You can talk to me about whatever you wish," she said. "I'd prefer that my students talk *with* me."

Good grief. If she was going to give me that much of a hard time over a stupid preposition, maybe it was pointless to talk to her. Or with her. Or at her. But I had to give it a shot. I was not a D student. Not in English. I pulled the test from my backpack. "I don't want you to think I didn't read the book," I said.

She glanced at the test. "I think you didn't read the book carefully," she said. "That's a fairly obvious inference."

"I love that book," I said. "I've read it twice. I swear."

"When?" she asked.

I told her.

She shook her head. "It was your summer-reading assignment. *This* summer. Not two summers ago, or however far back you crossed paths with it. You can't participate in a class discussion of a book that's at best a vague memory."

I was going to protest that the book was far more than a vague memory. But I realized the test in my hand was a lethal counterargument to that claim. "I know. I messed up. But I did love the book. Both times. And I love to read. I read a ton of books this summer."

"That is irrelevant. You neglected to read the right one," she said.

"I made a mistake. Is there anything I can do to get a second chance?" I asked.

She regarded me for a moment, as if trying to see whether I was a hopeless scoundrel attempting to scam her, or a miscreant worth saving. "Write an essay on arrogance," she said.

"Great. I love writing. I'm really good at it."

"Perhaps *irony* would be a better topic for you."

I stared at her, not quite realizing at the moment that I'd just been skewered. Though it all became clearer during the dozens of replays my mind forced me to suffer through.

"I see that subtlety is lost on you. We'll stick with the topic of arrogance. You certainly are filled with love for things," she said. Her tone hinted she thought I was filled with something less fragrant than love. "Since you love writing, you'll have no trouble delivering an essay of five hundred words tomorrow."

"No problem," I said. If she'd thought I'd flinch at the word count, she didn't know me at all. "I could do that with my eyes closed."

"I'm sure it will read as if it were written that way," she said.

I stared at her. Had she just smacked me down with an insult? It definitely felt like a jab. She wasn't finished.

"Since you are so confident—perhaps even *arrogant*?— about your ability to churn out a large volume of prose in a short span of time, let's make your assignment an even thousand words. I want there to be *some* problem. Otherwise, there's no point in this exercise."

"Sure, I can handle that. Piece of cake." Oops. That slipped out before I had a chance to give it any thought.

"Two thousand, then," she said. "Have we transcended slices of cake? Are we in the realm of soufflés, tarts, *croquembouche*, and other more challenging baked goods? Will two thousand words be a sufficiently grueling assignment to require the opening of at least one of your eyes?"

I clamped my mouth down on my reflexive response. It seemed like a good time to merely echo her words. "Two thousand."

When I got outside, Lee said, "So, how much worse did you make things for yourself?"

"I didn't make things worse. She's giving me another chance."

"What do you have to do?"

"Write a two-thousand word essay on arrogance."

"For it or against it?"

"She didn't say."

"Probably safe to assume you should be against it."

"But she didn't actually specify a position." I got excited when I realized I could have fun with the essay. I'd spent all of last year stretching and expanding my writing. I'd found unique ways to report on sports. During the summer, I'd fooled around with poetry a bit, and even started to write some plays, and one marvelously gory short story, "Corpse and Corpuscles," where a man drowned in his own blood. "Maybe I am in favor of it. This is going to be awesome."

Lee made a sound. It wasn't the sort that accompanies encouragement. When we reached the bus area, I found myself facing a mob of freshmen. "It's *him*!" one of them shouted. The group vibrated.

"'Him'? Did you form a band and not tell me?" Lee asked. "Or make a movie?"

"Nothing that impressive," I said.

Jeremy detached himself from the masses. "They want to buy copies."

"All of them?" I asked. It looked like nearly a dozen kids.

Their heads nodded. Their eyes widened. My brain went *ka-ching!* "Hands," I said. Hands went up. I counted. Nine more copies. Wow. "I'll have them for you tomorrow."

The cluster darted away, moving like a school of baitfish.

"That was you not so long ago," Lee said. "And yet, you smirk."

"What are you talking about?"

"That look of amusement on your face. You think of them as pathetically helpless and clueless. Right?"

"Sort of. What's wrong with that?"

"Nothing. I just find it amusing."

"You're amused at my amusement?" I asked.

"Constantly."

"I'll keep that in mind."

When I got home, I figured I'd tackle the essay first. After that, I'd print the nine manuals. Despite Lee's warning, I knew it would be fun to take a position in favor of arrogance. I found out pretty quickly that I'd made the right decision, because the words just flowed directly from my mind to my fingers. I was totally rocking the task. It was fun defending arrogance. The first time I checked the word count, after what seemed like only two or three minutes, I was already up to three hundred words. Then I got on a roll, and fell into the creative zone where time no longer exists. When I checked again, I was close to a thousand words, and I still had plenty to say. Before I knew it, I had two thousand words.

Take that, Mrs. Gilroy.

Okay—I guess that was an arrogant thought, but I'd earned the right to think it. And I'd proved, by way of a well-constructed and clever series of arguments, that arrogance was not a bad thing. Now to get back to filling the orders for my manual.

I'd already done the hard work of separating the survival tips from the personal stuff, and formatting everything to look good. All I had to do was print nine copies. I set things up on the computer, then clicked *PRINT.*

Our printer was kind of slow. But I didn't need to hang around and watch the pages ooze out. I went upstairs to do my homework. After I finished my bio and geometry, I checked things, and saw a thin stack of pages in the output tray and a flashing light on the control panel. The printer was out of paper.

I fanned through the sheets. Oh, crap. I'd printed nine cover pages, nine copies of page one, then nine copies of page two, and so on. And it had only gotten to page three. There were twenty-eight more pages to print. And I'd have to collate the copies. It would be better to print one copy at a time.

I found more paper in a drawer under the computer desk—about a quarter of a pack—and refilled the printer. Then I went to the computer, cleared the current print job, and told it to print one copy. There was probably some way to tell it to print multiple copies in the right order, but I didn't want to spend time hunting for that. It was easier to do it manually. I figured I'd just print the copies one by one. It would be tedious, but better than separating all the pages after everything was printed. And, as I liked to remind myself, I was making money with every copy.

On my way up the stairs, I realized I didn't need to print the cover and the first three pages again. I already had nine copies of them. Too late for this copy. But not for the rest.

I printed the second and third copies without those pages. By then, I was totally out of paper. Tomorrow, I'd walk home after school and buy some in town. Paper wasn't expensive. Six of the freshmen would just have to wait for their copies. It felt good to be in demand. I was probably J. P. Zenger High School's best-selling author. And its only one.

I put the finished copies in my backpack. "I'm in business," I said. Business. Maybe I could come up with another idea to sell to the freshmen. Or to everyone. There was no reason I had to limit my market to one segment. This looked like a real easy way to make money. Even better, it was a way to make money doing something I was good at.

When I came down for dinner, Mom said, "Well, you worked hard today."

"I had a lot of homework," I said. Not to mention running my publishing empire, and writing a pretty awesome essay.

"Too much to handle?" Dad asked.

"Nope. I'm on top of it."

"Are you sure?" Mom asked. "It's not too late to switch classes. Bobby did that all the time."

"I'm positive," I said. "You have nothing to worry about."

They both looked relieved.

EIGHT

When I got off the bus, the freshmen descended on me, their arms out like they were begging for alms. I pulled the three copies from my backpack.

"This is all I have right now," I said.

That produced frantic hand-waving, a flurry of pushing, and shouts of "Me!"

"Calm down! I'll have the rest tomorrow." I wondered what would be the fairest way to decide who got a copy today. I couldn't help thinking about how each year, there was a hot toy that all the little kids wanted for Christmas. And there was never enough supply, so parents would pay all sorts of money or do crazy things to get their hands on one.

I realized I had to do something quickly. The gerbils were getting frantic.

"Who needs this the most?" I asked.

All nine hands went up.

Okay. That didn't help. I tried a different approach. "Who had a problem with another student yesterday?"

Nine hands.

"Who got in trouble with a teacher?"

Nine hands.

"Who got lost in the building?"

Nine hands.

"Figure it out among yourselves," I said.

They went from calm discussion to shouts and threats in less time than it took for me to fully congratulate myself on my problem-solving abilities. People really are animals.

"Stop it!"

They froze. I had a crazy feeling that if I said, "Drop to all fours and howl like a coyote," they'd transform the parking lot into Yellowstone right before my eyes.

I picked a random number. "Each of you, think of a number between one and one hundred." I pointed to them, one by one, and let them tell me their numbers. After I'd heard from all of them, I gave the manuals to the three who'd come the closest to my number. While the winners were paying me, and grinning like they'd just been handed a million dollars, I could see the others staring at them with a mix of envy and hostility.

"Don't worry," I said. "I'm just temporarily out of stock. You'll all get yours tomorrow."

As I put the money away, I wondered why I bothered

worrying about grades. Nobody in my family had ever gone to college. My brother hadn't even finished high school. He was studying for his GED now, but he'd left the halls of Zenger High midway through his senior year. And he was doing just fine. So was my dad.

If I was already making money with my writing, without even really trying, think how well I could do if I gave it all my attention. On the way to homeroom, I pictured myself living on my own, in a cool apartment, writing stuff people would line up to buy. Maybe I'd be living with Lee. That thought quickly took off in its own direction, abandoning the literary world for earthier realms.

"Hey, Scott, where are you?"

I looked back. Lee was right behind me. "Huh?"

"I called your name three times," she said. "Whatever thoughts you were lost in must have come equipped with earmuffs."

"Sorry." I banished the imaginary cohabitational Lee from my mind and turned my attention to the real one. "I was thinking about the manual."

"And you made the shift automatically," Lee said with a smirk.

"Yeah." My brain was too busy switching gears and wading through pools of guilt to reply to her pun with one of my own. I felt like I'd narrowly avoided being caught with my pants down.

But the memory of the fantasy tickled at my mind. As I sat next to Lee in geometry, I reminded myself that I had no idea what sort of relationship I'd even have with her when I was old enough to move out on my own. Still, it was a seductive image.

The rest of the day was uneventful, not counting the growls produced by the growing hunger I felt from skipping lunch. When I got to English class, I dropped the essay on Mrs. Gilroy's desk. "Two thousand words on arrogance," I said.

"Oh, good," she said. "I was afraid I'd have to settle for reading one of the classics this evening. I guess poor Tolstoy will have to get through the night without my admiration."

I didn't bother to respond.

"Want to walk into town?" I asked Lee after school.

"I can't. My folks are picking me up to go to my aunt's house. It's her birthday. She only has one a year, so it's sort of special."

"Too bad she's not twins," I said.

"That's my misfortune, too. There'd be more presents for me, were that the case," Lee said. "We could drop you off in town."

"That's okay," I said. "I'll walk." I didn't feel like being around her dad.

Since I didn't have to worry about catching the bus, I swung by Mr. Franka's room on my way out. He was sorting a stack of comic books in hanging folders in a filing cabinet.

"How's it going, Scott?" he asked when I walked in.

"Mrs. Gilroy hates me," I said.

"I know," he said.

That hit me by surprise. I'd expected him to lead with something like *Of course she doesn't.*

"How did you know?" I asked.

"Because she hates everyone."

"Very funny," I said.

"But also very true. She feels the current generation of students has no respect for our language. So don't let yourself feel singled out."

"I can't help it. She hates me more than anyone else in the class," I said. "And I love English. You know that."

"So consider this a true test of your love," he said.

"Why does love always have to be tested?" I asked.

"That's just the way things work," he said. "If love never got tested, what would writers have to write about?"

"Lots of stuff," I said. "War. Dragons. Cookies. The possibilities are endless."

"Here's the truth, Scott. Mrs. Gilroy knows more about the English language and English literature than anyone else in this building. If you're smart, you'll learn everything you can from her, no matter how hard it might be for you to put your ego aside. Trust me."

"Ego?"

"Everyone has one," he said. "To claim otherwise would be egotistical. Put yours aside."

"I'll try."

I headed into town and bought the cheapest paper I could find. Mom was on the computer when I got home, looking up something about baby rashes. From the brief glance I got of the images on the monitor, I definitely didn't want to stick around. I went upstairs to start my homework. After Mom was finished, I'd print out the last six copies. Maybe tomorrow I'd even get more orders. Word would be spreading. Especially since there'd been a shortage. I thought about just printing three copies, extending the shortage and making the manual even more desirable. But I was afraid there'd be a riot.

Later, when I heard Mom emptying the dishwasher in the kitchen, I put aside my history reading and went downstairs, but then Dad was online, checking out the sports news, so I got back to work. It really sucked that we only had one computer. But at least it was a good one.

Just as I was finishing my homework, I heard Dad swear. He doesn't do that much at all. I went downstairs. He was trying to print out a coupon for twenty percent off one item at our local hardware store.

"We're out of ink," he said. "How could we be out of ink? I just put in new cartridges last weekend. There's no way we used all of it."

He spotted me before I could sneak off.

"Did you print something?" he asked.

"A couple things," I said.

"Couple?"

"Maybe a bit more than that," I said.

"Maybe a lot more?"

"Maybe."

"So maybe you should buy some ink."

"Sure. I can do that." *Oh, crap.* I didn't even know what ink cost. It couldn't be that expensive. After Dad left the computer, I checked the model number for our printer, then got online and searched for cartridges.

Oh, my God. Did they make it out of the blood of unicorns or the tears of pixies? How could a little box of ink cost that much? It looked like my profits were going to take a big hit, or maybe even disappear entirely. And it looked like I wasn't going to print those six copies this evening.

September 4

I told you this wasn't a journal, Sean. And it's absolutely not a diary. Did you figure out what you have in your hands? It's actually an *epistle*. That's a fancy word for a letter. What's the difference? In a journal, I'd be writing to myself. I'd basically be sharing my thoughts with myself. In an epistle, I'm writing to someone else. That would be you. Even though you are not, at this moment that I am actually writing this, capable of reading these epistles. But that's okay. Your shortcomings—hah, you're short in most departments, except moisture generation—anyhow, your shortcomings have zero effect on the tone of the epistle.

Anyhow, here's today's tip. You can learn stuff even from people you don't like, and people who don't like you. At least, that's what Mr. Franka told me. And I like him. So I'm going to try really hard to learn from Mrs. Gilroy. And from Ms. Denton, for that matter.

When I got off the bus, I looked around for the pack of freshmen who hadn't gotten their manuals yet. I wanted to slip past them. They were going to be really unhappy that I was empty-handed.

But they weren't there. Nobody was waiting for me. That was weird. Maybe their history homework assignment had been to reenact the disappearance of the Roanoke Colony. On my way to homeroom, I saw a kid—one I didn't even recognize—carrying a copy of my manual. Except the cover wasn't in color.

I tapped him on the shoulder. He screamed and jumped away. Then he started digging in his pockets, like he was eager to give me his lunch money.

"Hold it! I'm not trying to hurt you. I just have a question. Okay?"

He nodded.

I pointed at the manual. "Where'd you get that?"

"Online. All the kids have it."

"Online?"

"Yeah."

As I hunted for Jeremy, I saw lots of freshmen carrying copies of my manual. Bootlegged, pirated copies.

I found Jeremy outside, near the back door. I guess he'd ignored my advice and lingered there, because someone had picked him up and put him in the Dumpster. Fortunately, it was fairly empty. Unfortunately, it was fairly deep.

"I told you not to get caught here." I reached in and gave him a hand, so he could climb out.

"I stopped to tie my shoe," he said.

"That's one of the first tips in the manual," I said. "You never tie your shoe around a senior."

"They weren't around when I knelt," he said.

"This is a *high school*. They're always around."

"Good point. Thanks for the rescue."

"I had no choice. If I'd left you there, I'd probably get stuck riding the bus with someone even more annoying."

"Was that a joke?"

"If you want it to be. By the way, what happened to my manual?"

"What do you mean?"

"Everyone seems to have a copy," I said.

He shrugged. "I guess someone scanned it and posted the file."

"How could someone do that?" I asked.

"Easy. Especially if your scanner has an automatic

document feeder. You just load the pages—"

"That's not what I meant. I know *how* they did it. I just can't believe someone *would* do it. It's not right."

"Is it really any different from if I let someone borrow my copy?" he asked.

"Yeah. Sure. Only one person at a time can read your copy. This way, everyone gets it at once. That's just wrong."

I felt like I'd been robbed. I guess because I *had* been robbed. And there probably wasn't any way I could fix things. Even if I tracked down the kid who'd scanned the manual, what could I do about it? I wasn't going to beat up some freshman pirate. I doubted I could get money from him. Or her. It was done. Over. My publishing career had lasted less than a week. All my profit had turned into red ink. Actually, make that black, cyan, magenta, and yellow ink.

I went into the school through the back door and headed for my homeroom. Two kids stared at me as I walked past them. I heard one of them whisper to the other, "*I think that's Scott Hudson.*"

"*You sure?*" the other whispered.

Weird. A couple other kids stared at me later. I guess they'd downloaded the manual.

I'd gone viral.

And it hadn't gained me anything. If I ever wrote another manual, I was going to carve it on rocks in my backyard. Anyone who wanted to read it would have to pay admission and promise not to take photographs.

I decided to give lunch another shot. I was getting used to the smells and sights in biology. The choices were chicken nuggets or mac and cheese. As much as I liked mac and cheese, the cafeteria's version was pretty dense and gooey, and seemed capable of choking me if it came back up my throat. If I died in biology, I could just imagine Ms. Denton seizing the opportunity to turn my corpse into an AP specimen. So I got the nuggets.

Lee, Edith, and Richard had opted for mac and cheese. Bradley had opted for making friends with some JV baseball players, and was sitting with them now.

I took a seat and stabbed one of the nuggets with my fork, then held it up and stared at it, bracing myself for that first bite.

Lee snickered. I could tell from her expression that she was about to launch into a biology joke.

"Please don't," I said.

"I'll spare you," she said.

"Whoever decided that chickens belonged in nuggets was clearly confused," I said.

"Sophomore!" Richard shouted, punching me hard on the shoulder.

"Ow! What was that for?" I asked. I rubbed my shoulder.

"You used an oxymoron," Richard said. "'Clearly confused.'"

"So?"

"So, if you hear someone use one, you get to hit them on the shoulder and shout *sophomore*."

"When did that become a thing?" I asked.

He shrugged. "I don't know. Always, I guess."

I put my fork down. "Is that a wild guess?" I asked.

"No. It's an educated guess."

I could tell from his eyes that it had just dawned on him what I'd done.

"Sophomore!" I shouted, hitting him hard for his *educated guess*. I could get into this game.

"You're both acting like big babies," Lee said. "And *educated guess* isn't necessarily an oxymoron."

Big babies! That was probably an oxymoron.

Before I could even launch my brain into the train of thought wrapped around what my response should be, Lee looked me right in the eyes and said, "Don't even think about it."

"I wouldn't dream of it." I turned my attention to my nuggets and started eating. But I left half of them on my plate. If I was going to lose my lunch, I wanted to keep the splatter to a manageable amount. Lee had no interest in the leftovers, but Richard and Edith happily split the bounty.

"Mac, cheese, chicken mélange," Edith said, stirring everything together.

Right before we headed out, Lee offered me the rest of her soda. I passed.

"Deep breath," she said as we approached the door to

biology. "Then breathe through your mouth."

I made it to my seat. The nuggets squirmed a bit, but they remained in place. It looked like I'd be able to continue enjoying a horribly early lunch. At least until Ms. Denton dragged out the next specimen. But, for now, I could cross biology off my list of disasters.

NINE

Mrs. Gilroy stood up from her desk and handed back my essay when I walked into class. Her eagerness did not strike me as a good omen. My eyes found the grade, but my brain struggled to process the number. Sixty-five? No way. I stared at Mrs. Gilroy. She stared back without any expression.

I went to my desk and flipped through the essay. Every page was covered with red marks. There were so many circles, it looked like half of a football play.

Most of the scarlet circles were at the start or end of a sentence. Mrs. Gilroy had marked every "And" and "But" at the beginning, and every preposition at the end. At the bottom of the last page, she'd written, "It appears that somebody didn't read the style manual."

Style manual? I still had the stupid booklet in my backpack. I hadn't realized there was any sort of manual in it. I dug it out and thumbed through the crumpled pages. There, all the way in the back, I found a list labeled "Rules We Will Follow."

The rules on the first page of the section were well known to anyone who'd been speaking English for more than a week or two, beginning with "Make sure your subject and verb agree." That was followed by rules about the right ways to use commas and apostrophes. There wasn't anything unfamiliar. At the top of the second page, I ran into trouble. The first rule was "Never end a sentence with a preposition." The second rule was "Never start a sentence with a coordinating conjunction." And those two rules were where I'd screwed up.

But those weren't real rules.

I knew that from reading *5,000 Amazing Facts*. The rules had gotten shoved into grammar books ages ago, mostly by mistake or misconception.

I pointed at the preposition prohibition and whispered to Lee, "That's not a real rule."

"It might not be justifiable," she said. "But it's real."

"It's stupid."

"Doesn't matter. If she told us every sentence had to contain at least one *Q* and one *Z*, that's what we'd have to do."

"It's still stupid. After class, I'm telling her she's wrong."

"That would be stupid," Lee said.

Mrs. Gilroy cleared her throat in my direction, killing my conversation with Lee. By the end of the period, I'd calmed down enough to realize that Lee was right about one thing. It would be a bad idea for me to tell the teacher she was wrong.

But I could at least argue for a better grade. As soon as the bell rang, I headed to Mrs. Gilroy's desk.

"Shouldn't I get some credit for my ideas and arguments?" I asked.

"You did. I gave you a ninety-seven for that part," she said. "Otherwise, you would have had a much lower grade."

"But I really only made two mistakes." It killed me to call them *mistakes*. My heart and brain waged a brief battle over my urge to tell her how wrong those rules were. I glanced toward the door, where Lee stood. She shook her head slowly and mouthed the word "no."

I sighed and focused on my point that I shouldn't be repeatedly penalized for the same mistake. "It's like, if I had misspelled the same word ten times, you wouldn't take points off ten times, would you?"

"The way things are going, I'm sure you'll get a chance to discover that," she said.

"It's not fair," I said. I couldn't believe I'd been reduced to arguing like a five-year-old. Maybe I could fall to the floor and throw a tantrum. That would probably be just as effective as anything else I tried.

"Good day, Mr. Hudson. If you really care about your grade, I'd suggest you spend more time studying the manual and less time whining. You might also benefit from reading some good books."

The fact that I didn't instantly explode and shower the

room with Scottie nuggets has to be counted as some sort of miracle. There were times in my life when *all I did* was read books. Books were a huge part of my existence, and my identity. And she'd just told me I should read a good book once in a while. I'd bet I'd read more good books so far in my life than she'd read when she was my age.

When I reached the hallway, Lee yanked me out of sight of the door and gave me a hug. It was the sort of hug you give to someone whose dog has just died. It was also a huge violation of the Public Displays of Affection rules. Not that I minded. But if a teacher had spotted us, we'd both get detention, along with a letter for our parents to sign. And then Lee's father would execute me. Slowly and painfully. Even so, I was in no rush to end the hug.

Too soon, Lee let go. Before I could speak and seek company for my misery, she said, "*Ssshhh*. I know. That was like getting a steel-toed kick to the nether regions."

"But it's all so—"

"*Ssshhh*. You are not allowed to speak until we've left the building and moved at least one hundred yards from any open windows. Then, you may scream and rant as long and loudly as you wish, and I will listen with patience and understanding."

She placed a hand against my back and steered me away from Mrs. Gilroy's classroom, leading me out the nearest door.

We walked across the street, then kept going for another block.

"Now?" I asked.

"Now," she said.

"That was so freakin' stupid," I shouted. Except I might have used a different adjective. I ranted and raged until I ran out of synonyms for *ridiculous* and *arbitrary* and *uninformed*. I'm pretty sure *draconian* surfaced more than once during my tirade.

Lee stood there and listened through the whole rant. "Feel better?" she asked after I was finished.

"Somewhat."

"You forgot *picayune*."

"I wasn't going for a complete set. But you're right. That was definitely an oversight."

"We missed the buses."

"I could use a long walk."

"Me, too. But we might have to stop for fuel. You're buying."

"I recently suffered a business loss," I said.

"That's irrelevant," she said. "Are you penniless?"

"Not quite," I said.

"Are you grateful for my company?"

"Quite," I said.

"Do you appreciate my patience and understanding?"

"That goes without saying."

"Then you're buying. That, too, should have gone without saying."

"Agreed."

We walked in silence for a block before I muttered, "Stupid rules."

"*Rules* being the operative part," Lee said. "Now, to a more crucial issue—what are you feeding us?"

We'd reached the outskirts of town. The options within sight included pizza from a place where the slices were only slightly better than the ones in the school cafeteria, ice cream at the place where Lee had worked last summer, fast-food burgers, and the diner.

"You pick," I said.

She pointed across the street, to Bongo's Bagels. "How about that?"

The sign on the door read "Come on in." One verb, two prepositions.

"Somehow, that seems perfect," I said.

I did not get one with poppy seeds.

At least it was Friday. I'd have two full days to recover from my four days of school. After dinner, I followed Dad out to the garage. He'd traded the old Corvette he'd restored for an even older Chevelle SS 396. Apparently, those were really hard to find.

I took my usual seat on a stool, close enough to see what he was doing, but far enough not to get in his way.

Dad grabbed a wrench from the pegboard on the side wall. "Everything okay at school?"

"Yeah." I flinched at the way my voice rose half an octave in the process of speaking a single syllable.

Dad loosened a bolt on the alternator. Or the generator. Or maybe it was the hibernator. "You sure?"

"It's nothing I can't handle," I said.

"Bully problem?" he asked.

"Not while Wesley has my back," I said.

"I thought he graduated," Dad said.

"He casts a long shadow."

Dad nodded. "I can see how that would work."

"It's just one teacher," I said. "She doesn't like me."

"You, or something you did?" Dad asked.

"The latter," I said.

"Maybe because you use words like *latter*?" Dad said.

"That's not the problem," I said. "It's English class. She'd approve of that usage. Though maybe not from me."

"So what's the problem?"

I told him about the first test, and the essay. As I narrated the events, I listened to myself and realized I really couldn't defend my actions all that well. I hadn't read the summer reading during the appropriate summer, and I hadn't read the handbook. But still, the rules were stupid. I said as much after I finished my story.

Dad put down the wrench and sat on the worktable in front of the pegboard. He propped his chin on his fist. After a minute or two, during which he was obviously deep in thought, he said, "Sounds like you've been fairly punished. Time to move on. I think your best bet is to keep a low profile. Don't try to impress her. And definitely don't try to defend your position. Being right doesn't mean much if the person who's wrong is in charge. Lick your wounds and keep your head down. Let her find someone else to focus on, if that's what she needs."

"I'll try. Thanks. That's good advice."

He shrugged. "I had a lot of practice with Bobby."

"That's for sure."

"Any other teachers butt heads with you?" Dad asked.

"Nope." That lie only spanned a quarter octave. I decided not to tell Dad about biology. I'd received enough parental wisdom for one evening. And biology seemed to be under control.

TEN

My phone rang. It was Lee.

"Let's do something," she said.

She didn't work during the school year. Not even on the weekends. That was one of her parents' rules. They wanted her to focus completely on school.

"Like what?" I asked. It was close enough to noon that I didn't mind getting out of bed.

"You choose," she said.

"Slot cars," I said. It popped out.

There was silence on the other end, as if I'd suggested we go to the zoo and throw darts at the baby otters. After the silence grew dangerously close to reaching an uncomfortable length, I said, "You told me to choose."

"I should have told you to choose *wisely*," she said.

"That's okay. We can do something else."

"No. Let's do it. I'll survive."

"Not if you race me," I said.

"What?"

"Just kidding."

"Is this the place right outside of town?" she asked.

"That place closed. But there's a new one. It's pretty far. We can't really catch a bus there. We're at the mercy of parental transportation."

"Mom's home," Lee said. "She can give us a ride, if one of your folks can pick us up."

"So this is your favorite thing in the entire universe?" Lee asked when we walked into Slots and Rockets. The indoor track took up a quarter of the floor space. Model kits, RC cars and planes, and rocketry supplies took up the rest.

"It's my favorite thing in this building," I said. "And maybe on the planet. But not in the whole universe. I'm sure, somewhere in the universe, there's a place where kids our age can drive real cars."

"That's the magic of infinity," Lee said. "Or maybe South Dakota."

I went to the guy at the register and got two controllers. Then I opened my carrying case and handed Lee a car. "Here. This is my best one. I'll take the clunker. It's kind of banged up because Bobby likes to send cars flying off the track."

"It's pretty," she said, tapping my car.

"It's a Porsche 911," I told her. "Your car is a Karmann Ghia."

"I like that," Lee said. "It sounds like an opera."

We placed our cars on the track. Then, I explained how to use the controller. "Take it easy at first," I told her. "Especially in the turns."

"In other words, I should try to remember that my car obeys the laws of physics?"

"Basically."

"No problem."

"Ready?"

"Ready. How do we know when we're finished?"

I pointed at the lap counter. "Let's do a short race. Ten laps. Start when I say 'Go.'"

Lee nodded. I said "Go!"

I didn't race full-out at first. I didn't want to leave Lee too far behind. I figured it wasn't likely she'd enjoy this all that much, but I could try to make sure she didn't hate it.

Her car lurched, stopped, lurched again, slowed, sped up, then took the first curve just slow enough not to go flying. As she started to catch up with me, I reflexively boosted my speed—right before the second curve, which was a tight hairpin turn. My car went flying.

"Does that mean you lose?" Lee asked.

"No. I just have to put it back on the track."

I retrieved my car. Lee, meanwhile, had stopped hers.

"Why'd you stop?" I asked.

"It seemed like the sporting thing to do," she said.

"No need. Keep going." I almost caught her, but when I got close she started to widen the gap. She increased her lead on the second lap, and finished the race a lap and a half ahead of me.

"You're right. This is the good car," Lee said. "I guess yours isn't very fast. Want to switch? That way, we can take turns winning."

"No!"

"I thought this is what you did for fun."

"I *am* having fun."

"It doesn't look that way."

We raced five more times. I don't remember who won.

Dad picked us up.

"See you Monday," Lee said when she hopped out of the car.

"See you. . . ."

"Smart girl," Dad said after he watched Lee go inside.

"Yeah. For sure."

He pulled away from the curb. "Are you two . . ." He paused.

"Are we what?" I asked. Had I taken half a second longer to analyze the nature of the pause, I could have figured out where he was going and avoided prompting him to finish his sentence. Which, apparently, he wasn't eager to do.

"Are you two . . . you know . . ."

"No!"

"No?"

"Yeah, no."

He patted me on the leg. "Good."

There was no real response I could make to his pleasure at my lack of pleasure, so I remained silent. Dad had one piece of wisdom to share with me on the topic.

"There's no rush."

"I know."

"Take your time."

"I will."

"You have the rest of your life for that."

"I hope so."

He shot me a puzzled look.

"I mean, I know."

September 6

I'll let you beat me at stuff for the first six or seven years of your life, Sean. After that, the gloves are off.

By the way, Dad told me to take my time three different ways. I think parents have a hard time settling for one broadcast of any important message. I, on the other hand, have full faith that I only need to tell you something once, and you will totally absorb the information. At least, once you're old enough to become more absorbent than anything you're currently wearing.

As for what he told me to take my time about—we're not going there right now.

Monday, I headed out for my first full week as a sophomore. It looked like my mornings would be fine. Geometry was actually sort of fun, especially since Mr. Stockman liked wordplay. History wasn't bad, either. It was facts, after all. And I was all about facts.

When second period ended, I had to face the fact that I was less optimistic about the rest of the day. Four of the classes would be fine, but they were sandwiched between biology and English like tasty cold cuts stuck between two stale pieces of moldy rye bread. In bowling, you get to take a practice throw before you start keeping score. Too bad school didn't give you a practice week.

As I rounded the corner down the hall from the cafeteria, on the way to lunch, I heard a familiar squeal. Jeremy was standing outside the boys' room. Two seniors were blocking the door. Jeremy was trying to reason with them. That was a waste of time. They were feeding on his discomfort.

Stay out of it.

I'm not super proud that this was my first thought. My second thought was that people had stood up for me when I'd needed them. Bobby, Wesley, even Kyle back in the old days. I ran the options through my head as I walked toward the standoff. I could reach between them and push the door open. But that would make me pretty vulnerable. And I wasn't sure Jeremy would take advantage of the opening.

I could distract them, or get them to walk away by luring them somewhere else. But this wasn't a cartoon. And I didn't have a bloody hunk of raw meat to toss down the hall for the wolves.

I could reason with them. But I'd already seen how well that was working for Jeremy.

As I reached them, I got an idea.

I didn't even look at the two seniors. "Do you have to go?" I asked Jeremy.

"Yeah." The stress on his face eased slightly as he recognized me.

"So go," I said.

"What?"

"Go right here. If they don't move, piss on them. They aren't leaving you much choice."

"I'll kick the crap out of you," the senior on the left said.

"And you'll still be drenched in piss," I said. "As well as whatever crap splatters over you as you're kicking it out of us. Sounds like a fair trade."

I turned my attention back to Jeremy. "Go ahead. Let it fly." Jeremy blinked. "Really?"

"Yeah. Really."

He reached for his zipper and pulled it down.

"You're crazy," the senior on the right said as he scooted away. "Both of you."

"Out of your mind," the other one said.

I watched them walk off. "That was close," I said.

"I don't think I could really have done it," he said. "I'm kind of shy."

"Doesn't matter. *They* thought you'd do it. Though it's always better to bluff when you're willing to go through with it. I guess then it's not really a bluff, is it? It's more like—"

"Scott," Jeremy said.

"What?"

"That's fascinating, but I *really* need to go."

"Go," I said.

Jeremy dashed into the boys' room.

When he came out, I said, "You might want to rethink your timing, and not try to go between periods. Or learn to get through the day without a bathroom break."

"What do you think I am? A dog?"

"Nope. A dog would have ignored those guys and done his business."

I got to lunch a couple minutes late.

"Sightseeing?" Lee asked.

"Nope. I'm fostering a puppy who's not a puppy," I said.

"How Zen of you," Lee said.

Richard looked back and forth from me to Lee. "I'm glad I don't listen too closely to the two of you."

"I don't listen at all," Edith said.

I, on the other hand, was determined to listen. I figured the best way to respond to Ms. Denton's apparent disdain for blood relatives of Bobby Hudson was to excel in the class. When I got there, I paid attention, took notes, and tried to participate in discussions, even though she rarely called on me.

When it was time for English, I decided to try to take Mr. Franka's advice and allow myself to learn from someone I didn't like. I had a feeling it would be an even more useful life skill to cultivate than balancing a checkbook. I took my seat, eager to be a sponge, a blank slate, or whatever the task required. Okay, not really eager. But willing. Grudgingly. Sort of.

"Who can name a figure of speech?" Mrs. Gilroy asked.

Similes, metaphors, onomatopoeia, and alliteration were quickly tossed out by the class. Followed—no surprise, given our first day of class—by oxymorons. Things slowed after that, but we added hyperbole and personification.

After a dry spell, I dredged up assonance and consonance, which I'd learned about last year when we were studying poetry. And that was the end of it.

"Is that all of them?" Mrs. Gilroy asked.

"All we can think of," Julia said.

All we've been taught, I wanted to say. But I'd learned to monitor my thoughts before they became words in this class.

"Well, that is the proverbial tip of the iceberg," Mrs. Gilroy said. She went to the board and started writing.

I looked at the first word she wrote. If it actually was a word.

metonymy

Beneath that, she wrote *synecdoche.*

They reminded me of the jumbled strings of letters that had appeared when I tried to make a crossword grid.

"Anybody?" Mrs. Gilroy asked.

Silence.

She looked directly at me. "Nobody?"

"Isn't *metonymy* like self-rule?" Julia asked.

"That's *autonomy,*" Mrs. Gilroy said. "You get credit for trying. Never be afraid to make a wrong guess in this class. That's part of the learning process."

Nice try? If I'd said that, she would have mocked me without mercy.

"These two, metonymy and synecdoche, are frequently confused," Mrs. Gilroy said. "That will not happen here. I should add that they are far from alone in being misunderstood and misapplied."

She resumed writing. I counted as she wrote. When she stopped, she'd put forty-seven words on the board, including the meager assortment our class had come up with. Several others joined *synecdoche* and *metonymy* in resembling really unplayable sets of Scrabble tiles.

"'*Antanaclasis*'?" I whispered to Lee. I would have mentioned *bdelgymia,* but I had no idea how to pronounce it.

"Not a clue," Lee said. She pointed to the board. "I just realized she did that from memory."

That was pretty amazing. But I had a feeling Mrs. Gilroy was about to suck all the joy out of creative writing.

"These are our tools," she said. "There are many others, but these are among the most essential. We are going to get well acquainted with them. We will learn to recognize them, and we will learn to create them, skillfully and eloquently. We will learn to *write*. You may think you've been writing all along, but without real knowledge of your tools, without a true appreciation of figurative language, you've merely been scribbling in the darkness."

Yeah, this was going to suck. I *knew* how to write. People loved my articles in the school paper. I'd found all sorts of creative ways to describe a football game or a wrestling match. And I got good grades on my papers from Mr. Franka last year. I wondered whether I could switch classes. I didn't have to be in honors English. Mom had mentioned that it wasn't too late to change. Maybe Mr. Franka taught a sophomore class. I'd have to find out. It would be awesome to have him again.

Mrs. Gilroy circled *simile, metaphor,* and the other figures of speech the class had named. "We know these. They are familiar, and easy to recognize. Let's move to the unknown. We'll explore a new term at the start of each week. I encourage you to learn to use all of them, except for this one." She drew a line through *catachresis.* Then, as if a strike-through wasn't enough, she erased the word. That, of course, made me wonder what it meant. But I wasn't going to fall for her teacher trick.

"Throughout the week, we will stay especially alert for the technique in our spotlight—and under our microscope—both in our reading and in our discussions."

I sat back as she circled *anaphora*, and explained that it referred to the repetition of a word or phrase at the beginnings of a series of sentences or clauses for rhetorical effect.

Ten minutes before class ended, she tapped the board by the figures of speech and said, "Copy these down."

Good grief. Hadn't she ever heard of a teacher web page? Or a handout sheet? I started writing.

"Pick one," she said. "Research its meaning from a reliable source."

Hands went up. Mrs. Gilroy intercepted them. "If you don't know what a reliable source is by now, you probably don't belong in this class. To continue: Write a paragraph making use of your selection. Turn it in next Monday. We'll share your efforts in class during the week, and see who can identify the main figure of speech. After that, you'll bring a new one in each Monday for the rest of the year."

There were some groans among my classmates, but I wasn't daunted by the idea of writing an extra paragraph each week. Not that I'd tell Mrs. Gilroy the assignment was a piece of cake. That's one lesson I'd learned.

Mom was in my room when I got home from school. That was never a good sign. She knew roughly when I'd normally arrive. So if she was in my room, it wasn't by accident. It was by design. And intent.

"Scott," Mom said, "if you're going to eat in here, at least try to be neat about it."

That wasn't one of the seven thousand transgressions that had crossed my mind as possibilities. "I don't eat in here," I said. At least, not since I'd lost a piece of pizza behind my dresser last year.

Mom pointed to the corner, past the window, at the bagel Wesley had flung at me the other day. "Do you want the house to be crawling with ants? Or mice."

"Sorry," I said. "I won't do it again." There was no point trying to explain that the bagel had been hurled at me through the window. However it had arrived, I couldn't deny that I'd left it on the floor. Though, in my defense, I'd been half-asleep at the time it had ricocheted off my forehead and settled in the corner. Of course, I was half-asleep most of the time.

"I know," Mom said, flashing me the *you're-my-well-behaved-boy* look. She picked up the bagel and took it with her.

After I did my homework, I went down to the computer. As much as I promised myself not to get sucked too deeply into Mrs. Gilroy's list of figures of speech, beyond finding one to use for my assignment, I sort of got hooked, and ended up researching a dozen or so terms, based mostly on how goofy they sounded. But I pulled myself away before I'd spent too much time doing that. And I decided to play it safe, for a change, and not get too creative with my choice for the paragraph.

September 8

Sean, it turns out there are something like five billion different figures of speech. Okay, that's an exaggeration. Or hyperbole. Which is one of the handful I know. Though I didn't remember I knew it until someone else mentioned it in class. Which, I think, sort of proves that I don't need to know the name for everything I do.

Speaking of which, I found a word that describes my freshman year pretty well, and better not describe my sophomore year. <u>Catachresis</u>. You know what it means? I won't keep you in suspense, or force you to run to the dictionary. I'll bet it isn't even in a lot of dictionaries. It means a mistake. That's all. It's a big word for a common thing. Though it's really a mistake in word use, not in life. So it only describes my freshman year metaphorically, since it refers to a word-use mistake. If I used a word the wrong way, or if I made a badly mixed metaphor, that would be catachresis. But here's the thing. You can also use it on purpose. If you're really good, you can use the wrong word in a creative way. And I'm going to do just that. I swear. In one of my papers for Mrs. Gilroy, I'm going cata the chresis out of the English language. Why? Because she said that's the one figure of speech we won't be using. I will figure out a way to use it. I swear. I'll keep you posted. But I'm not ready for that, just yet. I'm going to go for an easy one this time, like tautology. I'll let you look it up, find the definition, and learn the meaning of it yourself.

ELEVEN

September 9

Good morning, Sean. A modest request, if I may . . .

I'd appreciate it if you would try to refrain from screaming at the top of your tiny lungs every time you wake up in the middle of the night. Your life is perfect. You have nothing to scream about. I'm the one who should wake up screaming. Thanks.

I was making my way to homeroom on Tuesday when I spotted a familiar spine. "Great book," I said. I pointed to the copy of *Unwind* that Danny Roholm was carrying.

"Really?"

"For sure." I was tempted to warn him about the creepiest scene, but I didn't want to spoil anything.

"That's good to hear. We're reading it in English class."

"Seriously?"

He nodded.

"Who do you have?"

"Ms. Orstrum."

"Lucky you. We're stuck with the old stuff." I envied him. On the other hand, I'd already read *Unwind*, and I'd seen what happened when I tried to skate along on the memory of a book. Still, I wouldn't mind at all if I had to read it again for class. It was good enough for a second visit. I guess the fact that individual teachers got to pick some of the assigned books could be good or bad, depending on the picker. I sure couldn't picture Mrs. Gilroy loosening up enough to assign a novel that was written after she was born.

When it was time for gym, Mr. Cravutto sent us off on our own once again, while he stood waiting for the girls' teacher, whose name, I'd learned, was Ms. Swan. We paced ourselves, since we had no idea how long we'd be running. I noticed that the girls went right to the field and started playing again. That gave me an idea. After the fourth lap, which totaled one mile of running, I jogged over to Mr. Cravutto. He was now deeply engaged in a conversation with his counterpart, who seemed less concerned about escape than she'd been last week. I guess he was wearing her down with his charm. I figured I'd be able to get a partial share of his attention by shouting the magic word. And, really, I didn't want his full attention.

"COACH!" I yelled.

Before he could look toward me, I said, "Want us to start a game?"

"Yeah. Sure. Good idea."

I jogged back to the track, just ahead of the largest cluster of runners, and waved everybody over. "Coach said we can start a game."

"Good job, Hudson," Renzler said. He rewarded me with a slap on the back which, had I not braced myself for it, would have rendered me incapable of joining any game for quite a while.

Since we had our last names on our gym clothes in black marker, most of us were on a last-name basis, unless we knew each other really well outside of gym. So I was Hudson to most of the class.

As for those I knew well, I caught Kyle glaring at me. He seemed displeased that I'd done something that everybody liked.

We formed two teams and played football. That did not require the supervision of a college-educated physical-education instructor. We'd spent large portions of our childhood in various forms of pick-up games.

I kept an eye on my watch. "We'd better go in," I said to Renzler when we were ten minutes away from the end of the period.

"Showers!" he shouted.

We jogged into the locker room, well exercised, and relieved not to be exhausted from running laps, or in danger of running late.

. . . running laps or running late . . .

The phrase tickled something in my memory. I realized it was an example of *antanaclasis*, one of the figures of speech I'd looked up. It was also one of the simpler ones to understand. After I showered and got dressed, I opened my notebook and wrote, "running laps or running late." I figured I could use that in an English assignment.

I showed the page to Richard. "For English," I said. "One word used in two contrasting ways."

"That's pretty cool," he said.

"You're such a nerd," Kyle said as he closed his locker.

"What do you care?" I asked. "We have nothing to do with each other anymore."

He laughed.

"What's so funny?"

"You'll find out soon enough."

I had no idea what he was talking about.

Wednesday, after school, I waited outside the newspaper room to catch Mr. Franka before he came in for the meeting.

"Do you teach a sophomore English class?" I asked him.

"No way," he said.

"No way?" That was definitely not among the responses I would have expected. I'm not sure, but it's possible he'd actually shuddered when he spoke. "What's wrong with sophomores?"

"They can be difficult," he said.

"For you?" I found that hard to believe. He'd been in the Marines before he was a teacher.

"For everyone," he said.

"So, then, you don't teach a sophomore class . . . ?"

"I just told you that. Emphatically. Are you trying to be difficult?"

At least he laughed when he said that.

When we got inside, Jeremy handed out copies of his crossword. "I can do one a week," he said. "Easily."

Sarah stared down at hers. "This looks pretty tough," she said. "Let's aim for one a month."

I looked at mine. One a year might have been better. It was definitely tough.

After Sarah went over the articles for the paper, she said, "Scott, are you working on anything?"

Oh, shoot. Last year, I'd had assignments. So I knew what I had to do. This year, I had a vague commission to write opinion pieces or features. I'd sort of forgotten about that. The basic layout for each issue was done after the weekly meeting, but articles could be turned in as late as the following Monday morning. The paper came out on Tuesday.

I could tell Sarah I was working on something, but I figured it was better to go with the truth. "I don't have an article for the upcoming issue," I said.

"What about the puzzle?" she asked.

Puzzle?

I went from puzzled to panicked as I remembered the last meeting. Right afterward, I'd gotten so involved in my publishing empire, I'd totally forgotten to look through the Tom Swifties I'd written last year. I'd even skimmed past some of them, when I was pulling survival tips from my journal. I dredged one up from memory and shared it with them.

"That's good," Sarah said. "Maybe we should call it something else, to make it more special."

"How about Zenger Zingers?" Jeremy suggested.

"Great," Sarah said.

"And we can use John Peter instead of Tom," I said.

Several kids shot quizzical looks in my direction, and one of the freshmen said, "Who's that?"

"John Peter Zenger," I said, drawing out the first and middle names. "As in J. P. Zenger High School. You know. The guy the school is named after. The famous American journalist. The guy who beat a libel charge back in colonial times. That John Peter."

Heads nodded. Eyes widened slightly in token recognition. And thus the Tom Swiftie morphed into the Zenger Zinger, which was an equally vague but much more relevant name.

"Get us something great for next time," Sarah said to me as the meeting ended.

"Such as . . . ?" I asked.

"Totally up to you," she said. "See what you can come up with."

"Thanks." As I walked off, the words *up with* resonated in my mind, reminding me of a famous quote. As I savored that quote, I knew exactly the sort of opinion piece I could come up with. *"A smile crossed my lips, revealing my teeth," Scott said, transcendentally.* This was going to be awesome.

TWELVE

Saturday afternoon, Wesley pulled up in the bagel truck.

"Where's your car?" I asked.

"Home."

"Did it break down?"

"Nope."

"So why are you using this?" I asked.

"It has gas," he said.

For as long as I'd known Wesley, he'd seemed to have a thing against paying for his own gas. Or lunch. At least I'd pretty much managed to convince him that it was wrong to steal gas from other people. Or lunch money. Though I guessed he was sort of stealing it now, except not from strangers.

"Not your gas," I said.

"It's okay. My boss wanted me to make a delivery." He pointed over his shoulder to a half-dozen boxes on the floor.

"Is it legal?" I asked.

"It's bagels," Wesley said. "He donates the leftovers to the food bank down off Division Street."

I thought about my last experience with surplus bagels. "They haven't spilled out, have they?"

"Nope. Not yet. They came close a couple times."

Wesley drove. I sat in back and kept the boxes from tipping over. Then, when we got there, I helped him bring everything in.

"That's cool," I said when we were finished. "It feels good to help people."

Wesley glanced back at the food bank, then smiled. "Yeah. It does."

I looked at the empty area of the truck, and thought about all the bagels Wesley must have delivered. He'd put in a long day. "Do you miss school?"

"Some of it," Wesley said.

"Seriously?"

"Yeah. The routine is nice. You always know where you're supposed to be, and you know when you're supposed to be there."

"But you cut class all the time," I said.

"You're right." His eyes clouded over with a look of nostalgia. Then he nodded. "Breaking the routine is sort of nice, too."

Tuesday, the first issue of the paper for the school year came out. One of my favorite things was seeing kids carrying a copy with their books, or even stopping to read an article when a headline caught their eye. The teachers give out copies in homeroom, but there's also a *Zenger Gazette* box by the front office, so visitors can grab one.

I stopped by the box on my way in, to check out the front page. Everything looked great. We'd led with a story about the budget.

"Good start," Mr. Franka said, walking up behind me.

"Thanks." I pointed to the box. "It's a good feeling."

"I'm glad you're keeping Tom Swifties alive," he said.

"Me, too. Hey, were you on the paper when you were in high school?"

"I wanted to be. But my grades weren't very good."

"Seriously?"

"Dead seriously."

"That's hard to imagine," I said.

"Not everyone shows up at the front door equipped for an easy trip," he said. "I had to learn how to learn. I did have several teachers who tried pretty hard to get some knowledge through my thick skull. That made a difference."

"Is that why you teach now?" I asked.

"That's part of it, I guess. But you can't really boil down big decisions in life into simple explanations, like we're fictional characters in one-dimensional novels."

"I guess not." I thought about some of my own decisions. Most of them were based more on whim and chance than inspiration.

When I got to homeroom, I was pleased to see that most of the kids were reading the paper. I even heard some of them discussing the Zenger Zinger. I was tempted to toss out cryptic hints, like *It will take you forever to find the answer.* But I decided not to do that.

Zenger Zinger for September 16
Find the missing word. The solution will appear next week.
"I love how cats respond to stroking," John Peter said
_____.

We were all pretty jazzed at the meeting on Wednesday. The paper had gotten a lot of good reactions. Kids were even trying to trick staff members into revealing the solution to the Zinger, or to Jeremy's crossword.

"Let's not rest on our laurels," Sarah said. "We need to keep up the quality."

"We will," Jeremy said.

"I've got something this time," I said. "It's an opinion piece."

"On what?" Sarah asked.

"The unfairness of pedantic and arbitrary rules," I said.

Sarah frowned. "Scott, this is a high school paper, not a college symposium."

"No worries," I said, waving a hand to dismiss the objection. "It's written in a very conversational style."

"I'll look forward to reading it," Sarah said.

■ ■ ■

September 17

Check out this legendary sentence, Sean. I should explain it first. When someone mentioned that you can't end a sentence with a preposition, this guy Winston Churchill, who was prime minister of the United Kingdom, super smart, and super sarcastic, replied, "That is the sort of errant pedantry up with which I will not put." That's such a brilliant comeback. Putting aside the vocabulary-busting phrase "errant pedantry," which just means "misguided, stupid, nit-picking," Churchill knocks it out of the park with an example of how awkward it is to follow that rule. Any normal person would say, "That's the sort of thing I wouldn't put up with." Anyhow, I opened my essay with that quote, and then explained how the "rule" got into grammar books. It's a killer essay. I totally demolish the stupid rules in the handbook. This is going to be awesome. I can't wait to see it in the paper.

THIRTEEN

Mr. Franka popped his head into study hall, pointed at me, and said to the teacher, "I need to borrow him for a moment."

I got out of my seat and followed Mr. Franka into the hall. "What's up?" I asked.

"I read your essay."

I was pleased he'd gotten to it already. "It's pretty good, isn't it?"

"It's well written . . ."

"But . . . ?"

"You're taking a shot at Mrs. Gilroy."

"I never mention her name," I said.

"You make it obvious enough."

"You aren't going to tell me we can't run it, are you?" I felt a surge of heat invade my cheeks at the thought of being censored.

"Never." He touched the Marine Corps tattoo on his arm. "A lot of people made large sacrifices for your freedom to speak your mind."

"So, why are you here?" I asked.

"To urge you to think carefully before you commit to publishing this. I understand why you wrote it. I understand how you feel. I know you believe those rules are arbitrary. Some scholars agree with you. Others don't."

"What about you?" I asked.

"I generally don't enforce them. But they're widely entrenched. When enough people accept a rule, its origin doesn't matter. That's how the academic world works. Students need to know these rules. It doesn't hurt to practice them. I respect Mrs. Gilroy's insistence on having her students learn and follow them. I respect her expertise. But that's beside the point. Look, I'm not saying we won't ever run the piece. I'm asking you to let it sit for a week or two. Give yourself a chance to think calmly about everything you wrote. Are you okay with that?"

I thought about the fantasies I already had of the student reaction. Kids would cheer for me as I walked down the halls. They'd rip up writing guides and shower me with confetti. "I was kind of looking forward to getting it in print," I said.

"Of course you were. We write to be read. But I know from experience that the angrier the article, the more time you should take before the point of no return. You should give yourself a bit of time to think this through. Would you do that as a favor to me?"

I didn't like the idea. There was no reason to wait. I was positive my opinion wasn't going to change. But he was the best teacher I'd ever had, and he'd given me a lot of breaks. "Sure. Why not? I'll hold off."

He clasped my shoulder. "Thanks, Scott. It's a smart move. I appreciate it. If the paper gets killed by the voters, you can save the piece for the last issue, and really go out with a bang."

"I hope it doesn't come to that," I said.

"That makes two of us."

I let Sarah know I was holding back the essay. So, once again, I would have nothing in the paper. But it was still early in the year. I'd rather take my time and write a great article than rush stuff into print for the sake of being in every issue.

On Friday in history, Ms. Burke smiled at me when she handed back my essay.

"Good job," she said.

"Thanks." This had been our first written assignment, and I'd put a lot of time into doing a good job. I stared at the grade. Not only had she given me a hundred, she'd written, "I love your writing."

Wow. I like to think I'm good. But this seemed a bit over the top. I guessed I should be happy I impressed her.

Sunday, after lunch, I kept thinking about the jerks who had invaded my life. I wasn't sure how they ranked, as far as claiming the trophy for who was the worst, but I knew I'd be a lot happier without Ms. Denton and Mrs. Gilroy around. I'd finished the rest of my homework, but I still needed my figure-of-speech paragraph. I was scanning the list in my notebook when I spotted the one I couldn't believe was an actual word. *Bdelgymia.* Seriously, do people need to make everything harder by giving impossible names to stuff?

When I looked up bdelgymia, I discovered it would give me a chance to write the perfect paragraph for my present mood, and fill the vengeance void I'd created when I'd agreed to hold back my newspaper essay.

Sweet.

All bdelgymia meant was a spewing of hatred. I grinned at the idea of having permission to do that. Still, why couldn't they give it a cool name like *hatespew* or *wordsword*? Oh, I liked that second one, especially since people might not notice the "sword" part at first. If I ever got made Emperor of English, I'd definitely change all the names to make them more fun.

Zenger Zinger for September 23
Last week's answer: "I love how cats respond to stroking," John Peter said perpetually.
This week's puzzle: "I like to make rhymes when I'm underwater," John Peter said _____.

Mrs. Gilroy didn't pull my paragraph from the pile until Thursday. It had been preceded by a sea of unexceptional *antistrophes*, mundane *distinctios*, a clueless *haiku* from someone who clearly misunderstood the assignment, and a clever *psittacism* that I knew was Lee's. Clever Lee. Yes, Lee is clever. Lee is very clever.

As soon as I heard the first sentence of my paragraph, I poked Lee in the arm and shot her a grin.

I have to give Mrs. Gilroy credit for reading my whole glorious and venomous hatespew without blinking. I loved the way the class, which started out only half-listening, gave her their full attention by the last sentence. This was great. When Mrs. Gilroy was finished, I waited for her reaction. To my surprise, she didn't say anything. Instead, she went to the board and wrote out my paragraph.

The English teacher was one of those harpy-like harridans who is always sure she is right, even when she is pathetically wrong. Happy to constantly flout her arrogance, she wrings every shred of pleasure from the study of the English language. Her horrible personality is matched only by her dreadful sense of style.

After quickly determining that none of my classmates recognized the figure of speech, Mrs. Gilroy said, "I'm not sure where to start. There are so many errors."

Her words hit me like a punch to the gut. *Errors?*

She tapped *harridans*, and said, "Plural subject." Then, she tapped the "is" that followed it and said, "Singular verb. This is a very common mistake, but that's still no excuse. Anyone with a true ear for the language would never do this. Let's move on."

I stared at the first sentence. Damn. I saw what she meant. It should have been "one of THOSE HARRIDANS who ARE always sure."

My smackdown had just begun. Mrs. Gilroy tapped *flout*. "Class?"

A half dozen hands went up. Oh, crap. I meant *flaunt*. I always get those mixed up.

Sticking with the same sentence, she tapped *constantly*. "I'm not even going to ask who knows this. You're all aware you shouldn't split infinitives."

This was another debatable rule. Before I could even get suitably annoyed about that, she grabbed the chalk and circled *wring every shred*.

Now what? That was a perfectly fine phrase.

Hands went up. Knitting needles entered my gut and colon.

"Mixed metaphor," Julia said. "You wring liquids from things, not shreds."

Mrs. Gilroy smiled at her like she'd just written a sequel to *Hamlet*.

"As for the last sentence," Mrs. Gilroy said, "amazingly, it is not peppered with errors. I suppose anyone can get the words right once in a while, although these tepid attempts don't rise to the caustic level one would expect from a well-crafted example of bdelgymia. I won't embarrass the author of this thin gruel by naming him. All of you should view this as a wonderful example of how not to write bdelgymia, or anything else, for that matter."

Lee was nice enough to treat me to French fries after school. It didn't help. Or they didn't help. Or that didn't help. I'm not really sure. One of those. Pick whichever sounds right. Or sound right. Or sound rightly. I, apparently, have no ear for prose.

I licked my wounds that night. Most of Friday slipped by pretty quickly. Mrs. Gilroy and Ms. Denton crushed my spirits in various nonlethal ways, and I still had nothing for the next paper, which came out on the last day of the month. But everything else was fine.

That afternoon, Danny had a new book. Before I could even ask, he held it up.

"*Stotan!?*" I asked. The author's name seemed familiar, but I was pretty sure I hadn't read any of his books. "What's that mean?"

He shrugged. "I haven't started reading it yet."

I held my hand out, and he passed the book to me. I read the back. It sounded good. And it explained what a Stotan was. We'd just started reading *Cyrano de Bergerac* in English. It was sort of cool in its own way, and there was a lot of wordplay, along with sword play, and a healthy dose of wordswords, but it's not something I would have picked for myself if I'd had a choice.

I handed the book back to Danny. "Let me know how it is."

"Sure."

It bugged me that Danny was reading a book I'd never read, so I swung by the library at the end of the day. They had a copy.

"Good choice," the librarian, Ms. Paige—really, that's her name—said when I checked it out. "It does contain some adult language. Are your parents okay with that?"

"My father's a mechanic," I said. "Have you ever hit your thumb with a wrench?"

"Got it," she said. "Enjoy the book. If you like it, he's written others that are equally good."

"And equally inappropriate?" I asked.

"You bet." She punctuated that with a wink. Librarians rock.

"Thanks." I tucked the book in my backpack. I was always up for discovering a new author. And Ms. Paige was pretty good at gauging my tastes. Last year, she'd introduced me to Stephen Gould and Peter S. Beagle.

As I headed out at the end of the day, I realized I was close to surviving my first sophomoric month. And Jeremy was almost finished with his first freshmaniacal one.

"Here's hoping next month is uneventful," I said as we took our seats on the bus.

"I've been hoping for that every month since I started kindergarten," he said. "So far, no luck."

...

Zenger Zinger for September 30
Last week's answer: "I like to make rhymes when I'm underwater," John Peter said subversively.
This week's puzzle: "The tomb is filled with blood-sucking insects," John Peter said _____.

FOURTEEN

When I took my seat in geometry next Wednesday, Lee handed me a package neatly wrapped in newspaper. "Here."

I was amused to note she'd selected the sports section. "Thank you for not using the obituaries."

"Too obvious."

"What is it?"

"Open it," she said.

It felt like a book. I ran a finger under the spot where the paper overlapped, and lifted the tape. It was a book. "*The Humor of Edgar Allan Poe*," I said, reading the title. "Humor?"

Lee grinned. "He was a bundle of laughs. You'll see."

"Cool. But why are you giving me a present?" I asked.

"You'll figure it out," she said.

I had no idea whatsoever. All day, Lee kept throwing meaningful, expectant glances in my direction. I remained clueless. On the bright side, it did give me an idea for the next newspaper puzzle. The staff loved the Zinger when I revealed it at the meeting.

That night, as I was drifting off to sleep, an image floated up from my mind. One year ago, on October 1, Lee had walked into homeroom. She was wearing a shirt with a decapitated teddy bear on it. One year ago. Exactly one year. Today was the anniversary of Lee's arrival at Zenger, and of the day we met. That's why she'd given me a present. And that's why she kept staring at me all day, like she expected me to do something. I never would have guessed Lee cared about anniversaries.

You'll figure it out.

Those were her exact words. Which meant she expected me to remember. Anniversaries are the sort of concepts that girlfriends care about. I mean, I have no idea what date Wesley and I became friends. Maybe one way to get Lee to be my girlfriend was to act more like she already was. Though I could see where that could turn into a minefield of awkward moments and misunderstandings.

However much or little this anniversary meant, I'd obviously not remembered soon enough. I needed to fix this. But I wasn't sure how. If I pretended I was totally clueless, she'd eventually either let it go or let me know why she was angry. But then I'd have to figure out whether to be apologetic or tell her how I felt about pseudo-significant moments. I was glad she'd come to Zenger. I was really glad we'd met and become friends. But, seriously, the anniversary of the day we met? It didn't seem like an occasion for a gift.

I could come right out and admit that I was slow to realize it was an anniversary. The fact that I'd finally figured it out should earn me at least a little bit of credit. Especially if I ended the admission by handing her a gift. Assuming I had any idea what to buy.

First thing in the morning, I looked up anniversaries. I was pretty sure that the one-year gift was supposed to be made of paper. A quick check online proved I was right. So, paper . . . a book was the obvious choice, and also the least imaginative, since she'd already given me one. A journal? Not bad, but not great. Origami paper? Nope. She had tons of it. Cardboard counted, too. I guessed anything in a box would sort of count. Crayons would be fun. No. Crayons would be stupid. But maybe Lee would think they were fun. I wondered whether there was a wax anniversary.

I realized I was in danger of driving myself crazy. I looked around my bedroom, seeking inspiration. I saw a deck of playing cards. Cards. They were paper.

Wait!

I could get her tarot cards. Those were cool and also kind of creepy—especially the ones involving death. Yeah. That was perfect. The only problem was that I'd have to wait until after school to go shopping, and then give the present to her that evening, or the next day. Showing up at her house with a gift would be really weird. But the longer I waited, the worse it would be. *Here's a gift to commemorate the time we first met, one year and two days ago. Aren't I thoughtful?*

But there was someone who always had my back. Someone I could count on when I really needed help.

I called Wesley. "You driving?" I didn't want to distract him if he was on the road.

"Nope. Just finished my route. What's up?"

"I need a favor."

"Name it."

I explained what I wanted him to do. The stores wouldn't be open yet. I figured the earliest Wesley could get the cards and meet me was third period. "I'll wait for you by the cafeteria doors," I said.

"You got it."

"Thanks."

When I saw Lee in geometry, I assumed I'd receive another of those expectant stares. But she greeted me normally. Which didn't mean anything, since she was really good at hiding her feelings. Still, it made me happy that I was going to acknowledge the anniversary. I was pretty sure she'd be pleasantly surprised.

At lunch, I waited for Wesley by the side door of the cafeteria and, sure enough, he pulled up in his truck. Except it wasn't the bagel truck. This was one of those street-sweepers. He got out, came over, and handed me a small bag.

"What happened to the other truck?" I asked.

"I lost that job."

"But you got another," I said.

"Yup."

"And you drove the sweeper over here, from wherever you were supposed to be."

"Sure. No big deal. I mean, all the streets are dirty, right?"

"Right. How much do I owe you?" I asked.

"My treat," he said.

"You didn't . . ." I was afraid he'd stolen the cards.

"Didn't what?" he asked.

"You didn't have to do that," I said.

"Hey, what are friends for? Catch you later."

I looked in the bag and was relieved to see a receipt. I guess there was hope for Wesley, after all. He'd gotten the deck wrapped. Appropriately, the paper was black. I took the present out of the bag and walked over to our table.

"I finally figured it out," I said, handing her the gift. "I'm a bit slow at this stuff."

Lee looked at the gift. "This is a nice surprise. And don't be too hard on yourself. Not everybody memorizes the death dates of famous writers."

Death dates? Famous writers?

"Yeah. Not everyone," I said. So that was the October event. This was so typical of Lee—give me a gift to celebrate Poe's death, not the anniversary of our meeting. And that's why she had said that the obituaries were too obvious.

"Cool," Lee said after she unwrapped the cards. "What's this have to do with Poe's death?"

Before I could invent an answer, a tell-tale slip of

paper flittered out of the wrappings. I recognized Wesley's handwriting. Lee picked the paper up and read the note. "Happy anniversary."

She frowned. "What anniversary?"

This was not going well.

"You thought my gift was to commemorate our first meeting, right?" Lee said.

"Right."

"But you didn't come to that mistaken conclusion until last night. Or this morning. Right?"

"Right."

"And then you scrambled to get me something. Right?"

"Right."

"That's sweet. And stupid. We could call it *glykomoronic*. Hey, I made a word."

She grinned at her coinage, opened the box, and slid out the cards. "Let me tell you your fortune." She shuffled the deck, then turned over a card. I expected The Hanged Man, but it was The Fool.

"I guess we can stop right here," Lee said.

October 2

Here's a tip for you, Sean. Keep a diary. I know guys don't do that. But if we did, we could look back and always know what had happened exactly one year ago.

By the way, as exhaustive as Mrs. Gilroy's list of essential figures of speech might seem, I realized she missed a lot of them. So I took some time and made my own list. The last one's especially for you.

Scott Hudson's Little-Known Figures of Speech
Hamonym—creative phrases for tasty parts of the pig
Bdelguppia—dozens of small words dashing about
    like little fish
Ablitteration—words so awesome they blow the reader
    away
Slimeli—any description or comparison using snot or
    mucus
Metafart—any descriptive phrase that includes a colon
Bananaclassis—writing about the same fruit at
    different times for different reasons
Cacaphony—any words used to describe rubber dog
    poop
Oopsphemism—unintentional swearing
Onomatopony—how toddlers ask for a horse

"Isn't it picture day?" Mom asked as I headed for the door on Monday.

"Yeah. So?"

"You're wearing a T-shirt," she said.

I glanced down. "It's clean."

"That's not the point. You want to look presentable."

"Why? We have lots of pictures of me."

"Your grandparents love the photos. So do your aunts."

"I can get Lee to retouch last year's picture. She can age me slightly. She's really good at that. They'll never know the difference," I said.

"Scott."

It always amazed me how a single syllable could carry so many different meanings simultaneously when uttered by a parent. This one, at the moment, carried a variety of commands, laced with several threats, and an ultimatum.

I played my last card.

"I'll miss the bus."

"I'll drive you."

Had I known what sort of nerve gas lurked in Sean's bowels, awaiting release in the car, I would have appeared at breakfast in a tuxedo.

I saw a lot of freshly scrubbed faces in the halls, and an abundance of well-ironed clothing, crisp pleats, and stiff collars, along with the usual variety of individual protest statements. I blended right in among the respectable buttoned-down majority. Jeremy, who I saw out front after Mom dropped me off, had been swaddled in a sports coat and tie. Poor kid.

"Nice shirt," Lee said when I walked into geometry.

I didn't bother to respond.

"Did your mom dress you?" she asked.

"Basically," I said. "I should burn all these shirts."

"I'll help. We can have a festival and call it Burning Shirt. It could start a trend. At which point, of course, we'll stop going because it became too trendy."

She was wearing a black T-shirt. But it didn't contain any horrifying images or defiant messages. "Did *your* mom dress you?" I asked.

"No. She merely advised me. We agreed, after heated negotiation, that this would be an acceptable compromise."

"That's what parenting is all about," I said.

"Hey, I have an idea. We've got that geometry test tomorrow. Let's study at my place." She gave me a calculating grin.

"You want your dad to see me dressed up."

"It will disturb his universe, slightly. Are you in?"

"Sure." I might as well get some mileage out of my outfit.

FIFTEEN

Lee and I ended up studying for a long time, because her dad worked late. But her mom brought us several nutritious, high-fiber snacks. She was a phlebotomist, so she was professionally oriented to be even more aware of nutritional perils than the average parent. When Lee's dad finally arrived, he came loaded with takeout Italian food from a place near his office. The food was well worth the wait.

As I was walking back from the bathroom after dinner, I passed Mr. Fowler's office. He usually kept the door closed. It was open this time. I guessed he'd dropped something off when he got home from work. I glanced in, curious about what the room would look like. No surprises leaped out at me. No statue of Beelzebub, or a cage full of weeping of orphans. No towering pile of Dalmatian skins. There was a large desk of dark wood. Maybe cherry or mahogany. There was a sturdy leather chair of the swiveling sort. There were bookcases filled with volumes that unanimously featured mundane spines. I saw a framed piece of needlepoint on the wall behind the desk. It looked like it had a sentence in fancy script in the center, but I couldn't make the words out from the hallway.

"Go ahead," Mr. Fowler said, walking up from behind me. "Take a look. Lee made it for me back when she was in eighth grade."

I walked in. As I got closer, I realized why I couldn't read it. It wasn't in English. I was pretty sure it was Latin. I sounded it out, to see if it meant more when the words were spoken, "*Aedificare in tuo proprio solo non licet quod alteri noceat.*"

"It's one of the many Latin phrases they make you memorize in law school."

"Why do they do that?" I asked.

"To thin the herd. To weed out those who lack sufficient will. It's an honored tradition." He touched the needlepoint. "Any guess what it means?"

"Except for *in*, *solo*, and *non*, I'm totally clueless. I can't even think of any words close to the rest of those." Usually, if I saw a sentence in a language I didn't know, I could figure out some of the words, based on the way they resembled roots or prefixes from English or Spanish.

"'It is not lawful to build on one's own land what may be injurious to another,'" Mr. Fowler said.

"But isn't that exactly what—" I caught myself. From what I knew, his clients wanted him to help them build things that were harmful to others. They skirted environmental laws, and he found ways for them to avoid fines or other forms of punishment.

I guess he knew what I was going to say. But he didn't get angry. He laughed. "Remember who gave it to me. . . ."

"Right. I'll bet she spent hours looking for the perfectly ironic phrase."

"That's my little girl." As he walked off, he said, "Nice shirt. You should dress like that more often."

I stood there and memorized the quotation. Knowing the meaning made that easier. I figured it would be fun to spring it on Lee someday, should she ever do something that might be *injurious to another*. Or maybe spring it on her at a totally unrelated time, which could be even funnier. And I happened to know the Latin phrase for that: *non sequitur*.

Zenger Zinger for October 7
Last week's answer: "The tomb is filled with blood-sucking insects," John Peter said cryptically.
This week's puzzle: "Edgar Allan wrote some less serious works," John Peter said _____.

Tuesday, I got a letter from Mouth. That's his nickname. We'd started freshman year together, but he'd left Zenger. We'd written to each other once in a while, after he left. I think we might have been the last two kids on the planet to write actual letters, not counting parent-mandated thank-you notes. I hadn't heard from him in a while. Since last summer, I think. And I guess he hadn't heard from me, either. But it was nice he got back in touch.

Dear Scott,

Remember me? Of course you do. We had a lot of good times at the bus stop last year. There's no way you'd forget me in a couple of months. Unless you got a girlfriend and can't think about anything else except her. And I sure couldn't blame you if that was the case. I know, if I ever get a girlfriend, that's all I'll be able to think about. But even if you were madly in love, you'd still remember me, since we hung out all the time at the bus stop, and at the newspaper meetings. Those meetings were great. Anyhow, I just wanted to say hi and let you know how I'm doing, and where I am, since you're the only one who cared about me back at Zenger High. Well, you and the school nurse. We moved to Nebraska. I guess you can tell that from the postmark on the envelope. Unless you already threw out the envelope. People are nice here. They smile a lot. Nobody tells me to shut up. Sometimes they don't stay until I'm finished telling them what I want to say, even if it's important, but they are very polite when they walk away.

That's enough about me. How are you? Did
your mom have her baby? That must be weird.
Some people think clowns are scary. I think babies
are scarier. I'd hate to have to sleep near one. How's
school? Are you on the paper? I loved your articles
last year. I cut all of them out and put them in
a notebook. I show them to my friends. Well, to
people I've met. People here are nice. I told you
that. But nice is sort of different from friendly. My
doctor told me not to think too much about friends.
Especially if it makes me sad. But I think about you.
And that makes me not sad.

    I have to go. I hope you write back.

        From far away,
        Louden "Mouth" Kandeski

Wednesday after school, I waited outside the meeting room,
again, so I could catch Mr. Franka.

    "I really wish I'd run that opinion piece right away," I said
when he reached the door.

    "Why?"

    "Mrs. Gilroy is nailing me for all kinds of stupid things,"
I said.

    "Like what?"

    I held out the essay I'd written during a free-writing

session, and pointed to one of the many sentences she'd circled.

Hoping it would be an amazing summer, my bicycle carried me down the street, leaving my home behind me like a fragile cocoon abandoned by a butterfly.

"That's good writing, isn't it?"

Mr. Franka responded to my question by staring at me. He didn't say a word.

"Well, isn't it?"

"Pretend someone else wrote that. Read it slowly and carefully. Read it out loud, for that matter."

I read it out loud, slowly. "Sounds fine," I said. "Sounds like good writing."

"The *bicycle* has hopes?" Mr. Franka asked.

"No. That's not what it says. Wait." I read the sentence again. Oh, crap. It did sound like the bicycle hoped it would be an amazing summer. My hand dropped. I felt like crumpling the essay.

"Hey, cheer up, Scott. Everyone makes that sort of mistake. It's very common. That's why there are teachers," Mr. Franka said. "The cocoon thing was pretty good."

"Thanks."

"You can write, Scott. You have talent. But it's a huge mistake to think you have nothing to learn."

"I guess. But it's a lot easier to learn from some teachers than from others," I said.

I expected him to accept that as praise, since he was

definitely one of the teachers I liked learning from. But he responded, "And it's a lot easier to teach some students than others."

"I'm not hard to teach," I said.

"I never said you were."

"You didn't say I wasn't, either."

"That's true, too."

"That's *parisology*," I said, dredging up one of the more easily memorized words from Mrs. Gilroy's list. Too bad all of them didn't contain parts that resembled the names of famous cities. "It's the intentional use of ambiguous phrasing."

He patted me on the shoulder. "I'm glad to see you're learning something."

"I'm learning something," I said ambiguously, as I followed him into the meeting.

As I took my seat next to Jeremy, I realized I still hadn't written an actual article that was going to run in the paper. That was okay. There was an issue every week. I just needed to think about something where I had a strong opinion. Or look for a good feature story.

October 9

Sean, my biology notebook is due tomorrow. This is a big part of our grade for the marking period. I spent three hours going over it tonight. I double-checked every fact against the textbook. And I checked everything against my class notes. It's perfect. There isn't a single thing I can lose points for. Even the grammar is perfect, not that Ms. Denton would care. If she's at all fair about grading, she has to give me a hundred. Maybe that will get her off my back. After school tomorrow, I can take a break. Believe it or not, Lee allowed Wesley and me to convince her to go to the Columbus Day football game at school. I don't think she's ever been to a game. I hope she likes it.

"Wow, look at all the little kids," Wesley said.

"Everyone looks little to you," I said.

"Where should we sit?" Lee asked.

"Near the top," I said. "We want to be able to see everything."

We threaded our way up the home team bleachers. A lot of people shifted when Wesley came near. I suspect more than a few of them had donated their lunch money to him during the years he was in school.

"It's going to be weird not covering the game." I spotted the two freshmen from the newspaper, Teresa and Doug, standing right by the fence at the edge of the field. So far, they'd done a good job reporting on the games. Though they didn't get very creative.

"Think of it this way: You can relax and watch the game," Lee said.

"I'm not sure I know how to do that," I said. "I spent all of last year trying not to miss anything important."

"Sounds stressful," Lee said.

"Nah. It was fun, once I got used to it."

The other team kicked off. One of our guys—I think it was Dominic Manzini—caught the ball just behind the five-yard line and started a run straight up the middle. Then, breaking a tackle, he cut to the left and plowed through an opening, right between two defenders.

"Whoa," Wesley said.

"He's going all the way!" I said as Dominic reached the fifty.

By then, the whole crowd was standing and screaming. Dominic nearly got tackled on the twenty, but he shook that off, too, slipped past the last defender's desperate dive near the ten, and cruised into the end zone.

"Sweet," I said.

I looked at Lee. She'd stood, too. Her face was alive.

"Fun?" I asked.

"Fun," she said.

I couldn't have wished for a better start to Lee's first football game. "He broke through the defense like it was made of moonlight," I said. I liked that phrase. It was a keeper. I reached for my pad to write a description of the run. I had no pad.

"Is every play this exciting?" Lee asked.

"Not exactly. But that's part of the fun."

■ ■ ■

October 11

You're actually making human speech sounds,
Sean. I thought it was babbling, but Mom said it's
called cooing because it all pretty much sounds like
vowels right now. But that gives me hope we'll be able
to belt out parts of "Old MacDonald" together pretty
soon. If people can teach parrots to recite the Gettysburg
Address, I don't see why I can't teach you to go "E-I-E-I-O."

"If you are interested in running for class president or student
council, pick up an information sheet at the front office," the
principal said during morning announcements on Tuesday.

When I got to geometry, Lee said, "Running?"

"Sitting," I said.

"As in sitting it out?" she asked.

"Exactly." I'd been on student council for a while last year,
for all the wrong reasons. I'd seen enough to know it wasn't
something I'd enjoy doing again.

"You might have a shot at president," Lee said. "You're not
exactly unpopular."

You just want to be first lady.

That was the joke that popped into my mind. Luckily, it
didn't all pop out of my mouth. I got as far as "You just want to
be" when I realized that *first lady* implied a much more serious
relationship than we currently had. I scrambled to think of a
neutral way to finish the sentence.

"Be what?" Lee asked.

"A campaign manager," I said.

"Dream on."

And so I did. But I had something I wanted to ask her. I thought about it all through geometry and history, and all through lunch. There was a school dance the Friday after next.

"Hey," I said as we were getting up from the table.

"What?" she asked.

The words should have flowed. Six words. Six syllables. Eighteen letters. *Want to go to the dance?* Nothing flowed. The words had formed a logjam. Lee frowned. The silence grew.

"What?" she asked again.

I pointed at her tray. "You didn't finish your fries."

"As usual," she said.

That was true. She rarely finished her fries. She tended to eat slowly, and as I'd mentioned, the fries tended to get exponentially less edible as they cooled.

"Did you want them?" she asked.

"Yeah. Sure." What else could I say?

"All yours." She put the tray on the table in front of me. "Eat up."

"Thanks." I took one of the cold, greasy fries and started to chew. It was like eating a buttered slab of congealed mayonnaise, wrapped in raw bacon.

As I swallowed my clotted-starch treat, I thought about Ms. Denton's class. *This is a mistake.* The single fry felt like it was expanding in my stomach. I could picture it sending tendrils throughout my digestive system. Or evacuation notices. Lee stared at me. I ate the rest of the fries.

As if the barely edible fries weren't enough of a burden on my gut, the dark look of glee Ms. Denton gave me when I walked into class was sufficient to make my stomach tighten. I was pretty sure she had something special waiting for me.

SIXTEEN

I hope you all like seafood," Ms. Denton said after we'd been seated.

I just knew she was going to bring out a preserved shark and give me the honor of making the first cut. What she didn't know was that I'd been fishing for most of my life. And one of the first things my dad insisted on was that if you were going to catch and eat a fish, you had to know how to clean it. So, while I was definitely not eager to explore mammalian anatomy, I was okay with the piscine sort. A shark, or a perch, or a trout would have been just fine with me. I could cut one open.

It turned out to be a different branch of sea life.

We each got an oyster. That was fine, too. I'd helped chop clams up for bait when I'd gone deep-sea fishing with my dad and my uncles.

"You going to be okay?" Lee asked when Ms. Denton plopped my oyster in front of me.

"I'm looking forward to this," I said, loudly enough so the teacher would hear.

"Now, I'm worried about you," Lee said.

We got to work. The fries still exerted some pressure, but it wasn't anything I couldn't control.

"I found a pearl!" Lee said after she began cutting.

"I found ooze," I said.

But I felt I'd turned a corner in this class. I was doing good work, participating, taking pages and pages of notes, and studying hard for each test. The only casualties in the room right now were the oysters. No matter how much Ms. Denton had it out for me, I could cross biology class off my list of problems. And that left just English standing in the way of an enjoyable sophomore year and a decent grade-point average.

Ms. Denton handed back our biology notebooks about five minutes before the class ended. When she gave mine to me, she smiled that same dark smile.

The oyster, it seemed, was a red herring. The notebook was her dark surprise.

I looked at the cover page. A sixty?

What the heck . . . ?

Under that, in red marker, she'd written, "Where are the illustrations?"

Illustrations?

I turned to Lee and spoke that word.

"Yeah. Of course. It's a biology notebook. It's sort of useless without drawings." She flipped hers open, but not before I spotted the ninety-seven on the cover. She thumbed to a page, revealing several neatly labeled drawings. She flipped past other pages, all heavily illustrated.

"I didn't know . . . ," I said.

"How could you not?" Lee said. "That was one of the first things she told us."

"When was that?" I asked.

"The first day."

"Probably at the same time I was taking the mop and bucket back to the janitor's closet," I said.

"After you puked."

"Thanks for reminding me."

Would there be any point in asking for a second chance? There wasn't any way I could do all the drawings. Maybe I could get her to show me a bit of mercy. It hadn't been my fault I was out of the room when she mentioned that requirement.

I walked up to the front table.

"No," she said.

"No to what?" I asked.

"Anything you are about to ask," she said. "Just *no*."

"But I was out of the room when you told the class there had to be illustrations," I said.

"It was also at the back of the guidelines," she said.

That put an end to my plea. I remembered getting the guidelines, glancing at them, and tossing them on my desk back home. As I returned to my seat, I spotted Ike's notebook. He'd also been out of the room. He had an eighty-five. I was pretty sure Chelsea had illustrations, too. I was the only unwise sophomore in the room.

Zenger Zinger for October 14
Last week's answer: "Edgar Allan wrote some less serious works," John Peter said politely.
This week's puzzle: "Fee, foe, fum," John Peter said
_____.

Wednesday, in English, we got our short stories back. This was the first time I'd had a chance to write fiction for Mrs. Gilroy. I didn't have high hopes that she'd like my story, but when she dropped it on my desk, I saw that even my lowest hopes weren't depressed enough to match reality. I'd gotten a seventy-five.

I was so used to getting shot down by her that I didn't even let out a moan. But I was curious which obscure, obsolete, or arbitrary rule I'd broken this time. Nothing was circled on the first page. Nothing on the second or third. I turned to the last page. Scrawled in red across the final paragraph were three words: "*deus ex machina.*"

Huh? I wasn't even sure how to pronounce that.

When I got to the newspaper meeting, I showed Mr. Franka that page. He glanced at it, then said, "God from a machine. In ancient Greek performances, the actors would get themselves into a mess. Then one of the gods would come down from above, lowered with ropes in a basket, and save the day."

"That sounds sort of cool." I guess the ancient Greek stage-crew guys were pretty strong.

"It probably was, way back then," he said. "But, these days, when your story problems are solved by someone who just shows up, or by some other sort of miracle, that's *deus ex machina*. And that's not a good thing."

"Is it bad enough to earn a seventy-five?" I asked.

"Do you think you'll ever make that mistake again?" he asked.

"No way."

"Then I think the grade served its purpose."

Two days later, I got called down to the guidance office.

Mr. Tivelli looked at the open folder in front of him as if it were an AP Bio cat. "Hmmmm." Then he looked up from the file and stared across the desk at me. "You're nearly failing both biology and English. How do you feel about your grades?"

"I feel bad," I said.

"Badly," he said.

He was wrong. *Bad* was correct. I wanted to stand up for myself. He was giving me a character test, and he wasn't even aware of it. If I corrected him, he'd get angry, and he'd probably find some way to make me suffer. Or maybe he'd write something really terrible in my records. Guidance counselors had a lot of power.

"I don't feel good about them," I said. I came dangerously

close to saying, "I don't feel *goodly*," to point out why *badly* was wrong. But that wouldn't have been good, either. Or goodly. The moment of crisis ended as he moved on from the impromptu grammar lesson.

"What do you think we should do about these grades?" he asked.

"Try harder?" I guessed.

"That would be a good start." He closed the folder with the triumphant finality of someone who has just solved a massive engineering problem. "Look at this as an opportunity to do better, Mr. Hudson."

"I'll do my bestly," I said. But I said it very quietly, after I left his office.

Painfully participating in the political process by producing poorly phrased passages and plodding poetry, people proposed platforms and pled for patronage. I survived the candidates' student-council speeches we sat through in the assembly on Monday. Later that day, in English, Mrs. Gilroy touched on *paroemion*, a term for excessive alliteration. The technique did not get her approval.

October 21

The first school dance is on Friday. I don't know what to do. I'd like to go with Lee. I want to ask her. I already tried, once. But I chickened out. Actually, I

French-fried out. It's kind of like a minefield with her, when it comes to social stuff. She made fun of dances last year. But then we ended up going to one. And it was an amazing night. There's no way I'll ever capture that magic exactly the same way. And I'm not trying to. But I'd like to dance with her again. And I think she'd like to dance with me. I keep thinking of that hug she gave me last month. A hug is like a very short dance. Without music. I want a longer dance.

Zenger Zinger for October 21
Last week's answer: "Fee, foe, fum," John Peter said defiantly.
This week's puzzle: "I love channel surfing from my couch," John Peter said _____.

"Who wants to cover the dance?" Sarah asked.

I realized that if I was covering the dance for the paper, I could tell Lee I had to go, and ask her to come along to keep me company. By the time I'd explored that thought and envisioned several outcomes, five hands had gone up. Including Jeremy's.

"You don't want to do that," I said.

"Why?"

"Imagine an adhesive bandage being ripped off your arm. You know what that feels like?"

"Sure."

"Now, imagine a thousand bandages."

"Ouch."

"Yeah."

I sat back as Richard and Edith decided to split the assignment, and write the article from two perspectives. I had to admit that was a pretty good idea.

Dear Mouth,

I'm glad you're feeling better. Sorry it took me a while to write back to you. I've been pretty busy. Things are good here. My mom had the baby. Sean isn't scary. Unless you're terrified of moisture and stench. I'm on the paper. I haven't written much yet. But I'm going to be doing opinion pieces and news features. I don't have a girlfriend. Lee and I are friends. Do you remember her? She had a lot of piercings and wore dark and gory shirts. You know who I mean. They all called her "Weirdly" when she got here. But she's not weird. She's really smart. She reads a lot. She likes the stuff I like. Except for slot cars. (Though I think she might like them, too.) So we have a lot in common. Her father scares me. But I think that's his job. I have to get going. I'm glad you wrote to me. It was a nice surprise.

From equally far away,

Scott Hudson

SEVENTEEN

Thursday night, right after dinner, the doorbell rang. I opened the door, and experienced that weird jolt you get when you see someone unexpectedly. I knew the face well, but never imagined I'd encounter it on my porch this year.

"Hi, Scott," Kyle's father said. "Haven't seen you in a while."

"Guess not. . . ."

"Kyle's been pretty involved with his wrestler friends." He poked my shoulder. "You're a strong kid. You should go out for the team."

"I'm not much of a wrestler," I said. I guess Kyle was as enthusiastic about sharing social updates or upheavals with his parents as I was.

"You never know until you try. Hey, I don't want to hold you up. I'm sure you've got stuff to do. I'm meeting your dad. Can you let him know I'm here?"

"Uh, yeah. Come in. Have a seat. I'll get him. He's in the garage."

"That's just like him. Can't keep his hands off cars."

I went to the garage. "Dad, Mr. Bartock is here."

"Thanks, Scott." Dad grabbed a rag and wiped his hands. He stepped away from the car with a wistful look. I think, in a perfect world, he'd just fix cars right here in our garage.

"He's your partner?" I asked.

"Yeah. You don't hang out with Kyle anymore, do you?"

"We drifted apart," I said. *Like the shell of a hand grenade.*

"It happens. Who knows? Maybe you'll drift together. Especially if I'm in business with his dad. You boys could become good friends again."

"Anything could happen, I guess."

It wasn't impossible, but it sure wasn't likely. Until the deal was done, and the contracts signed, Kyle could threaten to make trouble. He could tell his dad anything. I just didn't trust Kyle anymore, especially when he had some sort of power over me. As I headed up to my room, I thought about things that were more probable than a happy reunion with him. When I got upstairs, I jotted down my list.

Things That Will Happen Before Kyle and I Are Friends Again

Mr. Cravutto replaces laps around the track with poetry readings.

Hershey Park starts offering pterodactyl rides.

Mr. Fowler gives me $100,000 so I can run off to

Vegas with Lee and get married.

Slitty the Cat comes back to life and finds work as a purse.

The next day, in study hall, I watched to see if Kyle would give me any sort of knowing look. When he caught me staring, he grinned and mouthed the words *You're mine.*

Great. He knew that I knew.

He didn't say anything else to me that day, but I was sure there'd be trouble down the road.

When I got home from school, I headed into the kitchen for a snack. Mom was making a blueberry pie. She'd cut strips of dough for the top, and was weaving them in an open grid. She'd once told me it was called a lattice top.

I'd seen documentaries about Buddhist monks who make these large designs out of colored sand. They look totally at peace with the universe. That's how Mom looked. The pie was the center of her focus. The pie and the sand painting had another thing in common. Neither would be around for long. One strong wind, or one hungry family, and they were history.

"Looks good," I said.

"Thanks. It will smell even better than it looks."

"I know." I sat on a stool by the counter and watched as she finished weaving the strips. She took a piece of foil and wrapped the edge of the crust. That would keep it from burning while the pie baked. I couldn't make a pie myself, and I doubt I'd get much joy out of any effort in that direction, but I'd seen the process often enough that I knew the details. And I definitely knew the results. Mom's pies were as good as anything you'd get in a bakery or a restaurant.

"You didn't seem very happy to see Mr. Bartock," Mom said.

"He's an okay guy," I said.

"Has he ever done anything that made you uncomfortable?" she asked.

"No. Definitely not," I said. Kyle's dad was a little strict, but he definitely wasn't creepy or inappropriate. I guess it was part of any mother's job to track down the cause of strange reactions her kids had to other people.

"But something bad happened between you and Kyle," she said.

"Old history," I said. "It's nothing." I didn't share my fear that Kyle would try to exert some sort of control over me.

"Your dad never wanted someone to tell him how to run the business," Mom said. "Mr. Bartock is willing to be a silent partner."

"Silent partner?" I asked.

"He'll own half the business, and share the profits. But he has no say in how the business is run. He's purely an investor."

"Wow. That's a pretty good deal," I said.

"And hard to find," Mom said. "Most partners want control."

"So do most parents," I said.

Mom rewarded me with a frown.

"Just kidding," I said. Actually, *most people* would be more accurate.

October 24

No dance, Sean. I am so gutless. And distracted, I guess. I can't believe Dad is going into business with Kyle's dad. I don't want to talk about it. I don't want to think about it. I'm really not looking forward to gym next week. That's going to be Kyle's first chance to take advantage of me outside the civilized world.

"Hello, my servant," Kyle said when I got to the locker room on Tuesday.

"Very funny."

"You work for me now."

"Not really."

"Your dad works for my dad."

"Not yet. And not really. They're partners."

"No. My dad doesn't have partners. He has pawns. This is going to be awesome," he said.

As he said that, I realized there was really nothing he could ask me to do. He had power, to some limited extent, but no use for it. He was like a clunky old C-cell battery in a world of AA devices. I decided not to point that out to him. I didn't want him to try to find a way to prove me wrong.

Zenger Zinger for October 28
Last week's answer: "I love channel surfing from my couch," John Peter said remotely.
This week's puzzle: "I deduce that we have to take the left fork of the trail," John Peter said_____.

I got called back down to guidance the next day.

"Hudson, I have a suggestion," Mr. Tivelli said.

"Yes?"

"You have to admit you're in quite a sophomore slump," he said.

"Slump?"

"Quite a towering slump, actually," he said.

Towering slump. I resisted the urge to hit him in the shoulder.

He picked up my file and held it under my nose, "Look at last year. Good grades. Student council. Stage crew. All those articles in the paper. You were a ball of fire. What happened? Did you meet a girl?"

I met two women. One teaches English. The other teaches biology. They share a hatred for me. I didn't share that with him. "I'm still on the paper," I said.

"I don't recall seeing any articles by you," he said.

I opened my mouth. But none of my responses seemed worth the effort. I was pretty sure he wouldn't consider the Zenger Zingers a valid equivalent to everything I'd done last year.

"Since you don't seem to have a strong academic drive, maybe it would help your college chances if you went out for a sport. Is there anything you're good at?" he asked.

"I'm okay at fishing," I said.

He snorted. "Very funny. Can you run or wrestle, or do anything physical?"

"I guess."

"Well, give it some thought."

"I will." But it seemed crazy to think about it at all. I hadn't gone out for any sports freshman year. I was too short to play serious basketball. I'd wrestled in gym class, but that was it—except for a brief battle last year with Kyle that had been fueled by enough rage to tilt the outcome in my favor. I sucked at volleyball. Swim practice was at a fitness center at the edge of town, way too early in the morning for anyone other than vampires. We didn't have a hockey team or a bowling team. It looked like Mr. Tivelli was in for another disappointment.

Thursday, in the cafeteria, I heard a shout as I was walking over to get some mustard for my soft pretzel.

"Hey! Paper boy!" Kyle yelled at me from his seat at the table with his wrestler friends.

"What?"

He pointed at the French fries on his tray. "We need ketchup." I guess it had taken him half a week to figure out some way to prove he had power over me.

"It's right there," I said, pointing across the cafeteria to the table with the big pump jars of ketchup, mustard, and mayonnaise.

"So bring it here," he said.

We locked eyes. Pride and passion were at stake. My pride versus my father's passion. Could Kyle really screw things up? I had no idea. As I stood there, contemplating my next move, I spotted Lee out of the corner of my eye. She left our table, went to the condiments, and picked up the ketchup. She carried it across the cafeteria. As she walked past me, she said, "I have catlike hearing."

She plunked the bottle in front of Kyle. I could see some of the wrestlers cringing. A lot of them were creeped out by Lee. And I knew Kyle hated her. She held her palm under the dispenser, pumped a glob of ketchup on her hand, then slowly licked it.

"Yummm." She flashed the wrestlers a faux-bloody grin. *"Bon appetit!"*

I followed her back to our table.

"What was that all about?" she asked.

I explained the situation with the contract.

"I don't think he can really mess things up for your dad," she said.

"Probably not, but I can't take any chances. This is his big dream." I looked over at Kyle and his friends, who were occupied in drenching all of their food in ketchup. "I just have to tough it out until they sign the contract. I can handle it."

"You're so sweet," she said. She patted my cheek with her palm.

"Sweet and sticky," I said when I realized which hand she used.

"Hey, a bit of blush looks good on you," she said. "Don't wash. You can wear it tomorrow, for Halloween."

"Want to come over tonight and help hand out candy?" Lee asked me on Friday morning. "We get the cutest little monsters in our neighborhood."

"That would be fun, but I'm going out."

She stared at me like I'd told her I was entering a yodeling contest. "Going out?"

"I'm handing out flyers for the budget vote. I'll give you some. Maybe you can pass them to the parents who come with their kids."

"Sure. I can do that."

That evening, I went from house to house, threading among the dozens of little pirates and princesses. Each time I knocked on a door, the person answering would stare at me, and then start to sneer, just the same way any adult would sneer at an uncostumed high school kid going out to trick or treat.

I'd tried to get Mom to let me dress Sean up as a zombie and bring him with me. It seemed pretty much a perfect way to get people to listen to me. I'd even offered to make him a bulging eye out of a painted Ping-Pong ball. Who can resist a zombie baby? But she didn't think it was a good idea.

"Maybe next year," she'd said.

So I was forced to face a series of skeptical homeowners, armed with nothing but fast words and an earnest smile.

"I'm not here for candy," I'd say. "I just want to ask you to vote to save the school paper." Then, I'd hand them a flyer. And, much to my surprise, most of them would insist that I take a piece of candy. I didn't have a bag, so I had to put the candy in my coat pockets, until I ran out of room. At that point, I had no choice but to eat some of the treats. Politics is hard work.

One man told me, "It's nice to see a young person involved in the democratic process."

Another said, "Good for you."

Of course, I also got several versions of "I'm not wasting a penny of my hard-earned money on unnecessary luxuries for you young thugs."

No surprise—those people didn't offer me candy.

"How'd it go?" Mom asked when I got home.

"I don't know. It's hard to tell. You're voting, aren't you?"

"I'll try. Next Tuesday's looking pretty busy."

"It's important," I said.

"I know it is. I'll try. I really will."

Later, when I asked Dad, he said, "I'll vote on the way home from work. Unless I have to stay late."

I held out a mini Snickers candy bar. "Can you be bribed?"

"Not usually." He took the candy. "But you found my weakness."

October 31

Happy Halloween, Sean. Next year, I'm dressing you up and taking you trick-or-treating. I miss going out. I went out tonight, but I was asking for a lot more than candy. It feels strange asking people to vote for something. It feels good when they say they will. I don't like the way I feel when they say no. I'm pretty sure I could never be a politician.

EIGHTEEN

I was up in my room after lunch on Saturday when I felt my floor shake like someone was driving a tank down the road. I looked out the window. No tank. But close. It was a tractor. Not the kind of little tractors people use for mowing lawns or plowing driveways. This was one of those farm tractors you sometimes see chugging along the road toward a field at five miles an hour. Wesley was driving it.

I went outside. "You taking up farming?" I had to crane my neck to talk to him.

"Nope. Got a job delivering them," he said.

"Don't they usually put them on a flatbed truck?"

"The big dealers do. This is a small operation. They don't have a truck. So they hire people to drive them there."

"Where are you taking it?"

"Off County Line Road, about five miles past the old slate quarry," he said.

"And how are you getting back?" I asked.

Wesley shrugged, then said, "I'll figure that out when I get there."

"Want me to see if my dad can pick you up?" I asked.

"That would work."

"No problem." I ran in and checked, then told Wesley the good news. "He can do it. Just call the house when you're ready."

"Thanks. You coming?"

I was about to say no. But I realized that would be totally typical of me. I needed to do more stuff that wasn't typical. How often do you get a chance to ride a tractor?

"Sure. Why not?"

While I was climbing up, Wesley pointed over his shoulder. "There's room to stand behind me. Hang on. I'll try not to go too fast."

"That shouldn't be much of a challenge." I grabbed the back of his seat, and he drove off.

"Great view," Wesley said.

"For sure," I said. "It does look pretty cool from up here." And even at five miles an hour, with cars backing up behind us and honking, or zooming past and screaming swear words out the window, the wind felt good in my face.

There were times with Wesley when I felt scared, apprehensive, nervous, guilty, perplexed, or flat-out terrified. But even then, I usually felt fully alive.

■ ■ ■

November 1

This is National Novel Writing Month, Sean. I think it's also National Pet a Turtle Day, National Artificial Sweetener Week, and probably National Zucchini Fortnight. There seem to be more national days on the calendar than there are days in a year. Same thing for weeks and months. But NaNoWriMo, which is what they call it, is a pretty cool idea. People write a whole novel of at least fifty thousand words in one month. Fifty K isn't even two K a day. And we know that's a piece of cake. I'm going to give it a shot. Good thing this is Saturday. I can get a jump on things, just in case I have to slack off during the week. I'd hate to have to start a novel on a Wednesday. I'm not sure what I'm going to write about. Maybe dragons. Yeah. Dragons would be fun.

Here's a tip. If anyone ever offers you a tractor ride, take it. Oh, two more things. First, don't assume you can get cell phone coverage way out in the country. Second, a long walk on a country road on an autumn day is a great way to spend time with a good friend.

Saturday evening, I took my seat at the temple of the Chevelle. Last year, when I was adoring Julia from afar, I'd asked Dad how long it took for him to actually talk to Mom for the first time. He'd told me it had taken a couple months. I wanted to find out about the next phase of their relationship.

"Dad, do you remember the first time you asked Mom out?"

"Sure." He smiled the smile of recollection.

"Was it hard getting up the courage?"

"It was hard. But I did it."

"How long did you take before you asked her out on a real date?"

"That was a long time ago. Hang on. Let me think." He fiddled with the engine for a while, but I could see he was traveling through the past while his hands moved the wrench on autopilot. Or auto-mechanic. "Probably a month and a half."

"So you weren't like Bobby, either." My older brother had dates lined up before he was born.

"Not even close."

That was comforting. Physically, Dad and Bobby were a lot alike. But I guess, inside, when it came to dating, Dad and I were a bit closer. He'd told me he'd been real shy when he was my age.

"Were you afraid she'd say no?"

"Terrified," he said.

"But you still asked."

"Soon after I'd started talking with her, she went out of town for a week. I pictured that week, when I didn't see her at all, as how the rest of my life would be, if we weren't together.

I couldn't accept that. I needed her in my life."

"Where'd you go for your first date?"

"A movie." Then he laughed.

"What's so funny?"

"I thought it was an outdoor adventure. The title sure sounded like that. But . . ." He shook his head. "It was the wrong movie. Similar title. The actors didn't leave their clothes on very long."

"Oops."

"Yeah. Oops. Not the kind of film for a first date. Or a hundredth. It wasn't X-rated, at least. But nobody seemed to be interested in wearing a shirt."

"What'd you do?"

"As soon as I realized where the film was headed, I looked over at your mom and said, 'Let's get out of here.' She didn't need to be convinced. So we went for coffee. I apologized several times, until she told me to stop."

"So it worked out."

"We talked until well after midnight."

"That's a lot of talking for you," I said.

"Your mom has that power," he said.

Lee texted me at 2:00 A.M.

Use your extra hour wisely.

I could just imagine her waiting up all night so she could do that right when the clocks were supposed to be turned back.

I wisely used my extra hour, and many that followed it, for sleep.

November 2

Sean, I think all the good dragon ideas have been taken. Today, halfway through writing my first chapter, I realized I was totally ripping off <u>Jeremy Thatcher, Dragon Hatcher</u>. Maybe because I've read it seven times. I also spotted a smattering of <u>Dragonflight</u>. I guess it's easy to copy something without realizing it. I'm going to try writing something else today.

Monday was the last day of the first marking period. It also felt like the last day of the world. I could tell all my teachers were worried about the budget vote. I was worried about my grades. But it was too late to do anything about them.

I got another great essay grade from Ms. Burke, who seemed to love my writing. Maybe the key to high school success was to write essays for history, and history papers for English. Though I was pretty much convinced Mrs. Gilroy would shoot down anything I wrote, no matter what the topic or format.

I did my last bottle drawing in art. I had a whole stack of different drawings, sketches, and paintings, executed in a variety of techniques. We'd done extremely precise blueprint-like renderings, contour drawings, abstract representations, impressionistic wet-brush paintings, and a slew of other things. I'd felt it was stupid, at first, that we were drawing the same objects over and over. But after a while, I started to appreciate that my three bottles were the anchor for all the techniques. If I'd drawn a sketch of three bottles, but then made an abstract collage of a house, followed by an impressionistic watercolor of a basket of apples, I wouldn't have learned as much about the techniques. Or about the bottles.

November 3

You'd think, after all the books I've read, it would be easy to write one. But every time I get an idea, I immediately think up a thousand reasons why it won't work.

"Your girlfriend can't save you in here," Kyle said when we were getting changed for gym the next day.

"What, you want ketchup?" I asked. "I've heard it makes jock straps much tastier and easier to swallow."

"I want you to show me some respect," Kyle said.

"Sure. I'm happy to," I said. "How would you like me to manifest that?"

"For starters, you can talk like a person, and not a freaking encyclopedia."

"You mean, like a dictionary? Or a thesaurus?"

Kyle glared at me. "You used to be a normal kid, back

in middle school. I don't know how you got so messed up. My father's making a big mistake getting involved with your family."

"He doesn't seem to feel that way," I said.

"Things can change," Kyle said

"That's for sure," I said. "You know there are a thousand other people who'd love to be in business with my dad."

"Good luck finding one," Kyle said. He got up and headed out, giving me a push as he went by. I didn't push back.

November 4

I think I found the perfect idea. And it's still really early in the month. That gives me lots of time.

I watched election results on the local news that night, but they weren't covering anything except congressional races, and some scattered politically important campaigns for various mayors and governors. I couldn't find anything online, either. The next morning, I saw the results in the paper. The voters had killed both the main budget increase and Question Two.

I could have figured that out just as easily by the look on any of my teachers' faces when I got to school. To use a vocabulary word I hope I never have another opportunity to write, the atmosphere at Zenger High was funereal. When Mr. Franka walked into the meeting room after school, he looked like his dog had died trying and failing to rescue his best friend from a burning building containing the only existing copy of an unpublished novel by H. G. Wells.

"We lost," he said.

"I know. That stinks," I said. "Now what?"

"Now there's no paper," he said.

"But it's been published for seventy-five years," Sarah said.

"The school is named for a newspaperman," I said.

"They can't just kill something with all that history," Jeremy said.

"They just did," Mr. Franka said.

"So we're finished?" I asked.

"Soon," he said. "We can print two or three more issues with the remaining funds. That money is ours. We can maybe stretch things out through the end of December, if we cut costs. But there's no more money coming."

"What's the point?" Richard asked. "That's like being on life support."

"There's a point," I said. "We can't quit. We'll make them the best issues ever."

"Waste of time," one of the seniors said. "Bye, guys. It's been fun."

He walked out.

As I looked around the table, I had a weird image of people in the Alamo, deciding to stick together in the face of certain death. "Anyone else want to leave?" I asked.

Heads shook in the negative. They were staying.

"Maybe we can print it ourselves," Sarah said.

I thought about my adventure with the survival manual. I figured it would be cheaper to print a copy of the paper than a whole manual, but we printed a lot of copies. "How much does an issue cost to print?" I asked Mr. Franka.

He told me.

"Wow. That's a killer," I said.

"Why don't we publish online?" Jeremy asked. "We can put it on the school's server. The cost would be insignificant."

"That's a possible solution," Mr. Franka said.

I thought about how kids would get a copy of each issue and look at it throughout the day. That made it special. There was so much stuff online, and so little in print. "No. We need to preserve the tradition. There has to be a way." I grabbed a notepad. "Ideas? Say anything that comes to mind, no matter how absurd. Who knows what it could lead to?"

We spent at least half an hour listing everything we could think of, ranging from the practical to the absurd.

Scott Hudson's (and Friends') List of Ways to Save the School Paper

Sell ads.

Sell subscriptions for enough money to cover the printing cost.

Rob a bank.

Find a sponsor.

Get a grant.

Sneak into the offices of the local paper and use their
   equipment.

Win a contest where the prize is a high-speed printer
   and a year's supply of toner.

Print everything real tiny so it all fits on an index card.

Write it on our arms and stand in a row in the hall.

Sing it like bards of old.

End each meeting with a fight to the death, and
   charge admission.

In the end, after things started to move too far out of the box,
we ended up with the obvious things in the box.

"My mom makes amazing cookies," I said.

"Are you suggesting a bake sale?" Sarah asked.

"I guess. Yeah. I am. Her pies are killer, too."

"We'll put it on the list," Sarah said.

We didn't come up with a better idea. So we all agreed to
bring cookies.

I ran into Mr. Franka in the hall after the meeting. He was
coming out of the teachers' lounge, and he looked even more
disheartened than he'd been at the meeting.

"What's wrong?" I asked.

"We lost more than money yesterday. There were some
board members who've been trying for years to make drastic
cuts in areas they consider unimportant. They've always been

outvoted, five to two, or four to three, when it came to those measures. But three members were up for reelection. Two of our strongest supporters got defeated by people who aren't on our side. That will swing all the important votes against us."

"So the people who are against spending money on us are the majority now?"

"I'm afraid so."

"What else is going to get cut?" I asked.

"I don't know. We'll just have to wait and see. But I have a feeling it won't be pleasant."

"What about your job?" I couldn't imagine Zenger High without Mr. Franka.

"I'm in good shape," he said. "English and math are mostly safe, since they're required by the state. At least, for now. But art, music, wood shop, all of that could be in danger."

"That's just wrong," I said. "That stuff is important."

"We both know that. But some people feel differently. There are folks who think the schools should teach nothing except for the basics. There are even people who feel the government shouldn't be involved in providing an education."

"That's just stupid," I said.

"I agree. But the sad truth is that if fifty-one percent of the people who bother to show up at the polls vote for stupid, then stupid wins."

■ ■ ■

"We're having a bake sale," I told Mom when I got home. "Can you make some cookies?"

Her eyes glowed. "How many do you need?"

One of those super sped-up movie scenes flashed before my eyes, with Mom blurring around the kitchen, zipping from mixing bowl to oven to cooling racks, producing a growing mountain of cookies. "I don't know. Maybe a couple dozen. Is that doable?"

She was already pulling supplies out of the cabinet. "Piece of cake."

I detected no irony in her voice.

It wasn't until she'd set the oven to preheat and started pouring ingredients into the bowl of the electric mixer that she asked, "What's the sale for?"

"The newspaper," I said. "We lost the budget vote."

"Oh . . . I'm sorry. I didn't get a chance to vote. Was it close?"

She sounded guilty. As much as I was sad she hadn't voted, I didn't want her to feel bad. "No. It wasn't close, at all." That was the truth. The only people who voted were the ones who didn't want to pay for all the extra activities and programs. That made sense, in a sad way. People who didn't mind paying more had less incentive to vote than people who didn't want to pay more.

"Well, I'll certainly get you as many cookies as you want."

"Thanks."

I called Sarah to coordinate things, and she promised to get in touch with everyone else.

Zenger Zinger for November 4
Last week's answer: "I deduce that we have to take the left fork of the trail," John Peter said pathologically.
This week's puzzle: "Stacked deck for a straight," John Peter said _____.

NINETEEN

November 5

I didn't work on my novel, Sean. I was too bummed out about the paper getting killed. And I had to help Mom make cookies. I still think I have a great idea for the plot. I don't want to tell you about it here. At least, not yet. I've heard that if you discuss your idea too soon, you can kill all your creative energy. I'm pretty sure Hemingway talked about that. I'll get to work on it tomorrow. There's still almost a whole month left. That's plenty of time.

We're pretty lucky Mom loves to bake. And I was lucky she was home last year. She was working when she and Dad met, but she took time off when Bobby was little, and again when I was little. The year before you were born, back when I was in eighth grade, the local economy got real bad. A bunch of places went out of business. Mom had a part-time job, but she gave it up so one of the other workers, who's a single mother, could get more hours. She'll probably wait until you're at least a year old before going back to work. Then, she'll stick you in a day care with a cigar-smoking woman who's watching twenty flea-infested kids in her basement. You will scratch and cough quite a lot. I just realized that you won't even read this until you're way past that age, and well aware Mom doesn't do stuff like that. But at least I amused myself.

Thursday morning, I headed off to school with a large box of cookies, and dreams of a self-sufficient school paper. Actually, if we funded it ourselves, maybe it wouldn't even technically be a school paper. Which would mean we wouldn't be under the control of any school regulations.

I paused to absorb that thought. Total freedom. We could be like one of those great satirical newspapers from the past that poked fun at everything and fought for social justice.

Jeremy also carried a box. It was pink, wrapped with a white ribbon tied in a bow.

"Your mom didn't have to get fancy with the packaging," I said. "We're selling the individual cookies."

"That was a sexist assumption. My mom doesn't bake," he said. "She's too busy analyzing the structures of complex proteins."

"Okay, your dad, then. That's cool. My friend Patrick's

dad used to make these awesome funnel cakes for us. And he baked the best brownies ever. They moved last year."

"My dad doesn't bake, either," Jeremy said. "So he bought these for the sale."

"Hey, however we raise the funds, I'm happy," I said. "Thanks for bringing cookies."

"Cookies?"

Several kids at the bus stop favored us with lean and hungry looks. I responded with a hands-off stare. It was early enough in the day that nobody was willing to engage in an actual battle for an overdose of sugar.

I noticed Julia had a box, too. "Selling something?" I asked.

"It's for the chess club," she said. "We lost our funds. I wish my mom had voted."

"Good luck," I said. I wasn't worried about a bit of competition. There were more than enough snack-hungry sugar-craving students and teachers to support two bake sales.

But not two dozen.

When we got to school, it looked like we'd wandered into an indoor flea market. There were about ten tables crammed into the open area between the front entrance and the auditorium doors. I spotted other tables along the hallways on both sides.

They were all bake sales. There was one for the Academic Challenge team, another for the history club, the poetry club, the debate team, and so on. Even if my cookies were the best ones on the planet, they had little value in this crowded market.

"Back to the drawing board," Jeremy said.

"Definitely not back to the baking sheet," I said. "Or the cake pan."

I shared the cookies with the kids in homeroom.

November 6

My perfect idea fizzled out after three pages, Sean. It had seemed so great, until I tried to make it work on paper. It's kind of like playing chess. (Which I will teach you as soon as you are old enough not to choke on a pawn.) You reach out to make a move, and then you think about what moves that will lead to, and everything seems great as you look ahead a move or two. But then you get to the third or fourth move out, and all of a sudden, your whole strategy falls apart. The next thing you know, you're down two pawns and a knight. I'm going to take enough time to come up with a good idea that doesn't fall apart after three or four moves, and then I'll really think it through, all the way to the checkmate (to extend the metaphor).

I see now that it was a mistake to dive right in. That's okay for an essay or a story. But a novel takes a lot of planning. I don't want to write my way to the middle just to discover I have no idea how to finish it. I'll give my novel plenty of thought tonight and tomorrow, and then start writing on Saturday. Yeah. That'll work. There are still a ton of days in the month.

"The football team's budget never gets cut," Lee said as we made our way up the bleachers for the Friday-evening game.

"And it never will," I said. The only thing more sacred than football around here was wrestling.

"Maybe you should tap into their budget. Let the football team fund the newspaper," she said.

"I think that would be a bit tough," I said.

We grabbed seats and watched the kickoff. The ball hit just inside the five-yard line. Our kick returner let the ball bounce into the end zone.

"He didn't catch it and run," Lee said.

"He played it safe," I said.

"Last time, he ran with the first kickoff," she said. "I was looking forward to that."

"It's different every time," I said. "That's the beauty of it. You never know what will happen."

"Imagine if stage plays were like that," she said.

"I think that's called improv," I said.

"Oh, yeah. You're right. Maybe scripts are a good thing."

We failed to score during that possession. But five minutes later, we recovered a fumble. Two plays after that, we scored from the fifteen with a perfect pass, rifled between a pair of defenders. I could tell Lee was enjoying the game.

"I can't believe you're turning me into a sports fan," she said. "Next thing I know, you'll be asking me to the senior prom." She laughed.

I didn't.

November 8

All my ideas suck.

I think I need to let things jell in my brain. November's barely begun. I can do some serious brainstorming this weekend, and then get going on the novel on Monday.

After grappling with my guidance counselor's suggestion for a while, I decided to take a shot at wrestling. Tryouts were after school on Monday. The gym was packed. Mr. Cravutto had pulled in the other three gym teachers to help, and set up four mats. I beat the first kid I went against, but not by much. The next round, I found myself face to sneer with Kyle.

"You're going down," he said.

"Like last time?" I asked.

"No trash talk," the coach said. He blew his whistle.

Kyle came at me hard. I should have tried to deflect him, but I met him full force. Our heads were jammed close together as we fought for an advantage.

He whispered a threat. "I'll tell my dad you tried to kiss my sister."

"Even you wouldn't sink that low," I said. Kyle's sister was in sixth grade. A kid my age would have to be a total predator to try to kiss her. He'd never go through with that threat. And nobody would ever believe it. But the thought broke my concentration.

I was briefly in the air.

And then, briefly, on my back.

I didn't bother trying to win my next two matches. Even if I was good enough to make the cut, there was no way I wanted to spend a season on a team with Kyle.

Later, in the locker room, I couldn't help myself. "You wouldn't do that," I said to Kyle.

Instead of answering directly, he leered and said, "You always did suck at poker."

So, yeah, he'd bluffed me. But it was a rotten bluff.

Zenger Zinger for November 11
Last week's answer: "Stacked deck for a straight," John Peter said tenaciously.
This week's puzzle: "The weapon was a lead pipe," John Peter said _____.

The next morning on the bus, Jeremy was grinning so hard, I was afraid his cheeks would rip.

"What?" I asked.

"You'll see."

"Tell me."

"You have to wait until the meeting."

"I could dangle you out the window."

"You're not a thug."

"I guess I'll have to wait."

"It will be worth it."

TWENTY

I have an idea." Jeremy pulled a thick document from his backpack and dropped it on the table.

"We should wait for Mr. Franka," Sarah said.

"He's got a staff meeting," I said. "He told me to tell everyone to go ahead without him."

"Okay." Sarah pointed at the stack of paper in front of Jeremy. "What's that?"

"The school budget," he said.

"But the budget was defeated," I said.

"No. The discretionary items in the supplemental budget were defeated, as was the increase for the main budget. The school has to have a budget. They asked for more money for this year to cover increased expenses and a shortfall in state funds, which meant the voters would have to approve a rise in taxes. That got defeated, so the school has to get by on the same amount of money from the residents as last year. The district receives a specific amount of money from local taxes, along with state and federal contributions. All of those dollars are allocated by the school board into expenditures such as salaries, textbook purchases, building maintenance, and so on. That allocation becomes the budget. Get it?"

I nodded, as did the others around the table. I didn't totally get all the details, but I grasped the basic idea.

Jeremy flipped to a page where one line was circled in black marker. "This is the section for clubs and activities."

"I thought all the clubs got killed," Sarah said.

"Not all. Some stayed in the main budget. Nobody is going to kill clubs or activities related to popular sports." Jeremy pointed to the top of the page. "They still have the varsity-letter banquet, and funds for the cheerleaders to attend two out-of-state competitions. But check out what else is here."

I looked at the line he'd circled. "Latin Club? They don't teach Latin here anymore. I don't think they've taught it for years."

"Exactly," Jeremy said. "But there are funds set aside for it. A lot of funds. I'll bet, back in the old days, they went on some kind of expensive field trip."

Now I saw where he was going. "Since there's no Latin Club to use the money, can we get it for the newspaper?" I asked.

"No," Jeremy said. "But we can get the money for the Latin Club."

"I'm not following this," I said.

"If we *become* the Latin Club, we have access to its funds. Since the club currently has no members, we can basically take it over. The club can publish a newsletter. There's more than enough money to cover our costs. We can do anything we want, as long as our adviser approves."

"And that would be Mr. Franka?" Sarah asked.

"Assuming he agrees with the plan," Jeremy said. "Which I'm sure he will."

"I'll track him down right after the meeting," Sarah said.

"So, we're still publishing the *Zenger Gazette*, but we're calling it the Latin Club newsletter?" I asked.

"Yup. We can even still call it the *Zenger Gazette*, if we want. It doesn't matter what we call it," Jeremy said. "Or even what's in it. All that matters is that it has to be published by the Latin Club."

Sarah leaped from her seat and threw Jeremy a hug. "That's brilliant!" she said.

I was afraid he'd get snapped in half, but when she stepped back, he seemed intact, though his face was slightly ruddier than usual. I had a feeling he was going to have sweet dreams tonight.

I figured I'd surprise everyone and get things started, since I hadn't made much of a contribution to the paper, so far. On the way out, I stopped by the office and got a copy of the form clubs used to apply for their budgeted funds. I filled it out for the Latin Club when I got home, listing Mr. Franka as the faculty adviser, and Sarah as the president. I knew how much the paper would cost to print, so I listed that for the newsletter. There really weren't any other costs. I was tempted to ask for money for snacks, but I was afraid that if I got greedy, it would cause trouble. When I was finished, I signed the spot at the bottom where it asked who filled out the form.

November 12

I got sidetracked, Sean. But I still trust my sub-conscious to give me a great idea for my novel. And I have more than half a month left. I think as long as I start by Saturday, and really crank out the words, I'll be fine.

"I hope this works," I told Jeremy when I got to the bus stop.

"It has to," he said. "The money is there. We have an adviser. There won't be any problems."

When we got to school, I took the form to the office and handed it to the secretary.

"Latin Club?" she said. "We haven't had one in years."

"Latin is getting really popular again," I said. "I think it's because of that show set in ancient Rome."

She shrugged, and put the form in a basket.

We'd be getting our first report card of the year on Friday morning. And for the first time in ages, I was dreading that moment. The card itself was actually a slip of paper. And we didn't have to get it signed. My parents might not even ask to see mine. Bobby had pretty much scalded their eyes with his report cards, on those rare times when they managed to get their hands on one. In comparison, my usual B grades, spiced with a sprinkle of As, made them happy.

It was pretty much as I'd feared. I got decent grades in most classes, but a seventy-one in biology, and a sixty-eight in English. It didn't bother me as much as I'd thought it would. I knew I should have cared. I mean, yeah, it's good to care about grades. But not when the playing field isn't level. Mrs. Gilroy wanted me to fail, and Ms. Denton wanted me to suffer. All I wanted was to get through sophomore year.

"Bad?" Lee asked when I took my seat in geometry, where I'd earned a solid B.

"I never thought my gym grade would be one of the high points of my report card. I aced that class. And history." I had a feeling Mr. Cravutto, who was still a-courtin' his female counterpart with vigor, had taken it easy on everybody.

Lee held out her hand. "Let me see."

I gave her the card. She read it, winced, and said, "Poor baby. You need to heal your wounds with ice cream."

"It's November," I said.

"It's *ice cream*," she said, as if those two words ended all arguments. Which, of course, they did.

TWENTY-ONE

Saturday afternoon, I was in my room, wondering whether it would set a bad precedent if I got out of bed before 11:00 A.M. Sean had been more quiet than usual during the night, so I'd gotten some uninterrupted high-quality sleep. Dad was in the garage. Mom was midway between us, in the living room, when the phone rang.

Mom's shriek brought both ambulatory males running at full speed. I grabbed my baseball bat on my way out of the room. Dad was a bit closer, but I had gravity on my side as far as clearing the stairs, so we reached the living room at about the same time. Upon arrival, we both slid to a stop and contemplated my mom/his wife sitting there with a huge smile on her face and a phone in her hand. Based on the scream, I'd have anticipated the presence, at the very least, of an enormous spider, or a deeply evil person wearing a hockey mask and brandishing some form of bloodstained cutting tool. The fact that Dad was clutching a hammer provided one more bit of evidence that we were a lot alike on the inside.

Mom spoke, nodded, spoke, squealed, then finally noticed the hovering protectors.

"Bobby's engaged!" she said. She immediately returned her attention to the phone.

"Bobby's dating someone?" I asked.

"Apparently," Dad said.

He put a hand on my shoulder and backed me away from the couch. "We'll both go crazy if we try to pick up the facts from one end of the conversation. She'll fill us in soon enough."

"I can wait," I said.

"Me, too," Dad said. "But it is exciting."

"Uh, yeah." I doubted it. I'd been to only one wedding, back when I was in third grade. It was my aunt Zelda's second marriage. Pretty much all I remembered was that you could get as much food as you wanted, and that cherry punch doesn't do much to make vomit look any less nauseating.

"Want to hang out in the garage?" Dad asked. "This could take a while."

"I'm working on a novel," I said.

"How's it going?"

"Slowly."

Dad tilted his head toward the garage. "Sometimes, it's good to take a break and give your mind a rest."

"You're right." I followed him to the garage. "It won't hurt to take a breather." Maybe a change of scenery would inspire me. Maybe I could set the novel in a garage. That was worth thinking about. There could be an evil car. Yeah! A car that tries to kill people. No. Crap. Stephen King did that one already.

When Mom got off the phone, she tracked us down and shared all the details. "Her name is Amala Alverenga. He's actually known her for several years. She works as a publicist for small bands."

And that's all we knew.

"Bobby's kind of young to get married," I said.

"It might be good for him." Dad said. "Your mom and I got married pretty young, and that seems to be working out okay."

"Good point."

November 15

Bobby's engaged. That means we'll have a sister-in-law. If he actually goes through with the wedding. He doesn't have the best track record when it comes to finishing what he started, or establishing long-term relationships. Except with music. Even there, he needs a push sometimes. But he's a really good guitarist. He's starting to make a living with it, which is pretty cool.

Time flies. Or, as they say in Latin, *tempus fugit*. The weekend fugited away, and I was once again sitting in homeroom.

...

"Scott Hudson, please report to the office."

First, I'll report that sophomores are not mature enough to resist spouting variations of "*Ooooohhhh. Someone's in truhhhh-bullllll. . . .*" when the target of that announcement is within earshot. And eyeshot. And, I guess, mouthshot.

When I got to the office, the secretary told me to go see the principal. He wasn't alone. A middle-aged guy sat in a chair on the left side of the desk, wearing a suit and tie. He looked like he'd just eaten a lemon.

"This is Mr. Sherman," the principal said. "He is the head of the school board."

"Hi," I said. I'd never met him, but I knew who he was. Everyone in town knew his name. You could see *Sherman Construction* signs all around this part of Pennsylvania.

Mr. Sherman didn't bother to return the greeting. Instead, he waved the Latin Club application in my face. "Is this some kind of joke?"

"No," I said. "We want to make the club more active."

"They don't teach Latin here. We eliminated it years ago. You don't speak Latin." He smirked like he'd just caught a three-year-old in a lie. "Go ahead, say something."

As my brain started to slip into panic mode, I remembered the phrase I'd memorized. "*Aedificare in tuo proprio solo non licet quod alteri noceat,*" I said, letting the words from Lee's needlepoint gift for her father roll off my tongue. I had a feeling I could have just as easily mouthed a string of gibberish for Mr. Sherman, and he wouldn't have known the difference. But Principal Hedges would probably be able to tell if I was faking it. There was a diploma on the wall behind him from Montclair State for his bachelor's degree, and one next to it from Temple for his Master's in Education. Even if he hadn't studied Latin, he'd have been exposed to enough of it to recognize the real thing.

Mr. Sherman glared at me. "That's a pretty hefty budget for a newsletter," he said.

"It's within the amount allowed for the club. I broke down the expenses," I said. "Everything's been properly allocated."

"A weekly newsletter?" he said. "What's the point of that?"

"There's a lot to discuss. And we want to share the news. The more we tell people about the club, the more members we can get. We're very enthusiastic about keeping a dead language alive."

His frown deepened. From what I'd heard about him after the election, he really didn't like education. He didn't like knowledge. But I guess he realized, whether he liked what I was doing or not, I was within my rights. He tossed the application on the principal's desk, and said, "I'll be keeping my eye on you."

I appreciate that, sir. I kept my sarcasm to myself.

"We're finished," Principal Hedges said. "Good luck with the club."

"Thanks."

As I left the room, I heard the principal say to Mr. Sherman, "It could be a good thing."

The door closed before I could hear the reply, but I was pretty sure it wasn't enthusiastic. Mr. Sherman was a real grump.

First period had started, so I headed for geometry. I was tempted to open the door, fall on the floor, and drag myself to my chair like a kid who'd just been beaten close to death. But I decided that it probably wouldn't be as funny as I thought. And I didn't want to mess up the good relationship I had with Mr. Stockman. So I settled for walking in, taking my seat, and offering a shrug to the inquiring eyes of those who'd heard me being summoned to the office.

I waited until lunch to tell Lee how her needlepoint had saved the day.

"You're being very altruistic," she said.

"What are you talking about?" I knew Lee didn't misuse words, but altruism is when you make a sacrifice to help others. I was doing all of this as much for myself as for the rest of the staff.

"Aren't you—" She cut off whatever she was going to say next, and glanced away.

"What?" I asked.

"Did you look at your report card?"

"Sure. I looked at it, and it sucked. So I looked away. What's the problem?"

"Take a closer look."

I still had the report card in my backpack. I pulled it out and scanned the various numbers and letters scattered across the sheet. My eyes locked onto something I hadn't even noticed before. A single word at the bottom of the slip had snagged me and slain me.

Ineligible.

"That means . . ." I said.

"No clubs, sports, or activities for this marking period," Lee said.

I swore and ripped the report card in half. "That's not fair."

"Agreed," Lee said.

"I'm still going to the meeting Wednesday," I said.

"Good luck," Lee said.

I told Jeremy the same thing during the ride home. "Maybe they won't even know," I said.

"I'm sure there's a list," he said.

Zenger Zinger for November 18

Last week's answer: "The weapon was a lead pipe," John Peter said bluntly.

This week's puzzle: "It's a shame to burn the steak," John Peter said _____.

TWENTY-TWO

I expected an alarm to go off when I walked into the meeting and took my seat. Or maybe everyone would leap to their feet and scream, "Unclean!"

Nobody seemed surprised to see me.

"Hi, Scott," Mr. Franka said.

I heard giggling next to me. I looked over at Jeremy, whose face had been conquered by smugness. "What?" I asked.

"I was right. There was a list. Club presidents get it. So do club advisers."

"So why haven't I been kicked out?" I asked.

"I looked up the club rules," he said. "Any student can sit in on a session of any club. Nothing is secret or private. And the specific definition of *ineligible* only mentions club membership."

"So I'm not here as a member. But I can sit in."

"And participate in discussions," Jeremy said.

"Can I write articles?" I asked.

"No. Sorry," Mr. Franka said. "That's clearly out while you're ineligible."

"What about the Zenger Zingers?" I asked. "They're anonymous."

"We can't take that chance," Mr. Franka said. "We violate rules, we might get shut down. We can't risk that. Besides, it's just for one marking period. Right?"

"I hope so," I said. "Look, if someone else wants to write the Zingers right now, that's okay with me."

Nobody wanted to step in. I was glad everyone felt it was okay to wait until I could come back.

Later, when Mr. Franka headed out, I followed him. "Got a minute?" I asked.

"Sure."

"Do you have to go to college to be a writer?"

"No. You don't *have to* go to college for that. But if you plan to be a writer, you *should* go to college to study something. It's not just about knowledge. It's about experience."

"A lot of writers got their experience out in the world," I said.

"True. Some of them by choice. Some of them because they never had the opportunity to do otherwise. It really depends on the type of writer you want to be."

"I want to be a good one," I said.

"Then expose yourself to every experience you can find or afford. That definitely includes college, if possible. And it is almost always possible."

"Thanks."

■ ■ ■

November 19

I nearly had to make up some fake Latin the other day, Sean. Here's the crazy thing. If you toss out some Latin-sounding stuff to try to appear smart, amazingly enough, there's a word for that. <u>Cacozelia</u>. I love that, because it sounds like caca, which is slang for crap. There are a couple other words that are related to cacozelia. Here's the best one. If you use a word that sounds right but isn't, that's a <u>malapropism</u>. Like if someone said that self-rule was <u>metonymy</u>. As much as I'd rather have anyone else for an English teacher, some of the words Mrs. Gilroy introduced us to are, as they say in Latin, <u>retortocerebemic</u>. Guess what? I made that up. You've been <u>cacozeliad</u>. Looks like there's more than one Hudson who can deliver the caca, you little diaper stuffer.

Thursday, when I saw they were holding auditions for the play, I wandered down to the auditorium to watch. I was ineligible to try out. That was okay. I had no interest in acting. I just wanted to check things out.

When the director spotted me, a look of horror rippled across his face. I guess he hadn't forgotten my audition from last year. Then the horror was replaced with relief. He pointed at me and said, "Stage crew. Right?"

"Yup. But I might not be able to do it this year."

"That's a shame. What's keeping you away?"

"Grades," I said.

"Well, if you manage to fix that, you're welcome at any time."

"Thanks. What's the play this year?"

"We're doing a musical version of *Goodnight Moon*," he said.

"That's a picture book." I tried to imagine it being brought to the stage.

"Every object in the room has a story to tell. And a song in its heart." His grin was followed by a sigh.

"What's wrong?"

"I wanted *The Giving Tree Opera*, but it was too expensive. The new school board is killing us with their cuts."

"Hey, maybe next year . . ." I figured I should let him get back to work. I was about to join the stage crew members who'd come to watch the auditions when Kyle walked into the auditorium and headed in their direction. Great. He probably wanted to get on stage crew to be near Kelly, who was likely to get a role in the play. Whatever his motivation, if he was going to be part of the crew, I definitely didn't want to get involved.

I heard a car pull into the driveway. "I'll bet that's Bobby." I got up from the couch, where Dad and I had been camping, watching the college games.

Dad nodded. "Definitely him. He told me he'd rescued a '68 Plymouth Satellite from the junkyard."

I opened the front door. Yeah. Bobby was there, driving an enormous old muscle car I now knew was a Plymouth. He got out and headed for the trunk.

"Need a hand?" I shouted.

"Sure. Grab a bag."

A woman got out of the passenger side. She was tall and curvy. Nearly as tall as Bobby. I feel weird saying this about my future sister-in-law, and I'm only going to say it once, but she had a great body. Her skin was dark. Her hair was abundant.

"You must be Scott," she said.

"Somebody has to be," I said.

Bobby gave me a weird look. He doesn't always get me. But Amala laughed. "And you were chosen for the role," she said.

"Right. I beat out all the weaker contenders." I grabbed a suitcase from the trunk.

Mom and Dad joined us.

"Welcome to our home," Mom said. She held out her arms. They hugged.

Dad held out his hand. Amala took it. I realized I hadn't offered her either a handshake or a hug. I hoped she didn't think I was a jerk. Though Bobby had probably already told her every horrifying and embarrassing story from my infancy and childhood.

Mom swept Amala off for an in-depth tour of Sean World. Dad and I helped Bobby carry their stuff up stairs.

"Is she . . ." I pointed downstairs in the general direction of Amala, Then, I pointed to Bobby's room. ". . . here?"

"Unless you want me to move in with you," Bobby said. "We still have the old bunk bed stored in the basement."

"No way I'm ever sleeping in that thing again." I spent two years waiting for the top mattress to crash down and smother me into the deep sleep of death, while Bobby lay above, oblivious, sleeping the deep sleep of sleep. Maybe that's why I liked reading Poe so much.

"Don't worry," Bobby said. "You won't have to."

"Your mom and I had a long discussion about this," Dad told me.

"Mom's cool," Bobby said.

"I wouldn't go that far," Dad said. "But she's . . ." He looked at me for the right word.

"Tolerant?"

"Yeah." Dad put a hand on my shoulder. "But don't you get any ideas."

"No ideas," I said. *Dreams, yes; ideas, no.*

November 23

Sean, Bobby's fiancée is really smart. She has a degree in public relations from Kent State. I'm not sure where she's from. I mean, she grew up in south Jersey, but I can't figure out her ethnicity. If I had to guess, I'd say she's from south of the equator. But I guess I don't have to guess. She'll tell us. Or Bobby will. Or they won't. We'd learned in history about how at one time in parts of America, it was illegal to marry someone from another race. I can't imagine that. Talk about voting for stupid. . . .

■ ■ ■

Amala fit right in at Thanksgiving dinner. And she preferred thighs to drumsticks, so I didn't have to exercise altruism. Mom ground up a tiny piece of turkey for Sean, to go with his sweet potatoes and beans. She should have ground some up for Aunt Zelda, too. At least my messiest aunt and my messiest brother were seated near each other, so there was only one zone of repulsion for the eye to avoid.

Lee called me after dinner. "Don't make any plans for tomorrow," she said.

"I was going to work on my novel," I said.

"For NaNoWriMo?" she asked.

"Yeah."

"That's highly ambitious. How much do you have left?" she asked.

"Some . . ."

This was greeted with silence.

"A lot . . . ," I said.

More silence.

"Pretty much all of it."

"Do you even have a title?" she asked.

"I figured I'd save that for last."

"First chapter?"

"Nope."

"First paragraph?"

"Still working on it."

"Opening line?"

"Soon. I've come pretty close."

"You know the month is nearly over," she said.

"Yeah. I'm not sure how that happened."

"I give you my permission to fail," she said.

"I don't need your permission," I said.

"True. That's been emphatically demonstrated recently. But I'm still giving it to you. See you tomorrow. We'll pick you up around 12:30."

"We?"

"Dad and me."

"Yay. See you then."

"Wear comfortable clothing," she said.

"That's all I have."

November 27

There's a lot of satisfaction in writing short things, Sean.

TWENTY-THREE

Lee wouldn't tell me where we were going. All her dad would say was that this was their traditional day-after-Thanksgiving outing.

"Does it involve a human sacrifice?" I asked.

"Relax, Scott," he said. "If I were planning to kill you, I would have left Lee at home."

"Dad!" Lee said. "Not funny."

"Sure it is. Right, Scott?"

"Yeah, hilarious," I said.

We headed up the Northeast Extension of the Turnpike to the next exit, then drove along a road off 209 that wound northwest, skirting a stretch of state forest. Several miles later, we pulled into a parking lot in a large clearing by a four- or five-story metal building that turned out to be an indoor climbing gym.

"I thought you weren't big on sports," I said as we walked inside.

"This is not a sport," Lee said. "It's an adventure."

We took turns climbing far higher than anybody needed to go. It was actually fun. Though the thing I enjoyed most was watching Lee climb. I tried not to watch her too closely, or with too much admiration for her form, since I was sure her dad would be able to sense any heat waves emanating from me.

He held the rope when I climbed. I had a feeling he liked knowing my life was in his hands. Lee and I held his rope together.

"How fond are you of him?" I asked as he neared the top of the climb, and reached the spot where we'd all slipped at least once.

"You're as bad as he is," she said. But she said it with a grin.

"Hardly."

"Fond or not, I think my mom would be sad if we returned without him," she said.

"We can't have that," I said. "Let's not let him fall."

"Agreed. Let's not."

Mom and Amala had gone shopping. Along with almost every other person in the country. Dad was in the garage. I said hi to him, then headed up to Bobby's room.

"Where'd you go?" he asked. He was sitting on the edge of his bed, playing his guitar.

"Lee's dad took us rock climbing."

"Sounds risky," Bobby said.

"Girls' dads are scary," I said.

"Tell me about it. Amala's dad is like six foot eight."

"Seriously?"

"Close. He played football in college."

"What's he do now?"

"Mostly, he struggles to keep from killing me. In his spare time, he's a foreman at a company that makes caskets."

"Is that a joke?" I asked.

"I wish."

"Well, if he kills you, at least he'll probably feel guilty enough to make sure you're buried in style." I sat on his bed next to him. "It's nice having you here."

"It's nice being here."

Sunday was the last day of the month. And the end of NaNo-WriMo. Maybe next year I'd try again. For now, it was sort of a relief to accept that I'd failed.

Bobby and Amala were planning to head out after dinner. While Bobby and Dad were in the driveway playing around with something under the hood of the Plymouth, Amala poked her head into my room.

"Thank you for being so welcoming," she said.

"You're pretty easy to welcome," I said. I got up from my desk and walked over to her. "I like you. You're good for Bobby."

"How so?" Amala said.

"He's settled down. He used to be a bit . . ." I didn't want to say anything bad about him. But I wanted her to know he wasn't a choirboy.

"Wild?" she guessed.

"Yeah."

"So was I," she said. "So were *we*," she added.

"You and Bobby?"

"We go back a ways. We crossed paths a lot."

"Really?"

She smiled. "Do you remember last year, when Bobby was in Ohio?"

"Sure." I'd never forget the day he took off.

"That's where I was," she said.

"At college?"

"Right. He came out one time before that, too. We were wild. But we got all of that wild out of our systems. I think we calmed each other down. You know what it all comes down to?"

"What?"

"I love him. Totally. With all my heart. With all my soul. With all my being."

"*Anaphora*," I said.

She stared at me.

"Sorry. Bad habit. I've been sort of immersed in figures of speech."

She laughed and gave me a hug. "I love you, too, my little brother." She let go and stepped back. "Bobby chose well when it came to siblings."

"So did I."

As if on cue, Sean let out a wail.

"At least, the first time," I said.

TWENTY-FOUR

The gloom of our adolescent moods contrasted jarringly with the early December mid-afternoon sunlight that dappled the ledges of the waist-high bookshelves in the antiquated ninth-period English literature classroom (for it is in Zenger High School where our story begins), when the overly stern educator Mrs. Gilroy hefted a leather-bound tome and intoned an overly emotive rendition of the opening narrative.

"It was a dark and stormy night; the rain fell in torrents—except at occasional intervals, when it was checked by a violent gust of wind which swept up the streets (for it is in London that our scene lies), rattling along the housetops, and fiercely agitating the scanty flame of the lamps that struggled against the darkness."

"That's awful," I whispered to Lee. I hoped this wasn't an introduction to our next reading assignment.

"Impressions? Reactions?" Mrs. Gilroy asked.

Hands went up. I kept mine down. Teachers hate it when

you criticize the writing they bring into the classroom.

After listening to various responses, ranging from "highly poetic" to "literary," Mrs. Gilroy said, "Most people with an ear for prose feel this is an awful sentence."

I flashed Lee a grin. Mrs. Gilroy flashed me a glare, then continued talking. "This deathless prose is the opening sentence of a novel by Edward Bulwer-Lytton." She paused to write the man's name on the board. "It has inspired an annual contest that encourages people to write the worst possible opening sentence. I encourage all of you to give that exercise a try."

"Why would you want us to write something bad?" Julia asked.

"Would anyone like to venture a guess?" Mrs. Gilroy looked around the room. Nobody was willing to take a shot.

I was pretty sure I knew the answer, but I didn't raise my hand.

"To write something really bad, you have to know what makes something really good," Mrs. Gilroy said, echoing my thoughts. She looked right at me as she added, "That's a lot harder than it sounds."

That was when I decided I was going to win the contest.

Kyle's father came over to the house again that evening, with some papers for Dad to read through. He brought Kyle, who didn't look any more thrilled to see me than I probably looked to see him.

"Hey, Scott," Mr. Bartock said. "We're just running errands. You guys can hang out for a minute while I give these to your dad. Is he in the garage?"

"Yeah," I said.

Mr. Bartock scooted down the hall. Kyle and I stared at each other.

"Our dads seem to think we should get along," I said.

"That's one more reason not to," Kyle said.

"You sound like Lee."

"Who?"

"You know."

"Oh, yeah. Her. The guys on the team call her Weirdly."

"You've called her worse," I said. "She's my friend."

"You deserve each other."

"Why are you so mean?" I asked.

"Why are you so stuck up?"

The approach of our fathers cut the discussion off before we could reach common ground or critical mass.

As Mr. Bartock was leaving, he shook Dad's hand and said, "It's a relief to be back on my feet. It's been a rough year."

"This will be a good start for both of us," Dad said.

"Rough year?" I asked after he'd left.

"He had some real bad luck," Dad said. "Not his fault. Two of his businesses got sideswiped by the economy."

"That's brutal," I said.

"And it's scary," Dad said. "You work hard. You work smart. And then bad luck comes along."

"So what do you do?" I asked.

"Keep working," he said.

I heard Mr. Bartock's car starting up. I knew there'd been a lot of tension at Kyle's house last year. I realized we hadn't hung out there as much freshman year as we had through elementary and middle school. Last year, we'd usually gone over to our friend Mitch's house, until he'd dumped us. Or Patrick's. Until he'd moved.

I guess Mr. Bartock really wanted Kyle to learn about business, or rekindle old friendships, or something, because he brought him again the next evening, when he came to give Dad some good news.

"I know it's been a long wait. But we're finally in good shape," Mr. Bartock said. "I wanted to tell you in person. I have a deal with Sherman Construction for the Kingston units I need to sell. The guy's a jerk, but he always seems to have lots of cash on hand."

"I'm just glad we're almost there," Dad said.

"I'll be signing papers with him next week," Mr. Bartock said. "And we can sign ours as soon as he hands me that check."

"Great," Dad said.

They shook hands.

"Really great," I said, giving Kyle my biggest grin. He might still look for some way to hurt me, but at least soon he'd no longer be a threat to Dad.

■ ■ ■

December 8

Sean, I spent all week trying to write a bad opening for the Bulwer-Lytton contest. I totally failed. I suck at being bad. Ironically, that's not good.

TWENTY-FIVE

I'd managed to convince my parents that they needed to get out of the house once in a while. They were just going down the road for pizza. But it was a start. What I really wanted them to do was go out for New Year's, which was two and a half weeks away. I was hoping they'd let Lee come over, too.

"We'll be back as soon as possible," Mom said.

"Or sooner," Dad said.

"Relax. I've got this," I said, trying to sound more confident than I felt. Sean seemed just fine in his playpen.

"Are you sure?" Mom asked.

"Positive," I said.

I suspected she wanted to get seven or eight more reassurances from me, but Dad ushered her toward the garage.

"Totally sure?" she called from the hallway.

"Totally," I yelled back. "Enjoy your pizza."

I heard the door close.

"Looks like it's just you and me, little brother," I said, sinking deeper into my seat on the couch.

Sean started crying.

The very same kid who, an instant before, had been quietly chewing on a rubber ducky and drooling copious quantities of saliva, had morphed into a red-faced howler monkey. His eyes were shut tight, and yet still produced a stream of tears. Liquid snot magically began to stream from his nostrils as if he'd been tapped on an unseasonably warm day during maple-sap season. I walked over to the playpen.

"Hey, Sean. It's okay."

Apparently, those words meant nothing to him.

"Sean, calm down." I rubbed his back.

That's where the volume switch was hidden, I guess. Because he got louder.

I started to pick him up, but I immediately pictured a thousand ways in which that could go terribly wrong, from dropping him to getting sprayed point-blank in the face with baby puke. Nope. I wasn't lifting him off that nice, safe padding.

The phone rang. Great. It was Mom.

I thought about taking the phone to the bathroom and closing the door. But I was afraid to go where I couldn't see Sean.

I moved as far away from the crib as I could while still keeping Sean in sight, then pulled my sweatshirt up to just below my eyes. I slid the phone under my sweatshirt, so I could talk, and let the top end stick out past the collar, near my ear.

With luck, the sound of crying would be muffled enough to be unrecognizable.

"Hi. What's up?" I asked.

"Just checking in," Mom said.

"Everything's fine. If you keep calling, you'll drive Dad crazy."

"You sound funny," she said. "All muffled."

"I think I'm getting a cold."

"Don't breathe on Sean!"

"I'll grab a dust mask from the garage," I said.

By the time I convinced Mom to hang up, Sean had passed out. That was good, since I got five more calls from Mom before they finished their pizza.

It was also a good thing they didn't stay out late. We got slammed with snow that night. It was still falling late Saturday morning when I got out of bed.

Mom and Dad were at the kitchen table.

"Looks like we'll be shoveling for a while," Dad said.

I heard the plow go by. I might not be able to identify cars by the hum of their engines, but every kid who lives in a snowy region knows the sound of a steel blade scraping the street clear.

"We'll take turns," Mom said. "Two of us shoveling, one of us watching Sean."

"I don't mind shoveling. You and Dad can swap Sean-watching duties." I said. I didn't want to risk having Sean get hysterical when Mom and Dad went outside.

"Weird," Dad said, looking toward the garage.

He stood up. So did I. The plow sounded really close.

"Someone's in the driveway," I said.

Dad and I went to the living room window. One of the town's snowplows was clearing the driveway. That's not something they normally do. We headed for the door.

"Jackets," Mom called.

But we were already on the porch.

The plow driver waved at us. We waved back.

"New job?" I yelled.

"Yeah," Wesley said. "But I think it's seasonal."

He finished our driveway, came in for a cup of cocoa complete with tiny marshmallows, then headed out to get back to work clearing the town streets.

December 21

This is the first day of winter, Sean. I'll wait until you're older to explain seasons and solstices to you. For now, it's more important to know that Christmas is almost here. I'm hoping Mom will dress you in a silly elf hat. I can get Lee to take pictures, and we can embarrass you with them when you get a girlfriend. I don't think Bobby has anything like that to spring on me when I start dating. Of course, he might be in a retirement home by then.

■ ■ ■

Monday after school, I grabbed a snack, sat on the couch, and flipped on the TV. There was some kind of breaking news announcement on the local station. A vacant apartment building on Kingston Street that was being renovated had caught fire.

I watched for a moment before I switched the channel. The fire was already mostly out. *At least nobody was hurt*, I thought.

I was wrong.

TWENTY-SIX

Two days later, on the afternoon of Christmas Eve, the door-bell rang.

Mr. Bartock was on the porch, without Kyle.

He and Dad had a very short conversation.

"That apartment fire," Mr. Bartock said. "That was my project."

"Bad?" Dad asked.

"I was underinsured. I took a risk. What were the odds something like this would happen?"

"Now what?" Dad asked.

Mr. Bartock shrugged. "I wish I knew. I just wanted to tell you in person."

Dad held out his hand. They shook. Mr. Bartock said, "I'm really sorry." Then he left.

"Well, I guess that's that," Dad said.

Mom had come up behind us. "I'm so sorry," she said. She gave Dad a hug. "Maybe it will still work out."

"I don't see how," Dad said. He went to the garage.

"Think I should go out there?" I asked Mom.

"In a while," she said. "He needs time by himself. That's how he copes. He'll be okay."

"I know," I said. "But it hurts to see his dreams get crushed like that."

"He's lucky he has people who care so much about him. And you should be glad you have someone you care that much about," she said. "That's something money can't buy."

I nodded. Speaking didn't seem safe at the moment; I was afraid my voice would betray my feelings. But she was right. We were all pretty lucky. Still, it sucked to see Dad lose his dream.

Later, I heard the garage door open, and the increasingly familiar growl of the Chevelle as Dad drove off.

December 24

It's going to be a weird Christmas, Sean. Bobby and Amala went to see her parents in Mount Laurel. I'm sure Bobby's thrilled about that. Amala's dad sounds like Lee's dad on steroids. I did get you a present, even though you won't really appreciate it. It's a reindeer hat. I'm sure you won't remember it. But there will be pictures. Hundreds of pictures.

We unwrapped our presents before breakfast on Christmas morning. I got a video game system. The new one. And a gift certificate to the local bookstore. I guess Dad had bought it last night. Mom got a pearl necklace, and this fancy Calphalon pot she'd been coveting for ages, like the ones you see the real chefs use on cooking programs. It was way more than we'd expected. We told Dad he shouldn't have done it.

"We've been scrimping for too long," he said. "I wanted to bring home some happiness for us."

"What about you?" I asked.

"I'm good," he said. Mom and I had gotten him modest presents; nothing like what he'd bought for us.

My parents had gone out for New Year's Eve. Mom was reluctant, but Dad had put up a convincing argument that the best way to shake off a tough year was to greet the new one with enthusiasm.

Lee was here. To my amazement, her folks had let her come over. With Sean standing guard in his playpen, I doubt my parents or Lee's parents were worried anything serious would happen this evening. I was worried nothing serious would happen this lifetime.

"I always feel I should do something significant on the last day of the year," I said.

"It's just another day," Lee said. "Either you did significant stuff already, or you didn't. Why stress about it?"

"I don't know. I should write a poem or jog five miles or something."

Lee looked at the clock. "Go ahead. You have time."

"For what?"

"For either. Even if you do a lazy ten-minute mile, you'll be finished before midnight. Sweaty, frostbitten, and reeking, but finished. A poem would take even less time, as long as you're happy with a crappy one. Hey, *happy* and *crappy* rhyme. You can use them to get started."

She leaned over the crib and sang, "Happy crappy New Year to you, little Pooh Bear."

Sean, dressed in his Winnie-the-Pooh decorated jammies, appeared to like that. Lee's voice always made him smile.

She picked him up.

"Careful," I said. "He's covered with Pooh."

"Don't you ever get tired of saying that?" she asked.

"Not so far. It's a classic."

I thought about going out for a jog. It seemed like a really stupid idea. I thought about writing a poem. That seemed equally empty. I grabbed a handful of cheese curls, sat back down on the couch, and watched faded celebrities introduce the formerly popular bands that seemed to lie in wait to perform last year's hits on the last day of the current year.

"Ten!"

"Nine!"

"Eight!"

"Seven!"

"Six!"

"Five!"

"Four!"

"Three!"

"Two!"

"One!"

"Happy New Year!"

We both stood up from the couch.

I looked at Lee, wondering what to do. She leaned over, went up on her toes, and kissed me on the cheek. Boom. That was it.

"Happy New Year," I said. I hadn't meant to leave off the exclamation point, but I didn't think she noticed.

"Ready for a new chance to make the same mistakes and repeat the same bad habits?" she asked.

"I thought that's what sophomore year was for," I said.

TWENTY-SEVEN

New year. I squinted at my clock. It was eleven in the morning. Coincidentally, the same hour as last night when I'd decided against doing anything significant. Did I want to do anything significant today?

Maybe today. But definitely not this morning.

I rolled over and shoved my head under my pillow. Lee was right. If you did stuff all through the year, it was silly to try to make the first or last day something special. I guess the same held true if you didn't do stuff all year.

I called Wesley around 2:00, but he sounded like he'd partied pretty hard, so I took pity on him and ended our conversation. Lee had gone with her folks to visit relatives. It seemed that, for the moment, I was on my own.

January 1
    This is my first journal entry of the year. I guess
I should strive to make it prefect. I'll leave it at that.

■ ■ ■

I finally caught up with Wesley on Sunday, when he picked me up to go bowling. He was driving his own car for a change. On the way to the lanes, I told him about the garage.

"That's rough. Your dad must be bummed."

"Yeah. But he's not showing it."

"That's what dads do," he said. "It's got to be a tough job." We reached the lanes, and went to the counter to rent shoes.

"I wish I could do something for him," I said.

"You'll think of something," Wesley said.

"I hope so . . ."

January 4

Mark your calendar, Sean. We have a wedding scheduled. Bobby and Amala picked May 9. Bobby told me he chose that date because it was the day before Mother's Day. That way, he'd never forget his anniversary. When I pointed out to him that the date for Mother's Day changes from year to year, he laughed and smacked me on the head. Yeah, he was kidding. Actually, they picked it because it was the only date this year that fit the schedules of both families and that worked for the reception place they liked the most. They'd found a banquet hall on farmland in Flemington, which is halfway between here and south Jersey, where most of Amala's relatives live. Mom seemed to think that four months wasn't anywhere near enough time to plan a wedding, but the happy couple had already lined up not just the location, but also the food and the band. Neither of them saw any reason to wait until next year.

And once again, I was back in school.

"You're at the circus," Mrs. Gilroy said. "You see a clown juggling. Another clown hits him with a pie. How do you feel?"

At least half the kids in class raised a hand.

Why bother? I thought. But I decided to give it a shot. Hey, it was a new year and all. Fresh start. Clean slate. So I raised my hand, too. It's not like there were any wrong answers.

Mrs. Gilroy pointed at Josh, who said, "Amused."

It figured he'd take the easy one. Several hands went down; I guessed they'd also come up with just that one word.

Mrs. Gilroy picked three more kids, and received *delighted, happy,* and *terrified.* She frowned at the third one, but let it go.

She was holding off calling on me. I didn't care. I knew I'd be able to come up with a word nobody else thought of.

Finally, mine was the last hand standing. I got ready to impress her with my vocabulary. I actually had five words in mind. But I wasn't going to show off by listing all of them. One would do.

"Bemused," I said when Mrs. Gilroy pointed at me.

She strolled over to my desk. She was actually almost smiling. Cool. I'd impressed her.

"Bemused?" she asked.

"Yup. Bemused."

"You're a dunce, Mr. Hudson."

She walked off, leaving me, as I soon learned, thoroughly bemused.

"Bemused?" I said to Jeremy when we got on the bus.

"Only by the question," he said.

"No. What's it mean?"

"Puzzled. Stunned. Overwhelmed by an idea, as if struck by a muse," he said. "Or deep in thought."

"Oh, hell. . . ."

January 5

So I've been using a word wrong my whole life. Not that it's a word I use much. And not that it's accurate to say "my whole life" since I doubt I used it when I was little. But you know what I mean. I thought bemused was sort of like a fancy way of saying amused. It isn't. As for what it means, if you don't know how to use a dictionary by the time you reach this entry, there's no hope for you. Look it up. But don't use a new dictionary. If a lot of people misuse a word, which is certainly the case with bemused, and if they do that for a long time, eventually the dictionary people sigh, mutter, "Okay. We give up. You win," and accept the new meaning. Not that they're happy about surrendering. But Mrs. Gilroy pretty much adheres to the classroom dictionary, which has to be at least fifty years old, for her word supply. I checked once, and kilobyte wasn't even in it.

I wonder how many other words I'm misusing? There should be an app that listens to what you say, and compares it to the real meanings of the words. If I knew how to write an app, I'd bet that one would make a zillion dollars. That would be awesome. Not just for me. I'd give Dad as much money as he needed so he could buy that garage. Then he wouldn't have to wait, or find any partners.

A forced silence hung between Kyle and me when we were getting dressed for gym on Tuesday. I felt bad for his dad, and terrible for mine. I also felt relief. Kyle had lost his power over me. I wanted to tell him I was sorry things fell apart, but I was pretty sure he had no interest in my sympathy.

As we were leaving the locker room at the end of the period, he said, "Looks like you got your wish."

I didn't bother responding.

"Can I trust you kids to play nicely on your own?" Mr. Franka asked.

We gave him our assurances. We'd have our regular

meeting tomorrow, as usual, but we all thought it would be a good idea to start the year with a special meeting, to figure out what would change now that the Latin Club was active.

"Good. I have a staff meeting." He headed out the door.

"Welcome to the first meeting of the Latin Club," Sarah said.

We all stood and shouted random Latin phrases. I went for *excelsior*. I wasn't sure what it meant, but it felt good to shout.

"*Ad astra per aspera*," Jeremy said.

Richard giggled. "You said *ass*. Twice."

"I said *astra* and *aspera*," Jeremy said.

"That's even funnier," Richard said.

Eventually, everyone settled down.

"What's the name going to be?" Sarah asked.

"I think it should still be the *Zenger Gazette*," I said. "We need to keep the tradition alive. But we can add a subtitle, or a slogan."

"Like the *New York Times*," Jeremy said. "They use 'All the news that's fit to print.'"

"But it should have something to do with Latin," Sarah said.

"Got it!" I said. "The *Zenger Gazette*: From friends of a living dead language."

Richard shouted, "Oxymoron!" and reached past Jeremy to slam my shoulder.

Jeremy laughed. "That's also beautifully ambiguous."

"It will grab the zombie fans," Sarah said. She looked around the table. "Everyone good with that?"

All hands went up. Then I put mine down, since I wasn't

technically a club member. But that didn't matter. It was official. The *Zenger Gazette* would live on, uninterrupted.

We had a short discussion about what things we'd need to change. There wasn't much. Jeremy suggested we number the pages with Roman numerals. Everyone loved that idea.

When we were finished with the changes, I said, "We have total freedom, right?"

"It's a club," Sarah said. "I imagine we can do what we want."

"We should have some kind of radical humor," Edith said.

"We have cartoons," Dan said. "That's enough."

"No. We need written humor, too," I said. "Something real edgy."

"Yeah," Jeremy said. "It would be cool to do something funny."

"Like what?" Sarah asked.

I thought about the first day in history class. "We could have three facts. No, make it ten, about a teacher, and kids will have to guess who it is."

"What's so funny about that?" Sarah asked.

"We'll make up the facts. It will be a satire," I said. "We can all do it. Except me, of course. We'll have a suggestion box. Everyone who wants to will put in fake facts. We need stuff that will point to the person, but be ridiculous. Like, if we were doing Mr. Franka, since he has that Marine tattoo, one of the facts could be *I have a Hello Kitty tattoo on my butt.*"

"Or *I steal comic books from little kids,*" Edith said. "*If they complain, I make them read sonnets.*"

"Good one," I said. Everyone knew Mr. Franka had a whole drawer of graphic novels and comics. "That's exactly what I mean. At the meeting, we'll pick the best ones."

"Let's do it," Richard said. Everyone nodded.

"Don't sign your ideas," I said. "That way, we can be really fair when we pick the best ones."

"Good idea," Sarah said. "So, who is our first victim?"

"How about Mrs. Gilroy?" I said.

"Perfect!" one of the juniors said. "I had her last year, and she was brutal."

"She's kind of old-fashioned," Sarah said. "Do you think she might get offended?"

"I think she'll be thoroughly bemused," I said.

And so it was decided. I went right to work when I got home, since I planned to contribute. That's the real reason why I'd suggested we keep the submissions anonymous.

I needed to come up with some killer "facts" about Mrs. Gilroy. She always wore those white shirts with the long sleeves. That was a good target. I grabbed a pen and wrote, "I hide my heroin addiction from the world by covering my tracks."

To my credit, no more than five or six seconds passed before I muttered, "No way," and crumpled the paper. I'm happy to say I also sank a three-pointer into my wastebasket. The shirt was a good target for satire. Everyone was familiar with it. But I had to find the right approach.

I only buy the finest shirts made by sobbing six-year-olds in Cambodian sweatshops.

Crumple. Swish. Three points!

Child labor wasn't funny. Satire was tricky. I didn't want to harm innocent bystanders.

What else did a white shirt imply? Purity? Ewwww. No way was I going in that direction. The thought made me shudder. I put the shirt aside and looked for other ideas. Ten minutes later, I had three good facts, and two others that would be okay if nobody came up with anything better:

Fake Facts about Mrs. Gilroy

I was drawn to my profession after dating William
   Shakespeare in my youth.

My teeth aren't false. They're just undecided.

I got tossed off the Mayflower for correcting everyone's grammar.

I have a great sense of humor. I laugh when I hand
   out bad grades.

During the summer, I earn extra money working for
   local farmers as a scarecrow.

That seemed like plenty—especially since the rest of the staff was going to be contributing, too. As I was getting ready to move on to my real work, another one hit me.

I make all my own shirts from a pattern I found in Dressing Dreadfully *Magazine.*

Not bad. And I might be able to think up a way to tweak it a bit. After that, I'd print them out and cut each into a strip.

I figured that if I just put the whole list in the box, someone might recognize my style.

I went to the meeting room at lunch time and put my strips in the box. I hoped the first piece was a success. I had plans for suggesting Ms. Denton next. Latin Club vengeance is sweet vengeance. I'll bet that sentence would sound even sweeter in Latin.

When the meeting started, Sarah dumped the contents of the box onto the table. I was relieved to see plenty of other strips.

"Wow, lots of ideas," she said. "Let's do a quick sort, and then narrow it down. I'll read each one. Raise your hand if you want to keep it under consideration."

She started reading. I heard some pretty funny suggestions. Three of mine made the first cut, including the one about the shirt. From there, we kicked around our thoughts and cut the list to the ten best entries. Two of mine survived—the shirt and the *Mayflower*. Someone else had come up with a better one about Mrs. Gilroy's false teeth. Based on his smile each time it was read, I figured the author was Jeremy.

"Good job," Sarah said as she typed the ten survivors into her laptop. "This will be fun."

For sure, I thought, relishing the idea of hitting Mrs. Gilroy with some writing she wasn't going to be able to shoot down or slap with a bad grade.

TWENTY-EIGHT

January 9

We read "The Monkey's Paw" in English, Sean. It was creepy, but not really scary. I think, ages ago, when we weren't flooded with TV shows and movies filled with special effects, it would have totally freaked me out. I'll bet it was the first story to use that sort of twist. But a zillion writers have borrowed the idea since then. The more we move into the future, the harder it is to get scared by the old stuff. But there are always new fears to take the place of the old ones. And that classic advice—*be careful what you wish for*—is as good in the real world as it is in the fictional one.

Dad's ears perked up as the rumble came through the walls. It was Saturday, and we'd just finished lunch. Actually, it was lunch for my parents, breakfast for me.

"Ferrari," Dad said.

He got up from the table and headed for the front door. I followed. Nobody we knew had a Ferrari.

It was a red one. I think that's their natural color in the wild. Wesley waved at me from the driver's seat.

"Where'd you get that?" I asked.

"My dad's friend was over," Wesley said. "He asked me to get it washed."

"The car wash is right down the street from you," I said.

"The closest one is," Wesley said. "But what fun would that be?"

"I see your point," I said.

"Go for a ride?" he asked.

I was about to nod, but then I realized he was talking to Dad.

Dad looked at me. Then he looked at Wesley. They had a brief conversation made up entirely of glances and nods.

"Go ahead," I said. "I think you'll appreciate it more."

"Tell your mom I'll be back in a bit," Dad said. He slid into the passenger seat.

I went inside to deliver the news to Mom. She understood.

I heard the rumble again about an hour later. Dad was behind the wheel, and Wesley was in the passenger seat. Both of them were laughing. As they got out and walked past the front of the car, they exchanged a high five. Then Wesley got back in the driver's seat.

I caught Wesley's eye before he took off and mouthed, "*Thanks.*"

He responded with a grin.

"Fun?" I asked Dad.

He shook out his hand. Wesley had a hard slap. "Yeah," he said. "As long as your mom never finds out about the speeding tickets."

"Tickets?" I couldn't help noticing the plural.

"Tickets," Dad said.

In geometry on Tuesday, I opened Lee's copy of the paper and pointed to the "Ten Amazing Facts about Me" article. The art staff had added some killer illustrations. I watched Lee's eyes as she read. And I watched her mouth, waiting for a grin. Her expression shifted through a variety of responses, none of which conveyed amusement.

When she was finished, she closed the paper and said, "Kind of harsh."

"Kind of deserved," I said.

Throughout the day, I caught snatches of conversation about the piece. It seemed to be a hit. I forced myself to pause when I reached the door of English class. I was wearing the crazy smirk of vengeance delivered. That would give me away. I backed off, and tried to rein in my joy. When I felt ready, I walked into the room. As I turned toward my desk, I risked a glance at Mrs. Gilroy. She looked as stern as usual. But maybe there was an extra glint of displeasure in her expression. I couldn't be sure. Well, if she hadn't seen the article by now, she'd see it eventually. Or someone would tell her about it.

I took my seat and watched the door. At least half the kids who came in had the paper. Some of them must have read the piece. Josh pointed at it, then pointed at me.

"What?" I asked.

"Did you . . . ?"

"Did I what?" I asked, playing stupid.

"Never mind. But whoever did this is a genius."

It was hard, but I kept my mouth shut. When class started, Mrs. Gilroy swept her gaze slowly across the room, as if to connect with every pair of eyes. I stared back, unblinking as she locked in on me. I held steady until she moved on.

"We're going to put Eudora Welty aside for the moment," she said, "and examine a major aspect of literature."

She walked to the board and wrote "SATIRE."

Or most of that word.

Halfway through the E, she dropped the chalk. And then, she dropped. It was a slow fall. She clutched the edge of the chalk tray on the way down and knelt, like someone in church. From there, she crumpled over. She didn't hit the ground hard. But she ended up on her side on the floor. Her right hand clutched at her heart. I stood there, frozen, hoping she was playing some kind of cruel joke on me. I heard sneakers slapping tiles as kids raced to get the nurse.

Paramedics came. I stood there the whole time. After they took Mrs. Gilroy away, Lee put a hand on my back. I realized I was shaking.

"*My fault* . . . ," I whispered.

"Don't be ridiculous," she said.

"I gave her a heart attack."

"You're not that good."

My head snapped toward her.

"Sorry. Just trying to make you feel better," she said.

"It's not working."

"Seriously, you can't blame yourself. You don't even know if she read it."

I went to Mrs. Gilroy's desk and picked up the paper. I couldn't tell whether it had been opened. But she'd had time to read it. So she'd probably taken a look. The written word was her life. I hoped it wasn't her death.

"We killed her," Jeremy said after we got on the bus.

"She's not dead," I said.

"How do you know?" he asked.

"She can't be. There's no way we can live with that," I said. "She has to be alive."

"I hope you're right."

January 13
    I suck, Sean.

Before I left school, I'd asked Chuck Peterson to let me know if he heard anything. He told me he'd ask his mom when she came home from her shift at the ER. Late that night, I got a message that Mrs. Gilroy wasn't dead. That's all Chuck knew. The message didn't wake me. I was up.

"We're not murderers," I told Jeremy the next morning.

"Yeah. Just thugs and bullies," he said. "I never pictured myself as a bully."

"I never pictured you that way, either."

"Power is seductive," he said. "So is anonymity. It's easy to hurt people when they can't look you in the eye."

"I guess that's why the Internet is so popular," I said. "And so vicious."

When I got to English the next day, I saw a very familiar face.

"Oh, no . . . ," I said to Lee.

"What's wrong?"

I thought about the best way to explain the problem, but then I realized it would be more interesting to watch her expression as she discovered it for herself.

"Albayer substoot ferda raysta dawake, orayven langa" the man at the front of the class said. The whole time he spoke, he also enthusiastically chewed a wad of gum, punctuating the words with random wet smacks.

Most of the kids were obviously puzzled. Several, like me, knew what was going on. And we knew what was coming.

A kid in the front row raised his hand.

"I didn't understand you," the kid said.

Here it comes, I thought.

"Nwarries, smite!" the teacher said.

I knew he was saying *No worries, mate!* That was the only phrase of his I'd ever been able to decipher. I settled back in my seat.

"What's going on?" Lee asked.

"That's Mr. Kamber," I said. "He's from Australia. I had him for Spanish last year."

"Spanish?" Lee said. "That's unimaginable."

"Pretty much. And unintelligible."

"English isn't going to be much better," she said.

"I suspect you're right."

I thought about skipping the newspaper meeting. But I wasn't quite that big a coward. Mr. Franka was already there when I came in, sitting with his chin propped on his hand. He didn't look at any of us as we took our seats.

Finally, after what felt like a century, he sighed, as if he was about to start talking. Then, he dropped his forehead onto his hand, like he was totally at a loss for words. He shook his head.

"Forget it," he said. Though he used a different *F* word. He got up and walked toward the door. "You know exactly what you did. You don't need a lecture." He put his hand on the doorknob. "Do better. You're journalists. Just . . . do better."

He went out.

"It's my fault," I said. "I'll quit. I'll take all the blame."

"You can't quit," Jeremy said. "Because you're not a member."

"And you can't take the blame," Sarah said. "Or everyone will know we let an ineligible student come up with ideas for the newsletter."

"So, what do we do?" I asked.

"We write an editorial about satire and responsibility," she said.

"I'll do it." I blurted that out, and then wished I could blurt it back in. "Sorry. I'll just shut up."

I kept quiet for the rest of the meeting.

Throughout the week, all of us waited to be called down to the office. Or for the principal to disband the Latin Club. But nothing happened.

I never thought that not being punished would be such a painful punishment.

TWENTY-NINE

The last time I'd been to the hospital was right after Sean was born. That was a happy memory. But the time before that, I'd gone to visit someone who'd tried to kill himself. This time, it was someone I might have almost killed with my stupid idea for a satire.

I was relieved that Mrs. Gilroy seemed totally alert. I was also dismayed. I'd hoped for the saving grace of a bit of sedation to take the edge off her sword.

"Mr. Hudson," she said, "this is a surprise. I know you aren't here to tell me you're nominating me for teacher of the year."

"Yeah. I mean, no, I'm not." I seemed to have lost most of my basic English skills.

She didn't say anything.

"The thing in the paper . . . ," I said.

My unfinished sentence remained dangling.

"It's my fault. My idea. I didn't write all of it, but I wrote some of it," I said.

"I recognized your style," she said.

"So you read it?" I asked.

"I do have a professional interest in the writing of Zenger High students, many of whom find their way into my honors English class," she said. "Your flaws reflect poorly on me."

"I'm sorry."

"That was a plural pronoun. You are far from unique in being flawed. You owe me no apology for that."

"But I gave you a heart attack," I said. "I'm sorry. I'm really sorry. I didn't mean any harm."

"Of course you did. You meant harm. That was your purpose. This was personal. Don't try to deny it. You picked me as the target of your satire because you wanted to hurt me."

"You're right."

"Don't think something as silly as a sophomoric attempt at humor could affect my health in the slightest," she said.

"But you had a heart attack," I said. "I was there."

She shook her head. "For a professed writer, you are not a very keen observer."

I thought back to when she'd collapsed. I remembered her clutching at her chest. I'd assumed she was reacting to pain. But maybe she'd been doing something else, and I'd misinterpreted it. She always wore a necklace with a large locket. "Were you reaching for some kind of medicine?"

"That's better," she said. "What else do you notice?"

I looked at her. That felt weird. I was used to seeing her in her long-sleeved white blouses, not in a hospital gown. I noticed a needle in her right arm, on the inside, right past the bend of the elbow. But it wasn't a regular IV needle. It was like there was a tube in her arm, or some kind of port.

I pointed at it. "That's why you wore long, loose sleeves."

"You're clawing your way up from a C minus," she said. "I wish you didn't move at such a glacial pace. If you're putting me at risk of anything, it's death from old age and boredom. Try to accelerate your epiphanies."

"It's for medicine of some kind. Right?"

"Right."

"What kind?" I asked.

"You don't need to know that. Just rest assured that it has nothing to do with my heart. It is not something that could be exacerbated by reading a halfway-clever attack. If we are to be judged by our intentions, you are guilty, but if we are to be judged by the results of our actions, your conscience is clear. You failed to harm me."

"I think I'm leaning toward the guilty side right now," I said. I looked away from her unwavering stare. She had a stack of books on her bedside table: *The Elements of Style*, *Merriam-Webster's Dictionary of English Usage*, and several others.

"Don't you know all that stuff?" I asked.

"One never knows *all that stuff*." She picked up *The Elements of Style* and held it out. "This is my bible, and your penance. Read it carefully. Absorb it. Then read it again."

"Thanks. I'll bring it back as soon as I'm finished."

"Keep it. I have several copies. You'll be reading it many

times, if there is any depth to your enthusiasm for writing."

"Are you going to be okay?" I asked.

"My condition is chronic and unpleasant, but not known to be fatal," she said. "Thank you for your concern. I'll be away from the classroom for a while, but I will return to torment you before the year is over."

"Like the Ghost of Christmas Present Tense?" I asked.

She smiled, briefly, then caught herself. "That was almost clever, Mr. Hudson. There may be hope for you after all."

When I got home, I opened *The Elements of Style*. There was a bookplate pasted to the inside of the cover: "This book belongs to Lorraine R. Dewitte." Maybe that was her maiden name. Just for fun, I searched online for that name.

A book popped up. And it wasn't a grammar book. It was a novel. *As Breath into the Wind*. The author photo was definitely her. Much younger, but there was no mistake. I dug a bit deeper. The book was published forty years ago. All the reviews said stuff like "great new voice" and "promising debut." As far as I could see, she'd never written anything else. Weird. I turned my attention back to the book she'd given me. It was actually pretty cool. Though I was still feeling guilty enough that I would have read a carburetor-repair manual, if that's what she'd offered me.

I guess I'd been given a second chance.

That night, Dad said, "We have good news."

I paused with my fork halfway to my mouth, and decided

I wouldn't even try to guess what form this newest crushing blow would take.

"Bobby and Amala are facing a pretty high rent," Mom said. "They need to try to save more of what they earn. And even a simple wedding comes with plenty of expenses for the bride and groom, beyond what all of us parents are covering."

"With them traveling so much, it doesn't make sense for them to take out a full-year lease," Dad said.

I realized I was being softened up for something that didn't require softening. "Do you want them to move in with us? That would be awesome." I liked having Bobby around. And Amala. After Bobby's band's tour wrapped up at the end of January, they weren't touring again until July, so he and Amala had planned to get an apartment in town. He would be giving guitar lessons at the local music store, and working there part-time as a salesman. Amala was able to do most of her work from home, since it involved stuff like sending out press releases and arranging interviews. The key fact about both income streams was that they were close to a trickle.

"When are they coming?" I asked.

"The start of next month," Dad said.

"Great." It was nice to get good news that wouldn't lead to disappointment, like the garage news had.

Tuesday was the end of the second marking period. If I didn't screw up hugely, I'd be back on the paper in a week.

"I would have to mess up in inconceivable ways to blow my grades this time," I told Lee at lunch.

"Please tell me you're not thinking of that as a goal," she said.

"Of course not. But it's a great exercise for a creative writer. It's interesting to try to figure out a way that I could screw up at this point. I mean, if someone was writing a novel where he wanted a kid to destroy his grades at the very last moment, what would he do?"

We tossed around ideas. Edith and Richard joined in. I compiled a list, just for fun.

"I trust you won't put any of those to the test," Lee said.

"Nope. I'm eager to get things back to normal."

Happily, at the end of the day, I hadn't even come close to messing up. I'd made it. My grade-point average for the first half of the school year would still be pretty unimpressive, but I'd be fine for this marking period.

Scott Hudson's (and Friends') List of
Last-Minute Ways to Ruin Your Grades

Go back in time to steal your homework from yourself.

Take hostages. (Several of us felt this was too close to reality.)

Hack into the school computer and mess up while changing the grades.

Bribe the school board to flip the scale so a zero is the highest grade and a hundred is the lowest.

Wednesday, we were supposed to start learning about silk screening in art. But the budget for supplies had been cut so drastically that Mr. Belman had to choose between getting the stencils and inks for us, or buying oil paints for the seniors. The seniors had priority. For now, we were working with our choice of colored pencils or India ink, since the art department had plenty of those supplies on hand.

Mr. Franka came to the Latin Club meeting. He didn't say anything. But he stayed the whole time. Sarah's editorial about satire and responsibility was really good. As much as I'd wanted to write it to try to make up for what I'd done, and as much as I hate to admit it, I doubt I could have done a better job.

While nobody could understand Mr. Kamber, at least he gave us our writing assignments straight out of the textbook. So we all knew what we were supposed to do. I guess he liked my writing. I actually scored a ninety-two on the first essay, and a ninety-five on the second. He didn't even circle anything, or mark stuff as wrong. I wouldn't have minded some sort of comments—preferably positive ones—but I was definitely happy with the grades. Eventually, I realized I could stop even trying to listen to him. English became my favorite spot for daydreaming.

The second marking period had already ended, but I had high hopes for the third. Two good marking periods, and I could pull my final grades up from the basement.

■ ■ ■

January 31

Time's flying, Sean. A moment ago, it was the new year. Now, a whole month is gone. Sophomore year is more over than not. But there's good flux coming. Bobby and Amala are moving in, tomorrow. It will be nice to have them around.

THIRTY

February 1

Happy shortest month of the year, you shortest Hudson. Last year in English, Mr. Franka taught us about redundant statements, like *free gift* and *surprise ambush*. Those are kind of obvious. But I've noticed some subtler ones. In the short story I'm reading for class, I saw the phrase *dried husks*. But being dry is part of the definition of husk. I think it's really easy to fall into redundancy. People say stuff like, "When I first started high school . . ." But *first started* is redundant. If you look at it, you're sort of redundant, too.

I'd never been so nervous about a report card. When I got mine on Tuesday, my eyes went right to the bottom. It's funny—I think it's a lot harder to make sure something isn't there than to verify that it is there. But there was no sign at all, in any spot, of the word *ineligible.*

Lee was actually waiting for me outside of geometry.

"Well?"

"Eligible again," I said.

"Great."

"Yeah. Maybe this time, now that I'm back on staff, I can actually kill a teacher with my writing," I said.

"I'm pretty sure everyone is safe from your superpower," Lee said. "But just to be certain, maybe you should set your journalistic sights on something inanimate, like cafeteria food quality, or budget cuts."

"Good idea."

"Hey," Lee said as we headed in. "There's a pattern. You were ineligible. Then you became eligible. If the sequence holds up, next marking period you'll be igible. And you can finish up the year as ible." She laughed and repeated "ible" with various tones and stresses as we made our way to our seats.

The next day, after school, I had the pleasure of walking into the newspaper meeting, and saying, "I'm back."

"Yay!" Jeremy said.

I looked at Mr. Franka and added, "If that's okay with you."

"Welcome back," he said. He didn't smile, but he gave me a small nod.

My first official act wasn't to pitch an article. It was to ask Sarah to permanently kill that opinion piece I'd written about prepositions.

She was happy to do that.

...

"I have to figure out what to get Lee for Valentine's Day," I told Bobby. I would have asked Amala, but she'd gone into New York to meet with a prospective client. "Any ideas."

"That depends. Are you still *just friends*? Please say no. . . ."

"Yes . . ."

"Jewelry for her," Bobby said. "And a backbone for you."

"She isn't into that stuff," I said. Lee put a lot of effort into not falling into any stereotypes. Though a tiny backbone made of silver would probably please her.

"Scott," Bobby said, putting his hands on my shoulders. "Have you ever actually looked at her?"

"Uh, yeah. All the time. I'm pathetically incapable of not looking at her."

"And, uh, her face is sort of decorated with stuff, right?"

"Right."

"And what would you call that stuff? It's not rivets and bolts. It's not fishing tackle."

"Sometimes she wears a safety pin," I said. Though I realized she'd pared down the edgier hardware in the last several months.

"Forget that. All this other stuff. Rings. Tiny gems. Small objects made of precious metals. Tell us, Mr. Vocabulary, what do you think that might be called?"

". . . Jewelry . . . ?"

"Bingo! Do you get it? She might not want a gold bracelet or a pearl necklace. She sure wouldn't want the kind of jewelry Grandma likes. But she'd love the right piece."

"How'd you get so smart about girls?" I asked.

"By not wasting time getting smart about anything else," he said. "I decided to specialize."

"Good move." I headed out of his room. "Thanks."

"Any time, little brother."

"Middle brother," I said.

"Middle little brother," Bobby said.

"I like little middle brother better," I said.

"They sound the same to me," Bobby said.

"That's how I feel about guitars," I said.

So, now, at least I had a clue. And I knew a shop nearby where I could probably find something Lee would love.

Bobby didn't have time to take me there before he had to go to work. So I called Wesley. He picked me up in what looked like an oil truck.

"Are you delivering fuel now?" I asked.

"Nope. I'm pumping crap."

"What kind of crap?" I thought he was using it as a synonym for *stuff.*

"Crap crap," Wesley said. "What other kind is there?"

It took a moment for that to register. And for me to identify the smell that seemed to envelop us. We have a sewer line at our house, but some of the houses way out in the woods at the edge of town have septic tanks. So does my uncle Steve's place, up in the Poconos. And those tanks have to be pumped.

"That stinks," I said.

"Pays good," Wesley said.

"Why don't you work for your dad?" I asked. "Limos cost a ton to rent. I'll bet the drivers make good money. And tips."

"I want to. But I'm not old enough to get a limo driver's license. You have to be twenty."

"I've seen you drive trucks and stuff," I said. "How old do you have to be for that?"

"Just eighteen," he said.

"So you have that license?" I asked.

"It's never really come up. The people I drove for didn't seem concerned."

"You could do other stuff for your dad, like take care of the limos," I said.

"I already do. He doesn't think I should get paid for that. Not while I'm living at home."

"Are you thinking about getting your own place?" I pictured myself hanging out at Wesley's future apartment. Better yet, I pictured Lee and me hanging out there.

"I'm pretty comfortable at home," he said. "So, where are we headed?"

"That goth shop in South Side Bethlehem."

"Got it."

He drove down the street, turned left on the corner, then took the ramp for the highway.

at about the part of the town where the shop was.
g might be tough."

"I'm not worried."

I think *worried Wesley* would be an oxymoron. Or an impossibility. But, just as I'd feared, there weren't any spaces in front of the store. Not that a space or two would have helped. I estimated that Wesley would need three open spaces in a row to park the truck. I hadn't counted on him double-parking, but he stopped in front of the shop and turned off the engine.

"You're just going to leave it there?" I asked.

"Yeah." He glanced at the three cars he'd blocked in. "If anybody needs to pull out, I'm sure they'll make some kind of noise."

I looked at the sign above the door of the shop: *WHAT HATH GOTH WRAUGHT?* Beneath that, it read, *Handmade Gifts and Unique Clothing.*

"Good choice," Wesley said, looking around at the displays of grim merchandise as we walked in the door. "This is Lee's kind of stuff." The earthy scent of leather and the synthetic odor of vinyl battled for dominance.

There was a woman behind the counter to the left. She had full arm tattoos, and some impressive hardware on her face. "Lost?" she asked.

"Often," I said. "But not this time." I wasn't insulted that I didn't strike her as a typical customer. "I'm looking for a present for a friend."

"Sweet," she said. She licked her lips.

I jumped back when I noticed her tongue was split. I'd heard about people having that done, but I'd never seen it. Not counting a statue of a lizard man at a Ripley's Believe It or Not! museum.

Before I could tell her what I was looking for, I heard a shout from outside. "Who blocked me in?"

"Told you it would work," Wesley said. "I'll be right back."

"Careful," the woman said. "They tow cars around here."

"Good luck with that," I said.

I told the woman what I was looking for. She asked me a couple of questions about Lee, then pulled a tray out from under the counter. "These are nice."

There were various beads and rings, along with a lot of skulls. "She likes skulls," I said. As I stared at the assortment of pins, my brain handed me a gift. It struck with enough force that I said, "Oh, my God!"

"Easy there, kid. Don't get too spiritual."

"Sorry. Thanks. I figured out exactly what I need." I knew a place that had to have what I was looking for. I stepped outside the store and called them, just to make sure. Then I hunted down Wesley, who'd pulled around the corner.

"We need to go to Allentown. Okay?"

Wesley laughed. "Sure. I love opening this thing up on Route 22."

And so we went to a shop in the city next to Bethlehem,

and I bought the perfect, and perfectly affordable, present for Lee. And Wesley got to raise the blood pressure of several dozen more drivers, who had the pleasure of trailing us on the highway and wondering *What's that smell?*

February 7

Word geek alert, Sean. You can skip this entry without fear of missing important life skills. But if you read it, and can understand why I bothered to write it, you'll move a little closer to understanding me. I just realized something interesting. Well, interesting to me. I think Lee and Mr. Franka would also appreciate it. But it's bedtime, and I want to write it down while it's fresh in my mind. It's amazing how ephemeral an idea can be if you don't make a note of it. (Yeah, I'm still working hard to enhance your vocabulary.) So, lucky you, you're the first one to get my thoughts on this. A while back, I mentioned tautology. That's when you say the same thing more than once. For example: <u>I went home. I returned to my house. I entered the place where I live</u>. The other day, I reminded you about redundancy, where you use words that are unneces-sary because they're covered by the meaning of other words. Like if you say crossword puzzle, that's redun-dant since a crossword is a puzzle. But if tautologies and redundancies both refer to repeated information, why do we need two terms? Isn't tautology itself, as a term, redundant? As I was trying to figure that out, I realized there are subtle differences. The unnecessary word in a redundancy doesn't have to have the whole meaning of the other word. It just has to repeat part of the meaning. <u>Surprise</u> doesn't mean the same thing as <u>ambush</u>. But there also seems to be a lot of overlap between tautologies and redundancies. And tautology can be part of a writer's style. I guess I have to give all of this a bit more thought. But I'll give you a break and stop for now. I don't want your little head to explode. Or blow up.

Wait. One more thought. This is really cool. I just realized that a redundancy is the opposite of an oxymoron. Or maybe a tautology is. It's amazing my own head doesn't explode. Or blow up.

Hang on. Yeah. Yet another last thought. A redundancy slipped into this discussion. See if you can find it. I'll give you a couple days. It's sort of subtle.

THIRTY-ONE

"Hudson," Mr. Cravutto called as I was closing my locker. He'd stuck his head out the door of his office, and waved his hand to get my attention. Given the size of his hand, that was sort of like getting waved down by a yellow flag at the racetrack.

"Yes?"

"Come here."

"Okay." I walked over, wondering what sort of nightmare was about to invade my life.

"You wrote all those sports articles last year, right?"

"Yeah. That was me."

"Do you know anything about poetry?" he asked.

I'll admit I was briefly bemused by the totally unexpected direction the conversation was taking. I felt I knew a lot about poetry—thanks to Mr. Franka. I still wasn't sure where this was heading, so I didn't admit my passion for the subject, but I did nod and make an affirmative utterance along the lines of "Uh-huh."

Mr. Cravutto slid a notepad on his desk around so the scrawled words faced me. "Is this any good?"

I read the poem he'd written.

Your eyes are pools of starlight,
Your thighs are full of muscles,
Your laugh is like nice laughter,
You're as sweet as sprouts from Brussels.

"It's for Valentine's Day," he said.

"It's very nice." At first, I felt the opening line was a mixed metaphor, but I guess a pool of water could reflect starlight, or light could pool in other ways. I decided Mr. Cravutto wasn't going to be interested in a literary analysis that went to quite that deep a level. I moved my attention to the second line. "Do you think the person you give this to will want you to focus on her thighs?"

"She's very proud of them," he said. "She puts a lot of time in at the gym."

"Good to know." I rescanned the third line. "Maybe you can compare her laugh to something other than laughter?"

He frowned, and I had an image of myself being dribbled into the gym and stuffed through a basketball hoop. Some people don't cope well with constructive criticism. But then he nodded. "That's a good point. I'll work on it. What about the last line? Is it okay?"

"Well, you should feel good you found a rhyme for 'muscles.' I don't think there are a lot of them." I ran the other candidates through my mind: *bustles, hustles, rustles, tussles.* Nope, not much to work with. I wasn't going to advise him to keep looking.

"Thanks. So it's mushy enough?"

"Absolutely. Can I have a late pass?"

"You won't need it," he said, giving me a dismissive wave.

I headed off to art. Once again, all I had to do was start a sentence with "Mr. Cravutto," and my art teacher gave me an understanding nod and a sympathetic smile.

As I took my seat, I thought about all the pain caused by Valentine's Day. Maybe it was Cupid, and not Mars, who should have been the god of war.

Zenger Zinger for February 10
Last answer: "It's a shame to burn the steak," John Peter said sincerely.
This week's puzzle: "The preschool eye chart keeps sliding," John Peter said _____.

Since Valentine's Day was on a Saturday, the dance was tonight, Friday, after school. By lunchtime, I still hadn't figured out the best strategy for coordinating my moves. I had a present for Lee, and I wanted to ask her to the dance. I wasn't sure whether to give her the present and then ask about the dance, or ask about the dance, and give her the present there. But if she shot down my invitation to the dance, it would be weird to give her the present. And the present was so totally cool and amazing it would kill me to not give it to her.

Time was running out. I figured I'd just give her the present, and take it from there. I pulled the box out of my pocket. I'd wrapped it in plain green paper. Nothing pink or heart-strewn. I wanted it to be sort of casual.

"Got you something," I said, sliding the box across the table.

"For me?" She picked it up and tore off the paper.

I remembered a phrase she'd used last year, when she'd given me a bag of black jelly beans. I tossed it back at her, now. "Reciprocity is not mandatory."

Her grin told me she recognized the words. "Deferred reciprocity has its charms," she said. She opened the box and stared at the small piece of pewter jewelry inside.

"A fish?" she said.

"A special fish," I said. I contemplated tossing out the scientific name, *Cottidea*, but that would make the search for the meaning behind the gift too easy. I knew she'd search. I wanted it to take a bit of work, so the revelation would be that much more powerful and rewarding. I wanted her to gasp when she grasped the significance.

She took the pewter pin from the box and examined it from every angle. "Thank you."

I contemplated options for my next sentence:

If you're still perplexed, I'll tell you after the dance.

Hey, I think there's a dance tonight.
You can wear it to the dance.

That one might work.

I reached out to point at the pin. My hand hit her soda, knocking it over.

Lee pushed her chair back. "I'll get some napkins."

By the time she got back and mopped up the spill, we were rushing to biology.

February 13

Sean, would you like to go to the dance? I know dancing isn't part of your skillset at the moment. Neither is the ability to say yes or no. That doesn't matter. I just wanted to actually ask someone the question, to see how it felt. I realize, looking back, I never actually asked Lee to the dance last year. Yeah, I know we went. I won't go into all the details, but I said something stupid and I hurt her. To make up for it, I told her I was picking her up for the dance. When she scoffed, I told her I'd be at her house to pick her up, and I'd wait outside all night if I had to. Luckily, she answered the door when I knocked. That's how it played out. And maybe that's why this is so hard. It's a lot easier to tell than to ask. You're less vulnerable.

Anyhow, no need for you to take dance lessons or find some festive diapers. Neither of us is going to tonight's dance. You're going to take a nap. And I'm going to see if I can get a ride to the mall.

Wait. Before I go, did you spot the redundancy in the last entry? (Or did your head explode?) If not (neither?), here's a hint. It's in this part: "A while back, I mentioned tautology. That's when you say the same thing more than once."

Give it some thought.

THIRTY-TWO

Saturday, after lunch, I heard a car pull up out front. A moment later, I heard footsteps run up the porch, followed by the doorbell.

It was Lee. Her folks were at the curb. The pin I'd given her had replaced the three studs she'd been wearing in her right ear.

"That was brilliant," she said. "Best present, ever!" Her smile alone made all my effort worthwhile.

"I'm glad you figured it out," I said.

She grabbed my shoulders and gave them a squeeze. "Thanks."

I think she might have hugged me if we hadn't been under parental observation. Or maybe even kissed me. "Glad you liked it."

"I have to go." She raced toward the car. Then she stopped, twirled back toward me, and yelled, "Skull pin!" She emphasized the space between the two words. "Pure genius!" Laughing, she returned to her parents, who I imagine were totally puzzled by all of this.

I wondered how long it had taken her to identify the fish I'd given her as a sculpin. And then to figure out the pun. I was sad that the gift hadn't been my ticket to the dance, but happy that she loved it so much.

Amala walked up to me right after I closed the front door. "You like that girl a lot."

"Is it that obvious?" I asked.

"Only to someone who is highly empathetic and extremely observant." She awarded me with a wink and a gentle smile. "Don't worry, Scott, you aren't wearing your heart on your sleeve."

"That would not be a great place for it. Though I think Lee would love the idea." I pictured an actual heart on a sleeve. "Yeah. That would definitely charm her."

"Have you asked her out?"

"I've tried. It's not easy. I guess I'm just a coward."

"Don't be too hard on yourself. Shyness is real," Amala said. "People don't recognize that. If you slashed your finger, anybody who saw it would tell you to put a bandage on the wound."

"Sure," I said.

"But if you tell people you're shy, all they say is 'Get over it.'"

"That's what I tell myself," I said.

"Before you even try to get over it, you need to accept it. It's not a disease or a flaw or even necessarily a bad thing. It's part of who you are, at this moment in your life. Does that make sense?"

"Yeah. It does. Thanks."

"That's what big sisters are for," she said. "If you want me to talk to her, say the word. I speak her language."

"Not yet. But thanks for that, too."

February 14

It's Valentine's Day, Sean. You'll probably enjoy it, once you start school. I can already see that you have an abundance of Hudson charm. As for me, I still don't have a valentine, but I made Lee very happy. Which made me happy. I think when you find someone whose happiness makes your own life better, you've found something special.

I know that there's more to a relationship than gifts, but it made me feel so good seeing her reaction, I thought about other things I'd get her, if I could. Here's my list:

Some of the Things I'd Buy for Lee
if I Had Infinite Funds

A haunted castle

Books

Pluto (the one in orbit, not the dog)

Disney World (just in case she wanted both Plutos)

Bookshelves

A mummy

A top hat for the mummy

Bookmarks

The skull of a famous writer

A beret for the skull

The skull would come from a writer who is already dead. I probably didn't need to specify that.

Oh, in case you didn't spot it, the redundant part of the tautology definition (I loved writing that) was between <u>same thing</u> and <u>more than once</u>. Each implies the other. I should have written, "when you say the same thing in different ways." I think that's a better definition, anyhow, because different ways is a crucial part of the definition of tautologies.

"Oh, dear," Mom said.

"What?"

She handed me the local news section of the Sunday paper and tapped the headline of the lead article: *Developer Announces Plans to Revitalize Sibert Street.*

I read the article. Sherman Construction had bought all the buildings on Sibert Street. There were plans to tear everything down and put in an office building. Demolition was set to start in July. I guess Mr. Sherman wanted to focus all his energy on ruining things for students and teachers while school was in session, and then ruin things for everyone else in town during the summer.

"Does Dad know?" I asked.

"Probably not yet."

"It's going to reopen the wound," I said.

"There'll be other opportunities to find a place."

"But that place was perfect," I said.

"Nothing is perfect," Mom said.

"It was close to perfect," I said.

"You're right," she said. "It was."

Zenger Zinger for February 17

Last week's answer: "The preschool eye chart keeps sliding," John Peter said emotionally.

This week's puzzle: "I had to split my box of Valentine's chocolates with my friend," John Peter said _____.

February 23

Sean, maybe I don't want Lee to be my girlfriend. I mean, I want a girlfriend. Desperately. But maybe I don't want to mess up my friendship with Lee with the whole boyfriend/girlfriend thing. We've really got the friendship thing down pretty well. I see couples breaking up all the time in school, and it's horrible. But I guess friends break up, too. I hadn't thought about that. Pay no attention to this entry, Sean. I'm confused.

Zenger Zinger for February 24

Last week's answer: "I had to split my box of Valentine's chocolates with my friend," John Peter said halfheartedly.

This week's puzzle: "I wish hurdlers and sprinters got paid," John Peter said _____.

THIRTY-THREE

Lee showed up at my door Sunday afternoon. "Bookstore," she said. "Are you up for it?"

"Which one?"

"At the college."

I looked past her shoulder. Her mom was at the wheel. "I'm in." I told my parents where I was going, then followed Lee to the car.

"Happy hunting," her mom said when she dropped us off outside the student center.

Lee and I cut through the building and took the stairs up to the bookstore on the second floor. It mostly carried only the required books, but from what I'd seen, colleges required a lot of awesome reading material.

"This is like the first day of high school, freshman year," I said. The college students dwarfed us. Unlike high school upperclassmen, they ignored us. I guess they were well on their way to becoming adults.

"Without the *Heart of Darkness* feel," Lee said.

"'*Heart of Darkness*'?" I asked.

"Brutal jungle environment," she said. "You haven't read it?"

"Not yet."

"I'm appalled and dismayed. Call me dispalled." She cut across to the English lit section, speed-browsed the shelves for nine seconds, grabbed a paperback, and said, "My treat."

"Thanks."

She held up a credit card. "Actually, my parents' treat."

"Even better."

Lee headed deep into the literature aisles. I wandered. That was the best way to experience a bookstore. I ended up in the film studies section, which had a nice assortment of movie scripts. Lee eventually tracked me down there. She had a stack of novels in her hands. But she pulled another book from the shelves of the psychology section as we walked to the register.

"Check this out," Lee said, holding it out toward me.

"*The Birth Order Book*," I said, reading the cover. "What about it?"

"Well, yours has changed," she said. "You're a middle child now. So you'll act differently."

"No way. I mean, I know I changed from being the youngest to being in the middle. But that didn't change anything about *me*." I reshelved the book.

Lee laughed. I didn't pursue the topic.

···

March 1

February is over, Sean. I'm glad. It's a bleak month. Too dark, too cold. I think everyone in Pennsylvania would be happy to teleport to somewhere warm for those four weeks. But March is here. Technically, still winter. But a gateway to spring.

Speaking of progress, you impressed me today, Sean. Banging two blocks together is a pretty awesome achievement for someone who's been in the world roughly as long as he'd been in the womb. It borders on the entertaining. Keep it up.

Zenger Zinger for March 3
Last week's answer: "I wish hurdlers and sprinters got paid," John Peter said protractedly.
This week's puzzle: "Let's touch the bare wires together," John Peter said _____.

Take Your Child to Work Day is the fourth Thursday of April. Whoever picked that date years ago couldn't have known that Test the Crap out of Sophomores Month would also eventually fall in April. As well as parts of March and May. Our school decided to relocate the event that was less important to them to the first Thursday in March. As much as I'd enjoyed it last year, I wasn't sure I wanted to be with Dad at his job right now. Especially since this was the month the garage would have opened.

Lee had a solution. She unveiled it during the first Wednesday in March, which happened to be Try to Guess What's Really in the Chicken Cutlet Day.

"Let's switch," she said.

"Switch what?"

"Dads."

"No thanks. I want to survive to adulthood. And my dad is unschooled in parenting females."

"Not the actual dads, although that would be amusing. Their jobs. I've already experienced all the glory of a day at a law firm. I'd prefer all the gory of a day of phlebotomy, but doctor's offices have these stupid rules against stuff like that. I'd love to go somewhere else. Switch with me?"

"That doesn't seem like a good idea."

"Please?"

"No way."

"Pretty please?"

"It's hard to resist such a persuasive argument," I said. "But I'm standing firm. Wait. Actually, I'm avoiding a firm."

"If it's hard to resist, it's persuasive by definition. You're being redundant. You can thank me for pointing that out by switching with me."

"Your dad might say no."

"He already said yes."

"My dad might say no."

Lee hit me with the second- or third-best-known *Princess Bride* quote. "Inconceivable."

"I might say no."

"That would be a mistake," she said. "Let's do it."

"Okay. Sure. We'll switch." I knew that it would be pointless to resist. Besides, it might be interesting to observe the lion in his lair.

Mr. Franka pulled me aside after the newspaper meeting. "You know those figures of speech you were learning about before Mrs. Gilroy took ill?"

I was glad he was talking to me again. "Is that a rhetorical question?"

"Very funny."

"Thanks.

"Seriously, that's not sophomore material. Some of it isn't even high school material. When Mrs. Gilroy first put it in her lesson plan, several decades ago, she was told she couldn't cover it."

"Seriously?"

"Yeah. Lesson plans were a lot more rigid back then. She fought for it. Took the battle to the school board. That's how much she cares. Of all the things she teaches, as much as she loves the prose of Steinbeck and the poetry of Whitman, it's the tools of the craft that are her true passion."

"Yeah. I get that. But I still don't understand why she's jamming all of this down our throats," I said.

"You'll figure it out eventually," Mr. Franka said.

"If I don't die first."

"I'm pretty sure you'd already be on board if anyone other than Mrs. Gilroy was involved," he said.

"Maybe."

"Well, you'll get your chance to find out soon enough," he said.

"What are you talking about?" I asked.

He gave me a cryptic smile. "You'll see."

THIRTY-FOUR

Are you sure you want to spend the day with the devil?" Mr. Fowler asked when he picked me up.

"As long as I don't have to sign anything," I said. I slipped into the passenger seat. "I like the devil's wheels." Any time Lee's parents had driven us places, it was in an SUV. This was an Audi Spyder.

"The wages of sin are six or seven figures," he said.

I don't know a lot about clothing, but the suit he wore looked like it cost more than most people make in a week. Or maybe even a month. I had the feeling someone he knew by name had sewn it together, piece by piece, so it fit him exactly. We drove across the Delaware River into New Jersey. So did about ten thousand other people, who all wanted to get in front of us, or push us out of their way from behind. Mr. Fowler didn't seem stressed at all by the traffic. On the other hand, he was driving a car that could eat most other cars for breakfast and spit their remains out its tailpipe while purring along at 120 miles an hour. I loved watching the expressions of the drivers we passed when they spotted me. *Yeah, this kid rides in style.*

We ended up at an office building in Piscataway. The directory in the lobby listed *Geary, Fowler, and Goldsmith, Environmental Law* on the fifth floor. I noticed there were no other companies on that floor.

When we stepped out of the elevator, it was pretty much the way they showed big law firms on TV. There was a receptionist right past the elevator, offices along the outside walls, and dozens of cubicles in the center of the space. Mr. Fowler had a large office in one of the corners, with a view of the Raritan River.

"Impressive," I said.

"Impressions help land and maintain clients," he said.

There was a family picture on his desk, taken when Lee was about five or six. It looked like she'd been born with brown hair. Mr. Fowler interrupted my contemplation.

"So, how much are you here to see what I do, and how much are you here because it got you out of school?" he asked.

"It's seventy/thirty," I said. "I am sort of interested."

"That's about what I would have guessed. As for the work, I'm sorry to say that much of it will seem pretty dull. Books, reading, research, that sort of stuff."

"I like research," I said. "And I spend a lot of time reading."

"Don't try to suck up to me, Scott," he said.

"I wouldn't dream of it. I really do like research."

He pulled a chair over for me, then sat at his desk and started working. As he went through a stack of documents his secretary had brought in, he told me what he was working on.

"There's a company near Lake Havasu City in Arizona. They make high-tech batteries. They employ three hundred people, doing everything from cleaning the floors to researching new technologies. This is all good, right?"

I hesitated, wondering whether it was a trick question. But finally, I said, "Right."

"The current manufacturing process involves some heavy metals. Do you know what those are?"

I nodded. "Stuff like cadmium."

"Right. And, as with any process, there are waste products. The company does a responsible job of disposing of these products. But a rare species of toad lives near the factory. Environmentalists fear that this properly disposed waste will harm this toad or reduce its habitat."

"So what do they want to do?" I asked.

"They want to close the plant."

He paused to let that sink in.

"Close it?"

"Close it," Mr. Fowler said. He waved his hand to encompass the law firm around us. "We, on the other hand, do not want them to have to close the plant and put three hundred people out of work. That would be not just a personal tragedy for each employee, but also a great loss to the economy in the area. Many local businesses would suffer."

"What's the law say?" I asked.

"The law is slightly vague on some aspects of this, as is often the case. Laws are written with words. Those words are defined with other words, which are in turn defined by yet more words, some of which end up circling back to the initial words."

"Sounds like modern poetry," I said.

"It's not quite that bad. But a lot depends on the interpretation. It's my job to argue for an interpretation that favors my client. The government will attempt to argue otherwise. But I haven't told you the most compelling part. Are you ready for the kicker?"

"Sure."

"The company is investing a large portion of their research funds in developing a green battery—one that can be completely and inexpensively recycled without damaging the environment."

"So it's not a simple case of man against frog."

"Toad."

"*Frog* is funnier."

"You might not enjoy law school." He grabbed a notepad, wrote down some reptile and amphibian names, both common and scientific, then said, "Here. Do some research. See if there are news stories about any of these animals."

I wasn't sure if he was just giving me busywork, but I wasn't lying when I said I liked research. And Mr. Fowler's firm had totally kick-ass computers with access to all sorts of databases and news archives. He also had lunch delivered.

...

"Thanks. That was interesting." I reached to unbuckle my seat belt. I didn't know whether I wanted to be a lawyer, but I totally knew how I wanted to get to work.

"You're welcome," Mr. Fowler said. "Pay no attention to my suggestion that you avoid law school. I think the professors deserve a challenge once in a while."

"I'll give it some thought," I said. "I really did have a good time."

"And your research actually had some minimal value."

"I'm glad."

As I pushed open the door and started to step out, he said, "Scott?"

"Yes?"

"If you ever hurt her, I'll destroy you."

Talk about being caught off guard. I guess I should have said something noble, or assured him that I would never dream of hurting Lee. I'd throw myself in front of her to take a bullet, if necessary. As usual, all the good replies came to me later, when I was replaying the scene in my mind. At the moment, all I could come up with was, "That seems fair."

I really don't ever want to have a daughter.

We compared notes at lunch the next day.

"Your dad's awesome," Lee said.

"I know. So is yours. Sort of."

"What are you talking about?" she asked.

"He's trying to save three hundred jobs at a company that wants to develop an environmentally friendly battery," I said.

"Oh my god, you went over to the dark side," Lee said.

"What?"

"You swallowed the poison. You chomped on the bait. You fell for his line. You probably don't care at all about the toad. You'd make a perfect lawyer."

"Well, it's just a toad. I mean, I feel bad for it, but there are lots of toads."

"Not like this one."

"So?"

"What if there's a chemical in that toad's skin that can cure cancer?"

"You mean you'd want to save the toad so you can grind it up for medicine?"

"No. That's just an example."

"What about the three hundred people at the factory?"

"I feel bad for them," Lee said.

"But not as bad as you feel for the toad?"

"It's not that simple," she said.

"Exactly!"

"Why are you shouting?"

"Why are *you* shouting?"

Lee looked at me. I looked at her.

We both started to laugh. Richard and Edith exchanged glances, and shook their heads.

"I'm glad I'm not an adult yet," I said. "They have to deal with all sorts of stuff where you just can't win. Even if you do win, you sort of lose."

"Let's stay young forever, Peter," Lee said. "We'll be pirates."

"Very funny. I don't want to stay young forever. I just want to remain here a little bit longer."

Wesley picked me up after dinner. We were going to the movies. He was in one of those trucks they use to deliver big sheets of window glass.

"Wow, you really have to be careful driving that stuff around," I said when I hopped into the passenger side.

"Tell me about it," Wesley said. "Some of the roads are still icy from the last storm."

Sunday, as I should have expected, Lee texted me at 2:00 A.M.

Is it my imagination, or did the last hour seem to fly right by?

I was too sleepy to think up a clever answer.

On Monday, as always after the clocks were changed, things felt a bit out of sync. But for a moment at the start of ninth period, when I walked into the classroom, it was not the clocks but the calendar that had been set back. Mr. Franka was standing up front. There was no sign of Mr. Kamber.

I turned to Lee. "If everyone gets three wishes, I'm down to two."

Mr. Franka soon doused my hopes. "Mrs. Gilroy, who will be returning next month, asked me to make sure her favorite class still has a large amount of enthusiasm for the joy of words. So, just for today, I've swapped classes with Mr. Kamber."

"Those poor freshmen," Lee said.

I flashed her a smile and said, "Nwarries, smite!"

"Let's generate some joy." Mr. Franka picked up the chalk. "Black-and-white television, AM radio, mainframe computer, analogue recording." He wrote each phrase on the board as he spoke. "What do all of these have in common?"

"They're old?" Julia guessed.

Mr. Franka nodded. "True. But there's more to it than that." He wrote "yes" above the list of words, and "no" to the right of the list.

Under the "no," he wrote "slide rule" and "buggy whip."

"What's a slide rule?" Kelly asked.

Mr. Franka gave her a quick explanation. I knew what they were. My grandfather had showed me one, years ago. It was kind of cool how you could do math with it, even though it wasn't real accurate for big numbers.

Mr. Franka tossed the chalk from hand to hand. "Any more guesses?"

"They're all some sort of technology," Kelly said.

"True," Mr. Franka said. "So let's add a few more examples." Under "yes," he wrote "wild salmon" and "snail mail."

I thought about my letters from Mouth. "Snail mail" used to just be called "mail." I scanned the rest of the phrases on the left side of the list, to see if they fell into that same category. Yeah, they fit. At one time, there was just radio, and there were just computers. All radio was AM, and all computers were mainframes.

"Got it." I raised my hand.

"Yes, Scott," Mr. Franka said.

"All the words on the left, they used to not need to be modified. Right?"

"Right," Mr. Franka said. "The new coinages became necessary because of changes. At one time, there was just television. When color TV came along, it became necessary to refer to the old televisions as black-and-white TVs."

He paused so we could absorb this, then added, "Words of this sort are called *retronyms*."

"Cool," I said. And that word made me think of a retronym. Hot tea. I think all tea used to be served hot. There was just tea. But then there was iced tea.

And so I had a brief classroom reunion with my favorite English teacher.

■ ■ ■

Zenger Zinger for March 10

Last week's answer: "Let's touch the bare wires together," John Peter said shortly.

This week's puzzle: "A buffalo and half a score of lampreys," John Peter said _____.

THIRTY-FIVE

I'd decided to go with a green shirt, but regular jeans for St. Patrick's Day. Going all green seemed a bit excessive. Especially when you're short, and don't want to offer anyone openings for leprechaun jokes.

I guess Jeremy hadn't given it much thought, because he'd made that mistake.

"You're going to have an interesting day," I said.

"*Interesting* has become my least favorite word," he said.

When I got to school, I was surprised to see that Lee had dyed her hair green.

"You went with the obvious," I said.

"It seemed the subtlest way to go," she said.

It wasn't subtle in the locker room. Besides a sea of green shirts and pants, there was an ocean of green underwear.

"This borders on the excessive," Richard said. He'd settled for a striped shirt that was green and blue.

"This is nothing." I turned toward Kyle. "Remember how

crazy Patrick would get? One time—" I cut myself off. I'd forgotten we weren't talking.

I guess Kyle sort of forgot, too. "Yeah. And he was only half Irish."

I turned my attention back to Richard, and recounted some of Patrick's more enthusiastic wearings of the green.

As we left the locker room, Kyle said, "You ever hear from him?"

"Once or twice. But not for a while."

"That's life," Kyle said. "People go away."

"I still miss him," I said.

Kyle nodded. It was a tiny nod, but a real one.

After a long winter of indoor gym, we'd finally started going outside again. That was good for Mr. Cravutto, since separate boys' and girls' gyms meant he was kept away from his true love. And it was good for the class, because it meant we were back to self-rule. Which, as anyone could tell you, was not called *metonymy*.

According to school rumors, several independent sightings, and their current body language as they chatted, the two gym teachers were actively dating. That was good. I was happy for Mr. Cravutto.

On the way out of the locker room, I poked my head in his office and asked, "Need any more help with poems?"

"No. That one seemed to do the trick. No point taking a chance that the next one will mess things up." He shook his head. "Women are hard to understand."

"But you finally asked her out?"

"Yup. Finally."

Maybe he'd be a source of advice. I'd been seeking sophisticated wisdom from various corners. Perhaps what I needed was primal instinct. I risked a question. "What took you so long?"

"Women are scary," he said. "But loneliness is scarier."

"That makes sense."

"What about you, Hudson. Got a steady gal?"

"I'm working on it," I said.

"Good for you."

The bell rang. Damn. "Can I have a pass?"

"You won't need it."

Zenger Zinger for March 17

Last week's answer: "A buffalo and half a score of lampreys," John Peter said bicentennially.

This week's puzzle: "There's a big hint on the pirate treasure map," John Peter said _____.

March 17

 Sean, St. Patrick's Day is two days after the Ides of March. That got me wondering whether there was a word meaning "the day after tomorrow." I looked it up. There is. Overmorrow. That's sort of cool, even if it's not used anymore. I wonder whether two days ago would be overyester? Probably not.

The subspecies *Homo Zengerus faculatus* has two dominant lines, *instructorus* and *administratus*. Interactions among individuals or groups of these lines can be cooperative or aggressively competitive. In either case, their actions often have a strong impact on *Homo Zengerus studentes*.

When I walked into biology on Monday, there was something other than a splayed cat occupying center stage. The principal was arguing with Ms. Denton.

"No," she said, at a fairly high volume.

Normally, I wouldn't pay attention to anything a teacher and the principal were discussing. I'd walked past dozens of those conversations, and knew they held no interest for me. But this was different. That one word—"no"—seemed to carry a lot of weight, as if it conveyed sentences, or even paragraphs.

I almost tripped when I reached my seat, because I was trying hard to walk like someone who wasn't eavesdropping.

"You have to," the principal said. "The board voted on it. Those new members came with an agenda."

"No," she said again. "I won't. Absolutely not."

"It's one module. It won't take any work on your part. They sent the material. You can cover it in fifteen minutes. Fit it in next week sometime."

"I'm not doing it."

"You have no choice. I wish you did. You know how I feel. But my hands are tied," the principal said. "I'm just doing my job."

"I do have a choice," she said. "And I'm just doing *my* job."

She stared at him. He stared back. Five or ten seconds passed. Each of them seemed to be thinking hard.

I didn't want to miss a single moment of the action, but I risked a quick glance at Lee. "Any idea what's going on?" I asked.

"Nope," she said.

I turned my attention back to the drama unfolding at the front of the room.

Ms. Denton took off her lab coat and tossed it on the table, finally giving Splitz a decent shroud. "I feel sick. I'm going home."

"You can't go home in the middle of the day," the principal said.

Ms. Denton barked out a laugh and left the room.

The principal finally noticed that he had a class full of biology students staring at him. He pulled the walkie-talkie off his belt, and said, "Brenda, I need someone to come up to room 316 and cover Ms. Denton's class for the period."

After he reholstered the walkie-talkie, he said, "Do something productive. Read some biology or something." Then, he stood by the doorway, looking down the hall.

Two minutes later, Mr. Cravutto walked in.

"What's up, Vic?" he asked.

The principal pointed at us. "Cover this class for the period."

"Sure. What is it?" the coach asked.

The principal glanced around the room, at all the myriad

clues to the nature of the topic taught therein, including posters of plant and animal taxonomy, several animal skeletons, a small bronze bust of Carl Linnaeus, and a shelf filled with microscopes, then said, "Biology."

Mr. Cravutto shrugged. "No problem."

The principal left. Mr. Cravutto told us, "Read something."

I resisted the urge to reply, "Yes, COACH!"

He reached toward the lab coat. "Someone's not picking up after themselves."

As he lifted the coat, Lee tried to catch his attention. I guess she wanted to warn him. I put a hand on her arm. I wanted to see this.

The coach had the coat all the way off the table before he noticed what he'd uncovered. He let out a shriek about three octaves higher than I would have expected, and probably four octaves higher than he'd ever want any of his friends to hear, and then jumped back.

"What the heck!" he shouted. Though the word he used wasn't even close to *heck*. "Who put that there?"

Someone said, "Ms. Denton."

"Well, no wonder she's gone. That's sick!" He tossed the coat back over the cat, and walked to the other side of the room. For the rest of the period, which we all spent pretending to read the textbook, I noticed that every two or three minutes, he'd shudder, like someone had drenched him with an icy bucket of Gatorade. I guess I have to give him credit for not puking. Even so, I think I had a memory I would treasure forever.

"Thanks, Slitzskers," I said as I walked past the table on my way out of the room.

It didn't take long to find out why Ms. Denton had taken sick. Coincidentally, I was in the locker room before gym the next day when I learned the first sketchy details.

"You hear about Ms. Denton?" Renzler asked.

"I was there when she walked out," I said.

"No way."

Several other heads turned toward me.

I didn't bother to point out that it wasn't exactly like being a participant in the first moon landing. A whole class had seen it.

"It's that evolution stuff," Kyle said. "They wanted her to teach both versions."

"Both versions?" I asked.

"You know," Kyle said. "Darwin and the other one. Something creative . . . ?"

"Intelligent design," Richard said. "Yeah. That's it."

"Who wanted her to teach that?" Renzler asked.

I knew the answer. It was the school board. What a mess. Ms. Denton shouldn't have walked out. She could have presented the material, and explained that it was a theory. She could do a lot more for science and knowledge by being the one who covered the material than by leaving it to someone else who might not care as much. But I guess the thought of being forced to teach something she felt wasn't based on real science just made her too angry.

•••

Zenger Zinger for March 24

Last week's answer: "There's a big hint on the pirate treasure map," said John Peter exclusively.

This week's puzzle: "I got his heart beating again," John Peter said _____.

THIRTY-SIX

This is a direct assault on the First Amendment," Sarah said.

"But not the part we care about, as reporters," Richard said.

Everyone on staff looked at him like he was crazy.

"I'm serious," he said. "The First Amendment has two totally separate parts. Freedom of the press is one part. Freedom of religion is the other. They just happen to be together."

"Let's go to the source." Sarah slid one of her textbooks onto the table. It was covered with a shiny purple wrapper, imprinted in glowing red letters with "Congress shall make no law respecting an establishment of religion, or prohibiting the free exercise thereof; or abridging the freedom of speech, or of the press; or the right of the people peaceably to assemble, and to petition the Government for a redress of grievances."

"Wow, it's actually three things," I said. "Speech, religion, and assembly." It had never really occurred to me before now that they were all lumped together.

"Four, I think," Jeremy said. "Assembly and petition are separate rights. At least, that's the way I read it."

"No wonder there are so many arguments about the law," I said. I remembered what Mr. Fowler had told me. "You'd think they could have expanded on their ideas a bit, and maybe defined some of the words."

"All they had were quill pens and inkwells," Jeremy said. "That's a good incentive for brevity."

"People, we're getting off topic," Sarah said. "Do we, as a newspaper, have an editorial position on the issue? Do we speak out in defense of Ms. Denton?"

"She's kind of mean," I said.

"I think it's too early," Jeremy said. "There's a board meeting Friday. Let's see what happens."

"Good idea," I said. This was getting too complicated. I was hugely in favor of free speech and a free press. But I'd never thought about whether all the parts of that Amendment were one thing, or separate issues.

Why did this stuff have to be so complicated?

After the newspaper meeting, I went over to Lee's place to study for our geometry test. Her mom invited me to stay for dinner. Her dad was bringing takeout from a place in Easton on his way home from work.

Lee's folks actually did something with Chinese food that I'd never seen before. They took the food out of the cartons and put it in serving bowls. As I was helping myself to some roast pork lo mein, I asked Mr. Fowler, "Did you hear about the biology teacher who's getting fired?" I couldn't get it out of my mind. No matter what we'd discussed in the newspaper meeting, I still thought free speech was part of the issue. And I liked free speech a lot more than I disliked Ms. Denton.

"I read about it in the paper," he said. "And Lee filled me in on some of the details. There are definitely some constitutional issues in play."

"I'll bet she could use a good lawyer," I said.

"Her union will take care of that," he said.

"Will it be a *good* lawyer?" I asked.

"Maybe." Then, he paused, and said, "Actually, it might just be a union representative."

"So it definitely won't be a *great* lawyer," I said. "Not someone like you."

"Scott, bull crap and dinner don't mix well."

"Lawrence!" Mrs. Fowler said.

"I was merely stating a fact," Mr. Fowler said to his wife. "I doubt Scott actually considers me to be a great lawyer. But he seems to want to help this teacher. And I'm certainly sympathetic to her cause. The new school board is nuts. On the other hand, her actions have made the whole issue more complicated. I'll look into it and see who's representing her. If I can be of assistance, and I feel my presence would improve her chances, I'll do what I can."

"Thanks," I said.

"You can thank me by passing the lo mein," he said. "But keep the bull to yourself."

I expected Mrs. Fowler to protest again. But she laughed and said, "Stop that. You know we only serve bull crap when we're having barbecue." Then she flashed me a wink. I guess she'd been joking when she pretended to be shocked. And I guess I knew where Lee got some of her edgy sense of humor.

The school board meeting, at the town municipal building, was packed. All the people who hadn't bothered to vote were now dealing with the results of their apathy. The conservative faction had proved eager to trim programs with the vigor and inaccuracy of a landscaper pruning a hedge with a chainsaw during an earthquake. And all the people who had voted against the budget, including the contingent that disliked anything that didn't mesh perfectly with their beliefs, had come to see a witch burned at the stake. Or whatever passed for the modern equivalent of that practice.

I wedged my way in, and found a spot against the back wall, next to Jeremy. The room was warm with all the bodies. The air felt angry. I heard mingled snippets of conversation containing the buzzwords of both sides.

Ms. Denton was sitting in the front row, with two of the other biology teachers. There was a woman in a business suit at the end of the row. I didn't recognize her. Right behind

Ms. Denton, I saw several more teachers from the science department. Other staff members were scattered throughout the room.

Mr. Sherman, at the center of the table of board members, banged a gavel and called the meeting to order. "I see we have more people here than usual. Please keep in mind that we have rules to follow."

What came next was a half hour of deadly boring discussions that nobody in the room cared about except for the board members. And I wasn't even sure they cared. As I sat there, I thought about the cat on the table in biology, and the way Ms. Denton had waited for us with mops and buckets ready. That cat hadn't been put out there for the AP class. It was the first day of school. The cat wouldn't have been halfway dissected. She'd put it out just for the fun of finding out who couldn't handle the sight. And that sure had been the case with me. I didn't know whether to be angry or impressed. She hadn't been targeting me, specifically. It had just been her good luck, and my bad luck, that the fly she'd snared in her web was one she'd taken special relish in devouring.

Now *she* was tangled in a web.

Finally, Mr. Sherman said, "Next issue: the disciplining of Marianne Denton, biology teacher at Zenger High School."

A murmur rose from the crowd, swelling in volume past a buzz on its way a roar.

Bang!

The gavel had descended.

"I will not do this again," Mr. Sherman said. "If you people can't act like adults, I will clear the room."

"*He can't do that*," Jeremy whispered to me.

"No?"

"No. There are sunshine laws," he said.

"I have a feeling he makes the law here," I said.

"Then he can shove that gavel where the sun don't shine," Jeremy said.

I stared at him.

"Too much?" he asked.

"It seems a bit out of character for you."

"Agreed. But I'm pretty steamed about this."

He was far from alone. People got in line to speak. I didn't see any students join in. That wasn't right. We were the ones who'd be affected. We were the ones being hurt by every decision the board made. Someone should speak for us. I hesitated, trying to figure out whether I had the guts to join the line. Finally, I went up, even though I wasn't sure what I wanted to say. As people spoke, I was amazed at the range of comments. Some people made good points, but a lot of the speakers were more interested in promoting their agenda—whether that was from a scientific or a religious viewpoint—than in addressing the issue of Ms. Denton's actions. I guess I had an agenda, too.

Finally, it was my turn. I passed Ms. Denton on the

way up to the podium that faced the board members. She seemed surprised to see me. I wrapped my hand around the microphone, stared straight at Mr. Sherman, and froze. The next ten seconds lasted about ten years.

"If you have nothing to say, please step aside for the next person," Mr. Sherman said.

I hadn't realized anyone had joined the line behind me. Not that it mattered. I gave myself a pep talk. *You can do this.* I suck at pep talks.

"Son?" Mr. Sherman said.

I was *not* his son. I was my father's son. I pictured Dad standing here, speaking with the calm voice of Atticus Finch from *To Kill a Mockingbird.* I was *his* son. I was Wesley Cobble's friend. He was fearless. I was Jeremy Danger's friend. He was fearful, so I had to be fearless for him. I was Mom's son, Lee's friend, Sean's big brother, Bobby's middle brother, and Amala's soon-to-be brother-in-law. I imagined each of them, except for Sean, standing here in my place. But they weren't at the podium. I was speaking for them. And for my classmates. If I could manage to find my voice.

I glanced at Ms. Denton, who seemed relieved that her least favorite student was about to fail to speak out about her.

There were murmurs from the audience behind me.

"Please step aside," Mr. Sherman said. He toyed with the gavel.

Jeremy's voice echoed in my mind. *Sunshine laws.*

That was it!

"Adenosine triphosphate," I said, spitting out the term.

It was as if I'd uncorked the viaduct that ran from my brain to my mouth.

I let the words flow. "That's a coenzyme that is crucial in the process of photosynthesis. It eventually reduces to adenosine diphosphate. During this process, which absorbs carbon dioxide from the atmosphere, a plant produces energy for itself, and oxygen as a byproduct."

I expected Mr. Sherman to tell me to shut up. But he seemed to be trying to figure out what I was talking about. I was tempted to toss in some Latin. But that wouldn't do anything for my current cause.

I pointed at Ms. Denton. "I learned those scientific facts in biology class. And I learned a whole lot more. I won't draw this out by proving my grasp of Linnaean taxonomy or describing the molecular structure of the human cell. I'm not great at science. And I'm definitely not a science geek. At least, I didn't think I was. I struggled through chemistry last year. This year is different. Ms. Denton motivated me to study harder than I've ever studied in my life. She is an excellent teacher. You can't take her away from us."

I glanced to my side. Ms. Denton seemed as stunned by these words as Mr. Sherman had been by my brief foray into the realm of photosynthesis.

"People have spoken about their beliefs. That's fine. We all have beliefs. But Ms. Denton's job is to teach us the facts and theories of science. However we were created, and whatever I believe, whatever my *faith*, whatever your faith, that is not the issue. Ms. Denton got in trouble for refusing to teach something that she felt is not part of a science curriculum. She is a scientist." I pointed to the other teachers in her row. "They are all scientists. They were hired to teach us science. Let them do their job. Thank you."

There was scattered applause as I stepped away from the microphone. And there was someone behind me, waiting for his turn to speak. He gave me a nod as he took his place. I stood nearby and listened.

"My name is Lawrence Fowler. I am a parent of a student in Ms. Denton's biology class. I am also a managing partner in the law firm of Geary, Fowler, and Goldsmith. As a parent, I have to echo the previous speaker's sentiments. Ms. Denton has lit a passion for biology in my daughter. I appreciate that. The objects of my daughter's passions don't always meet with my approval. But let me speak to you not as a father, but as someone who is as familiar with the law of the land as Ms. Denton is with the laws of science. We are not here to decide whether creation science is a suitable topic for a public school biology classroom. Even if that matter hadn't already been decided in a landmark ruling by a United States District Court, it wouldn't make a difference. We are here to determine whether the school board can fire a teacher for leaving school in the middle of the day due to an illness. That, and that alone, is the issue at hand."

He paused. I guess he wanted to let his words sink in. A couple people shouted their disagreement. Mr. Sherman banged his gavel, but didn't say anything.

Mr. Fowler held up a document. "This is the standard contract signed by all teachers in the district. The wording in section twelve, paragraph three, subsection C, is clear. She was fully within her rights to leave the classroom if she felt ill."

"She wasn't sick," Mr. Sherman yelled.

"And your proof?" Mr. Fowler asked.

"I know she wasn't," Mr. Sherman said.

"That's an excellent example of the difference between faith and science," Mr. Fowler said. "And since you are so fond of faith, I want you to have faith in this. If the board doesn't immediately overturn the motion to fire her, and instead proceeds with this farce, I will offer her my services and file a lawsuit against the board." He pointed at Mr. Sherman. "I might even be able to file suits against individual members. Thank you for your time."

The board members looked like they'd just opened their bedroom doors and found a half dozen zombies facing them.

"We're going to take a short recess." Mr. Sherman banged his gavel. Then he and the rest of the board got up from the table and went into a smaller room off to the side.

The woman in the business suit, who was the last person

in line, put her hand on Mr. Fowler's shoulder and said, "I'm Ms. Denton's union representative. I want to thank you. I think you just saved everyone from a long, unpleasant legal battle."

"I'm happy to help," Mr. Fowler said.

He followed me to the back wall. Lee was there. I guess she'd come in with him. She gave me a thumbs-up.

"Wow," I said to him. "That was impressive. Thanks."

"It's what I do."

"You're very good at it."

"Don't suck up to me."

"Sorry."

"You weren't bad yourself. You just picked a more difficult argument to support."

"I'm new at this."

"Despite what I said earlier, you should give serious consideration to being a lawyer."

I thought about the gut-churning experience of speaking to the board. "Do they let lawyers wear diapers?"

As the words left my mouth, I flinched. That was not the best sort of joke to make to the father of the good friend you hope will become your girlfriend.

But he smiled and said, "I usually recommend that to my opponents. They make extra-absorbent ones these days. That's another miracle of science."

"Thank you, Scott."

I looked to my left, at Ms. Denton, who'd just joined us.

"You're welcome," I said.

"I would never have expected you to defend me," she said.

"I was defending a principle. But everything I said was true. You definitely motivated me to study hard."

"Though not in the best way," she said. "I wasn't being very professional."

I shrugged. I wanted to rub it in a bit. She really had treated me unfairly. But she'd been battered pretty roughly this week for sticking to her principles. I'd heard she'd gotten some pretty nasty phone calls. Her eyes were moist. This was getting awkward. "No worries."

She turned to Mr. Fowler. "And thank you," she said, holding out her hand.

"I was defending a principle, too," he said. "And a good teacher. Lee loves your class. Though she tries not to reveal her passions to me and her mother."

"She's a wonderful student. She has a good mind for science. Were you serious about representing me? I don't have a lot of money."

"You wouldn't need any. And I doubt you'll need representation. The board may have taken a shift to the extreme right, but they aren't foolish. Whatever most people believe, however devout or irreverent they are in their daily lives, whether they spend Sunday in church or at the stadium, most of them still worship money. If the board is arrogant enough to believe they can defy the terms of your contract,

I'll be happy to demonstrate how expensive their mistake is for them, and how rewarding it is for my clients."

The door of the side room opened. After the board members were seated, Mr. Sherman called the meeting to order. "All those in favor of stopping the termination process?"

Four hands went up, including Mr. Sherman's, though he didn't look happy about it. Four mouths said, "Aye."

"Opposed?" he asked.

Three hands rose. I guess they'd decided that they could save face among their supporters, as long as the majority ruled in Ms. Denton's favor.

"The ayes have it," Mr. Sherman said. "Is there any other business?"

There was none. Ms. Denton hugged Mr. Fowler. Then she hugged me. Her fellow teachers came over. More hugs were exchanged. Lee came over and hugged her dad. Then, she offered me a high five.

Zenger Zinger for March 31
Last week's answer: "I got his heart beating again," John Peter said repulsively.
This week's puzzle: "I have my father's eyes," John Peter said _____.

THIRTY-SEVEN

Appropriately enough, the third marking period ended on April Fool's Day. I was pretty sure I'd maintained my eligibility. Better yet, we had another teacher swap in English.

Mr. Franka went for an English lesson in the truest sense, telling us about something called Cockney rhyming slang, which was a combination of wordplay and a simplistic secret code. We also discussed other secret languages and codes. Mr. Franka ended the lecture with an explanation of *shibboleths*, giving me another cool word and concept to add to my collection.

Near the end of the period, he said, "Good news. Mrs. Gilroy returns right after the break."

I walked over to him on my way out. "I'm glad she's coming back," I said. "I'm glad I'll have another chance to show her what kind of student I am."

"Everyone deserves forgiveness and a second chance, Scott," Mr. Franka said.

"I appreciate that," I said. "Did you ever mess up badly?"

"Constantly." His jaw clenched slightly several times, as if he were paging through a series of mistakes, in search of one suitable for sharing with a teen audience.

"I blew up my best friend," he said.

"You killed him?" I asked.

He shook his head. "Nope. Luckily for both of us, I was pretty bad at chemistry."

"What happened?"

"It was junior year. We were trying to make our own fireworks. I definitely do not recommend this. I overestimated my skill in creating fuses. And underestimated the stupidity of holding an enormous homemade firecracker in my hand. When I realized the beast was about to explode, I tossed it."

"At your friend?"

"Not intentionally. But, yes, at my friend."

"Did he forgive you?"

"Not back then. Not for maybe ten years. It takes a while to get over a lost toe. His dad forgave me a lot sooner. And that was probably more important. Although at the time, I didn't really appreciate what that took. Dads are highly protective of their offspring."

"So I've heard. It could have been worse. Imagine if it had been his daughter."

"In that case, I doubt I'd be standing here," he said. "As for you, basically, you screwed up, but nobody died, or was permanently damaged. You weren't even responsible for Mrs. Gilroy's collapse. Count yourself lucky. I suspect you suffered a bit of anguish, which seems fair. You learned a lesson. Time to move on. But take the lesson with you."

"I will."

"You are probably going to be writing throughout your life. You're going to have a chance to hurt people with your skills. Choose your targets wisely."

"Speaking of targets, which toe?" I asked.

"Second to last," he said. "Right next to the smallest."

"Penultimate?"

"I never thought of it that way. But yes, in that sense, it was the penultimate toe."

"Penultimate toe," I said, savoring the sound of it.

If I ever formed a band, I had a name for it.

We were off on Friday. Spring break had started. I went to the playground with my basketball. It was cold, but I felt like getting out and burning off some pent-up energy.

Kyle was there. I was about to turn away when he rolled his ball off to the side and held his hands out. I tossed him mine and joined him on the court.

We played one-on-one, to twenty. Playground rules. Make it, take it. One point per basket. You had to win by two.

It got rough.

And then it got brutal.

Kyle won, but only by four points.

By the end, as we dropped to the grass at the side of the court, I had a bloody nose, thanks to getting a jump shot stuffed back in my face, and a torn shirt.

Kyle had a twisted ankle. I'm pretty sure he also had some sore ribs, thanks to an elbow of mine that got out of control.

When I got home, Mom instantly asked, "Did you get in a fight?"

"Quite the opposite," I said.

Saturday, when we went bowling, Wesley picked me up in a flatbed truck with a giant statue on the back. The statue was one of those painted plaster things you see in front of restaurants. This one was a huge, smiling bee, painted in yellow and black stripes, wearing a chef's hat. It must have been eight feet tall. I didn't bother to ask Wesley about it. I had something else to discuss. I needed advice.

"I want to ask Lee out," I said.

"You go out with her all the time," he said.

"Out on a date," I said.

Wesley stared at me like I was a puppy he was trying to train to do a basic trick. "So ask her out on a date."

"What if she says no?"

"Then you won't go out on a date with her."

"But that could screw up our friendship," I said.

"Not if she's a real friend."

I wasn't sure things worked that way when dating was involved. I stared at the clouds for a while, then asked, "What do you think I should do?"

"I don't," he said.

"Don't what?"

"I don't think about what other people should do."

"Maybe that's the secret to happiness," I said.

"It works for me. I have no idea whether it would work for you."

"So, what's up with the statue?" I asked.

"New job."

"Oh."

"I have about ten more to deliver. It's kind of fun."

"I can see that."

"Except when they slide off . . ."

April 5

Happy Easter, Sean. I can't believe Mom let me put bunny ears on you. They were totally worth the fifty cents I spent on them at the thrift shop. You're still too young to hunt for eggs. I think next year might be the turning point.

Mrs. Gilroy is coming back pretty soon. I feel like I'm getting a second chance. I think, maybe, studying all those figures of speech is sort of like drawing three bottles for a whole marking period. You start to appreciate techniques, styles, and interpretations. Last month, when we were studying famous paintings in art, we learned the names for a lot of techniques, like chiaroscuro and sfumato. I guess that's sort of the same thing as in English class, except everything sounds cooler in Italian.

I reread my freshman sports articles last night. Most of my figurative language was similes. Seriously, nearly everything was like or as something else. I found some scattered metaphors, along with a sprinkling of the usual suspects—alliteration, onomatopoeia, hyperbole, etc. Though a few more sophisticated techniques crept in, especially in the later pieces. I spotted one nice chiasmus. Hey, don't look that one up yet. I know you're dying to learn the meaning, but the origin of the word is pretty cool. I'll tell you about it when I have a chance. I need to get going in a moment.

Anyhow, as I was saying, it was good writing. I'm proud of my work. But with all those similes, it was like I'd been using the most basic LEGO set, with just a few pieces, or I'd opened a giant assortment of crayons and extracted a single color. I have a whole arsenal now.

I made a serious effort to do nothing productive during spring break, and mostly succeeded. Sloth, when practiced with sufficient diligence and attention to detail, can be an art form. I did pick up a book on rhetorical terms at the used bookstore, but I barely glanced at it.

I went back to the playground on Saturday. I thought about going earlier in the week, but it had taken that long for all the bruises to heal. I made sure it was around the same time as before. Kyle was there.

"One-on-one?" he asked.

"How about we avoid contact sports for a while?" I said.

"Fine with me. Let's just shoot." He threw the ball to me. Hard. But not killer hard. Not brutal hard. Just Kyle harder-than-necessary hard.

"I'm sorry your dad had all those problems," I said.

"He'll be okay. He always bounces back. I'm sorry your dad didn't get to buy the garage," he said.

"Thanks."

"He'll get it someday," Kyle said.

"Yeah, he will. He was originally aiming for the year after next. Then Sean came along. That set things back."

"Babies are expensive," Kyle said.

"For sure. I tried to talk them into selling him. They couldn't be persuaded."

"Maybe they could rent him," Kyle said.

"That's not a bad idea. And the rental agreement could specify that he had to be returned fully cleaned. That would save a ton of work."

We speculated further on the details of a rent-a-baby contract, and gave some thought to pricing. At one point, as we were both laughing, I realized that this was something Kyle and I hadn't done since the start of freshman year. We were talking. Kidding around. He caught me looking at him, and stared back. We both stopped laughing. The shroud dropped over us again. But for a moment, it had been like all the bad stuff had been erased. It was nice to see a glimmer of healing. I knew better than to try to artificially extend it.

"I'd better get to work," I said after we'd played for about an hour. "I have a ton of reading to do." Our teachers had made sure our break was well spent.

"That's what you get for being a brain," Kyle said.

"Nice example of metonymy," I said. "Or maybe synecdoche. I can't keep them straight."

"I think you mean lunacy," Kyle said. But he smiled when he said it.

"You're probably right," I said.

Sean Hudson Lease/Rental Agreement

1. All rentals must include at least one overnight period. No returns can be made after 10:00 p.m. or before 10:00 a.m.

2. Sean must be returned with a full stomach and an unfilled diaper. Any stomach contents ejected before the end of the rental period are your property.

Attempts to include such post-peristaltic material in the return package is a violation of this agreement.

3. There will be a $1,000 damage fee assessed if, while in your possession, Sean has learned to hum, intone, chant, coo, warble, or babble songs from any animated movie featuring rodents, birds, or princesses.

4. Should you lose or misplace Sean, do not attempt to substitute another baby of equal value. For acceptable substitutions, please see the attached chart labeled "Toddler/Exotic Sports Car Conversion Rate."

April 12

Last day of spring break, Sean. Back to school tomorrow. And back to class with Mrs. Gilroy and her figures of speech. I think I've made it pretty obvious that I feel the names of a lot of these figures of speech are absurd. I mean, meiosis? That's vowel soup. But there's one term that is totally cool. I mentioned it the other day. Chiasmus. That's when two parts of a sentence or a clause have been flipped. Like in the well-known phrase that Mr. Cravutto has probably shouted ten zillion times: When the going gets tough, the tough get going. It's pretty easy to construct. Here, I'll make one up right now. You can take Scott Hudson out of the library, but you can't take the library out of

Scott Hudson. And it usually sounds deep, even if it isn't. So it's a great technique for persuasive essays and campaign slogans.

But here's the coolest part. The name comes from "chi" which is the Greek word for their letter x̲. And that's sort of what happens with the words themselves, in the two clauses or sentences. They cross. Okay, maybe right now that's not as cool, from your perspective, as the squeaky horn on the toy steering wheel Dad got you. But, someday, it will be.

Monday morning, I enjoyed a whopping one-twelfth of an hour of extra sleep. We'd gotten a notice that my bus schedule had changed. But only by five minutes. It was still at the same place.

Jeremy ran up to me as I was walking there. He looked like he was fleeing Godzilla.

"What's wrong?" I asked.

"They combined some of the routes," he said. "There are a lot more kids at our stop. They're kind of scary."

So that's why my pickup time had changed. It looked like the school board had found another way to save money and make our lives less pleasant. When I got closer, I saw that the new kids were from the other side of the development. "You'll be okay," I said. "Just stick close to me."

I walked over to Kyle.

"Where'd you get the puppy?" he asked.

"He followed me to school one day," I said. "Which, apparently, wasn't against the rule."

"Did the teachers laugh and play?" he asked.

I was pleased he'd caught the literary reference. "No more than usual."

I introduced Jeremy, and told Kyle, "He's a friend. Nobody messes with him."

"Got it," Kyle said.

"Thanks," Jeremy said.

"The universe keeps throwing us together," I said to Kyle.

"So the bus will probably break down," he said.

"That's the most likely scenario," I said.

Kyle grabbed a seat right behind Jeremy and me. By the time we left the last stop, every seat was full. I guess it made sense to be efficient with the buses, but I didn't like the way that we got hit with constant changes. I wondered what the board would do next.

THIRTY-EIGHT

Mrs. Gilroy walked slowly to the front of the room. *No, wait.* Mrs. Gilroy shuffled to the front of the room. Writing laboriously on the chalkboard, she carefully formed a sentence. *Hang on.* Laboring over each word, she crafted a sentence. She tapped the board enthusiastically to fully attract our attention. *Scratch that.* She smacked the board to capture our attention. She spoke the sentence solemnly. *Just a sec.* She intoned the words she'd written: "Adverbs are not always our friends."

Yeah, she was back. At least the marking period had ended, so I knew I'd have one good grade to average into the others, thanks to Mr. Kamber. The first thing Mrs. Gilroy did, after banning the lazy use of adverbs, was tell us to resume our exercises writing figures of speech. She also put all the terms we were studying back on the board.

I'd given my selection a lot of thought. If I tried to be nice and to make up for what had happened, she'd crucify me. I needed to be clever, instead. I needed to dazzle her.

I knew exactly what I was going to do. It made me nervous. But not because I was doing something wrong. I was scared because I wasn't sure I could pull it off. If I failed, I'd look like an idiot.

Thursday morning, when Jeremy, Kyle, and I got off the bus, Lee headed toward me. Her new bus had a slot near ours.

"Later," Kyle said, scooting off.

"He certainly vanished in a flash," Lee said.

"I think you scare him," I said. But I knew that wasn't the reason he'd split so quickly.

After school, when Lee and I were walking toward the bus, I noticed Kyle hanging back. When we took our seats, I turned to him and said, "I never told her it was you." He'd written something pretty nasty on her locker last year.

"No?"

"No."

"I still feel bad about it," he said.

"Let it go," I said. "It's long past."

"Maybe I should do something nice for her," he said.

I laughed. "That's a lot harder than it sounds."

The next morning, Kyle put his hand on my shoulder as we got off the bus. "Wait here."

He went ahead to intercept Lee. They talked for a while.

Not real long. Kyle's not a talker. But I guess he felt he needed to make things right by confessing.

"All is well?" I asked Lee when she joined me.

"All is well between Grapple Boy and Freaky Girl, as we now call each other," she said. "I'm glad we talked."

"Me, too."

Tomorrow was opening day for trout season. Unfortunately, today was opening shout-a-bad-word day when I got side-swiped, bushwhacked, and gobstopped by my report card in two directions at once. I might as well have shouted, "What the Dickens?"

It was the best of grades. It was the worst of grades.

I slipped into my seat next to Lee and checked out her report card. "Mommy and Daddy are going to be proud," I said.

"That's the downside of being a natural-born genius," Lee said. "How'd you do?"

I handed her my report card. Lee stared at it for a moment, as if digesting something that didn't quite make sense. I knew the feeling.

"Mr. Kamber clobbered you," she said. "How could he give you a seventy-five?"

"I have no idea. I got great grades on all my papers."

"But Ms. Denton gave you a hundred? Wow."

"Yeah. I feel sort of guilty. She's rewarding me for speaking at the hearing."

"And for getting my dad to speak for her," Lee said.

"There's no way she'd know about that," I said. "Your dad didn't mention me when they were talking."

"There are other ways she might have found out." Lee gave me a smug grin.

"But I don't want a grade I don't deserve," I said.

"Scott, you have too many rules. Accept the gift. Allow the universe to toss you a bone, or a bonus, you didn't earn. It's only fair, given how often the universe hits you in the face with a pie."

"It doesn't feel right," I said.

"What grade would you have given yourself?" she asked.

I did the math, based on my test scores. "I'd say about a ninety-three."

"So you're stressing out about seven points?" Lee asked. "Points that are helping you stay eligible for clubs?"

"No. Well, maybe. Yeah, I guess so." I took the report card back from Lee. Did I want to say something to Ms. Denton? Or was Lee right? Did I have too many self-imposed rules? I needed to think about that.

When biology class ended, I stayed in my seat.

I'd given my phrasing a lot of thought. I didn't want Ms. Denton to feel I was accusing her of doing something wrong. She'd had enough of that. After everyone else had left, I went up to her and said, "I was surprised by my grade."

"I was surprised by your enthusiasm for the minutiae of photosynthesis," she said. "It's not all that often a teacher can discover her lessons have made a lasting impact."

"I do like biology," I said.

"You earned that grade, Scott. You might have impressed me out there, at the board meeting, but you earned it in here, even if you aren't like your brother."

I couldn't think of a response beyond, "Huh?" How could it be bad that I wasn't like Bobby?

"I never had a more focused student," Ms. Denton said.

"Bobby?" I asked.

"Absolutely. He absorbed every word I said, never took his eyes off the board, and participated in the discussions. He had a knack for seeing how things connected. I'm sure he would have done great on the tests if he hadn't skipped school so much."

"That was sort of his hobby," I said. As surprised as I was by this, it made sense. Bobby was great with mechanical things. Biology wasn't all that different. Stuff connected and interacted. There were power sources and various means of converting energy into motion. Even so, not everyone could have held Bobby's interest. It looked like I'd spoken the truth when I'd told the board that Ms. Denton was an excellent teacher. "I'm glad there was one class he enjoyed."

"I enjoyed teaching him. I was so disappointed when you acted like such a slacker," she said.

"You can't blame me for throwing up," I said.

"I didn't. I blamed you for not paying attention. For not taking class seriously."

"That's not really who I am," I said.

"I've come to learn that," she said. "Although you have a hard time tearing your attention away from Lee."

"I'm working on that." This seemed like a good time to change the subject. I pointed at Splitten Kitten. "Why the shock treatment?"

"To discourage the unfit," she said. "In college, they do a brutal job of culling the herd of wannabe doctors who don't have the heart or mind for the role. I'm just starting the process early."

"That's pretty cold," I said.

"So is life." She shrugged. "Still, you're probably right. It's cold. But winter is over for you. Enjoy the grade. Work hard. Keep learning."

"Thanks. I will." I headed out.

"Did you talk yourself into failing?" Lee asked when I joined her in the hallway.

"Not this time," I said. "But I'm sure there will be plenty of other opportunities."

"That's just part of your charm, Scott."

"It's a Hudson thing," I said.

I headed off to Life Skills. Though I had a feeling I was learning the real life skills outside the classroom.

■ ■ ■

After school, I hunted down Mr. Kamber. I'd heard he was sub-bing in chemistry. There were still about ten kids in the room when I got there, staring at him from their seats as if, after an extended period of observation, they would suddenly be able to understand what he'd been talking about during the period. I waited by the door until the last of them gave up and left.

When I walked in, Mr. Kamber flashed me a smile of recognition and said, "Skaught Hadsen!" We'd crossed paths many times.

"Can I talk to you?" I asked.

"Roit," he said.

I took that for a yes. I pointed to my grade on the report card, where I'd been Kamber-clobbered. Then I pulled my last paper from my backpack and pointed to the grade on that. "You gave me great grades on my papers, and a terrible grade for the marking period."

"Smoren jessure pipers," he said.

"What?"

"Sherattitude anyer hievyur."

I could see it was pointless. Still, I couldn't part without saying, "It's not fair."

He grinned, slapped me on the shoulder, and said, "Nwarries, smite."

THIRTY-NINE

The mist above a trout stream on an April morning is like a whispered echo of the running water. It shifts shape slowly, fluidly, while mimicking the curves the creek has allowed the land to suggest. The sun will burn the mist off by midmorning, but the memory of it will linger in the rivers of the mind.

I love opening day.

Dad, Bobby, and I went farther afield than usual this year. Normally, we'd hit the Bushkill or the McMichaels. The former would be mobbed. The latter would be less crowded, but far from isolated.

We headed deep into the game lands, to a perfect fishing stretch along a branch of the Tobyhanna. You could only reach it by hiking a narrow trail for half an hour.

We got there well ahead of the legal time for the first cast. None of us fished yet. We could easily have done so. There were no wardens out here. But that was not the way Hudsons fished.

When the time came, we all cast together.

"No matter what happens, we have to always do this," Bobby said.

"Always," Dad said.

"Always," I said.

We caught fish. The number and size doesn't matter.

"Life is good," Dad said, late in the afternoon, as we pulled back into our driveway.

"Life is good," Bobby and I said.

April 18

Sean, I can picture the future. Someday, maybe in three or four years, there will be four Hudson guys on the stream bank on opening day. That will be nice. As long as you don't try to poach off my spot.

Things are starting to get busy here. The wedding is less than a month away. Mom and Amala are doing all sorts of things involving dresses, food, candles, flowers, and endless spools of ribbon. Amala's mom is here all the time. Or Mom is over there. Everyone consults with Dad once in a while. He pretty much tells them he's happy with whatever they decided, and then disappears into the garage. I've been relatively safe from it all, except I had to get fitted for a tux. Much to my surprise, it's a lot more comfortable than a suit. They make them stretchy so people in a range of sizes can rent the same one.

Bobby's bandmates are coming up a couple days

before the wedding. They're throwing him a bachelor party. I'm pretty sure that's not something I'll be invited to. Amala's friends already threw her a bridal shower. Needless to say, I wasn't at that celebration, either.

Zenger Zinger for April 21
Last week's answer: "I have my father's eyes," John Peter said inherently.
This week's puzzle: "My ballpoint pen melted and drooped into a semicircle," John Peter said _____.

Mrs. Gilroy didn't get to my paragraph until Wednesday, which also happened to be Earth Day, not that there was any connection between those two things. I had a copy of it with me. I followed along, reading mine silently as she read hers out loud to the class.

Unlike simians, metronomes, and other familial fixtures of screech, catachresis flails to stripe the ear in a peasant and euphoric way. Perhaps in fear that any exorcise utilizing this reportorial technique might encroach bad habits, the teacher delighted it from the list of permeable fixtures, forboding its use.

She'd frowned, briefly, before she started. But after that, I couldn't read her expression at all. When she was finished, she said, "Who can name the rhetorical technique this passage was meant to illustrate?"

There was a pause. Nobody seemed to have a clue, despite

the fact that I'd mentioned it. I guess the word was lost in the jumble of mistakes I'd pumped into the paragraph. Finally, Julia raised a tentative hand. "Isn't that the one you told us not to use? Cataleptic?"

"*Catachresis*," Mrs. Gilroy said. "You were close." She turned her attention to me. "How do you justify using the one figure of speech I told the class not to use, Mr. Hudson?"

"Because my paragraph is not an example of catachresis," I said.

I expected her to shoot me down, or shout me down, but she nodded, pointed to a spot on the floor in front of her desk, and said, "Please come up here and continue your explanation."

I took my place facing the class. "Catachresis is basically about breaking rules. Specifically, the rules of meaning. But there was a rule against using it. So, by using it, I broke a rule against using a figure of speech about breaking rules." I paused to savor the moment. I knew how Mr. Fowler must feel when he was arguing a case in front of a judge and jury. "Therefore, what we have is an example of . . ." I pointed to the class.

They responded with the correct answer: "Irony!"

"I rest my case."

To my surprise, Mrs. Gilroy said, "Very clever."

To my further surprise, I devoured this gift of praise.

To my furthest surprise, Mrs. Gilroy said, "However, in your attempt to create irony, you have created a problem for yourself."

It was her turn to pause, and to look at the class to see if anyone could fill in the blanks. After a moment of silence, she said, "If the central rhetorical concept of your paragraph is irony, then it isn't based on catachresis. Correct?"

"Right. I just said that."

"If it isn't based on catachresis, you haven't broken a rule against using catachresis. Correct?"

"Uh . . . wait . . ." I had a feeling I was being schooled. Then I saw where this was going, and realized there was no escape.

Mrs. Gilroy plunged the dagger into my paragraph. "If you haven't broken a rule by using an example of a method involving the breaking of rules, you haven't created irony."

It was my turn to say it. "Correct." I looked at the class. Some of them were following this. I could tell that Lee was. Mrs. Gilroy was waiting, as if there was one more step, and she expected me to discover it.

I let out a gasp as everything clicked. I had created a prison. But it was the most beautiful, elaborate, twisting prison imaginable, like a jailhouse drawn by Escher. "If it isn't irony, then we're back at it being catachresis, so I did break a rule, which means it *is* irony." I felt like I'd been hunting for a paper clip, and found a nugget of gold.

Mrs. Gilroy actually smiled. "We go around and around and around. If it is irony, then it isn't. If it isn't irony, then it is. Congratulations, Mr. Hudson. You've created a paradox. Who follows this?"

I raised my hand, along with about half my classmates.

"The rest of you, give it some thought. You'll see what's happening. Those of you who have grasped the nature of this paradox are to be congratulated on making your first baby step from sophomore to philosopher."

Yeah, I was gloating.

"Mr. Hudson's selection has a unique benefit," she told the class. She turned back to me. "Do you see it?"

I spoke my thoughts, trying to see where they led, beyond the looping paradox. "I wrote a paragraph filled with intentional mistakes—"

A motion distracted me. Richard punched his own shoulder, mouthed the word *sophomore*, and then pointed at me. I guessed he was planning to hit me later for *intentional mistakes*. I pulled my attention back to my explanation. "But even if I committed some accidental mistakes, you can't mark me down for them. Every mistake, accidental or intentional, is correct. All mistakes count as examples. So you have to give me a hundred."

"Unfortunately," Mrs. Gilroy said, "that is true. That is also a first for this year."

The class awarded me scattered applause for my achievement, tempered, I suspect, with a bit of envy. I walked past Richard on my way to my seat, so I could get the punch over with. After I sat down, and digested what had happened up there, I realized that this might explain why she'd banned catachresis. Maybe she'd hoped one of her students would see that as an opportunity.

On my way out of class, Mrs. Gilroy said, "Mr. Hudson . . ."

"Yes." I braced myself for the inevitable deflation.

"Well played."

"Thank you."

Since I'd wimped out as far as stage crew, I figured I could at least support the *Goodnight Moon* musical by being an audience member. Lee and I got tickets. I also got tickets for Wesley, Bobby, and Amala. Just like it felt strange to watch a Zenger football game that was being covered by other reporters, it was weird to watch the play from the audience.

Weird or not, the play was a lot of fun.

"Oon," Lee said as we were leaving.

"What?" I asked.

"Oon, just oon. Oon all day. Oon all night. Oon, always and forever. Oon eternal. Oon everlasting. Oonce oonpon a time."

I guess she had a point. The songs did lean heavily on the whole *moon* thing. But the cast did a great job with them.

Bobby and Amala headed home. Lee and I went out to the diner with Wesley.

"I liked the red balloon," Wesley said when we settled into a booth.

"Yeah. That was Edith. She really made you feel her balloonness."

"Oon . . . ," Lee said, pointing at her spoon.

"The chair was good, too," Wesley said.

"For sure."

"But not as good as the balloon."

"Agreed."

"Oon . . ." Lee had spotted a cartoon on the placemats.

I stopped listening. I knew she'd get tired of the game eventually. Of course, when Wesley dropped her off, I couldn't resist saying, "See you oon."

April 25

Sean, I think the year got away from me. There's less than a month and a half left for school, and I've pretty much dropped the ball on everything. I have more to say about this. I'll get back to you later today.

FORTY

I wake and eat and walk and board the bus and ride and disembark and start my day at school. In English, we might read or write or debate or listen. On this day we were introduced to *polysyndenton*. It struck me as a dangerously wordy technique, and one best used sparingly.

> **Zenger Zinger for April 28**
> **Last week's answer:** "My ballpoint pen melted and drooped into a semicircle," John Peter said ubiquitously.
> **This week's puzzle:** "I'm against plays where the performers have to scale the walls," John Peter said
> _____.

"It would be great to put out a color edition once in a while," Sarah said when we were wrapping up the meeting.

"We're lucky we can put out any edition," I said. "Maybe

there's another club we can resurrect. We could do a joint newsletter."

"Good idea." Jeremy went over to the laptop connected to the SMART Board and logged into his student account. Then he used the browser to pull up the budget from the district's web site.

"Well, this is fascinating," Richard said, "but numbers make my head hurt. I'll leave you math types to it." He got up and walked out.

There were a couple more scattered "me, too"s, which triggered a mass exodus.

"Looks like it's me and you," I said.

"That's all it will take," Jeremy said. "Hey, here's one." He pointed to a line on the display. "Future Farmers Club. I've never heard of that."

"Me neither."

We found eleven other clubs that didn't seem to exist anymore.

"Wow," I said. "All that money could have been used for things the school needs. What a waste."

"Hang on." Jeremy scrolled to a different section of the budget.

"Look at this," he said. He tapped a section labeled "prior-year surplus." "That's any unspent funds. See here? The Pep Club didn't use all their money last year. So it showed up as a surplus this year. Everything has to add up. For every dollar allocated, there has to be a dollar spent. That's how budgets work. But there's no surplus listed for the phantom clubs."

"So the money for the Latin Club—for all these clubs—was spent?" I asked. My scalp tingled as my brain caught up with what Jeremy was implying.

"Somebody spent it," he said.

I heard the janitor rolling his mop and bucket down the hall. They'd be kicking us out soon. "Let's finish this at my place," I said.

"Do you have good Internet access?" he asked.

"Not really. It's okay."

"We'll go to my place." He pulled out his phone and called home for a ride.

I was enough of a reporter to know we were on to something big. There was a small chance we could find an honest explanation for the missing money. But there was a lot larger chance that someone had been stealing the money that was allocated for all the clubs that no longer existed.

As we rode in the backseat of Jeremy's mom's car, I remembered what had happened when I'd been called to the principal's office. Mr. Sherman had not looked at all happy about having me revive the Latin Club. But he also looked like he didn't want to protest too loudly. I guessed, if he was involved with all of this, he didn't want to risk me finding out exactly what Jeremy and I had just found out. He knew that if I got the funds, I'd go away happy, and never give it another thought.

"This could be a real scandal," I said.

"Definitely," Jeremy said. "I feel like Woodward and Bernstein."

"Both of them?" I asked. Those were the reporters who had discovered the Watergate scandal back in the 1970s that brought down President Nixon.

"No. You can be one."

"How about Hudson and Danger?" I asked.

"That sounds even cooler."

When we reached his house, Jeremy set up two laptops, then downloaded the school budgets for the past fifteen years to one of them.

"That seems like a lot," I said.

"We need to find out when the embezzlement started," he said. "And we need to see when the inactive clubs were eliminated."

"We could check yearbooks," I said.

"That might be tough," Jeremy said. "I'm not sure they're searchable."

"What about the local paper?" I said. "Most clubs get mentioned once in a while. I can search by year, to see when each club stopped being active?"

"Great idea."

We got to work. Jeremy pulled a list of all clubs from the budget and printed it out for me. I searched the newspaper, crossed off the clubs that were still active, and noted the years the other clubs had stopped meeting.

"The oldest budget I grabbed is legitimate," Jeremy said. "The clubs are all real. And the money left over by three of them was accounted for in the budget for the next year."

"So, no crimes happened that year."

"Right. Let's move on."

The next several budgets were fine, too. Then, midway through the batch, Jeremy said, "Found one! Eight years ago, there was no active Latin Club. But there was a budget for it."

"How could that happen?" I asked.

"People are lazy," he said. "They try to do as little work as possible. Maybe nobody on the board even knew the club was gone. Either way, at the end of the year, someone should have noticed that none of the money allocated for the Latin Club was ever spent."

"I think somebody *did* notice," I said. "And they decided to take advantage of it."

"For sure." Jeremy pointed to the list. "Look at this. One club wasn't enough. Somebody got greedy. Three clubs were eliminated the next year. But they weren't removed from the budget."

He checked through the rest of the budgets. All together, the misused money rose close to six figures.

Terror and excitement can feel pretty similar. I think they were wrestling in my stomach for control. "This really is huge," I said.

"Enormous."

"Who do we tell?" I asked. "The police?"

"They won't listen to us," Jeremy said. "We're just kids."

"Lee's dad is a lawyer," I said. "We could give all of this to him." I looked at my watch. "He won't be home yet. He works late a lot."

"Stay for dinner," Jeremy said. "My folks will drive us over after that."

I called my parents to let them know I was under the supervision of responsible adults. After dinner, Jeremy's dad drove us across town to Lee's house.

When we got there, he pulled to the curb and turned on the ball game on the radio. "Take your time."

Lee's mom answered the door.

"Hi, Scott. Lee's up in her room," she said.

"Actually, we came to see Mr. Fowler."

She hid her surprise well, and led us into the living room.

"I think we uncovered a major crime," I said.

He hid his surprise well, too. After Jeremy had gone over the evidence, Mr. Fowler said, "This is serious. And you were smart to bring it to me. With local issues, there's no way to know who might be involved. I'll take it to the state district attorney. He has forensic accountants who can analyze all of this."

Jeremy turned to leave.

"I'll catch up with you in a minute," I said.

After he headed out, I checked to make sure Lee hadn't come out of her room. The thump of music pulsing through her closed door removed any fear my words would be overheard.

"I need advice," I told Mr. Fowler.

"Shoot," he said.

"Actually, before I started, I was going to make you promise not to shoot," I said.

"Are we specifically talking about firearms, or are you including archery and slingshots?" he asked.

"All of those. And trebuchets," I said, naming my favorite type of catapult.

"You actually know what those are?" he asked.

"Doesn't everyone?"

"Sadly, no. Although, were one of those involved, I'd be more likely to shoot you *from* it than *with* it. That would greatly increase the chance of satisfying results. What's your question?"

"I like Lee." I paused to let that sink in.

"I was not unaware of that," he said.

"*Litotes*," I said.

"What?"

"Litotes. A figure of speech where an opposite is negated. *Not unaware*. Saying more by saying less. Sorry. Bad habit. I've been force-fed a lot of this. A little learning. Dangerous thing. But, yes, I'm not surprised that you are not unaware. Parents tend to know more than kids realize. Very observant of you."

"You're babbling," Mr. Fowler said. "And I know the definition of *litotes*. I was just surprised to have a rhetorical term pop up in the middle of what started out as a serious discussion of adolescent angst and indecision."

Good grief. He was right. I was turning into Mouth, right before my own ears. And I was sweating. And feeling cold. And dizzy. And hot. And shivery.

"Say it," Mr. Fowler said.

"I want to ask her out," I said. "But I have no idea how she'll react to anything."

"That sounds about right," he said. He seemed to be enjoying my discomfort.

"Look, can you give me any advice?"

"You're seeking advice on asking Lee out from the one person on the planet who doesn't want her to date?" he asked.

"It seemed like a good idea." I tried to remember how to breathe. He was playing me like I was a half-pound sunfish on a ten-pound line. He could keep letting me run and reeling me in all day. Or like a heavyweight boxer going ten rounds against a toddler. Or like—oh, hell. Now my brain was babbling thoughts worse than my mouth had babbled words.

From the side, Mrs. Fowler spoke. "Lawrence, the quality of mercy . . . ," she said. "Help the kid out."

"Okay," he said to her.

If I'd known quoting Shakespeare would do the trick, I'd have already been back in Jeremy's car. I gave Mr. Fowler my full attention.

"Be honest," he said.

I waited. He didn't expand on his statement. I was reminded of a crucial moment in *The Hitchhiker's Guide to the*

Galaxy, when the computer spits out a long-awaited answer.

"That's it? 'Be honest?'"

"That's it. Whatever else is perplexing or unpredictable about Lee, however cryptic she might be when the stakes are low, she values honesty. I'd like to think that, perhaps, this is something she learned from her parents. Maybe so. Maybe not. Either way, that's really all I can tell you. Other than a gentle reminder not to hurt her. But we've already covered that."

"Yes, we have. Uh, thanks for the advice."

"Are you planning to follow it?"

"I don't know."

"Well, that was an honest answer. Good start."

FORTY-ONE

I heard you stopped by the house last night," Lee said when I got to geometry. "You could have said hi."

"There were parents waiting in the car," I said. I explained what Jeremy and I had discovered. "Your father seemed like the best person to give it to."

"He was," Lee said. "He might help people turn rivers into sewers, but he's honest."

"Honesty is a good quality in a river sewer man." I pictured Lee's dad with a Mark Twain kind of mustache in a Mark Twain kind of scene with white coats, riverboats, rafts, and very muddy water filled with small brown bobbing objects. "It would be a good quality in a school board member, too."

"It will be interesting to watch this evolve," Lee said.

"*Paronomasia* intended?" I asked.

"Intended and savored," Lee said.

My success with the catachresis paragraph, and a consequent easing of hostilities between Mrs. Gilroy and me, had given me the courage to ask her something that had been on my mind ever since curiosity and ambition had driven me to look up a ton of rhetorical terms, well beyond the forty-seven figures of speech she'd listed on the board.

"Wish me luck," I whispered to Lee.

"Good luck."

"If I die, you can have my slot cars."

"Yippee."

"Here goes . . . ,"

I raised my hand, interrupting our discussion of ellipsis. When Mrs. Gilroy called on me, I pointed at the terms on the board and said, "It's a mess."

"Can you elaborate on that, Mr. Hudson?" she asked. "A pronoun in an isolated sentence is generally not very informative. *What* is a mess?"

"The figures of speech are a mess. There are terms all over the place with overlapping meanings," I said. "And some terms have different definitions, depending on where you look. I picked up a book at the used bookstore. Some of the definitions are totally different from the ones I've seen elsewhere."

To my surprise, she nodded in agreement. "All of this is true. The Romans adapted from the Greeks. The medieval scholars took their turn, followed by centuries of university professors. Even people who tried to reclassify everything couldn't resist leaving the old terms in place. On top of that, in part with thanks to our friends the ancient Greeks, the same terms appear with different meanings in other fields. In philosophy, a *tautology* is a statement that is self-evidently true. *Hypothera* is a rhetorical term, and also an obsolete word for part of an insect wing. *Meiosis* is understated irony, and a type of cell division. Rhetoric is a mess, a stew, a hodgepodge," she said. She wrote that sentence on the board:

Rhetoric is a mess, a stew, a hodgepodge.

"Class, what do we have here?"

"Tautology, maybe?" I said. That was easy. She'd tagged it with three similar terms.

Mrs. Gilroy wrote that word on the board, including my question mark. "Yes. What else?"

"*Stew* is used as a metaphor," Julia said.

Mrs. Gilroy added that to the list. "What else?"

"*Hodgepodge* has assonance and consonance," Lee said. "And it rhymes."

"I wonder whether there's a term for internal rhyme," I said.

"Don't just wonder and wait for an answer," Mrs. Gilroy said. "Research and investigate." She tapped the words on the board. "All of your answers are correct. There's also a literary allusion. My phrase owes a debt to the marvelous and well-known opening of a work you probably haven't read yet: *Cannery Row*. Mr. Hudson is correct when he points out that the study of figurative language is a mess. Every one of you has now looked at this simple sentence as carefully as a surgeon studies a heart he is repairing. You haven't just read it or heard it; you've grasped it. Rhetoric is a mess, but it is our mess."

...

May 5

Sean, I just wrote "nice benefit" in an essay. But I've been more aware of Latin ever since we formed the club. And benefit has <u>bene</u> as a root. I'm pretty sure bene means good. So I suspect nice benefit might be redundant. The problem is, I often want to add words that way when I'm writing. To my ear, benefit by itself feels undressed. I wonder whether that means my ear needs more tuning. On the other hand, you could use nice benefit for irony if you got something you didn't want. Like, "Gee, Mr. Cravutto, rope burns are a nice benefit of playing tug-of-war." I always thought irony meant when something happens that smacks you in the face or goes completely opposite from the way you'd planned. Like pretty much everything I did freshman year. And it does mean that. But it also means sarcastically saying the opposite of what you mean.

That's enough for now, you charming and eloquent little bundle of bowel and bladder control.

Zenger Zinger for May 5
Last week's answer: "I'm against plays where the

performers have to scale the walls," John Peter said anticlimactically.

This week's puzzle: "Well-mannered men love word-play," John Peter said _____.

Wednesday at the newspaper meeting, Jeremy and I strutted out our discovery.

"That's big," Sarah said.

"If it's true," Mr. Franka said.

"Do you think it isn't?" I asked.

"I think it is *probably* true. Maybe even very likely. We won't know until after the experts investigate the flow of the funds, and the legal system makes a judgment. We can never act before the fact." He paused and frowned, as if he'd noticed the unintended rhyme. "If we call suspects criminals before they're convicted, we've committed a crime ourselves. What's our best friend when discussing crime?"

We all shouted the answer to that question. "'Alleged'!"

"Scott Hudson, please report to the office."

Now what? It was the middle of second period on Thursday, and I had no idea why I'd been called down. Dad was waiting there for me. Before I could even speculate about some disaster, he said, "Your mom forgot to tell you she made a doctor's appointment for you." He shot me a wink with the eye that wasn't facing the school secretary.

I followed him out. "There's no appointment, is there?'"

"No. But we're giving Bobby a bachelor party, and we didn't want you to miss out."

Now I was really puzzled. Dad led me around the corner, out of sight of the school office windows, to a van from a local roofing contractor. Wesley was at the wheel.

"New job?" I asked.

"No. We just needed room for all the passengers. I borrowed this from a friend."

I looked inside. Bobby was there, along with his bandmates, Wayne and Charlie. I gave him a quizzical look. He responded, "No clue."

I got in, and Wesley took off. Wherever we were going, I was pretty sure it didn't involve kegs of beer, cigars, or adult entertainment.

We went up Route 33 toward the Poconos, and cut off toward Saylorsburg. Eventually, we left familiar roads. After several miles, Wesley drove through a wooden gate and followed a dirt road.

"Whoa!" I said when we stopped.

I was not alone in my exclamation.

"It's a racetrack," I said.

"Private," Wesley said. "One of my dad's friends owns it."

"The guy with the Ferrari?" I asked.

Wesley shook his head. "He's not talking to my dad right now. Or to me. He ran out of gas on the way home."

"I can see where that might have annoyed him," I said.

"At least the car was clean," Wesley said. "This is another guy. We've known him for years."

We got out and walked over to an old man wearing a bright yellow suit and a cowboy hat. He was standing by a car.

A car.

Those words are so inadequate for encompassing what we faced. It's like calling a hot-fudge and vanilla ice-cream sundae on a brownie "a sweet." Maybe *The Car* would be better. Maybe primal grunts and screeches would be the best of all. The Car was a Lamborghini Gallardo. I don't know cars the way Dad and Bobby do. I'm clueless about the mechanical parts. But I knew this car from video games. I never thought I'd be standing next to one.

Wesley introduced us to the man, who told us to call him Stumpy. He had a wide smile, a Texas accent, and a firm handshake. I did not speculate on the origin of the nickname.

"Who's first?" Stumpy asked.

Bobby, being the bachelor, had the honors.

Stumpy drove him around the track for several laps. Then they switched seats and Bobby drove. Dad took a photo of Bobby's face when he stepped out. He looked like he'd seen all seven wonders of the ancient world laid out before him.

Dad went next. Then Wayne. Then Charlie. Then Wesley. Then Stumpy looked at me and said, "Climb in, sport."

It was my turn to see seventeen or so wonders.

And then, after Stumpy took me around the track . . . they let me drive. Yeah. I had to keep it slow. But in a Lamborghini, even *slow* is still pretty awesome.

Bobby took another turn.

After he got out, he and Dad looked at each other. Some form of communication happened, but I was clueless.

"Can you pop the hood?" Dad asked Stumpy.

"Sure. Just be careful with the groom. A guy about to get married shouldn't let his eyes enjoy anything this hot for too long." He let out a guffaw.

Dad and Bobby studied the idling engine for about two seconds, then nodded.

"Alternator belt's slightly too tight," Dad said. "It's putting more strain than necessary on the engine."

Stumpy stared at Dad for a moment. Then he stared at the engine. "By gosh, I hear it now. Didn't notice it at all until you pointed it out." He slapped Dad on the back. "Thanks."

"Got tools here?" Dad asked.

"Has a kitten got whiskers?" Stumpy said.

"Trust us to adjust it?" Dad asked.

Stumpy slipped behind the wheel and switched off the ignition. "Be my guest."

We had the rehearsal dinner on Friday, just for the families and the wedding party. I was part of both since Bobby had asked me to be an usher. I kept telling people my name was Roderick, and I kept getting puzzled glances, except from Amala, who'd read the Poe story to which I was alluding. Her father wasn't quite as scary as Bobby said, but I'd definitely never want to end up on his bad side.

It was nice getting together with everyone. Amala's bridesmaids flirted with me. I could tell they were just having fun. That didn't diminish my pleasure.

Saturday, we went to the church early to get ready.

After Bobby got dressed, I said, "Thanks."

"What for?"

"For getting me a sister."

He smiled. "Got you a good one, didn't I?"

"The best."

I watched him fiddle with a cuff link. "Nervous?"

"Terrified."

"You don't look it," I said.

"What if I screw this up?" he said.

"You won't."

"I've screwed almost everything up in my life."

"If you're half as good a husband as you are a brother, you'll have the best marriage ever," I said. "Next to Mom and Dad's."

Instead of saying anything, Bobby gave me a hug.

■ ■ ■

May 10

The wedding yesterday was great, Sean. Amala was beautiful. Bobby looked like a dashing hero. Mom and Dad cried. I didn't. At least, not where anyone could see. After the reception, the happily married couple drove off for a honeymoon at a bed and breakfast in North Carolina. It didn't look like there was much to do around the place, but Bobby and Amala didn't seem to be concerned by that.

There was no honeymoon from school for me. I was back at it on Monday. Ms. Burke managed to fit one of her favorite poems into the history lesson, and Mr. Stockman tossed out a limerick in geometry. We studied a Langston Hughes poem in English, and a Pablo Neruda poem in Spanish class. I guess you could call it a day of rhyme and reason.

And I guess poetry was still on my mind on Tuesday, in the locker room after gym, when I asked Kyle, "Did you ever think about writing poems? It's a wonderful way to explore your feelings."

"Did you ever think about mating with a pencil sharpener?" he asked. "It's a wonderful way to experience new feelings."

"Yeah. But they always insist that I take them out for dinner and a movie first," I said.

He actually smiled at that. "It's getting harder to insult you."

"That's one of the many benefits of humility," I said. "I excel at being humble and modest."

Irony is enhanced by subtle use of tautology.

Zenger Zinger for May 12
Last week's answer: "Well-mannered men love word-play," John Peter said pungently.
This week's puzzle: "I lost my favorite board game," John Peter said _____.

A week after we shared the news about the budget, everyone on the paper wanted to know what was happening with the investigation.

"My friend said her dad had given all the information to the district attorney, and someone in his office is investigating," I said. "It could take days, or weeks, for something to happen. It could even take months."

It turned out it took only one more day.

FORTY-TWO

Thursday morning, I glanced in passing at the newspaper on the kitchen table. I was halfway to the fridge when the headline sank in and yanked me back. "School Board Member Arrested for Embezzling Funds." Beneath that, in the subhead, as we journalists call it, I read, "Long-time school board member and relative in business office implicated in nearly decade-long fraud."

I read the story. Mr. Sherman had been arrested, along with his sister, who worked in the school's business office and was able to help transfer the money. Nobody else was involved. The district attorney was charging them with embezzling funds in a scheme that dated back eight years. He was also seeking full restitution for the large sum that had been stolen. That was great. Maybe the school would get some of the money back. There was even a mention near the end about how the crime had been discovered by two high school students.

My phone rang.

"See the paper?" Lee asked.

"Yup. Just now."

"You're a hero," she said.

"Not really." But I did sort of feel heroic. And I realized I had finally found my feature story. How wonderful that the tale of an embezzlement that began with the Latin Club would soon appear in the Latin Club newsletter.

"We should do something to celebrate," Lee said.

"Sure. Hey, tell your dad I said thanks."

"If I have to . . ."

After I hung up, I wondered whether mentioning a celebration was her way of getting me to ask her out. Probably not.

I thought about the stuff Lee and I did. Was it all just friends hanging around together or could some of it be considered boyfriend/girlfriend stuff? I didn't mean kissing or hand-holding. I meant the activities themselves. What did I do with my friends? What would I do differently if Lee and I were dating? There'd be school dances, I guess. But they didn't come around all that often. Long walks? We already walked places. Movies? We did that. Usually with Wesley. It looked like dating wasn't about what you did, but how you felt about what you did.

No. That was nonsense. Dating was when the evening ended with a kiss. Not a high five or a pat on the back. Not a peck on the cheek, but a kiss on the lips. A lingering kiss. I had no idea how to make that transition. I guessed I could just kiss her, at the right moment. Even the thought of that excited me. But if I tried to kiss her and that wasn't what she wanted, it would definitely hurt our friendship. Maybe even kill it.

I looked back at all the missed signals and mixed messages I'd experienced this year. I couldn't believe I'd assumed the Poe book was an anniversary gift commemorating the first time Lee and I had set eyes on each other.

Anniversary!

There was another anniversary Lee and I had. Unlike our first meeting, this anniversary was significant and memorable. Last year, we'd gone to the final school dance. I could ask her to the dance again. She'd go for that. It would be like we were reliving an amazing day. Better yet, the actual date of last year's dance was also Sean's birthday. This year, his birthday was on Saturday. The dance was the Friday after that. So I could ask her to an anniversary dance on the actual anniversary of our first dance. That was the sort of resonance she'd find pleasing.

The phone rang again that evening. I was on the couch, recovering from my AP U.S. History test. But I managed to find the strength to answer the call. The guy on the other end asked for Dad.

"Who's calling?" I asked.

"Fred Regent from Regent Commercial Properties," he said.

It sounded like some kind of sales call, but I figured Dad didn't need my help to get rid of the guy. He was very good at telling people that he didn't want a quote for life insurance, a better credit-card interest rate, or an exciting time-share vacation opportunity.

"For you," I said, handing Dad the phone. "Fred . . . Reagan?"

"Regent?"

"Yeah."

He snatched the phone from my hand. "Thanks."

As I walked away, I heard him say, "Back on the market? Really . . . ?"

There was an edge of excitement in his voice. I turned around and listened to the rest. "I'd love to. More than anything. It's a perfect spot for me. But I don't know if I can get the financing." The excitement dropped. "Can you give me a couple days to think about it?"

"The garage?" I asked after he'd hung up.

"Yeah. The current owner has to sell it. That guy from the school board. He's facing lots of legal bills. And probably some huge fines. So it's going on the market at a big discount."

"Big enough?" I asked.

"No. It's still out of reach."

"What about a partner?" I asked.

"I can't think of anyone," Dad said. "Mr. Bartock is getting back on his feet, but he's in no shape to finance a business. Nobody else I know has a pile of extra cash sitting around."

"I wish the whole thing hadn't fallen apart," I said.

"I know." Dad put a hand on my shoulder. "It will happen when it happens. Meanwhile, we carry on. Speaking of which, come out with me. I need a hand adjusting the rear axle."

I followed Dad into the garage. There had to be some way I could help him get the money he needed. He deserved to see his dream come true. I thought about it all evening. I didn't see a solution, but I saw a better way to look for one.

It is a fascinating fact, known to few, that the lyrics to the happy birthday song are protected by copyright. Jeremy and I were discussing that fascinating fact immediately after we two fact-holders, along with my family and assorted friends, sung those very words that can't be put in print without paying a fee, and watched Mom help Sean blow out his candles. She provided the air. He provided a thin stream of spittle, which only sullied a small portion of the cake.

I hadn't slept much. I'd spent most of last night thinking about my failed attempts to ask Lee out, and trying to figure out why it was so hard. I'd finally decided I'd walk her home after the party, and just take the plunge.

Lee was her usual self, holding intense conversations with Sean and snapping photos of everyone. She had no idea I had so much on my mind. On top of the dance, I had something devious I needed to avoid signaling or giving away. Not to Lee, but to Dad. I'd crafted a plan and would soon spring it, with Wesley's help.

It felt a bit strange to have Kyle there, like we'd warped back to eighth grade. But I'd invited him for a reason. I was surprised, and pleased, that he'd showed up.

Right after we ate our cake, along with the ice cream that had served as its essential companion, and watched Sean open his presents (with Mom providing most of the ripping and Sean providing a slightly more impressive stream of drool, along with squeals of delight), the alarm on Mom's car went off in the garage.

"I got it," Dad said.

"Need help?" I asked. I flinched. That definitely was out of character for me. But Dad didn't seem to notice.

"I'll give a yell if I do." He grabbed the keys from the hook by the door and disappeared into the garage.

"Okay, everyone," I said. "We don't have a lot of time."

"Sure we do," Wesley said. He pulled Mom's extra set of car keys, with its electronic panic button, halfway out of his shirt pocket, flashed me a grin, then slid the keys back.

"Even so, we should get started," I said. That was my plan. I figured if all of us put our heads together, we could think up a way for Dad to buy the garage. I heard the alarm stop. But I knew Dad would look all around the car, and the garage, to see what had triggered it. And then maybe he'd clean some tools or gap some spark plugs, because Dad likes to take breaks and savor some solitude when there are a lot of people around.

Everyone started tossing out ideas. It was a great mix. Mom

was practical. Wesley was outrageous in his ability to think big. Bobby was pretty smart about garage details. Amala knew all about business. Jeremy was full of all sorts of knowledge. Kyle had grown up around investors. And Lee had a talent for seeing things from unique perspectives.

About five minutes later, Dad walked in from the garage. "I checked all over. I can't find a reason for—"

He was interrupted by the alarm. He let out the mildest of swear words, and headed back to the garage. I noticed Wesley had his fingers pressed against his shirt pocket.

We resumed brainstorming. Dad was away for ten minutes this time.

During the third session, which lasted twenty minutes, we struck gold.

"Limited partnership," Kyle said.

He spoke so quietly, I wasn't sure whether he was making a suggestion or just talking to himself.

"Yeah!" Jeremy said. "Good thinking. That's not a bad idea."

"What is it?" I asked.

Kyle looked over at Jeremy. "Go ahead."

"No," Jeremy said. "I barely know the basic concept. You explain it."

Kyle seemed a little uncomfortable about being the center of attention. "A limited partnership is like a company with a lot of owners."

"Sounds like too many cooks," Mom said.

"And too many bosses," Wesley said.

"No. That's the thing," Kyle said. "It's a *lot* of owners, so nobody has a big share, except for the person in charge. And in most LLPs, the partners have no say at all about the business itself."

"LLP?" I asked.

"Limited liability partnership," Jeremy said.

"So we'd have to find a lot of people to chip in," Bobby said.

"Invest," Amala said. "*Chip in* makes it sound like a poker game."

They exchanged smiles. Bobby didn't seem to mind that she'd corrected him.

"Half the companies I've worked for would probably want to invest," Wesley said. "Especially if investors got a discount at the garage."

"That's a wonderful incentive," Amala said.

"And I'll bet the exotic car guys would love to have access to Dad's skills," Bobby said.

"That's a great idea," I said. I pictured Dad working on tractors, septic trucks, and Lamborghinis. "It would also help guarantee a lot of customers."

This was getting exciting.

"These partnerships can be tricky to set up," Amala said. "You need someone with a business law background. Those folks can be very expensive."

I could feel the excitement level in the room drop several

degrees. The deal would never leave the ground if it took a lot of money to get started. "Wait," I said. "That could be a sort of partnership, too."

I pointed at Lee. "Law." Then I pointed at Kyle. "Business." Then I pointed at both of them. "Could your dads work together on this? Maybe for a share of the partnership?"

Lee and Kyle looked at each other.

"Sure," Lee said.

"I don't see why not," Kyle said.

"We can't tell Dad until we know it's happening for real," Bobby said. "We don't want him disappointed again."

A few minutes later, Dad came back in. This time, as he stood in the middle of the living room, staring toward the garage as if waiting for the fourth shoe to drop, Wesley said, "Oops. Look what I was sitting on." He reached behind himself and plucked the keys from the couch cushion. "Sorry, Mr. Hudson."

"That's okay, Wesley. It gave me an excuse to toss out some stuff I'd been meaning to get rid of. And I reorganized my socket sets. Come check it out."

Dad headed back to the garage, along with Wesley and Bobby. It looked like the party was winding down. But I'd accomplished the first of two goals on my list.

So much for the easy one.

"Isn't there something called *cake makeup*?" I asked Lee.

She joined me in admiring the way Sean had managed to

apply a huge quantity of birthday icing to his face. "I think it's *pancake makeup*," she said.

"It's not just for breakfast anymore," I said. "Walk you home?"

"Sure."

We left the house, strolling side by side. This was it. I was going to ask her to the dance. There were no interruptions or distractions. No school bells. Words from people whose advice I'd sought, and images of their faces as they spoke, floated through my head like flashbacks in a movie.

Amala . . . shyness is real . . .

Wesley . . . so ask her out . . .

Mr. Cravutto . . . women are scary, but loneliness is scarier . . .

Mr. Fowler . . . she values honesty . . .

Dad . . . I needed her in my life . . .

I promised myself I'd ask Lee to the dance before we reached the midpoint of our walk, which was roughly at the corner of Locust Avenue and Bayard Street.

I wavered between *Would you like to go to the dance?* and *Let's go to the dance.* The question allowed for rejection. The imperative sounded a bit bossy. Maybe there was some middle ground.

"Happy anniversary," Lee said.

There goes my train of thought, Scott said to himself distractedly.

Lee must have misread my expression for confusion,

384

because she added, "We went to the dance exactly a year ago. So Sean's birthday is our anniversary. Remember?"

"Vaguely. I have fuzzy memories of racing from the cops in a limo and facing down a bully in the gym. There might also have been a birth that drastically altered my family's dynamics. Is that particular May 17 the anniversary date to which you refer?"

"That's the one," Lee said. "And I have bad news."

"What?"

"I didn't get you anything."

"Thus making reciprocity a piece of cake," I said.

"Cake is always appreciated." Lee laughed. "Hey, I have an idea. Let's go to the dance."

Just like that, she'd asked me. Or suggested. Or something. Good enough, for now. Part of me realized I'd just slipped off the hook. But all of me realized I had a date with Lee for the dance.

"Well?" Lee asked.

"Sure. But no cops or babies."

"What about baby cops?"

"That's fine. I think we can outrun them," I said.

Zenger Zinger for May 19
Last week's answer: "I lost my favorite board game," John Peter said cluelessly.
This week's puzzle: "They took away the knight's title," John Peter said _____.

385

FORTY-THREE

Bobby dropped us off at the school. That was my crafty way of avoiding parental involvement.

"You sure you don't need a ride home?" he asked.

"Nope. I've got that covered." I'd arranged for Wesley to pick us up after the dance.

"This feels a lot different from last year," Lee said.

"Back then, we were fresh," I said. "Now, we're smart and stupid." I looked at the familiar trappings of a school dance. Nothing within the gymnasium had changed. The snack table, the couples and the clusters of single kids, the decorations—it could have been any year at any school in any town in America. But we'd changed.

We danced several fast dances. Lee didn't seem to mind that I was at about the same skill level as Sean. Except that I didn't frequently fall down. They played a slow song. I held out my hands. She held out hers. We stepped toward each other and danced.

"I like this," I said. Her body felt as if it belonged within my embrace.

"You're supposed to." Her own embrace tightened. "I like it, too."

As we danced, I couldn't help thinking about the year I'd wasted. How many slow dances had I missed because I hadn't found the courage to ask her out? How much easier would this school year have been if I hadn't walked through the doors of Zenger High with an overabundance of arrogance?

The dance ended.

"What are you thinking about?" Lee asked as we stepped apart.

"I was pretty much a nonstop bungler this year," I said.

"True. But you provided a lot of entertainment for the rest of us."

"Then it was worth it, I guess." I spotted Jeremy, standing by himself. He was staring across the gym at a group of girls seated on chairs along one wall.

I consulted with Lee as we walked over to Jeremy, then pointed at a girl in a knee-length skirt, whose expression seemed to show she'd accepted the sad truth that spectating would probably be the highlight of her evening.

"Ask her," I told him. "The one with the ponytail."

"Really?"

"Yeah. She wants to dance," Lee said.

"What if she says no?" Jeremy asked.

"Ninjas will leap from the walls, slice you open, and hang you from the ceiling by your intestines, causing unimaginable pain and unbearable regret," I said. "But it's worth the risk."

"If you say so."

Lee and I watched Jeremy cross the gym.

"This is more exciting than football," she said.

"That's because the risk of injury is greater," I said.

"He's doing it!" Lee said.

"Score!" I shouted.

"No, Scott," Lee said. "Don't take the metaphor there."

"Sorry."

We danced some more. We talked. We mingled with friends and classmates. We'd become a couple.

"That was definitely a lot more low-key and uneventful than last year," I said as we headed out to meet Wesley.

"Are you disappointed?" Lee asked.

"Not at all."

She took my arm. "Low key is nice sometimes."

"It is," I said. "But so are surprises."

"What do you mean?"

"You'll see."

I smiled as I pictured her reaction when she discovered Wesley's new job.

"You think of all my needs," she said a moment later, as he pulled up to the curb in an ice-cream truck.

"I try."

...

May 22

Good things happened, Sean. I'm not sure I want
to recount the magic of the dance here. Maybe I'll
write a poem. Or carve a mountaintop.

Memorial Day weekend followed the dance. Once again, I
went with my family to Lee's place for a cookout of epic proportions. And portions.

"Lee's changing," Mr. Fowler said when I walked over to
him at his Vulcanlike place of power. He pointed toward the
house with a massive two-tined fork.

"I doubt it," I said.

He almost smiled at the joke.

"How's the toad case going?" I asked him.

"It's over," he said.

That surprised me. I'd gotten the impression it would
drag on for months. I wondered how the trial went. I couldn't
read anything from his expression. "Did you win?"

"No."

"Sorry you lost," I said.

"I didn't lose," he said.

Okay, now I was wondering whether I had no understanding
whatsoever of our legal system. "What do you mean?"

"The owner got an offer to sell the company to an overseas

competitor in Malaysia that is working on a less ecological but more profitable battery. They bought all the patents so they could bury the technology. The plant's already been closed."

"What about the employees?" I asked.

"I doubt they'll want to transfer overseas, even if they were offered jobs."

"So, pretty much the only ones who made out okay are the owner and the toad."

"That's one way to put it," he said. "The owner would have preferred not to sell. But the penalty if he lost the case would have ruined him. I made out well, too. Although I would have preferred to win the case."

"How primal," Lee said as she walked up next to me. "Men and fire." She wore her compromise clothing, devoid of dark images, but the sculpin was fastened to the collar of her shirt.

"Hi." I put my arm around her shoulders. It was a casual move I'd rehearsed in my mind a thousand times. It took a major gut check on my part to actually go through with it, but I wanted to let Mr. Fowler know some things *had* changed.

"Hi," Lee said, reciprocating my show of affection with a non-mandatory but highly supportive arm across my back.

I stared at Mr. Fowler. He stared back and hefted the deadly fork. After a moment, he said, "Be careful." It wasn't exactly a congratulatory expression, but at least he hadn't tossed out any reminders of the threat of destruction.

"I will."

Lee and I walked across the lawn, toward a bench.

"He likes you," she said. "Usually he stabs boys who touch me."

I pushed away the flickers of jealousy her words had evoked, and reminded myself that she was kidding. "How many dozens of stabbings have there been?"

"Dozens? Hardly. At last count, it was hundreds," she said. "Half the backyard is reserved for shallow graves."

"All well-deserved," I said.

I glanced over my shoulder. Mr. Fowler had turned his attention back to the grill. That was good. He'd accepted things. Not that he would stop challenging me and testing me. But Lee deserved a boyfriend who could face those challenges and tests. Later, when we sat down to eat, Mrs. Fowler smiled at me.

Just as the dance felt different, so did the cookout. I hadn't realized how heavily the weight of wanting to ask Lee out had pressed on me all through last summer and the school year. I guess I hadn't been so much a basket case as an *ask-it!* case.

That evening, after the guests had left, we found ourselves once again on the front steps, just like way back on Labor Day. Well, not exactly like then.

I started telling Lee my regrets about the school year. "I should have worked harder. I should have paid more attention in class. I totally wrecked my English grade. I slacked off all over the place. Even in history, I skated through a lot of the assignments once I saw Ms. Burke liked anything I wrote. I failed miserably on the newspaper. I blew off stage crew. I didn't run for office. I failed to write a novel, and I failed to write a bad opening. And when I actually carried through with a plan and did something, it was my horribly bad idea for a satire. I screwed up from top to bottom."

"Scott," Lee said, putting a hand on my shoulder, "I never thought I'd say this to anyone . . ."

"Yes." I held my breath and wondered what her words would be.

"You think too much," Lee said.

"What?"

"You're smart. Very smart. And creative. But not everything needs to be analyzed and thought through. Not everything has to be viewed as a major thread in the plotline of a gigantic novel called *The Life of Scott Hudson*. Sometimes, you just have to act. You have to live in the moment. You just have to *be*."

As I tried to think up a response, Lee put her hand behind my head, pulled me forward, and kissed me. It was a long kiss. A wonderful kiss. To describe it at any greater length, or in any greater detail, would be to kiss and tell. And that's against my code.

"That was a nice surprise," I said.

"For both of us," Lee said. "I think I liked that."

"We'd better make sure." It was my turn to initiate a kiss.

Later, lazing in the afterglow of tender moments, I laughed as a thought hit me.

"What?" Lee asked. She stroked my cheek. That, too, felt perfect.

"I just realized something," I said.

"Go on," she said.

"It's a good one, but the first part isn't totally accurate. Still, I like the sound of it, though I'm not sure how it would be classified, rhetorically."

Her hand slid from my cheek to my lips, sealing my mouth. "Shut up and say it," Lee said. She removed the hand, freeing me to speak.

"The Labor Day cookout was laborious, but the Memorial Day cookout was memorable," I said.

Lee snuggled closer to me and let out a fake sigh. "Cute and smart," she said. "What more could a girl want?"

Or a guy.

We kissed again before I headed home.

May 25

The magic grows, Sean. Kissing someone you're crazy about is an amazing feeling. Not that I have anything to compare it to. I really haven't kissed a girl before. Not like this.

Tuesday on the bus, Jeremy said, "Thank you for giving me the courage to ask Gina out."

"You gave yourself that," I said. "I just gave you a prod. Did you ask her for her phone number?"

"Nope. I wasn't that brave. It's hard to ask girls for personal stuff." He shook his head. Then he grinned. "But she asked me for mine."

I gave him a high five.

Back at school, I guess kids picked up pretty quickly that Lee and I were together in a new way.

"Cute couple," Edith said at lunch.

"About time," Kyle said in the locker room.

Ms. Denton gave us an amused smile and suggested we didn't have to sit *quite* that close together in class.

Mrs. Gilroy looked directly at us as she read the class "Unending Love" by Rabindranath Tagore. I was glad she hadn't gone with Poe's "Annabel Lee."

People at home noticed, too. They were happy for me. And for us.

May blended into June. Lee and I spent a lot of time together, though I made an effort not to allow too blissful an expression to linger on my face when we were within sight of her dad. And she made it clear that she still needed time to herself. I guess I did, too, though not as much as her. I suppose when you're an only child, you get used to solitude. Either way, I cherished the moments we spent together, even though they seemed to have influenced me to use words like *cherished* far too often.

FORTY-FOUR

Come over?"

"Sure. But only for the snacks. You aren't very good company."

As we got off the bus after school, I noticed Kyle staring at Julia. "I can't believe we all hung out together in kindergarten," I said.

"Remember the time she started crying?" Kyle asked.

It came back to me in fragments.

"Wow, I'd totally forgotten about that." We'd been at the easels, painting. I was absorbed in whatever I was creating. Then I heard whimpering. The teacher went over to comfort Julia. "I had no idea what was going on when it happened."

"You always were pretty clueless," Kyle said.

"I still am." I'd noticed a puddle on the linoleum at her feet. But it wasn't until a year or two later, thinking back, that I'd realized she'd had an accident.

"Think she remembers?" Kyle asked.

"I'm pretty sure that's the sort of thing you don't forget."

"This is weird," Kyle said. "I don't think I want to talk about kindergarten bladder-control problems."

"Yeah. Let's never mention it again." I held out my fist. He gave it a bump. We walked the next block in silence.

"She sure is hot now," Kyle said.

"For sure . . ."

"I don't think she's dating anyone."

"Not as far as I know."

Kyle sighed. "What a shame."

"She and Kelly are still good friends," I said.

"That could be a problem," Kyle said. "Maybe I'll just pull a Hudson and settle for stalking her."

"I never stalked Julia. I worshipped her from afar."

"Same thing."

"Nope."

"Yup."

"No way."

"Way."

By then, we'd gotten to my place, so we let the debate die a natural death, smothered by oatmeal raisin cookies and milk.

There was an article in the local paper about how the school board was hopelessly deadlocked on any issue involving money. And a lot of other issues, as well. There was going to be a special election this summer, to fill the empty position. Whoever won the seat would be the tiebreaker. I hoped it would be someone who cared about education, and didn't have an ultra-conservative agenda to push. Maybe more people would vote this time.

> June 1
>
> It's the last month of school, Sean. And not even a full month. I'll be pretty busy studying for finals this week, and taking them next week. That's sort of an ominous word. Finals. Especially since tests seem to be endless. Both in school and in life.

At lunch, Richard and Edith were talking about some television program.

"I already had it previously recorded," Richard said.

Finally. I'd been listening to him for weeks, waiting for my chance.

"Second-year sophomore!" I shouted, punching him hard on the shoulder.

"Ouch! What the heck was that about?"

"*Previously recorded* is redundant," I said.

"Yeah. So what?"

"When someone says something redundant, you get to hit him on the shoulder and say *second-year sophomore*."

"When did that become a thing?" he asked.

"About thirty seconds ago."

Who said only teachers could make arbitrary rules?

Zenger Zinger for June 2

Last week's answer: "They took away the knight's title," John Peter said uncertainly.

This week's puzzle: "I'm puzzled why there are two separate places to moor your boat," John Peter said

_____.

Final exams started on Monday, and lasted through mid-August. Actually, they were only three days long, but they sapped the life out of all involved, both test-takers and test-givers. I studied hard. I was in good shape for most of my classes. The only downside was English. Even if I nailed the final, and bumped up my grade for this marking period, the best I could hope for as a grade-point average would be about a seventy-eight. That's a C+. No colleges that were strong in liberal arts would take me seriously when I applied. Whether I wanted to be a reporter, a writer, or a lawyer—an idea I'd started toying with more seriously recently—it would help to get into a good college. I could have lived with a bad final grade in bio, had I not ended up on Ms. Denton's good side, but the English disaster would be hard to recover from, unless I really aced everything during my junior and senior years. And who knew what sort of teacher I'd get next time?

···

Zenger Zinger for June 9

Last week's answer: "I'm puzzled why there are two separate places to moor your boat," John Peter said paradoxically.

This week's puzzle: "I need an ocean to slake my thirst," John Peter said _____.

June 14

It's the last week of school, Sean. You had a much better year than I did. You're learning to stand on your own. Maybe you can teach me to take baby steps.

The last edition of the paper for the year carried a full-page feature story by Jeremy and me about the budget scam. So I finally had something in the *Zenger Gazette*, even if I shared the credit. Jeremy and I also got a lot of praise for uncovering the crime. Next year, the money budgeted for those clubs that no longer existed could be allocated to things like art and music. Principal Hedges had assured me that the newspaper would be put back in the main budget, so it would never be at the mercy of the voters again. I guess, if I'd only achieved one thing this year, that was a pretty good thing for it to be.

Lee took a copy of my article to the school library and asked Ms. Paige to laminate it for me. From what I've seen, librarians love their laminators, and are overjoyed at any opportunity to use one.

...

Zenger Zinger for June 16

Last week's answer: "I need an ocean to slake my thirst," John Peter said sequentially.

Today's puzzle: "I have an innate talent for rebuttal," John Peter said _____.

June 16

    Tomorrow is the penultimate day of school, Sean.
I have nothing special to tell you tonight, but you know
I never miss a chance to use that word.

"I've been thinking," I told Kyle when we were waiting for the bus on Wednesday morning.

"You need to stop doing that," Kyle said.

"I'll think about it." I paused to savor the joke, and then I told him, "You should ask Julia out."

He glanced in the direction she'd be coming from, as if she might overhear us from three blocks away. "Why?"

"Because you're afraid to," I said.

"I'm not afraid of anything."

"That's mostly true. You're probably the bravest guy I know, next to Wesley. But *everyone* is a little afraid of asking Julia out. Right?"

"Yeah. Except for you. You weren't a little afraid. You were terrified."

"Thanks for the reminder," I said. "But the point is, the fear of asking her out is universal."

"That's no surprise. She's pretty much out of reach."

"But if everyone thinks she's out of reach, who's asking her out?"

Kyle digested that for a moment. "Nobody . . ."

"Exactly! So, yeah, it's scary to climb Olympus and present your petition to a goddess, but it's not a crowded climb. There's no competition when you get to the summit."

"So I should ask her out."

"You should ask her out." The suggestion rolled off my tongue, as if this were the simplest thing in the world. I was so much better at giving advice than taking it.

"She's *really* smart."

"You don't seem to be intimidated around anyone else who might be sort of smart."

"I said *smart*, not *nerdy*."

"Either way, give it some thought."

"Maybe I will."

"Good. And I'm not a nerd. I'm an enthusiast."

Since there wouldn't be another issue of the paper until September, the last meeting of the year was a staff party. Mom had armed me with these killer caramel-fudge cupcakes. Jeremy's folks had supplied a large assortment of tiny fruit pies.

Some of the staff felt it was cruel to make everyone wait until next year for the answer to the final Zenger Zinger.

But I didn't want to print the answer right under the puzzle, especially since I thought it was one of the best I'd come up with. I was pretty sure someone would figure it out and spread the word around. And that word was "counterintuitively."

Sarah gave us all parting hugs. I noticed that hugs from others feel different when you have a girlfriend. This was just one of many ways my life had changed.

After the festivities broke up, Mr. Franka said, "Congratulations, Scott."

"What for?" I sifted the possibilities through my mind. Nothing stood out as a clear winner. He'd already given Jeremy and me sufficient praise for the article.

"Your English grade. I checked it out when I was entering the grades for my students. You got a 93.75."

I'd hoped for something like that. Though, given my experiences this year, I knew better than to make assumptions about grades. "I worked really hard this marking period. And parked my ego a bit more, which seems to be the key to getting along with Mrs. Gilroy."

"I'm not talking about this marking period." He pulled up a file on his tablet. "You got a ninety-eight for the fourth marking period. But you averaged 93.75."

"No way."

"Way," he said, grinning, I imagine, at the pleasure of slipping into the typical debate/discourse style of my peers. He held out the tablet. "See for yourself."

The lines he pointed to displayed my English grade for each marking period, along with my final grade.

Marking period	1	2	3	4	Final	Honors adjusted
English 2	85	97	95	98	93.75	103.125

"That can't be right," I said.

"It can't not be right," he said.

"I have to talk to her." I headed for the door, then turned back. "Thanks for . . . everything."

"My pleasure."

"Do you teach juniors?"

"No. They're too serious."

"Seriously?"

"Get out of here."

Mrs. Gilroy wasn't in her room. I'd have to wait until tomorrow to ask her about the grade.

FORTY-FIVE

June 18

Good morning, Sean. This is the last day of school. It's hard to believe another year is almost finished. Or that I'm at the midpoint of my path through high school. I'm not going to summarize the year, or reflect on it. You can read this journal any time you want.

Father's Day falls on the overmorrow. Good news: you bought Dad a nice present. Bad news: your piggy bank is now empty. Great news: besides the expensive bottle of aftershave you bought him, Dad is going to get a present he'll never forget. We managed to get everything put in place to go ahead with the limited partnership. It's going to happen. A lot of people are eager to sign up for a share. Lee took a photo of the garage, and put *Hudson and Sons, Mechanics and Wizards* on the sign. It could just as easily have been called *Hudson and Friends*, since Kyle's, Lee's, Jeremy's, and Wesley's folks each have a share. Mom got a frame for the photo. I can't wait to see Dad's face when he unwraps it.

It turned out I had a bit of matchmaking skill. Mr. Bartock and Mr. Fowler discovered they enjoyed working together. They liked it so much, they were going to look for other deals to put together.

Mom had a surprise of her own to spring on us at dinner. She's going to run for the vacant position on the school board. We were all awash in amazement at the announcement. Except for you. You were awash in apple juice.

As for my own personal future (yup—*my own personal* was doubly redundant), that's looking good. I know I'll always have family to watch my back. And friends. Even a girlfriend.

Everyone says you work your hardest during your junior year. I guess I'd better do as much relaxing as I can this summer. I'm not going to slack off again in the classroom. You worked pretty hard this year, too, on fine motor skills and linguistic acquisition. I wish you'd hurry up with the latter, so we could have these discussions in a more interactive format. But there are small signs you're turning into an actual human being. So am I.

Hey, I'm babbling. Or, as Mrs. Gilroy would say, committing macrologia. Yeah, there's a word for that. There's a word for just about everything. The trick is to know when to use that word. And when not to. Because these are funny words. Not in the "what a weird spelling" sense. But in how they function. Sure, if I want to discuss poetry with Lee or Mr. Franka, I can point to where the poet employed antistrophe or epanalepsis (don't even bother looking them up). But really, these are my wrenches. Dad looks at an engine in need of repair, and knows which wrench to take from the toolbox. He doesn't hold it up and say, "Five millimeter metric socket," for the benefit of others who might be in the vicinity. And he doesn't try to drive a nail with a pair of pliers. If I'm writing a humorous story, I know antanaclasis would be a good tool. A persuasive essay is one place where chiasmus is very powerful. That's it in a nutshell. Writers have tools. The tools need names. Not for anyone else. For the writer. For me.

I have to go. I have a bus to catch.

Kyle didn't say much while we waited at the bus stop. He seemed distracted. Right before the bus pulled up, he walked over to Kelly and whispered something. She smiled and nodded. Kyle smiled back.

That surprised me. He hadn't said anything about trying to get back together with her. But if that was what he wanted, good for him for stepping right up to the plate.

When we got on the bus, Kelly walked past her usual spot. Kyle took the vacant seat next to Julia, and started to talk with her.

Gooder for him.

It was a half day. I could tell all the teachers were as ready for vacation as the students. Each teacher had some parting wisdom for us. Each one wished us luck. Each one told us it was a joy to get to know us.

Anaphora.

In geometry, Lee smiled at me and said, "I don't know if the year rocked, but our worlds sure did."

"Yeah. It's been an adventure."

Up front, Mr. Stockman said, "Trig is tricky."

Alliteration.

In history, Ms. Burke told us . . .

No. I'm not ending the year with a flood of rhetorical styles, terminating each class with a cleverly appropriate figure of speech. That's too easy, too obvious, and too much of a gimmick.

Damn. I seem to have sunk into an anaphoric rut.

Let's swap the anaphoric for the euphoric, and cut to the final bell, after our sophomore honors English class had been wished farewell and Godspeed by Mrs. Gilroy.

"I'll meet you in a moment," I told Lee.

"You can't resist taking one last shot at digging your own grave, can you?" she said.

"It's become sort of my hobby," I said. "But it beats cutting classes. Besides, you're fond of graves."

"True," Lee said. "Be sure to leave this grave to me in your will."

"Of corpse." I walked over to Mrs. Gilroy's desk.

"Yes?" she asked.

I pictured myself thrusting a spade into soft cemetery soil. "I think there's a mistake in my grades."

"And how would you know that?"

"Someone showed them to me."

"Let's see." She pulled a file folder from her desk drawer, and removed a sheet of paper with my name at the top. The grades were handwritten. Maybe that's how the mistake had happened. Whoever put them in the computer had messed up.

"Is this what *somebody* showed you?"

The numbers on the sheet matched the ones on Mr. Franka's tablet.

"Yeah, that's what I saw. But that's not what they used to be. You changed them."

"Your powers of observation are increasingly impressive," she said. "Perhaps you could seek summer employment spotting forest fires from a lookout tower."

"I didn't know you could change grades after a report card

came out." As the words left my mouth, I could already hear her response in my mind. She didn't disappoint me.

"There are many things you don't know, Mr. Hudson."

"But . . . why . . . ?"

I expected her to ask if I'd prefer for her to change the grades back. Instead, she said, "You have a gift. I gave you a difficult time after your disappointing performance the first week. I pushed you beyond the bounds of what would be viewed as the rubric of the sophomore English Honors curriculum. You showed spirit. My health may have affected my temperament earlier in the year. In my defense, I'd been told before school started that you were a gem, and yet you made an entrance that reminded me more of a turd."

The coarse word from an unexpected source had a lot of power. "I can't argue with any of that. I was a turd."

"As was I," she said. "That's enough scatology. Let us return to the topic at hand. I believe the adjusted grades I gave you are a fair reflection of your work. You also did well in classroom participation, despite facing some challenges."

"Challenges? You shot me down every time I spoke!" I didn't shout. I wasn't feeling angry. Just relieved, grateful, and perplexed.

"I can get a bit overzealous in my peregrinations."

"Peregrinations?" I said. "That's not the right word." I froze. I had to be careful not to ruin everything by getting her angry.

But she smiled, and I realized she'd made the mistake on purpose. "Nicely done, Mr. Hudson. Be careful. Most people don't appreciate being corrected—especially people who are tasked with instructing you."

"I know."

"I do have to say that your opinion piece on terminal prepositions was well thought out, well written, and thought-provoking."

"You read it?" I asked.

"One of my coworkers was kind enough to share it with me," she said. "He felt I'd appreciate the enthusiasm with which you approached the topic."

"Mr. Franka?" I asked.

"That would be the most likely *somebody*."

"Well written?" I asked.

"Don't grovel for praise. You heard me the first time. Don't you have somewhere you're supposed to be? Don't you have someone young and lovely waiting for you?"

"I do. Thanks for this." I pointed at my grades. Then I pointed at the figures of speech on the board. "And thanks for that."

"Thank me by doing something with your gift," she said.

"I will." I thought about my grades again. "This is sort of a *deus ex machina* way to end the year," I said.

"Sometimes, Mr. Hudson, if you are very fortunate, or very deserving, life imitates bad art," she said. "When that happens, take the gift and be grateful."

Before I left, I reached into my backpack and pulled out my copy of *As a Breath into the Wind* and asked for her autograph. She thought for a moment, and then wrote two words below my name and above her signature: "Amaze me." I promised I'd try.

As I walked through the corridors of J. P. Zenger High School, with Lee by my side, I thought back over our history. One slow dance last year, one long hug last September, pats on the hand, a kiss on the cheek. An embrace. Finally, a whole evening of dancing, and an act of courage in front of her dad. A first kiss. More kisses. More embraces. It was good. But I needed to stop being a slacker in one more aspect of my life.

"We should celebrate," I said. I remembered when she'd used that phrase, and I'd failed to follow up.

"We should," Lee said.

"How about a movie?"

"Sure."

I realized *a movie* could mean anything. Two friends just hanging out. A dance, a walk, a trip to the library—all of those were socially ambiguous. I seized the clichéd, stereotypical date, so there'd be no doubt what I was asking.

"How about dinner and a movie? I'd love to take you out tonight."

Lee smiled, faced me, and took both my hands in hers. "It's a date," she said.

I enjoyed the warmth of her hands in mine. Dad had nailed it. I couldn't picture a world without Lee. "Yes," I said. "It is."

So, finally, clearly, unmistakably, and far later than I should have, I'd asked Lee out on a date. That might seem like a distinction without a difference to anyone who doesn't live inside my head. But it was important to me.

We flouted the personal-displays-of-affection rule, and walked hand in hand to the bus lot, flaunting our relationship. "And here, we part," I said.

"But not for long," Lee said.

As I floated toward my bus, a long white limo pulled up in front of it. Wesley, wearing a chauffeur's outfit, got out and waved me over.

"You have to finish the year in style," he said.

"I thought you were too young to do this," I said.

"I can't drive customers. But I can drive friends."

"You mind a few more passengers?" I asked.

"The more, the merrier," he said.

I called Lee, Jeremy, Kyle, Julia, Kelly, Edith, and Richard over.

As everyone settled onto the long seat in the middle of the limo, I motioned for Jeremy to join me way in the back.

"I have the perfect nickname for you," I told him. It had come to me just moments ago, inspired by my conversation with Mrs. Gilroy.

"Great. All I need is for you to stick something belittling

on me," he said. "A nickname from you is like an uppercut from the world heavyweight champ."

"No. I'm serious. It's awesome."

"Okay. Let me have it." He squeezed his eyes shut and hunched down, as if my words would have enough mass and velocity to cause damage.

"Deuce," I said.

"Deuce?" He opened one eye and frowned. "Like in the tennis score?"

"No. That's not what I had in mind."

"Playing card?" he asked.

"Nope."

"Bathroom reference?"

"Ewwww. Absolutely not." That one hadn't even crossed my mind.

"Then I don't get it," he said. "And that's a rare situation for me."

"You saved the paper. You brought down Mr. Sherman. You came out of nowhere, like in the old Greek plays."

"*Deus ex machina!*" Jeremy shouted. Both eyes were open now. "How cool. Yeah. You can call me Deuce. I like that. Deuce Danger. You're tweaking the pronunciation a bit, but that makes it like our own secret code."

"That was my plan, Deuce."

"Scott and Deuce, dynamic freshman and sophomore crime fighters."

I put a hand on his shoulder. He barely jumped. "Sophomore and junior," I said.

"You're right! I'm a sophomore. I survived my freshman year, thanks to you." His grin of achievement gave way to a wavering smile of uncertainty. "There's a whole new world of terror and obstacles for me to conquer."

"Fear not, Deuce," I said as I realized I'd neglected to give myself credit for one major sophomore-year accomplishment. "I have a manual I can sell you."

ACKNOWLEDGMENTS

There are people to thank. This book would not exist were it not for Julie Strauss-Gabel, who said to me, "Let's make this book exist." (I'm paraphrasing.) It would not have existed on the tenth anniversary of *Sleeping Freshmen Never Lie*, were it not for Kathleen Doherty, who urged me to take a risk and take on the tough deadline Julie proposed, and for Susan Chang, who gave me a pep talk at a crucial time, and taught me many ways to become a better writer. I would not exist, were it not for my wife, Joelle, who pretty much did everything around the house, and delivered food at key moments, while I stayed in my chair and rediscovered Scott Hudson. She is also my expert resource on things as diverse as culinary arts, plant biology, and muscle cars.

There are others who were essential in various ways. My daughter, Alison S. Myers, is my go-to source for anything that happens in an English literature classroom, and my go-to peer for philosophical dialogues and epistemological explorations. She also dispenses calmness and wisdom far beyond her years at essential times when Dad is feeling stressed or frantic. (This seems like a good place to thank Mark Myers for a suggestion that became a key theme in the book.) Shannon Tyburczy is my source for the workings of AP History class, the sociology of sophomores, and all things historical. Doug Baldwin is my grammar guru. His wisdom was especially crucial as I navigated the hodgepodge of rhetoric. He also excels at the difficult and demanding task of being one of my close friends. Assistant editor Melissa Faulner served as the perfect central command for what, at times, was a very hectic process, and copy editor Rosanne Lauer's keen eye kept me from looking like a total dunce. I am in their debt.

The people to whom (possessive pronoun in the objective case!) this book is dedicated didn't necessarily have anything to do with this particular volume of my work, but they, too, deserve thanks. All have been called upon for help, advice, support, or companionship at critical times. None (singular!) has ever been too busy to be there when I needed aid, advice, or the second sitter at a table for two. It would take many hours to list all that they have done for me. I fear I have left someone out. But my friends are forgiving, and there's always the next book.

Last, and first, there would be no sequel, were there not a demand for it from you, the readers who embraced Scott, Lee, Wesley, and the gang, and the teachers who made that book a part of their curriculum (and who may very well prefer you don't end a sentence with a preposition, as is their right). I thank you for your enthusiasm, and for sharing my joy of exploring the magic that is our English language.

You can take the writer out of the sequel, but you can't—

. . . never mind . . .

KEEP READING FOR A NOTE FROM
THE AUTHOR ABOUT THE MAKING OF
SOPHOMORES AND OTHER OXYMORONS

OH, REALLY?

When I speak at schools, I'm often asked whether the events in my books are based on my own experiences. Since my work includes a fair number of horror stories with dark and ghastly endings, my immediate instinct is to reply, "I hope not." But, whether used in whole or as a seed of inspiration, all any of us knows is what we have experienced. The key for writers is what we do with these experiences. For my real-life young adult novels, the truth is that I draw from at least four different sources: my own experiences in high school; my observation of my daughter's experiences both as a student when she was young and as a high school teacher now; my current experiences as I visit schools; and filling in the gaps when experience isn't enough, I draw events from my imagination. (Though even seemingly pure imagination is connected to experience.) Since many of you who just finished reading *Sophomores and Other Oxymorons* came to this book after reading *Sleeping Freshmen Never Lie*, I'll start with a look at some of the sources for the freshman book. (Side note: I refer to the first book as *SFNL*, which pleases me because it sounds a bit like the abbreviation for *Saturday Night Live* and a bit like the NFL. I call the second one SO_2. Those of you who have studied chemistry will understand why this amuses me.)

I did know a girl in kindergarten who, like Julia, blossomed during the summer before freshman year. And I did run for student council. I was much more like Mouth than Scott. I talked too much and had few friends. But I was pretty good at conceiving wild and creative ideas. I actually did come up with the idea for the student-council speech that Scott used. Unlike him, I came up with the idea weeks after the election, when it was too late to do any good. But here's the magical thing. There's a famous and somewhat cryptic quote from F. Scott (no relation) Fitzgerald: "There are no second acts in American lives." I like to say that there *are* second acts, and second chances, in American fiction. (And in all fiction, for that matter, but I had to toss in "American" here for the sake of symmetry.) I might have conceived of the speech too late to get elected, but I can give it to my main character as a gift. If you fumble the ball, or think up a great response to an insult far too late to use it, you can let your character make the catch (or better yet, allow the fumble to lead him or her to something wonderful and life changing). You can give those belated words to your character, who can deliver a smackdown with awesome results.

Speaking of smackdowns, a rather dangerous fellow befriended me during my freshman year in high school. I have no idea why he did that, and I was always waiting for him to decide it would be great fun to punch me in the face. This was my inspiration for Wesley, though Wesley's personality and actions come from my imagination. As I mentioned, my imagination is fueled by my experiences. Even if I have a character do the opposite of something I've observed, the initial observation is still the source.

Let's shift to indirect experiences. My daughter had a Spanish teacher who came from Russia. The teacher was fluent in Russian and Spanish, but far less skilled in English. I never met the teacher, but I heard about her. We can call this a secondhand experience. But it was a valuable one. It inspired Scott's sequence of Spanish teachers, and spawned one character so memorable, and so much fun to write dialogue for, that I had to bring him back. My daughter is also the coach of her school's Academic Challenge team, which allows me to present a smooth transition from *SFNL* to SO_2. The second year that my daughter coached the team, their funding was moved from the regular budget to Proposition 2. The voters turned it down. So the team had no money. My daughter, who was determined to keep the team alive, had a bake sale to raise funds. The whole idea of budget cuts eliminating the newspaper, and the effect the cuts had on all aspects of school, came from my awareness of her experiences. I also see the impact of budget cuts all around the country as I travel to schools. I felt I needed to make that a central aspect of the book.

Jeremy showed up because I wanted to have a first-day bus scene in SO_2 that would parallel the one in *SFNL*. At the start, Jeremy was just a kid wearing a hat. His personality emerged as I wrote the scene on the bus. This happens a lot. I'll put characters together, let them talk, and see what develops. Even there, small things could come from my experiences. Jeremy plays with a calculator. I have a calculator on my desk.

Speaking of calculators, little things in my life trickle into my books in hundreds of ways. I suspect Scott's father's job in a car dealership's repair department might have been inspired by the fact that I'd just brought my car in for maintenance right before I had to decide what work to give him. Some of this is done through conscious effort, especially when it comes to background material like describing locations or buildings, but much of it is done without any awareness on my part. Things mix, meld, and morph in the subconscious, then bubble up into my mind when needed for a scene. Either way, my experiences, both large and small, color my work.

Finally, fans of Splitty the Cat will be happy (or horrified) to know I saw a similar splayed specimen in my own high school biology class. And, when the class reacted to a strong odor from the autoclave, our teacher actually used the line about the baby. I could offer many other examples, but I think that books, like cats, are best enjoyed intact and alive. Besides, you're finished here. You need to go out and have your own experiences. Here's hoping they give you lots to write about.

TURN THE PAGE TO READ SAMPLE CHAPTERS
FROM THE COMPANION NOVEL—

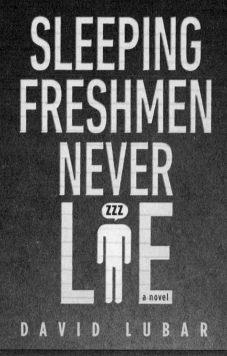

KEEP AWAY FROM SENIORS. KEEP AWAY FROM JUNIORS.
IT'S PROBABLY A GOOD IDEA TO AVOID SOPHOMORES, TOO.

SLEEPING
FRESHMEN
NEVER
LIE

a novel

DAVID LUBAR

{one}

We plunged toward the future without a clue. Tonight, we were four sweaty guys heading home from a day spent shooting hoops. Tomorrow, I couldn't even guess what would happen. All I knew for sure was that our lives were about to change.

"Any idea what it'll be like?" I asked. My mind kept flashing images of cattle. They shuffled up a ramp, unaware that their path led to a slaughterhouse.

"A *Tomb Raider* movie," Patrick said. "Or *Indiana Jones.*"

"It'll be the same as always," Kyle said. "Boring and stupid."

Patrick shook his head. "Nope. *Tomb Raider,* for sure. We'll get eaten alive if we aren't careful, but we'll be surrounded by amazing stuff."

"Right. Amazing stuff," Mitch said. He rubbed his hands together as if he were about to dive into a juicy burger. "High school girls. Hundreds of 'em."

"Like we have a chance with them," Patrick said. "I heard the seniors snag all the hot girls."

"Not when I'm around." Kyle slicked his hair back with his right hand, then made a fist and flexed his biceps. "Girls melt when I get near them."

"Mostly from the fumes," Patrick said.

"What about the classes?" I asked as Kyle shoved Patrick toward the curb. "Think they'll be hard?"

"Who cares?" Mitch said. "You just have to show up and you'll pass."

We reached my house. Second from the corner on Willow Street. The guys lived on the other side of the neighborhood. I realized that the next time we saw one another, we'd be freshmen at J. P. Zenger High.

Freshmen. Unbelievable. Fresh? Definitely. Men? Not a clue. I turned toward my friends.

"Bye," Patrick said.

Mitch grunted a farewell. Kyle's hand twitched in a lazy wave. I wanted to say something more meaningful than *See ya later.*

There they were, right in front of me—Kyle, who I'd known since kindergarten, Patrick, who I'd met in second grade, and Mitch, who'd moved here in sixth grade. We'd done everything together, all through middle school. The perfect words were so obvious, I couldn't help smiling as I spoke. "One for all and all for one."

The phrase was greeted with silence. Around us, I could hear the last crickets of summer chirping faintly. The crickets, too, seemed puzzled.

"One for all . . ." I said again.

Mitch frowned. "One for all what?"

"Is that like a Marines slogan?" Kyle asked.

"No, I think it's on coins. It's that Latin stuff, right?" Patrick said. "It's *E Pluto Pup* something or other."

"It's from *The Three Musketeers*," I told them. "It's a famous book."

Three pairs of eyes stared at me without a glimmer.

"There's a movie, too," I said. "These guys stuck together no matter what."

Kyle looked around, tapped his thumb against the tip of each of his fingers, then said, "But there are four of us."

"Absolutely. That's what's so perfect. There were four Musketeers, too."

"That's stupid," Mitch said. "Somebody couldn't count."

"Well, anyhow, let's stick together tomorrow," I said.

"You bet," Patrick said.

"For sure," Mitch said.

"One for all and all for me," Kyle said. He turned to go.

"See ya later," I called as they walked off.

Mom and Dad were side by side on the living-room couch. The TV was on, but it didn't look like they were watching it. They stopped talking when I walked in.

"What's up?" I asked.

"Hi, Scott," Dad said. "You have fun with your friends?"

"Yeah." I noticed his eyes kept shifting from me to Mom. "Is something going on?"

"Tomorrow's the big day," Mom said. "You must be excited."

Now I got it. They were stressed out from worrying whether they were headed for another disaster, which was one of the milder ways to describe my brother Bobby's high school experience.

"I'm sure I'll do fine." I could almost guarantee I wouldn't skip history seventeen straight days in a row, get nabbed nine times for public displays of affection—with nine different girls—or pull off any of the other stunts that helped end Bobby's high school experience half a year earlier than planned. "I'm really excited about school."

"Good." Mom smiled with way more joy than the situation seemed to call for. "Do you want me to make you a lunch? I bought your favorite rolls."

"No." I tried to hide my shudder as I imagined carrying a paper bag into the cafeteria. "Thanks."

"I think he'd rather buy lunch," Dad said.

I nodded, shot Dad a grateful look, and headed upstairs. I wanted to get my stuff ready, and they probably wanted to talk more about how there was nothing to worry about because I was different from Bobby.

Man, was that ever true. Bobby was almost as tall as Dad, good with tools, and strong enough to carry two sacks of concrete at once. Eighty pounds on one shoulder. That sort of load would snap my spine. Girls chased him like he was some kind of movie star. He'd gotten all the good genes. I was a runt who had to think hard to remember which way to turn a wrench.

I put my stuff in my backpack. Then I grabbed the books I'd bought last Saturday. Dad and I had gone to the flea market up near Stroudsburg. We go there at least once a month when it's open. He looks for tools. I look for books. I'd snagged a whole stack of Robert Heinlein novels for two bucks, and a *Field Guide to North American Game Fish* for fifty cents. Dad had gotten some huge clamps for five bucks. That's the weird thing about flea markets—books and tools seem to cost about the same amount per pound.

I crammed the novels into one of my bookcases, then sat on my bed and leafed through the field guide, looking at the color photos of smallmouth bass and imagining landing a four pounder while wading in the Delaware.

Before I went to sleep, I called Bobby at his apartment to see if I could get any advice from him about school. Which I guess was like asking General Custer for combat tips. It didn't matter. He wasn't in.

That night, I dreamed I was field-testing flamethrowers for the army. In a supermarket. I awoke to the smell of bacon.

First day of high school.

I couldn't believe it was finally here. Dad had already left for work. Mom was sitting on a stool by the kitchen counter, reading a magazine. But as my nose had told me, she'd been hard at work creating breakfast. "Good morning," she said. She slipped the magazine under the newspaper. "Hungry?"

"Starved."

Mom always made blueberry pancakes and bacon on the first day of school. As she loaded up my plate with enough protein and carbs to fuel a Mars mission, I glanced at the corner of the magazine where it stuck out from under the paper. Mom didn't usually hide stuff. It was probably one of those supermarket things, with stories about aliens who looked like Elvis and kids who'd been raised in the desert by giant toads.

Mom got herself a plate and joined me as I tried to make a dent in my stack. We didn't talk much while we ate. She seemed to be a million miles away.

"You okay?" I asked.

The too-big smile reappeared. "I can still make you a lunch. There's plenty of time."

"Maybe tomorrow." I glanced at the clock. "Gotta go." I grabbed my backpack and headed for the bus stop.

I was the first one there. I should have brought a book to help kill the time. But that would immediately mark me as a real geek.

Eventually, I heard a noise in the distance. "Hey, Scottie," Mouth Kandeski shouted when he was still half a block away. "Whatcha think? High school. It's the big time. We're in high school. Man, that's cool. That's sooooo cool."

He dribbled a trail of words like a leaking milk carton as he closed the distance between us. My best guess is that he can only breathe when he's talking.

"Hi, Mouth," I said when he reached me. His name's Louden. Bad move on his parents' part. He got called Loudmouth the moment he started school. It was shortened to Mouth soon after that. We didn't hang out or anything, but I guess since I was one of the few kids on the planet who'd never screamed, "Shut up!" at him, he figured I was interested in what he had to say. I was more interested in wondering what would happen to him if I clamped a hand over his mouth. Maybe he'd swell up and explode. Maybe the top of his head would pop off, sending his dorky orange ball cap into orbit where it belonged. Maybe the words would shoot out of his butt with so much force his pants would rip.

Left unclamped, Mouth had plenty more to discuss. "I'll tell you, I can't wait. This is awesome. I'm kinda nervous. Are you nervous? I mean, I'm not scared, or nothing, but just kinda nervous. You know, nervous isn't the same as scared. It's sort of like the buzz you get from lots of coffee. I drank eight cups, once. I started drinking coffee this summer. You drink coffee? It's not bad if you put in enough sugar."

Past Mouth, I spotted more freshmen. Familiar faces from Tom Paine Middle School, looking like Easter eggs in their new clothes. Then one unfamiliar face. A goddess. An honest-to-goodness goddess. At the first sight of her, even from a distance, I felt like I'd been stabbed in the gut with an icicle. I wanted to gather branches and build a shrine, or slay a mastodon and offer her the finest pieces, fresh from the hunt.

"Whoa, it's Julia," Mouth said, breaking the spell. "Hey, Julia, you look different."

Wow. Mouth was right. It was Julia Baskins. I'd known her most of my life, and I hadn't recognized her. She was one of those kids who blend into the background. Like me, I guess. Well, the background had lost a blender. She was gorgeous.

She'd always kept her dark brown hair in a braid. Now it was cut short and shaggy, with a couple of highlights. She was wearing makeup that did amazing things to her eyes, and a sweater and khakis that did amazing things to the rest of her. She looked taller, too.

"You're wearing contacts, right?" Mouth called to her. "I

wanted contacts, but Mom said I had to wait until I got more responsible. Just because I let my braces get gunked up and had all those cavities. And lost my retainer three times. Well, really just twice. The other time, my dog ate it, so that doesn't count. You have a dog?"

Julia shook her head and managed to squeeze in the word "Cat."

"I don't have a cat. I have an Airedale," Mouth said. "He's not purebred, but that's what we think he mostly is." He jammed his hand into his jacket pocket, fished around, and pulled out a broken Oreo. "Want a cookie?"

"No, thanks." Julia slipped away from Mouth and joined her friend Kelly Holbrook near the curb. I worked my way closer and tried to think of some excuse to talk to her.

I never got the chance.

{ two }

a hush fell over our cluster of freshmen, cloaking us with that same sense of dread that ancient civilizations must have felt during a solar eclipse. But we weren't awestruck by a dragon eating the sun. We were facing a much less mythical danger.

Older kids. An army of giants. I'd just spent a year in eighth grade, towering over the sixth and seventh graders. Okay— that was an exaggeration. I only towered over the short ones. But I wasn't used to being at the bottom of the food chain. Or the wrong end of a growth spurt. I felt like the towel boy for the Sixers.

As the loud, joking, shoving mob reached us, I slipped toward the back of the group and pretended to adjust my watch. Out of the corner of my eye I noticed a kid kneel to tie his shoe. That earned him a kick in the rear from a member of the mob as it passed by.

Mouth kept talking. Big mistake. The giants closed in on him, dumped the contents of his backpack onto the sidewalk, and threw his hat down a storm drain.

"Hey, come on, guys," Mouth said as his possessions spilled

across the concrete. "Come on. Hey. Stop it. Come on, that's not funny. We're all classmates, right? We all go to the same school. Let's be friends."

The scary thing was that the big kids didn't seem angry. I'm pretty sure they trashed his stuff by reflex, like they were scratching an itch or squashing a bug. Some people step on ants. Some people step on freshmen. I guess it was better to be a freshman than an ant. At least the seniors didn't have giant magnifying glasses.

Mouth was spared from further damage by the arrival of transportation. With an ear-killing squeal of brakes, the bus skidded to the curb, bathing us in the thick aroma of diesel fuel, motor oil, and a faint whiff of cooked antifreeze. The driver opened the door and glared at Mouth as the mob pushed their way aboard. "Pick up that mess, kid!" he shouted.

When I walked past Mouth, I thought about giving him a hand.

"You're holding us up!" the driver shouted. He kept his glare aimed in my direction while he took a gulp of coffee from a grimy thermos cup. Great—of all the types of bus drivers in the world, I had to get a shouter.

I hurried on board, hoping to grab a seat near Julia. No such luck.

As dangerous as the bus stop is, at least there are places to run. There's no escape from the bus. It's like a traveling version of a war game. All that's missing is paintball guns and maybe a couple foxholes. I could swear one of the kids in the back was in his twenties. I think he was shaving.

I sat up front.

That wasn't much better, since every big kid who got on at the rest of the stops had a chance to smack my head. I should have grabbed a seat behind Sheldon Murmbower. There was something about his head that attracted swats. Everyone within two or three rows of him was pretty safe.

For the moment, all I could do was try to learn invisibility. I opened my backpack and searched for something to keep me busy. Now I really wished I'd brought that field guide, or anything else to read. All I had was blank notebooks, pens, and pencils. I grabbed a notebook. The driver was shouting at a new batch of kids as they got on. Then he shouted at Mouth, who was sitting in the front seat.

"Shut up, kid! You're distracting me."

Last year was so much better. I had the greatest driver. Louie. He used to drive a city bus. That gave me an idea. I started writing. It didn't cut down on the smacks as much as I'd hoped, but it kept my mind off them.

Scott Hudson's Field Guide to School-Bus Drivers

Retired City-Bus Driver: Unbelievably skilled. Can fit the bus through the narrowest opening. Never hits anything by accident but might bump a slow-moving car on purpose. Spits out the window a lot. Never looks in the mirror to check on us. Knows all the best swear words.

Ex-hippie (or Child of Hippies): Has a ponytail, smiles too much, uses words like *groovy*. Likes to weave back and forth between the lanes in time to Grateful Dead music.

Wears loose, colorful clothing. Smells like incense.
Refuses to believe it's the twenty-first century.

College Student: Similar to the hippie, but no ponytail.
Hits stuff once in a while. Studies for exams while
driving. Sometimes takes naps at red lights or does
homework while steering with knees.

Beginner: Very nervous. Goes slowly. Can't get out of
first gear, but still manages to hit stuff pretty often.
Makes all kinds of cool sounds when frightened.
Occasionally shuts eyes.

Shouter: Very loud. Goes fast. Slams the door. Likes
country music, NASCAR, and black coffee. Hands tend to
shake when they're not clutching the wheel. Often has
broken blood vessels in eyes. Usually needs a shave.
Always needs a shower.

Twenty minutes and one full page later, we reached J. P. Zenger High.

"No pushing," the driver shouted as we scrambled out.

"High school," Mouth said, staggering to the side as someone pushed him out of the way. "Here we come. This is going to be great. We're going to rule this place."

Wrong, Mouth. Wrong, wrong, wrong, wrong, wrong.

There were so many buses, the parking lot smelled like a truck stop. On top of that, the lot was jammed with a long line of parents dropping off kids and a wave of seniors driving their own cars with varying degrees of skill.

I stood on the curb for a moment, my eyes wide and my head tilted back. I'd seen it a thousand times before, but I'd never really looked at it. Zenger High was huge. It sprawled out like a hotel that had a desperate desire to become an octopus. Every couple years, the town built another addition. The school mascot should have been a bulldozer.

My homeroom was located as far as possible from the bus area. I got lost twice. The first time, I asked some older kid for directions, and he sent me off to what turned out to be the furnace room. I assumed this was an example of upperclassman humor. The janitor, who I'd wakened from a nap, yelled at me. I reached my desk just before the late bell rang.

I didn't see a single familiar face in homeroom. The teacher passed out blank assignment books. Then he gave us our schedules. I scanned mine, hoping to get at least a clue about what lay ahead.

Period	Class	Teacher
1st	H. English	Mr. Franka
2nd	Gym/Study Hall	Mr. Cravutto/Staff
3rd	Art	Ms. Savitch
4th	Lunch	
5th	C.P. History	Mr. Ferragamo
6th	C.P. Algebra	Ms. Flutemeyer
7th	Life Skills	Ms. Pell
8th	C.P. Spanish	Ms. de Gaulle
9th	C.P. Chemistry	Ms. Balmer

I had no idea what the *H* or the *C.P.* stood for. Since there was no teacher listed for lunch, I grabbed a pen and wrote *Mr. E. Meat.*

My first class turned out to be as far as possible from homeroom, and nearly impossible to find. But at least I knew enough not to ask for directions. Ten minutes into my freshman year, I'd already learned an important lesson.

When I reached the room, I finally saw a face I recognized. The same face I hadn't recognized earlier. Julia was in my English class, along with Kelly, and a couple other kids I knew. Still no sign of Kyle, Patrick, or Mitch.

I grabbed a seat two rows away from Julia. Things were looking up.

"Welcome to Honors English," Mr. Franka said. He was a short guy with a beard and sideburns and the sort of rugged face you see on the cable hunting shows. Instead of a camouflage outfit, he was wearing a light blue button-down shirt with the sleeves rolled up, but no tie or jacket. "I hope you all love to read." He grabbed a stack of paperbacks from his desk and started tossing them out like literary Frisbees. I noticed a Marine tattoo on his left forearm.

He also passed out a textbook, which weighed about nine pounds. Fortunately, he didn't toss it. Otherwise, there'd probably have been a death or two in the back row.

Instead of reading in class, we started discussing how to define a short story. It was actually fun. I didn't say too much. I didn't want anyone to think I was some kind of brain—which I'm not. I wasn't even sure how I'd ended up in the honors class. Maybe it was because of the tests we'd taken at the end of last year.

Mr. Franka kept asking us all sorts of questions to keep the discussion going. At one point, he said, "What do you think is easier to write, a short story or a novel?"

I almost raised my hand. I'd read so many of both, I figured I had a good answer. A story was harder because you couldn't wander around. You had to stick to the subject. At least in a good story. It was a matter of focus.

Most of the kids said that a novel would be harder because it was longer. I wasn't sure whether to speak up or just keep quiet. Then Julia raised her hand. "I think stories are harder," she said. "In a novel, the writer can wander. In a story, the writer has to stay focused."

"Right!" Oh great. I hadn't meant to shout. But it was so amazing to find we felt the same way. Everyone was looking at me. "I agree," I said in a quieter voice as I slunk down in my seat. Wonderful. Now she'd think I was some kind of suck-up.

At the end of the period, Mr. Franka wrote our homework on the board and passed out a vocabulary book. One class— three books. This was not a good sign.

There was a dash for the door when the bell rang. The hall was jammed with freshmen walking in circles, ellipses, zig-zags, and other patterns that marked us as clueless members of the lost generation. Or lost members of the clueless gener-ation.

I saw Patrick in study hall, but the teacher wouldn't let us talk. For some reason, he thought we should be studying.

We made color charts in art class, which was pretty interesting. On the way out, Ms. Savitch gave us a photocopy of an article about Van Gogh. I was beginning to calculate my reading load by the pound instead of the page. But that was okay. I could handle it.